PONY CLUB
Stories

JOSEPHINE PULLEIN-THOMPSON

PONY CLUB
Stories

containing
PONY CLUB CUP
PONY CLUB CHALLENGE
PONY CLUB TREK

complete and unabridged

DEAN

Pony Club Cup was first published in 1983
Pony Club Challenge was first published in 1984
Pony Club Trek was first published in 1985
All by Fontana Paperbacks

This special omnibus edition first published in 1994 by Dean
an imprint of Reed Consumer Books Limited
Michelin House, 81 Fulham Road, London SW3 6RB
and Auckland, Melbourne, Singapore and Toronto
Copyright © Josephine Pullein-Thompson 1983, 1984, 1985

ISBN 0 603 55372 9

A CIP catalogue record for this title is available form the British Library

Printed in Great Britain by The Bath Press

PONY CLUB CUP

CONTENTS

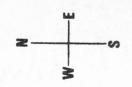

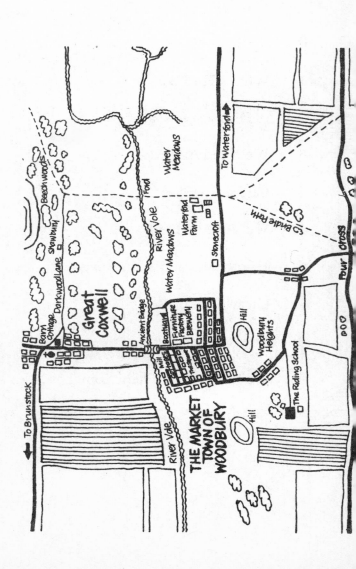

ROADS
LANES
BRIDLE PATHS
WATER

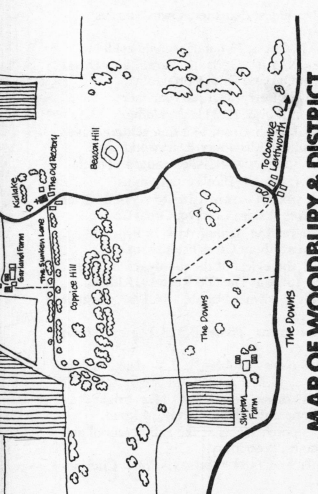

Kidlake

The Old Rectory

Beacon Hill

Garland Farm

The Sunken Lane

Coppice Hill

To Coombe
Leathworth

The Downs

The Downs

Shipton
Farm

MAP OF WOODBURY & DISTRICT

Members and Officials of the Woodbury Branch of the Pony Club

DAVID LUMLEY, ex steeple-chase jockey. Lives at Garland Farm.

MRS. ROOKE, Hon. Secretary. Lives at 20, The Heights, Woodbury.

LESLEY ROOKE, her eldest daughter. Owns Stardust, 14-hands chestnut mare.

SARAH ROOKE owns Chess, 13-hands piebald gelding.

MR. & MRS. ROBERTS run Garland Farm for David Lumley. They live at Garland Farm Cottage.

LYNNE ROBERTS owns Berry, 13.1 red roan mare.

PAUL ROBERTS owns Banjo, 12.2 black gelding.

ALICE DRUMMOND hires Saffron, 14.1 dun gelding. Lives with her uncle and aunt at Shawbury, Darkwood Lane.

MARGARET & PETER HUTCHINSON, Alice's aunt and uncle.

CLARE HUTCHINSON, one of Alice's four cousins.

HANIF (HARRY) FRANKLIN owns Jupiter, 14.2 liver chestnut gelding. Lives at Barn Cottage, Great Coxwell.

JAMES MORGAN shares Ferdinand, dark brown gelding, with his mother. Lives at Four Cross Fruit Farm.

RUPERT WHEELER, the eldest of the family, owns Rosie, 14.1 light bay mare. Lives at The Old Rectory, Kidlake.

ELIZABETH WHEELER owns Rajah, 14.1½ chestnut gelding.

ANNETTE WHEELER owns Tristram, 13.2 grey Welsh gelding.

OLIVER WHEELER owns Hobbit, 12.2 dark brown Dartmoor gelding.

JENNIFER BLACKER owns Sea King, 14.2 bright bay gelding. Lives at Stonecroft on the Waterford Road.

TINA SPENCER. No pony. Helps at the riding school and lives at 5 Mill Cottages, Woodbury.

JULIA CARTWRIGHT and JANET GREEN. Pony Club instructors.

CHAPTER ONE

"What's He Like?"

"I shouldn't think it *could* get worse. I mean fewer and fewer people are turning up, and you can't blame them when the instruction's so useless," said James Morgan gloomily, as he rode dark brown Ferdinand along the lane, walking stride for stride with Jennifer Blacker's Sea King. "Rallies weren't much fun when Mrs Smythe was D.C., but at least you learned a bit."

"Yes, and she always got really good people to instruct the top ride, but now we're in the top ride we still have Janet or Julia or Mr Foster's working pupils taking us. And those working pupils are *pathetic*, all theory. They don't ride as well as we do," complained Jennifer in a voice of deep disgust.

"We're only in the top ride because all the older members have stopped coming," James pointed out. "I do hope this new bloke fizzes things up a bit."

"But I don't see how an ex-jockey for D.C. *can* improve things. They only know how to ride in races."

"He's an ex-*jump* jockey, so with any luck he'll have us belting over steeplechase fences," said James, his solid face brightening.

"Well I'm not going to risk spoiling King just as he's begun to win," Jennifer spoke decidedly, as she patted her pony's bright bay neck. "I'm going to have another go at Mummy about transferring to the Cranford Vale. They're a decent pony club, much the best round here. They had a team in practically all the finals last year. The trouble is that their rallies are such miles away. It's too far to hack and Mummy says that with petrol the price it is, she can't afford to use the trailer for rallies as well as shows."

"Hadn't you better hang on for a bit and see if things improve?" suggested James.

9

"No, I'm not going to bother with it any more. If Mummy won't let me transfer I'll just give up the pony club," said Jennifer, her pale, flat face set in obstinate lines. "How can a smashed-up jockey know anything about proper riding."

"David Lumley knows a lot."

James and Jennifer turned in their saddles to see Paul Roberts jogging along behind them on his little black pony, Banjo. Paul was small for his age, which was eleven, had a small neat face which matched the rest of him, and serious grey eyes. He had listened to their conversation and now forced himself to speak up.

"David was in the pony club when he was young. He did a lot of ordinary riding and then he took to breaking and schooling and riding in horse trials *before* he became a national hunt jockey. He was top class, and all set to be Champion Jockey when he had his smash."

"You know this Lumley bloke?" asked James in surprise.

"Yes, you see my sister Lynne and I live at Garland Farm. Well, David Lumley lives in the farmhouse and we live in the cottages and my father runs the farm for him," explained Paul, wishing that Lynne, who was a year older, would stop giggling with Netti Wheeler and Sarah Rooke and help him stand up for David.

"All the rallies are going to be held over at our place, at Garland Farm, in future," he told them.

"Yes, we know that, Mrs Rooke announced it. But what's he *like*?"

"My mother knows all about him," Lesley Rooke, who'd been riding alone as usual—no one really liked her—pulled up when she heard James's question. "He wasn't all that keen to be D.C.," she went on, the sun glinting on her thick-lensed glasses as she kicked her pretty chestnut pony, Stardust, closer to the group. "Someone on the pony club committe heard that Mr Lumley had shut himself up and was moping, because he can't ride any more, so they decided he needed something to occupy him and talked him into it."

"He's not going to be much good if he's not really interested," said James gloomily.

10

"Well, there isn't anyone else. People round here won't take on thankless tasks like the pony club. My mother doesn't really want to be secretary—it's a lot of work—but no one else will do it." Lesley's wide, slightly cow-like face, with its broad nose and thick lips, looked pleased at this proof of meanness in local people.

"I think David *is* quite interested now that he's made up his mind to it," objected Paul. "He and Dad have been talking over which fields they'll use and things like that. But it's how he's going to manage, being so lame and having an arm that doesn't work at all; he can't lift a jump or buckle a bridle . . .".

"He sounds a bit of a wreck to me," grumbled James.

The four Wheelers, who had had to go back to the field where the rally was held to find Rupert's forgotten head-collar, clattered in pursuit of the other pony club members. Long-legged Rupert, the eldest of the four, was riding Rosie, a light bay mare with a mealy nose, a strong-looking pony of fourteen-two. Lizzie, who was next to Rupert in age, owned Rajah, a lean, sober, chestnut gelding, darker in colour and more solidly-built than Lesley Rooke's Stardust. You could tell that Rupert and Lizzie were brother and sister, they had the same pink and white faces, blue eyes and pale, straw-coloured hair, but Rupert's face was longer, his blue eyes dreamy, his hair short and curly. Lizzie had an anxious face, as though she expected things to go wrong, and she wore her hair in one long, thick, flaxen plait.

Behind, came the two younger Wheelers. Annette, she was always called Netti, had short curly hair like Rupert, but her face was heart-shaped and her eyes weren't dreamy or anxious, they had a sparkle which suggested that she enjoyed life and excitement and adventures. Netti was riding Tristram, a little grey Welsh pony who had been outgrown by Rupert. Beside her, Oliver, the youngest of the Wheelers, bounced about on Hobbit, a dark-brown Dartmoor who had once been Lizzie's pony.

"If he's a jockey perhaps he'll let us race instead of all this awful, boring schooling," shouted Oliver, who rode very badly but hated being taught.

"Mrs Rookery didn't really tell us anything about him," complained Rupert. "Lynne," he shouted, "wait for us, we want to know what this new guy is like."

Lynne Roberts was quite different from her younger brother Paul. She had wavy, light-brown hair which stuck out from her plump, cheerful face, and when she laughed, which was most of the time, her hazel-coloured eyes disappeared into the plumpness and became slits. She wasn't a very good rider, but she loved Berry, her red roan pony, and didn't mind that she wasn't very well-schooled and couldn't jump.

"What's he like, really, this David Lumley?" Rupert asked again as he caught up.

"He used to be very nice, always full of jokes," answered Lynne, "but the accident's changed him. Mum says it'll pass off, that it's only the pain and frustration that's making him irritable, but the doctors don't think he'll ever recover completely. They said he'd probably never ride again."

"What exactly happened to him?" asked Oliver, who enjoyed gruesome details.

"It was in some big race, not the Grand National. He's ridden in that lots of times. The Gold Cup, I think. The horse in front fell and brought his horse down and then a third one landed on top of him. It was terribly sad, two of the horses had to be shot and David was unconscious for over a week. Then, when he came round, he was partly paralysed: he couldn't walk or use his left hand, and, on top of that he had lots of broken bones."

"Poor him, how awful," said Lizzie, her voice full of concern.

"Is anyone going to the Brunstock show?" Sarah Rooke changed the subject. She was much prettier than her elder sister, Lesley, and didn't have to wear glasses. Her face was narrow and she wore her dark hair in a fringe. But it wasn't a friendly face, and her rather thin-lipped mouth gave her a determined look, as though she always got her own way.

Chess, her pony, was a stout little piebald of about thirteen hands.

"No shows for us these holidays," answered Lizzie. "Mummy's gone on strike over entry fees and anyway we never win anything.'

"I'm going in for the gymkhana, there are masses of events for twelve and unders. You ought to come, Netti."

"I don't really want to, not without the others. It's no fun hacking miles on your own. And with the Cranford Vale Prince Philip-ers there I wouldn't stand a chance. Even their B team is absolutely brilliant."

"The Great Sarah thinks she's good enough to beat them," sneered Lesley Rooke in a very spiteful voice, as they caught up with the group ahead.

"I didn't say anything of the sort," Sarah snapped back.

"Well, Mummy thinks you are. She's paying your entry fees."

She'd have paid yours, only she knows you haven't a hope in the under sixteen classes."

"I can't help my age . . ."

"Oh, shut up. Little Rookes in their nest should agree and not keep cawing in spiteful voices," Rupert told them.

"I do wish there was a jumping class for *small* ponies," sighed Paul. "Show-jumping is Banjo's best thing, but he can't go in Under 14.2 classes and its no fun going in Clear Round Jumping, show after show. You haven't really won the rosette and anyway I want to jump off against the clock."

"Daddy say's we're wet and that we should run our own gymkhanas and *get* as good as the Cranford Vale," Netti Wheeler told Paul. "But Rupert and Lizzie have gone off competitions now that they've got new and bigger ponies which aren't much good at anything, and Ollie and I aren't exactly brilliant at organization."

When the lane brought them to a road, the Rookes turned the opposite way to the rest of the riders, and trotted, in silent single file towards Woodbury Heights, the Victorian part of the old market town of Woodbury, where they lived in a tall, red-brick house.

At the next crossroads Jennifer Blacker rode on alone. She lived in a modern house called Stonecroft on the Waterford road. The remaining seven riders turned right and took the narrow, winding uphill road which led deep into the country. James Morgan was next to go. Calling that he would see them on Wednesday, he turned in at his white gate, beside a huge notice announcing Four Cross Fruit Farm.

The Robertses and the Wheelers jogged on together as the road meandered between fields, ploughed and sown. Smooth green, friendly-looking hills encircled them and far away on the horizon, they could see the blue line of the Downs.

"It's going to be gorgeous having the rallies right on our doorstep," Lizzie told Lynne. "We won't be late any more and Rajah will be much livelier when he hasn't had to hack miles. This morning he was worn out before the schooling started."

"I wonder what David means to do about schools and jumps." Paul sounded worried. "We've got a few poles and drums, but they're not up to much, and James is expecting steeplechase fences."

"He'll have to do something," said Netti. "A rally without jumps would be unbelievably dreary."

"Well, that girl Angela who took the D ride this morning would only let us trot over the poles," said Oliver Wheeler indignantly. "And we spent simply hours touching our toes and going round the world. Not one single race. If this pony club doesn't improve soon I'm going to give up."

"I expect Dad will sort something out," said Lynne comfortably. "He always says he's David's left-hand man and now he's finished with the spring planting and the cattle are out on the hills, the hard work is over until the hay-making starts."

"You'd better tell him that the pony club members will riot," suggested Rupert. "They'll all start chanting and throwing things if they come to a rally and find no jumps. Not that I mind much. Rosie's so completely clueless. I don't think her mother ever told her how to take off."

14

"Do ponies' mothers tell them things?" asked Netti, ꓮ
the Robertses turned up the Garland Farm lane, leavir
the Wheelers to ride on to Kidlake, where they lived in a
tumbledown old house that had once been a rectory.

"I suppose you may as well join the pony club if that's what
you really want," said Mrs Hutchinson grudgingly as she
drove out of Darkwood Lane and took the road to Woodbury. "The subscription's gone up and up since my children
were members, and everyone says that the Woodbury
Branch is pretty useless. Since Mrs Smythe gave up they
haven't done a thing in any of the inter-branch
competitions."

"I thought I might make some friends," said Alice
Drummond, trying not to be cast down by her Aunt
Margaret's perpetual pessimism.

"There aren't many girls of your age round here. The
Rookes live on the other side of Woodbury and the
Wheelers right out at Kidlake. With petrol so expensive I
couldn't possibly keep driving you over there."

"But once we've collected Saffron I won't need driving.
I'll be able to ride everywhere," Alice pointed out.

"I can't see the pony tied up outside the dentist's," said
Aunt Margaret as the lights changed and they were able to
cross the river Vole by the narrow, ancient bridge. "I do
hope it's quiet in traffic and easy to catch," she went on,
driving past the boat builders and the brewery and the
furniture factory, which made up Woodbury's light
industries. "Mr Crankshaw has only the one pony and his
terms are quite reasonable. I tried Neville Foster at the
riding school first, but he charges the earth. And the price
of riding lessons nowadays, you wouldn't believe it!"

As they left the town Alice tried to visualise Saffron. A
dun Connemara pony, her aunt had told her, fourteen
hands one. She had never had a pony of her own. Well, no
pets at all. Not a dog or a cat or even a hamster, because her
parents had always been on the move. Her father had
worked for a multi-national company and they had travel-

led the world, never spending more than two or three years in the same place: Washington, Mexico City, Rio de Janerio. She'd ridden a lot at riding schools and then, a year ago, when her parents had sent her back to an English boarding school, she had spent several weekends with pony-owning friends. She had loved catching up the pony and grooming it, having time to talk to it after the ride. It had all been much more fun than an hour's ride at some grand riding school. Now the thought of having a pony for the holidays and looking after it herself seemed the best thing that had happened to her since that cold winter morning when they'd broken the terrible news to her. She remembered the horrified faces and hushed voices of the matron and housemistress as they told her the plane had crashed.

"Ah, this is it, Waterford Farm," said Aunt Margaret, slowing down and turning in at an open gate. As the car sloshed its way up the muddy lane Alice took a look at her aunt's unsmiling face. It always seemed rather grim and aggrieved, pale against the dark red of hennaed hair. She didn't look a bit like Daddy, thought Alice sorrowfully, but then of course she was much older.

While her aunt went to the farmhouse to look for Mr Crankshaw, Alice searched the farm buildings for Saffron. She found him tied in a stall and her first feeling was a shock of disappointment.

She'd been imagining a beautiful pony, with a shining dun coat and a bright eye, but Saffron looked rough and unkempt, his ribs showing through his patchy, half-moulted winter coat, his neck and quarters thin, his eyes wary. Alice gave him a piece of bread and half a carrot as she fought with her disillusionment. Aunt Margaret re-appeared, accompanied by a very tall, thin man. Alice looked up from gumboots, corduroys and macintosh and came to a small face with sticking-out teeth topped by a tweedy cap.

"I'm afraid he's a bit poor," admitted Mr Crankshaw. "He didn't winter too well, but he'll soon pick up now that the grass is coming. I've wormed him and I'll drop in a couple of bags of pony nuts with the hay so that you can feed him up a bit."

Mr Crankshaw looked as though he needed feeding up too, thought Alice, as she patted Saffron and said, "He's lovely."

"I bought him for my younger daughter. She was always moaning that the country was dull and she had nothing to do, but she didn't take to riding. Always hankering after the bright lights, is our Sandra."

"Two of mine were pony-mad for three or four years, then they lost interest," complained Aunt Margaret. "That's what I keep telling Alice. I'm not going to all the expense and bother of buying a pony just to find that she's off on some new craze."

Mr Crankshaw produced a saddle and bridle. "Need a good clean, I'm afraid," he said, looking at them disapprovingly. He handed Alice the snaffle bridle and standing martingale. "He carries his head on the high side so we've always ridden him in a martingale. Do you know how to put it on?"

"Yes, I think so," answered Alice, fumbling nervously. Though she had ridden large horses in covered schools, trekked across plains and climbed rocky hillsides on wiry ponies in foreign lands, she hadn't done much saddling and bridling. Three fingers in the noseband, she reminded herself, and a clenched fist in the throatlash.

"Now, you know the way," said Aunt Margaret, when Alice had mounted. "Out of the yard, through the back gate and follow the track straight down to the river. It's fenced most of the way and you can't miss it because it was once the old road. You cross the river at the ford. I suppose the pony's used to water?" she asked, turning to Mr Crankshaw.

"Oh yes, no problem there. We're up to our knees in it half the winter."

"Then you can see our woods," Aunt Margaret went on. "You follow the track for about three quarters of a mile before you bear left and take a smaller path that'll bring

17

you out in Darkwood Lane. If you don't get lost you'll be home before I am; fighting my way through the town and hanging about at the bridge."

Alice waved goodbye and set off. It was lovely, she thought, as Saffron squelched down the muddy track towards the river, lovely to be riding again, to have a pony as a friend. You didn't miss people so much if you had a pony for company. She patted the thin, dun neck. Saffron seemed very willing. He walked briskly with pricked ears and didn't seem at all worried about setting off into the unknown with a complete stranger. Life on the farm must be very dull, thought Alice. Dull and lonely. Perhaps Saffron was also longing for friends; hoping for some sort of change in the dismalness of his day-to-day life.

The Brunstock Show was turning out to be even more of a misery than Hanif had feared. Jupiter, his handsome liver chestnut pony, was almost delirious with excitement and completely uncontrollable. The riding school's instructions were having no effect. Hot and exhausted, with arms which felt as though they had been pulled out of their shoulder sockets, Hanif longed to give up and go home, but he could here his stepfather's voice calling for him. Tall, fair and very English-looking, Charles Franklin has driven the hordes of gymkhana children away from the practice jump and built it into a solid, three feet six high hog's back.

"Come on, Harry," he called. "Don't mess about, put him straight over."

Hanif abandoned an attempt to circle. He pointed the pony at the fence and, accusing himself of cowardice, took a firm hold of the mane. Jupiter raced for it at terrifying speed and hurled himself over, clearing the top pole by a couple of feet.

"Well done. That's the stuff," shouted Mr Franklin encouragingly. "You'll be all right."

Circling wildly and tugging with all his strength in a hopeless attempt to slow Jupiter down, Hanif knew that his stepfather was being stupidly optimistic.

18

"Do you know the course? You'd better take another look at the board. You went wrong last Saturday, remember."

"I know the way. The problem is persuading Jupe to take it. I can't stop him except by circling," said Hanif in a despairing voice.

"Oh, for heavens sake! You've got a double bridle and two nosebands. If you can't stop him in that lot you must be as weak as water. Now keep him walking round until they call you. There are two to go, including the girl in the ring."

Hanif sighed with relief as his stepfather strode away to join Mrs Franklin who was watching from the ringside car park. She wasn't like the English mothers, who, with jeans tucked into gumboots, warm in their uniform of head-scarves and green husky coats, sloshed through the mud of the collecting ring, thought Hanif. In her pink and gold Sari and flimsy little shoes she *had* to watch from the car. He was wondering what it would feel like to have an English mother when he heard the collecting steward shouting his number impatiently. "Come on, sixty-three. We're waiting for you and we haven't got all day."

Flustered, apprehensive and with his hands uncomfortably full of reins, Hanif trotted into the ring. He didn't see the watching faces of the spectators, only the twelve, huge, brightly-painted fences and the impossible twists and turns he was supposed to make between them. Jupiter's head had disappeared into his chest, but at any minute he would see the jumps and there would be no holding him. Never mind, it'll soon be over, Hanif comforted himself as he turned Jupiter for the brush. With one determined tug the pony snatched control and flung himself at the first jump. Then he raced on, sailing over the gate and parallels with careless contempt. He steadied himself for the combination at the top of the ring, Hanif hauled him round and pointed him diagonally across the wall. They hurtled on, clearing the red wall and rustic gate with ease, but now they had to turn again and they were going far too fast.

"Whoa, boy. Steady," shouted Hanif, tugging on the

19

reins. But there was no response. "Whoa," he called again, pulling on one rein with all his strength and hoping to turn the pony, but they were heading straight for the ring rope at full gallop.

"Look out!" he shouted at the single line of spectators. "Look out, I can't stop!"

For a moment he saw the frightened faces, then Jupiter took off, sailing high into the air. People and ponies scattered, leaving a clear path as they raced on down the showground. It was in the horsebox and trailer park that Hanif finally managed to circle to a halt. He waited for a little to get back his breath and calm his pounding heart. Jupiter, prevented from grazing by his two bits and two nosebands, twirled restlessly.

He'll be furious, Hanif thought despairingly of his step-father. He won't lose his temper, he won't shout and rage, but he'll be furious inside. He bought Jupe so that I could be a success. He wants to see me beating other fathers' proper English sons, and I'm turning out hopeless. No good at riding or any other sport. It was no good putting things off, he told himself with a sigh, and, turning Jupiter, he rode back slowly.

As he came to the collecting ring he saw a small crowd gathered round an elderly man who was sitting on the ground. Hanif pulled up. "Oh Jupe, *don't* say we hurt someone," he said aloud.

"You didn't kick him or anything, I think he just fell over trying to get out of the way and he's rather ancient," answered a voice, and a thin girl in jeans and a green polo-necked sweater came up and patted Jupiter's neck. "You are an awful pony, jumping out of the ring like that when you were going so well," she told him. "You're a terrific jumper, the way you sailed over those people's heads."

Hanif took a second look at her. She was probably small for her age, he decided. She had a thin, pale face with freckles, faintly red hair that was cut short and curled close to her head, and greenish eyes. She didn't look as though

20

she was despising him for having no control over his pony.

"Is he your own pony?" asked the girl, walking beside him.

"Yes, my stepfather bought him for me at vast expense and now I can't ride him," answered Hanif sadly. "I'm just not up to Jupe's standard. He won a lot with his last owner, so I know it's my fault."

He could see his stepfather's head above the rest of the little group which clustered round the old man.

"Do at least let me drive you home," Charles Franklin was saying.

But the old man was shaking his head. "My daughter and grand-children will look after me," he answered, allowing himself to be helped up.

"Ah, here's the culprit, Harry, come and apologise for yourself," said Mr Franklin, catching sight of his hovering stepson. "You gave poor Mr Orton the fright of his life."

As Hanif said how sorry he was and explained that he couldn't control Jupiter however hard he tried, two of the collecting ring mothers and a very horsey-looking father surrounded Mr Franklin.

"The pony's too big and strong for a boy of his age. You ought to have got him a thirteen-two."

"Or have him taught how to ride the pony before you turn him loose on the unsuspecting public."

"The pony's won a lot in juvenile classes, I bought him with a good reputation," Mr Franklin defended himself. "And my stepson's been having lessons with Mr Foster."

"He's still a public danger. Have you tried the pony club?"

"The Woodbury's not much good. We're lucky, we're all from the Cranford Vale."

"But I've heard that David Lumley, you know, the National Hunt jockey who had a crashing fall at Cheltenham, is taking over the Woodbury, so things may improve."

"And the Secretary's here somewhere, a lady with glasses. She's called Mrs Rooke."

21

"You'd better get off home," Mr Franklin told Hanif, "and for goodness sake keep that pony under control."

Hanif waved goodbye to his mother and set off across the showground. The gymkhana events had started in Ring Two.

"You're going, then?" The small red-headed girl was beside him again.

"Yes, before I do any more damage. Are you riding in the gymkhana?"

"No such luck. I don't have a pony. We couldn't possibly afford one. Besides, we live in a flat. I just biked over with Mr Foster's riding school. I help there sometimes."

"I liked riding at a riding school better. At least I could manage the ponies," said Hanif sadly. "I thought I rode quite well until we moved to Coxwell and I got Jupe."

"Mr Foster's riding school's not much good," said the girl, looking across at the gymkhana ring. "You can see which are *his* pupils. They're all cantering at one mile an hour. They haven't a hope against the people from the Cranford Vale. What's your name?" she asked suddenly.

Hanif thought before he answered. He supposed his stepfather was right, Hanif was too complicated for English people, it was better just to fit in with their ways and call yourself Harry.

"Harry Franklin," he answered. "What's yours?"

"Tina Spencer," answered the red-headed girl, "and I live in Woodbury, in one of those little streets by the river, so, if you *do* join the pony club I may see you around."

CHAPTER TWO

A Disgrace to David

Perhaps the rally will change everything, thought Alice, rubber-curry-combing out huge handfuls of dun winter coat. If only I could make just *one* friend. It's lovely having Saffron but it would be even more fun if I had someone to ride with.

She had tried hard to fit in, but life at Shawbury really was rather dismal. Aunt Margaret was kind in her way, but she was only interested in her dogs. She bred springer spaniels, but they were all kept in kennels with concrete runs and not allowed in the house, so they didn't have much character. And she'd told Alice not to pet them as she might spoil their manners for the show-ring. Uncle Peter was rather fat and dull. He seemed to be interested in stocks and shares and cricket, and never wanted to talk, but hurried home from work and settled down in front of the television. The Hutchinson children, Andrew, Jane, Nick and Clare, were all years older than Alice. Andrew and Jane were working, Nick and Clare still at college. When they came they talked about their jobs and travels and exams. The three older ones couldn't be bothered with Alice, but Clare had been friendly and fun. If only she'd stayed, instead of loading herself with an enormous backpack and setting out to explore Turkey with a party of friends. Still, Saffron had certainly improved life. Alice had ridden him on every one of the four days for which he had been hers and had spent hours grooming him and cleaning his tack. If only I had had a brother or sister, she thought as she saddled up. It was difficult even to have friends when you moved about the world so much. She had made two at boarding school, but they lived such miles away.

23

To Hanif, too, it seemed a very important day. If this Mr Lumley can't help, I give up, he thought as he oiled Jupiter's hoofs. Dad will just have to swallow his pride and sell Jupe.

"It's nothing personal," he said, patting the strong, liver chestnut neck. "Just that you're the boss and it ought to be me."

Mrs Franklin, wearing one of her morning saris, came out to the stable as Hanif finished tacking up, and watched as he led Jupiter into the yard and prepared for the usual struggle to mount. She watched helplessly as Jupiter twirled and pranced, and Hanif, one foot in the stirrup, hopped in pursuit. At last he trapped the pony in the corner by the gate and scrambled into the saddle.

"Goodbye, Mum," he shouted, setting off at a hammering trot along the road. "Don't worry, I'll be all right." He knew that such a fast trot was bad for Jupiter's legs, but trying to insist on a slower pace would be hard on his own arms and, anyway, they were late starting. He had never ridden on the far side of Woodbury before and his step-father had said that Hanif would certainly lose himself if he went by the woods and fields and that Jupiter might refuse to ford the river, so there was nothing for it but the long, boring way round by the bridge and the town.

Lesley and Sarah Rooke weren't speaking. Sarah had won a rosette, only a third, in the Twelve and Under Egg and Spoon on Saturday and Mrs Rooke had been bursting with pride ever since.

"The only Woodbury child to come *anywhere*," she told all her friends, "and against the whole of the Cranford Vale Prince Philip B. Team. It was really quite something. I mean, they get to Wembley year after year. But of course Sarah's a natural, good at everything. Poor old Lesley has to learn the hard way. No natural aptitude at all."

It had always been like that, thought Lesley, seething with unspoken resentment as she groomed chestnut Stardust for the rally. Sarah was the pretty one, the clever one, best at everything. Julian was the baby, the boy. He was perfect in Mummy's eyes too. She was the ugly one, no good at anything, the one who didn't count.

She groomed fiercely, too absorbed in her hatred for Sarah to notice Stardust's gentle nuzzling. Only the unsatisfactory things forced themselves upon her attention. Stardust's forelock, which she had cut with scissors, still looked stupidly unnatural and like a fringe, her four white socks were grubby and refused to come clean.

Oh well, what does it matter? she thought angrily. It's only the pony club and no doubt David Lumley will spend his time praising Sarah, telling her what a brilliant little rider she is.

Lesley tacked up, and then finding with pleasure that her sister wasn't ready, started for Garland Farm alone.

Sarah's little piebald, Chess, hated being left behind. He neighed deafeningly, trod on Sarah's toe and refused to keep still while she saddled and bridled him.

Lesley's so jealous. It's mean of her to be so horrible whenever I win anything, thought Sarah, slapping Chess and shouting at him to keep still. It's not my fault if I'm good at things, better than she is. And, anyway, she couldn't win anything when she didn't even enter.

Tina Spencer was bicycling slowly out of Woodbury. It was uphill all the way to Garland Farm, she thought drearily, but still, it didn't matter if she was late, no one noticed the dismounted members. It was her mother who had insisted on her joining the pony club and who had paid her subscription. "Then you'll have something to do in the holidays when I'm working," she had said. And she'd saved the money out of the wages she earned at Fanny's Food and Wine Bar in Cross Street. It hadn't been much fun, standing in cold fields in January and watching other people ride, thought Tina, and she hadn't been able to afford the extra money for the trip to Olympia, but she pretended to her mother that she enjoyed rallies. She didn't want her to know that she had wasted her hard-earned cash. Next year

25

I'll tell her I'm too old, or something, she decided, as the red town houses ended and the fields began.

Then, hearing frantic neighs, she looked over a hedge and saw Sarah Rooke cantering across the field on an excited and indignant Chess. She leaned her bike against the hedge and opened the gate. "Are you going to the rally?" she asked.

"Yes, and Lesley was in one of her moods and wouldn't wait for me, so now Chess is going mad."

Jennifer Blacker was in a bad mood too. Though she had shouted and sulked and argued for three days she had still not managed to persuade her mother to let her transfer to the Cranford Vale. Mrs Blacker, who was an equally determined character, said that Jennifer needn't go to Woodbury rallies if she didn't enjoy them but that *she* was only prepared to drive her to a show every Saturday, and that was that.

Lesley, seeing Jennifer coming out of the bridle path at Four-cross, slowed up the already dawdling Stardust. She was still seething with anger and she didn't want to ride with anyone. But, as she dawdled along keeping a good distance between herself and Jennifer she heard hoofs and voices coming up from behind and, looking back saw that Sarah and Tina were overtaking her. She kicked Stardust into a trot. But the Rooke ponies were fond of each other, unlike the Rooke sisters. Stardust shuffled slowly, Chess produced his briskest trot and they managed a whinnying reunion as they turned up the Garland Farm Lane.

"Lesley, I forgot to tell you. Mummy says we're to be kind to this new girl, Alice Drummond. Her parents have been killed in an air crash. And there's a new boy too. He's foreign. He's come from Singapore, but he's really a Pakistani." Sarah told her sister.

"*You* can be kind to them," snapped Lesley, her eyes glaring angrily from behind the thick-lensed spectacles. "*You're* the clever one."

Paul was not very happy with the arrangements for the

rally. His father had dumped a large number of oil drums, an old pig trough and several worn-out tyres in an untidy heap in Long Meadow. The local builder had delivered six cavaletti and the Forestry Commission twelve immensely heavy fir poles, but there was no course, no steeplechase fences, nothing to impress James. It won't be much fun having a pony club if all the big ones give up coming, he thought despondently as he saddled Banjo.

Lynne was determined that red-roan Berry should be the best-turned-out pony there. She didn't care much about jumping or schooling and the only race she ever won was trotting, but she loved grooming and looking after ponies.

"And for once they're all going to see your oiled hoofs and your freshly water-brushed mane," she told Berry as she polished her with the rubber. "When we had to hack over to Woodbury, Paul said it was all a waste of time, but now it's definitely worth it."

Paul hated grooming, but then they were opposites in most things. He took after Dad and she took after Mum. She looked across at Banjo who was tied to a ring in the cattle-yard wall. His coat was awful. He wasn't losing it properly, and, when he did all the horrible bald patches caused by sweet itch would show up. They'd bought him very cheap because he'd looked so awful, but though they kept him in the yard all through the spring and summer and didn't let him eat a blade of grass, the hair didn't grow again. Luckily Paul didn't seem to mind. Jumping was all he cared about.

Mrs Rooke, the Secretary arrived, bringing Julia Cartwright, one of the junior instructors, who was to take the D ride. Julia was twenty-one, with a plump cheerful face and her brown hair worn in a pony tail. She waited, talking to Lynne and admiring Berry. Mrs Rooke, severely dressed in grey, lay in wait for the members, looking sharply from her watch to her lists and back again.

Suddenly the lane was full of the scrunch of hoofs, and the pony club members came riding past the back of the farmhouse, with its small, square stableyard. Mrs Rooke ticked her list busily, then she found Alice.

"Your badge and fixture card," she said, handing them over. "Now, do be *sure* to put your name down when you are coming to rallies. Is that the pony you've hired for the holidays? He looks a bit poor, you must worm him at once. Now, these are my daughters, Sarah, who's the real rider, and Lesley."

Alice searched her mind desperately for something to say. You didn't make friends by sitting on your pony in stupid silence, but then David Lumley came driving round the corner from his house in a specially adapted Land Rover with a disc announcing 'Disabled Driver' on the rear window. He stopped in the midst of the ponies and people.

Mrs Rooke hurried over. "I'm afraid they're not all here yet," she fussed. "It really is disgraceful."

"Well, let's make a start," said David Lumley. "Can Julia get her ride into the small paddock first?"

He was wearing corduroys, a thick, navy blue polo-necked sweater and a padded waistcoat that was a lighter blue. He sat with the Land Rover door open, but seemed reluctant to get down among the milling crowd of ponies.

"Here come the others," called Lynne, as James, looking unusually hot and flustered, came trotting up the lane, followed by the Wheelers, whose voices, all talking at once, drowned the sound of their ponies' hoofs.

"Late as usual," Lynne taunted them.

"Rupert lost his boots." Lizzie looked round anxiously. "I hope Mr Lumley's not cross."

"I think he is a bit," said Netti, taking a quick glance at the white, unsmiling face. "At least he doesn't look wildly pleased to see us."

"Well, we're not last for once," announced Oliver. "Here's someone arriving at the sideways canter."

"The sideways canter?" Sarah and Lynne hurried to look as a limp, exhausted Hanif and a sweat-lathered Jupiter came clattering into the yard.

"What *have* you been doing to that pony?" demanded Mrs Rooke, eyes glaring behind her glasses. "I've *never* seen anyone arrive at a rally in such a disgraceful condition."

"Sorry," answered Hanif who had no strength left for argument. "He went mad when he saw the other ponies ahead."

Oliver Wheeler, who looked like Rupert, but with a rounder, cheekier face and blue eyes, bright with self-confidence instead of dreamy, began arguing with Mrs Rooke.

"But it's not fair that I should always be in the D ride. I'm only two years younger than Paul and Netti and half the D's are years and years younger than me. Some of them are only six . . ."

"Oh, come on, Ollie," interupted Julia Cartwright. "You know you're my leader and I can't manage without you. And poor David's already got eleven. He can't cope with any more."

Oliver went off to the small paddock, muttering indignantly. David Lumley, trying to escape from an anxious and very talkative mother, shouted to Paul to lead on. Hanif struggled to remount the twirling Jupiter. Alice turned back, grabbed his rein and tried to hold him still.

"Are you new too?" she asked as they rode into their field, which ran, long and narrow, beside the lane and was fenced with thick hedgerows, well studded with trees.

"Yes," agreed Hanif breathlessly, as Jupiter jogged sideways, fighting for his head and, at intervals, pulling his rider half out of the saddle with his violent snatches at the reins. "This is my first rally and I have a feeling it may be my last."

The other riders had been arguing about their positions in the ride, but Hanif and Alice merely joined on at the back. Then, looking across the school at Jennifer on bright bay Sea King followed by James on the stouter, taller, but equally well-turned-out darkbrown Ferdinand, both decided that they were hopelessly outclassed and waited gloomily to be sent to join the D ride.

David Lumley parked the Land Rover in the centre of the school and climbed out slowly.

The pony club members tried to inspect him without staring too obviously as he limped a few steps and then stood, leaning on his shooting stick. He was slim and wiry and about middle height, a good bit taller than some jockeys, thought Alice, who had been to the Jockey Club in Rio de Janerio. His hair was nice, thick, mouse-brown and vaguely curly. His eyes were blue but his face was white and drawn and looked older than the rest of him.

David Lumley looked critically at his pony club members.

The first two looked competent and well-mounted. Behind them came Rupert, gazing into space. His anorak was unzipped, his crash cap on the back of his head and his pony, which was half Exmoor, decided David Lumley, noticing the mealy nose and toad eye, wandered along with its nose poked out. Then there were two girls on chestnuts, one anxiously fiddling with her pony's mouth and looking down, the other dawdling along, sitting in the back of her saddle and not trying at all. A nice-looking little grey led a collection of smaller ponies. Roan Berry, piebald Chess and Black Banjo, all drifted along on each other's tails, while their riders flapped their legs uselessly. At the back came a girl on a stargazing dun, and a liver chestnut, sweating with frustration as he fought his equally unhappy-looking boy rider for his head.

David Lumley sighed. What a collection! he thought. Where *does* one begin?

"Good morning, everyone." He spoke briskly to hide his despondency. I'm David, your new D.C. Now from the front, can you tell me your names. First names will do."

Except for Rupert, who had drifted into a dream and had to be answered for by Lizzie, everyone shouted out his or her name in turn.

"I don't suppose I'll get them all straight off. You'll have to remind me," said David, repeating them. "Now, can we have those two large ponies at the back a bit further forward. Lizzie, would you make a large circle and the rest of you follow her, except for Alice and—was it Harry? Right, you two close up with Rupert. Good. Now prepare to trot on."

They trotted, or at leat the two leaders did. Jupiter, cantering sideways and throwing his head about, was upsetting Rosie and Saffron.

"You'd better keep off my tail. Rosie's not totally reliable, she kicks sometimes," Rupert told Alice, who was trying to sit on the stiff-backed, stargazing Saffron.

"Sorry." She tried to slow the pony up by feeling his mouth, but he simply carried his head higher and higher until his ears were almost in her face. It was a horrible feeling and she seemed powerless; out of control and quite unable to do anything about it.

Suddenly Rosie decided that she had had enough. Taking Rupert by surprise, she opened her mouth wide and charged off down the field in the direction of home. Saffron followed her and Jupiter soon overtook the pair of them and thundered on round the field, ignoring Hanif's tugs and 'whoas'.

Alice stopped first, she managed to circle Saffron and, not being at all fit, he was soon quite pleased to stop cantering round. Red-faced, she hurried back to her place in the ride. Rupert stopped at the far end of the field by riding Rosie into the hedge, and he too slunk back into his place, but everyone was too busy watching Hanif, galloping round the field at full speed and completely out of control, to bother about them.

"Don't worry, just keep him going round until he's tired," shouted David. "Don't bother about stopping, steer."

After four circuits of the field Jupiter showed signs of slowing up. "Keep him going," shouted David. "Go on, round again. You mustn't let him stop the moment he wants to."

He turned to Rupert. "How old is your pony?"

"Six, but she hasn't been schooled."

"I can see that. Are you going to school her?"

"Me?" asked Rupert doubtfully.

"Yes, *you*. Ponies don't school themselves and it's no use hoping for a miracle. If you worked on her for the rest of the summer you might get somewhere."

Hanif appeared looking very crestfallen. "Sorry about that," he said to David, "I'm afraid I've no control."

"So I observed. Is your pony stabled?"

"Only at night. He was clipped when we bought him."

"What do you feed him on?"

"Hay, nuts, oats, bran, chaff. The usual things."

"Well, the first thing is to cut out the oats and nuts. Until you've learned to ride him he doesn't get a single oat or nut. Not *one*. O.K.?"

"O.K."

"Right. Number two. Why have you got the wretched animal strapped down like that? Look at you, a double bridle, two nosebands, a curb chain and a running martingale."

"I've never been able to stop him so we've gradually added more and more."

"And you still can't stop him, which proves you're on the wrong track, Let's get some of it off. The dropped noseband and the running martingale to start with, and let the curb chain out a couple of links. "You'll have to do it, I can't. I've got a useless hand."

Hanif dismounted and felt very relieved when Tina appeared to help him.

David had turned his attention to Alice. "How long have you had that pony?" he asked.

"Four days. He's hired for the holidays."

David groaned. "Can you send him back and ask for something rideable?"

"No." Alice shook her head. "I'm afraid not. But he's not as bad as this usually. He's just excited."

"You can cure stargazers, but it takes months rather than weeks," said David with a sigh. "I'm afraid you're in for a rotten holidays."

He turned back to the rest of the ride who were beginning to feel bored and neglected. "Well, now we've got the lunatic ponies under control, let's see what you lot can do. Change the rein, Jennifer. Now I want you to canter on, one at a time, circle at a convenient point and join on at the back of the ride."

Jennifer prodded Sea King into a canter with her heels, circled smoothly and re-joined the ride with a smug expression on her flat, pale face.

David looked at the rest of the ride. "What was wrong with that?" he asked.

"Nothing."

"It was a gorgeously slow canter."

"Perfect," they answered.

"You didn't see anything wrong with the circle?"

"No." They were all shaking their heads.

"Which way should a pony be bent on a circle? Which way should he look?" asked David.

"Inwards," answered Lizzie.

"He should be bent round the rider's inside leg," added Sarah.

"Your turn, James. Now watch carefully this time," David told the members.

"He isn't looking inwards."

"Ferdie's not bent enough."

"Too stiff," they shouted now that they knew what to look for.

Lizzie was next and she had a job to get Rajah cantering. She kicked and whacked energetically and felt quite triumphant when he finally lurched into a canter. "Too fast, he's unbalanced," David was shouting. "Sit up, look up. Take your hands off the withers." Then he waved Lesley on with his good arm. She set off grim-faced and, flapping her legs energetically. She managed to keep Stardust cantering round the school, but the moment she circled the pony fell back into a trot and the rest of the circle was a wild flurry of arms and legs as Lesley tried to get going again.

"No impulsion," shouted David. "It's no use kicking, you've got to sit down and ride. Why's that pony wearing a vulcanite pelham?" he demanded, as Lesley, looking hot and cross, re-joined the ride.

"She always had one she's quite easy to stop in it."

"It's crazy, a pelham on a pony that's behind the bit and

carries its head too low. Don't you understand that with a pelham, whichever rein you use activates the curb chain and therefore has a lowering effect on the pony's head? With a double bridle you have a choice—the bridoon is separate from the curb chain—but your pony needs a snaffle."

"Next," he shouted at Sarah. She was ready and giving Chess a sharp kick broke straight into a canter. She looked down to check that he was on the correct leg, circled neatly and joined the back of the ride.

"Too fast," said David. "Why kick and why look down? We don't want to see your aids. A good rider on a schooled pony gives invisible aids. Only beginners kick."

Netti's little grey Welsh pony, Tristram, had been well-schooled before he belonged to the Wheelers and he went round very neatly, but David said that Netti's circle was more like a banana than a circle and that re-joining the ride was a transition and should be made with elegance. She had stopped with a lurch, using Chess's hindquarters as a buffer.

Lynne made a mess of her turn. Berry trotted faster and further than Rajah, raced round the circle twice and then went half way up the ride before Lynne could stop her.

David sighed. "We know she's been in harness, but you could school her. Hacking may be more fun, but it doesn't improve ponies. You've got to work at it if you want to get anywhere. Go on, Paul."

Paul bustled round on Banjo, who had a very short stride, but was obedient and willing.

"Yes, you do it, but you don't do it well," David told him. "You are all the same," he went on, looking up and down the ride, "You sit on top of your ponies, steering. You kick your heels and you flap your legs and you think you're riding, but you're not. A good rider sits deep, influences the horses hindlegs, gets him moving with impulsion so that he goes on the bit. Some of you are sitting too far forward, some too far back, none of you are sitting deep."

The pony club members all shifted in their saddles. David went on, "Now those of you who have sensible ponies can cross your stirrups and in a moment we'll see if we can get you riding better, but first I'd like the three lunatic ponies to circle and join on. Only at the trot."

Rosie set off with her head low and her nose poked out, and the moment Rupert asked her to circle, she opened her mouth wide and charged off across the field.

"She's so unbalanced and stiff that it's difficult for her to circle," David explained to the rest of the ride. "And she's quite crafty. She's discovered that she can escape from anything difficult by opening her mouth, evading the bit and charging off. What she needs is a properly adjusted dropped noseband." He remembered Hanif. "Can we borrow yours? I'd like to see if it does the trick."

"Yes, of course. Tina's got it."

David left Tina and Lizzie to re-organize Rupert and told Alice to trot on. Saffron trotted, stiff-backed, with a jerky uneven stride and his head carried so high that his face was almost horizontal.

"It sets my teeth on edge to look at him," said David. "Bring him over here and walk round me in a small circle. Now try to take up a contact with his mouth. No, that's no good. Try again at the halt. Use your legs. On a pony like this you must use your legs at every stride, very gently. Never surprise him with them. Now feel his mouth again. Use the legs and try to bring his head down. Good. That's the idea. Now he's accepting the bit. See if you can move off into a walk. Use the reins and legs together."

Alice managed a few strides at the walk before Saffron turned inside out and she had to halt and put him back on the bit. She was delighted to find that she could persuade him to change and she walked and halted happily, but the other pony club members were very bored.

Jennifer produced a Cranford Vale fixture card and showed it to James. Rupert was circling, trying to find out if the dropped noseband made any difference. Netti and Lynne were giggling over something that had happened at school, while Paul and Sarah were engaged in a mounted fencing match, using their whips as foils.

"Come over here and look at this pony," shouted David, suddenly becoming aware that he was losing control. "You can learn a lot from watching other people's ponies. One day you may have to ride a stargazer. This pony was probably born with a weak neck and not much muscle along the crest, but whoever broke him in didn't notice, didn't take extra care to keep him calm and quiet until his neck muscles developed. He was obviously hotted-up and galloped about, he became frightened of his mouth and found he could escape the bit by carrying his head high. Then, the more he stargazed, the more he developed the muscles along the bottom of his neck, which we *don't* want, while the ones we *do* want, the ones that give a pony a beautiful arched neck, which enable him to carry his head correctly and proudly, were allowed to wither away. Now he's spoiled and it's going to take months of patient schooling to change the shape of his neck so that he carries his head in the right place comfortably and naturally."

David patted Saffron's shoulder. "You'll have to keep him very calm, Alice, and remember that every time he gets his head up he's making those lower muscles stronger. It might be an idea to try him in the vulcanite pelham. Where's the pony that ought to be wearing a snaffle?"

Lesley asked, "Do you mean Stardust?"

"Yes, she's the one. You two change your bits over, while I look at Harry."

Tina hurried over to help them. This was turning out quite an interesting rally, she thought, unbuckling Saffron's cheekpiece. She wasn't just standing about and she liked hearing what was wrong with the different ponies and how to cure it. She listened to what David was telling poor Harry.

"A *gentle* squeeze, and don't clutch at the reins. Look, you must realise that if you let it come to a trial of strength, he'll win. He's far, far stronger than you are. You have to control a pony by teaching him to answer your signals, by

36

keeping him clam and balanced so that he's in a position to answer them, and then rewarding him when he does so. Your pony knows the signals, he's well-balanced enough to answer, but he isn't calm. All your bits and nosebands have driven him wild with frustration and, because his whole life has become a pulling match, he's never rewarded. He can't change this, ponies don't have the sort of brains that can work out what's gone wrong and what ought to be done about it. That's the rider's job. Now, it takes two to pull and you're *not* going to be one of them. Trot around the school, and if he starts going too fast, circle or change the direction, don't pull."

"A worried looking Hanif was soon circling feverishly as Jupiter, delighted to have his head, tore round and round.

"Do you know how to make a half-halt?" asked David.

"No."

"Can any of you tell him?" asked David, observing the bored faces of the rest of the ride.

"Yes, it's when you nearly halt, but not quite," answered Jennifer.

"That's the idea. By using your legs, back and seat and your hands very lightly, you go through the motions of halting, but the moment the horse obeys you, by putting his hindlegs under him and shortening or collecting, you reward him by giving with the hands. There is no change of pace. With a difficult pony like Harry's you can make a dozen half-halts in one circuit of the school. And, because you are rewarding him each time he obeys he will gradually come to accept your control. Do you understand, Harry? You do *anything* but pull."

"Yes, I'll do my best," answered Hanif in a dispirited voice. This advice didn't seem to be working either, he thought, and the circling was making him giddy.

"Very green ponies like Rupert's, or very stiff ones like Lizzie's, can't half-halt, but the rest of you should use it to get your pony's hindlegs under him and to increase impulsion. Right, form up the ride and let's see if things go better now."

The well-behaved ponies cantered and circled in turn while David roared at the riders to 'sit deep'. When Stardust's turn came she was greeted with a shout of triumph. "Look at that pony, she's hardly overbending at all and she's got far more impulsion."

Hanif and Alice, struggling to carry out their instructions, were quite pleased to find themselves ignored as David concentrated on the rest of the ride. He had them all riding a large serpentine, three loops covering the whole school. As they crossed the centre line they were supposed to straighten their ponies and then take up the correct bend for the next loop. Jennifer was roared at for holding her pony out with the outside rein so that he always had a wrong bend. All Lizzie's loops looked like triangles instead of circles and Sarah and Netti were told they were idle, while Paul was sitting crookedly, hanging over one side and trying to force his pony into the correct bend, instead of sitting deep and trying to influence the hindlegs.

Lynne, holding on to the pommel and shrieking that no one could be expected to sit to Berry's trot, simply followed the pony in front, and James, who was also bouncing about and looking hot, was shouted at for always being late in changing his bend and not anticipating.

A general cry of relief went up when at last they were allowed to walk.

"Well, we haven't much time left, and I suppose I'd better see what you're like at jumping," said David. "I'll need some strong characters to haul poles and drums. Could the less strong hold the ponies?"

Except for Jennifer, who immediately offered to hold Ferdinand, everyone wanted to build jumps. Hanif found himself with the Roberts's ponies. Berry took an instant dislike to Jupiter, stamping her fore-foot and squealing if he dared to look at her, and Hanif, being pulled in several directions at once, had to be rescued by Tina.

"She's always awful with strange ponies," shouted Lynne, happily engaged in dragging poles from the Land Rover. "Why don't you ride her round, Tina?"

A delighted Tina rushed round trying to find a crash cap to fit her. Sarah's was almost the right size and she mounted and rode proudly away round the field.

Hanif watched dismally as the course emerged. The jumps were nothing like the size he was expected to jump at home, they were only about two-feet-nine in height, but there were all the usual fatal twists and turns. But, when the course was ready and everyone was mounting, David drove over in the Land Rover and said, "We've put three cavaletti in the centre of the school for the lunatic ponies. I don't think it's any use trying to jump them at the moment. You're just going to undo any improvement you've made this morning."

The other riders, excitedly shortening their stirrups, looked at the banned three with shocked pity. But Hannif was ashamed at his feeling of relief and Alice announced firmly that jumping inside out would be no fun at all and she liked cavaletti work.

They trotted round and round, changing the rein at intervals. At first the ponies were excited. Saffron stargazed, Jupiter tried to rush at the poles and fling himself over, Rosie tried to avoid the whole business by charging past them, but gradually the steady trotting round and round calmed them, they began to lower their heads, round their backs and even Rosie, to Rupert's delight, produced a slow cadenced trot.

When they felt the ponies had done enough they stopped and watched the jumping. It was a good course, very solid-looking, with the pig trough, tyres, straw bales and a log making the various arrangements of poles and drums more interesting. But David didn't sound very satisfied with the standard of riding.

"You're all far too busy," he was shouting. "*You* don't have to get the pony over. Your job is to get him going in a balanced manner and with plenty of impulsion. Let *him* do the jumping. Sit *still*. How can a pony concentrate on jumping if you're kicking and steering right up to the fence? Get him going properly before you put him at it. You all ride like beginners. I don't want to see your aids. Use your legs *quietly*, in time with his stride."

Finally he sent them round the course one behind the other, with instructions to keep going and jump every fence three times.

"They do look a bit wild," observed Hanif, watching them critically. Alice felt a huge pang of envy. She did long to be flying round there too.

As David dismissed the ride and then limped to the Land Rover, Mrs Rooke came hurrying down the field.

"I've an announcement to make, David," she called. "Quite an important one."

"You carry on," answered David, going through the awkward, twisting motions that would get him into the driver's seat.

"Listen, everybody," Mrs Rooke commanded the members. "As you know, the pony club is divided into Regions, Areas and Branches and I've just received a letter from our Area Representative telling me about a new competition which is to take place these holidays. It's intended for younger members and those who don't have good enough ponies for the main inter-branch events; in fact, anyone representing their branch in the horse trials or Prince Philip is ineligible. It's to be called the Area Cup, and each team competes in all the phases: dressage, cross-country, turnout and quiz, but there are five members in each team and only four perform in each phase. I thought it sounded just the thing for us."

"*These* holidays?" asked David from the Land Rover.

"That's right."

"Not a chance. None of them can ride a circle yet, much less a dressage test, and their jumping's abysmal. We don't want to disgrace the Woodbury the moment we take over. Give me a year and I'll produce a reasonable team." He started the engine. "Goodbye everyone. See you next week. And *please* school those ponies."

He drove away up the field, leaving them all too surprised to shout their thank yous for the rally.

40

"Well, he won't see *me* next week," said Jennifer indignantly.

"Oh dear, he was rather brusque. I do hope he hasn't overdone things. He did look rather grey," worried Mrs Rooke, starting after the departing Land Rover. "I hope he's well enough to take on the job of D.C."

"Yes, and some of us could perfectly well go in for this cup," Jennifer went on, her indignation rising. "I know half the ride was completely useless. There ought to have been another instructor to stop them holding things up and spoiling it for the rest of us, but we could make up a team of five, Mrs Rooke."

"You, James, Sarah," agreed Mrs Rooke, "and then I suppose Netti and perhaps a Roberts. Yes, I'll talk it over with David again when he's less tired."

The other members were looking at each other despondently.

"He doesn't think much of us," said Lizzie sadly.

"He thinks we're dim."

"Dim and wet."

"Well, I'm afraid we didn't put on a very good show," James admitted solemnly.

The D Ride had finished earlier and only Oliver Wheeler waited in the yard. Everyone else had gone home.

"We had a great time," he announced. "Hobbit won the Handy Pony and Musical Sacks and my lot won the Relay. How did you get on?"

"Ghastly," answered Rupert sliding off Rosie. "My legs are in a state of collapse from overwork and I don't think this silly pony's improved at all."

"It takes time," Lizzie told him. "And the noseband did help a bit."

Hanif dismounted. "Would it be all right to eat lunch here, before starting home?" he asked Lynne.

"Yes, of course. Would you like to water your pony at the trough? It's over there. And, if you haven't got a headcollar I'll lend you Berry's and you can tie him up while you eat."

"Thanks." Hanif took off his crash cap and rumpled his thick, blue-black hair. "What about the noseband, Rupert? Would you like to keep it for a bit?" he asked.

"Well, yes, if you don't need it. Can I borrow it until next Wednesday? If it really works I may be able to persuade my parents to buy me one, but it won't be easy. They're a bit broke at the moment."

"What about your pelham?" Alice asked Lesley.

"I don't care one way or the other. I can't see that it's made much difference to Stardust."

"Well, if you really don't mind, can I keep it?" asked Alice. "I think it really does make quite a big difference to Saffron."

Only Hanif and Alice stayed to eat their lunches. Tina wished she had thought of bringing hers. I will next week, she decided, as she bicycled down the lane behind the Wheelers. Everyone was much friendlier this time and Lynne let me ride Berry.

"Do you live a long way away too?" asked Hanif, as, with the ponies tied up and munching the wisps of hay scattered over the barn floor, he and Alice collapsed on straw bales and unpacked their food.

"Yes, Darkwood Lane. It's on the other side of Woodbury, but my aunt's taught me all the short cuts so it's a lovely ride. All woods and fields until you get to Four Cross."

Hanif, looking at Alice's face, decided that he liked her. She wasn't a pink and white English blonde like the Wheelers. Her hair was dark gold, her skin brownish, her eyes dark blue. She had a big mouth, a straight nose and a decided expression. She looks Swedish, he thought.

"I live at Coxwell," he told her. "It's not far from you, so perhaps you'll show me the good way home. I wasn't sure that I'd ever get Jupe to ford the river so I came all the way by road."

CHAPTER THREE

We Need Advice

After the rally, Mrs Rooke was very anxious that Sarah should school.

"David did ask that you should all train your ponies, and we do want you in top form," she said. "I know there isn't much time, but supposing I did persuade him to relent and at least *consider* entering for the Area Cup, you must have Chess going well. Perhaps you should go round to Mr Foster's. I know the instruction's not up to much, but you have the use of the jumps and the dressage arena, and if you have your own pony they only charge a third of the cost of a proper lesson."

So, next morning, Sarah went off to the riding school, and Lesley, who had paid more attention to David's advice than she had admitted, doubled the oats and nuts in Stardust's feed and made two jumps out of straw bales and a old door. Later on, when Stardust had digested, she had pulled up her stirrups and tried going round the field at the gallop.

"Inspire that pony," David had said. "Don't kick her, get her going with impulsion. She's a nice-looking pony. She shouldn't be dawdling along behind the bit. Go on, wake her up. Make something of her."

Well, at least he hadn't told Sarah that she was a brilliant little rider. He had swept aside Mummy's suggestion that Jennifer, James and Sarah were better than the rest. That had kindled a faint spark of hope in her. I'll try for a week, she decided, and then, if he doesn't notice, I'll go back to hacking.

Alice had shown Hanif the way home by the Four Cross bridle path, Waterford Farm and the woods. They hadn't talked much because they had both been worn out by the

43

rally, and she was very surprised when Hanif telephoned next morning at breakfast-time.

"Are you going to school today?" he asked, "because if you are, why not come over and ride in our field? I've got some jumps and a school marked out. Jupiter keeps neighing. I think he's missing his pony club friends."

"Oh, terrific," said Alice, who knew that Aunt Margaret was sighing over the muddy track she was making in the paddock. "Shall I come as soon as I've groomed?"

"Yes, that'll be great," Hanif sounded pleased. "See you."

When Alice arrived, Hanif was attempting to mount a spinning Jupiter. Saffron, excited by his lively companion, followed them out to the field stargazing horribly.

"Oh, what lovely jumps," Alice exclaimed, amazed at the sight of six professional-looking show jumps arranged in the centre of the field. "You are *lucky*."

"Am I?" asked Hanif, already hot and harrassed by Jupiter's behaviour. My stepfather's bought me a brilliant pony which I can't ride and made me perfect show jumps which I can't jump. Well, not properly. I crash over out of control." He sounded very bitter and despairing.

"Does he know anything about riding?" asked Alice, walking round the school and admiring the letters which marked it, neatly painted on white plastic buckets.

"A bit. He belonged to the pony club when he was a boy. He was in the tetrathlon team. I think he was better at running and shooting and swimming than at riding, but he's good at all sports."

"Tough," said Alice. "On you, I mean. Still, he seems very generous."

"Yes, but then I feel I'm letting him down," explained Hanif. "If he gave me less I might not feel such a failure."

"Well, I'm afraid I'm a great trial to my relations too," said Alice, glad to tell someone. "You see my aunt and uncle thought they had finished with children. Theirs are all grown-up, the youngest is twenty, and now they've had to give me a home. My mother was an only child and my father had this one, much older sister, so she feels she has to take me in. Things are a bit better now I've got Saffy. At least I can go for long rides. I'm not under my aunt's feet *all* day."

"Our lives are full of problems," said Hanif, "and you ponies should help us, not add to them. Do you hear, Jupiter? Now do stop messing about and walk on a loose rein."

They schooled at the walk. Alice was pleased with Saffron. The pelham was being a great help and she could almost always keep his neck the right way round walking and halting. Jupiter was still jogging and looking round for excitement. He still seemed over-fresh, but gradually he calmed down and began to walk on a long rein.

When they were tired of walking they agreed to try a trot. Jupiter set off immediately at a sideways canter and Saffron, catching his sense of excitement, began to star-gaze. Alice walked, halted and started again, this time smoothly and on a circle. She practised circles on both reins and then, becoming bolder, attempted a serpentine.

Hanif, tired of battling with his snatching, bouncing pony, stopped for a rest and stood in the centre, watching her.

"You're doing quite well," he said. That's a big improvement. When Saffy's going properly he looks quite a superior sort of pony."

"It's partly the bit. He's not afraid of it in the same way that he was of the snaffle. I suppose being large and round and not having a joint it feels quite different."

"When you're worn out, will you stop and watch me?" Hanif said. "I'm not getting anywhere and you may be able to see what I'm doing wrong."

Alice's legs were already aching. She had to squeeze so hard to keep Saffron on the bit, and glad of an excuse for a rest, she halted carefully, beside Hanif.

"He's not bad at the walk. Look." Hanif set off round the school on a long rein.

"You see, I'm giving him his head at the walk, no problems, but when we try trotting..." He picked up the reins and a pulling match began. Soon Jupiter was cantering sideways and flinging his head about.

"Try circling," said Alice. But Jupiter merely proved that it was possible to circle at a sideways canter. Swinging his quarters he bounced round and round until Hanif began to wrench at the reins angrily.

"Walk," said Alice. "Try and get him to relax again."

"It's no use," Hanif sounded despondent. "The same thing happens every time."

"But supposing you start off with a completely loose rein, exactly as though you were walking. Don't shorten them this time. Leave them lying on his neck and start off very gently."

"I'll probably gallop twice round the field," said Hanif gloomily. "Trot on, Jupe."

Jupiter started fast, but then he seemed confused to find he had nothing to pull against. He gradually settled to a shambling trot with his head low.

"It feels very peculiar, unbalanced," said Hanif, "but it's restful for the arms. Though how I'm supposed to circle or jump like this is beyond me."

"It's beyond me too," agreed Alice. "But I should go on riding like that. At least he's stopped being a fiery charger."

They schooled on. Experimenting, Hanif found that he could persuade Jupiter to walk or halt by word of mouth and taking his weight back and he could make vague circles with a slight feel on the inside rein.

"I don't see what the next stage is," he said when they both stopped for a rest. "I suppose I can go on trotting round like this until next Wednesday."

"We need more advice. We're doing what David told us and it's working, but we need to be told what to do next. Do you think he'd take another look at us?"

"Before Wednesday?"

"Yes."

"It's asking a lot. I don't think he enjoyed teaching us, we were too awful. I think he'll just say no."

That wouldn't kill us," said Alice. "Do you think if he knew we were really *serious* about schooling he might agree to help us?"

"I don't know," answered Hanif. "We've only met him once and we didn't really get to know him."

"The Robertses know him best. We might ask them what they think," suggested Alice. "And if Rupert and Lizzie are trying to school they may be desperate for advice too. I'd telephone them all, only Aunt Margaret's in a great fuss about her bill. Why don't we ride over? Are you doing anything tomorrow?"

"No, just trying to tame Jupe."

"Will you come then? We could take our lunches. Let's visit Lizzie and Rupert first, and if they agree we'll ask the Robertses whether we dare ask David. We don't want to put him off the pony club altogether."

It was a sunny April morning with a pale blue sky and small scudding clouds. A good omen, thought Alice, looking up through the still bare branches of the beech trees as she waited in the lane for Hanif. Aunt Margaret was training one of her dogs, walking it up and down the paddock and making it stand at attention in front of imaginary judges. They both looked rather bored.

Hanif came down the lane, walking on a loose rein. "Sorry I'm late," he said. "I didn't dare try trotting."

Along the narrow path through the wood both ponies wanted to lead, and whichever was behind jogged and pulled or jogged and stargazed, but once they had crossed the river and could walk side by side up Mr Crankshaw's muddy track, they settled down.

The Wheelers' house was old, and it peered out from beneath a mass of ivy. Half-attached trellises dangled from its walls, unsupported creepers and climbing roses grew downwards instead of up. They rode into the cobbled yard at the side of the house. The stable doors sagged on their hinges and needed painting. Headcollars, buckets and grooming tools lay scattered everywhere.

It was very different from Harry's weedless gravel, clipped hedges and perfect loosebox, thought Alice. Very different from Shawbury with its gloomy, dripping trees and the smell of dogs' meat cooking. She liked it better.

"I can hear their voices," said Hanif. "Do you think we should look for them down there?"

They took a path through the overgrown laurels and came to a field. It was a very bald field. The grass was eaten right down to the earth, and it was scattered with bits of jumps and battered oil drums. Rupert was riding Rajah and Lizzie Rosie. They seemed to be schooling earnestly.

"You're right, he is like a board," shouted Rupert. "In some ways he's worse than Rosie."

"She's so *long*, she seems to go on for ever," Lizzie shouted back. "I've tried everything, but I can't seem to push her together!"

Lizzie was looking down with a worried expression, completely absorbed by her schooling. It was Rupert who saw Alice and Hanif at the gate.

"Visitors," he shouted, obviously welcoming any interruption. Kicking Rajah into a canter, he came thundering over. "As you can see we're obediently schooling. But, as you may also have noticed, we are not making much impression."

"We've improved a bit," Alice told him. "We can both walk, but we need more advice. We can't wait until Wednesday."

"It's no use coming here for advice," said Lizzie, arriving at a fast, unbalanced trot. "We need it more than anyone else."

"We hoped you might be feeling desperate too." Alice looked at Hanif.

"What Alice means is, do we have the courage to ask David for another schooling session for the lunatic ponies before next Wednesday," said Hanif quickly.

"Oh, we *can't*." Lizzie sounded horrified at the idea. "He was quite worn out by the last one. And we were all so dreadfully bad. I don't think he liked teaching us one bit."

"I was afraid you would say that," admitted Alice sadly.

"Of course, you could make out a case that it's in his own interest," said Rupert. "I mean, if we improve we won't be so ghastly to teach and we won't drive him potty. Once we're all riding well on our beautifully schooled ponies, he'll be able to hold up his head among the other D.C.s."

"But you can't possibly ask for an extra rally," objected Lizzie.

"No, not a rally, just advice. I can walk and trot on a loose rein. What do I do next?"

"My question's about the canter, I can keep Saffy on the bit at walk and trot, but he turns inside out the moment we canter," added Alice.

"I still don't understand what to do about Rosie's nose. I've schooled her all morning and if anything its worse, so I could certainly do with advice if there's any going," said Rupert.

"We could consult Lynne and Paul," suggested Alice. "They know David best."

"Yes, let's do that," agreed Rupert. "Anything to stop schooling. Here, take your ramrod Ra, Lizzie. I think he's un-bendable and you've got to accept a lifetime of square circles."

"No, I won't give up," Lizzie answered firmly. "I'm sure Ra is really as good as all the other ponies. It's probably just me."

They rode back down the winding road towards Garland Farm.

"It's lovely here," said Alice looking at the primroses on the banks and the circle of smooth green hills.

"It's a great place for riding. Netti and Ollie have gone for a gallop up Beacon Hill." Lizzie pointed. "The tall one, over there. But of course the beech woods are best in the summer; cool and shady and the ground doesn't get so hard."

As they drew nearer to the farm they all became silent, for the favour they were about to ask seemed to be growing larger, while the importance of their reasons for asking it was shrinking to nothing. They found Lynne and Paul painting their jumps. They had the poles propped along the fence and Lynne was painting sections in white, Paul in red, both leaving spaces for the other colour to go on later. They seemed very pleased to see the pony club members.

"We thought we'd smarten things up a bit for Wednesday," Paul explained, "and since David bought rustic poles, we thought we'd have ours coloured."

"Has he recovered from the rally?" asked Alice.

"Looks like it. He's been round the farm in the Land Rover this morning," Paul answered.

"He told Mum he was absolutely whacked after coping with us lot, but I think he's over it now," added Lynne.

"Where is he?" asked Rupert, looking round the farm buildings.

"Gone for his lunch, I should think. It's half-past-twelve."

"We can't disturb him at lunchtime," said Lizzie, glad to grab at any obstacle.

"We've come to ask him for some more advice," Alice explained. "We've all been doing the things he told us and we've improved a bit, but now we've all run into new problems and we've got questions to ask. It'll be a terrible waste of time to wait until next Wednesday."

"And when he's got a whole ride he can't spend much time on us, it holds everything up," added Hanif.

The Robertses looked at each other. "Mum's always telling us we mustn't bother him," said Lynne, but you're the pony club and that's different. If you like I'll pop round and tell him you're here."

"Yes, and you might explain that we've come for advice," Rupert told her.

"And that we've brought our lunches so we don't mind waiting until it's convenient," added Hanif.

Lynne ran round the corner of the dutch barn and vanished.

"It looks a nice house, old," said Hanif, studying the back, for it had been built to face south and the Downs.

"Yes, it's very old," Paul sounded quite proud. "And David's made it very posh inside. He was going to get married, you see. Everything was settled and then he had the accident. His girlfriend chucked him when he was in hospital. It was when they thought he would never be able to walk again."

"What a horrible girlfriend," said Lizzie indignantly.

"Dad always thought she was a good-looker, but Lynne and I didn't like her much. Mum says David's well out of it," added Paul.

"Poor David, he must have been miserable. That on top of everything else," said Alice, "though I suppose you've got to look at it from her side too."

"Well, at the time he was fighting to get better. He was determined to get out of his wheelchair. Dad used to go and see him in hospital. He said he was really brave. Then, when he got home it all seemed to hit him, and he got really depressed."

"It was a good thing he'd bought the farm and lucky he'd got all of you," said Alice.

"Well, jockeys don't go on for ever, so, if they've any sense they save when they're doing well and buy a place where they train a few horses later, when they retire. David's got a row of boxes by the house. But now no one knows whether he'll be capable of training. The kick he got on the head is the worst of it. His brain was damaged and that's why his left arm doesn't work and he still gets headaches."

"He's welcome to use us as guinea-pigs," said Hanif.

"It's quite different training racehorses to teaching the pony club," Paul began, but Alice interrupted him.

"Here's Lynne coming back."

"He says he'll come and see you in about twenty minutes to half an hour when he's had lunch," Lynne told them.

"How did he take it?"

"Did you tell him we wanted advice?"

"Did he seem cross?" they asked, crowding round her.

"I don't know really. He seemed a bit put out to start

with, but then he said O.K. and went on cooking his chops. Everything takes him such a long time with only one hand that works, but he doesn't like it if you keep offering to help."

The pony club members looked at each other doubtfully. It didn't seem very hopeful.

"Oh well, we'd better eat our lunches," said Hanif despondently. "Can we tie the ponies to the barn, Lynne?"

Hanif was packing his picnic box away in his rucksack when David appeared round the corner of the barn. His limp looked even worse than on Wednesday, thought Alice, trying not to stare. His walk was a sort of crabwise movement. Perhaps they really ought not to bother him.

"You wanted to see me?" asked David, sitting down on the nearest hay bale.

"Yes," they all answered at once, and then they stood round speechless, each hoping that someone else would begin.

Alice took the plunge. "We've been schooling, doing all the things you told us, and the ponies have improved a bit, but now we need more advice and next Wednesday's such a long way off. We wondered, well, if you could take another look at us and our ponies."

"Just to see if we're on the right track," Hanif added hastily, "and where we go next. I've got Jupiter to walk and trot on a loose rein, but I've no control and I don't see how it works show-jumping."

"And I've cornered and circled Rajah for hours, but it doesn't seem to be doing much good so I can't be doing it properly," wailed Lizzie.

"And I can go round and round the school now. We don't charge off at all, but Rosie doesn't show the smallest sign of going on the bit," complained Rupert.

"Three of you were the lunatic fringe, weren't you?" asked David. "I seem to recognise the worst behaved of the ponies."

"Yes, I'm afraid so," agreed Alice sadly. "But we are determined to improve. We've all been schooling very seriously."

52

David looked round at their doleful faces and suddenly smiled. "All right, you've convinced me. I didn't expect to see any of you again after the rough time I gave you on Wednesday, but if you're that keen I'd better try to help. We'll go in the small paddock and take a look at all these problems."

"Oh thanks."

"Great," they said, rushing to buckle nosebands and tighten girths.

"Could someone fetch my shooting stick from the Land Rover?" asked David as they mounted.

"I will." Lizzie trotted off towards the house and returned in a few moments, bearing the stick proudly. "You go on and start walking round," said David, getting to his feet painfully.

The riders were all grimly intent on showing improvement, but the ponies were excited and uncooperative. Saffron was jogging and stragazing, Jupiter fighting for his head. Alice turned away from the others and circled, Hanif rode round in the opposite direction from the Wheelers and dropped his reins. David reached the centre of the paddock and sat watching them.

Then he said, "Look, they're all so completely different I think I'd better see you one at a time. Alice first. The rest of you come into the centre and watch."

Alice circled, using her legs desperately, determined to prove that she could keep Saffron's head down at the walk, whatever happened at the trot.

"You've got the idea," David called to her. "He's happier in that bit and you've persuaded him to accept your contact with his mouth. But you must remember that it's difficult for him to carry his head the correct way, you've got to allow time for the muscles to develop. When they do, everything will become easy for him, but until then you must give him frequent rests. After every spell of going on the bit, give him a spell of walking on a long rein, let him stretch his neck right out."

"Supposing he puts it up?" asked Alice.

"If he's calm he won't. But go on, give him a long rein now. Good. This applies to all of you." David turned to the stationary riders. "When you've schooled for, say, ten minutes, give your pony a long rein and if he walks round stretching out his neck as Saffron is, that shows your schooling has been on the right lines."

He gestured towards Alice. "Keep him going. It's his neck muscles we're resting, not your legs. Remember that on a lively pony you must use your legs very quietly every stride. Now, pick up your reins, very gently, put him back on the bit and, when you're ready, try a trot."

Saffron threw up his head and set off at his jerky stiff-backed trot.

"Keep rising," shouted David. "It's no use trying to sit on a stiff-backed pony, you only make him worse. Use your legs together as you touch the saddle. No, it's no use. You've lost him. Come back to a walk and try again. Now this time I want you to squeeze your inside rein in time with your legs. Give a squeeze at the same moment as you ask him to trot. The idea is to keep his jaw soft and flexed, to persuade him not to stiffen or resist as he changes pace. The trouble about horses is that their jaws, necks, backs and hindlegs are all attached and if anyone of them is stiff the whole lot are affected. Off you go, Alice, and keep squeezing." He let her trot around several times.

"Well done, now see if you can change the rein through the circle and go round the other way. Good, you've got the idea. And I'm afraid that you've simply got to go on and on like that until he develops the right muscles. It's a long and boring business."

"I don't mind said Alice, patting the dun neck. "I've got nothing else to do these holidays so I may as well try to re-school him even though he's not mine."

"Right, well we'll have Rupert next. Bring that pony over here, I want to have a look at the noseband. Good grief!" he went on indignantly. "You've pulled it up so tight she *can't* flex her jaw. Of course she's not going on the bit, you've made it impossible."

"I thought they weren't supposed to open their mouths," said Rupert, his pink and white face flushing scarlet. "I thought that was the whole point of a dropped noseband."

"No, it's to stop them opening their mouths *wide* and evading the bit. To have a soft mouth and a supple spine a pony must flex or relax his jaw and gently chew his bit. Jump off and let it out. You must leave room for three fingers."

"You all seem to have the idea that if a little of something is good, more of it must be better," he complained, as Rupert re-mounted and began to walk round. "It's not true. We want as few gadgets and bits as possible. We want to use the lightest possible aids. We want to make everything look easy and simple. That's the sign of a good rider."

"But lots of leg," suggested Alice.

"No, not more than is necessary. None of you have learned to use your legs and seats properly yet. You're not 'active' riders. Everyone is a beginner for at least two years and then, as you become more experienced, you have to change into an active rider, who influences his horse, instead of just sitting on him. Once we've got you all riding forward, using your legs and seats automatically, and you've developed the right muscles, it won't be such an effort."

He turned to Rupert. "Leave her nose alone. Stop thinking you can *pull* it in. Ride her forward, think about her hindlegs. If you get them working she'll start to improve. Your hands *feel* her mouth, but they follow it. There musn't be any backward pull. You wouldn't ride a bicycle pedalling like hell with the brakes on, would you?"

When Rupert began to look exhausted he was called in and Lizzie took his place. They could all see how stiff Rajah was on the circle, and Lizzie, looking down, seemed to have become equally tense and rigid.

"Relax," David shouted at her. "Loosen your elbow joints, stop fixing your hands on his neck. You won't get anywhere if you try to *force* him into the correct position, in fact you'll make it more difficult. Relax, put your reins in one hand, look at the scenery." When he had Lizzie and Rajah both looking less tense, David called them in.

"Your pony has been spoiled," he said. He's not like your brother's youngster, who's just green and unschooled. He's acquired bad habits and being middle-aged he's set in his ways. You can't *force* him into another shape, force him to bend his ribs, but with suppling exercises we can certainly improve him. Have you heard of shoulder-in?"

Lizzie nodded.

"Well I think he'd find that too difficult at the moment, so I'd like to start with something called leg-yielding. It's quite simple," he added as Lizzie's expression became anxious. "Just walk round on the circle, now turn his head in a little more with your inside rein and at the same time push his quarters out with your inside leg. No, no, no. Sit up, look up, relax your elbows. If you stiffen up and sit badly you make it harder for him. All right, ride on, and when you've come round the circle, try again.

Lizzie had to struggle so hard against her own habits of looking down, leaning over and stiffening her elbows, that she couldn't do much about Rajah, and the more David looked at her the stiffer and more self-conscious she became. He turned back to the others.

"Rosie's not ready for this yet, but let's try the dun. Walk him round on the same circle as Lizzie and when you've got him going nicely, increase the feel on the inside rein and push his quarters out, just for a couple of steps."

Saffron was good at it and Lizzie, seeing that it could be done, stopped worrying and suddenly Rajah got the idea.

"Well *done*," shouted David in tones of triumph. "Did you feel that? He took and extra large step with his hindleg and at the same moment flexed his jaw. That's what we want. Give him a pat and then try again. You see it's the inside hindleg coming under the body and taking the weight that *enables* them to bend."

He told the two girls to practise on the other rein while he looked at Jupiter, and Hanif set off, holding his reins at the buckle and pleading with Jupiter to behave.

"Well, that's certainly an improvement," announced David. "What about the trot?"

"We sort of lumber round," answered Hanif, gingerly urging Jupiter into a gentle jog.

"Good, you've taught yourself not to pull at him. Now you've got to acquire control by using the legs."

"Legs?" repeated Hanif. "We'll be off down the field if I do."

"That's another bad habit then," said David. "You can't let your pony think that legs only mean 'go faster'. They don't, they also mean 'put your hindlegs further under you', 'go slower, but more collectedly', and, as we tried to teach him the other day, 'half-halt'. You can't do anything with a pony that runs away from the leg. We have to teach him to accept it, just as we have to teach him to accept the bit. Now start using each leg in turn at the walk, slowly in time with his stride. Never mind if he jogs, tell him to walk. Relax, give him a pat, go on using your legs. Now pick up your reins, very quietly, go on using your legs. You've got to ride him forward. Forward, on to the bit. Try a halt, and again remember to ride him *forward* into the halt. Your hands and your weight give him the signal, but there's no pulling. You go on riding him forward and finally he stops. Do you begin to understand?"

"Yes, I think so," said Hanif doubtfully.

"Well, you carry on schooling, I'll just watch. Use your legs one at a time when walking, both together at the trot, and don't attempt cantering for the moment. The trot is much the best pace at which to school."

Presently he called them all over. "Well, that's enough for to-day. I'm sure they've all got aching muscles and I hope you have. Are you pleased with them?"

"Yes." Alice spoke first. "He's going far better at the trot and he loves leg-yielding."

"I *think* I'm beginning to see a faint glimmer of light at the far end of the tunnel." Hanif didn't seem very certain. "But I still can't quite see myself jumping round a ring under control."

"Nor can I," agreed David. "The answer is don't attempt to jump until you can ride him on the flat."

"Is it all right if I tell my stepfather that you say I'm definitely not to enter any more shows for the moment? You see, he thinks I'm being wet, but he regards you as an expert. He'd take it from you."

"That's big of him," said David. "Well, tell him that I'd rather you didn't show-jump until I've sorted the pair of you out, and that to do so will only delay the sorting-out process."

He turned to the Wheelers "Lizzie did you get anywhere?"

"Yes. Ra's bending a tiny bit and he's chewed his bit several times and he's got the idea of leg-yielding."

"Rosie's still pretty ghastly," complained Rupert.

"She's young. You can produce quicker results with a spoiled horse; a young one always needs plenty of time. The trouble with you is that you go round and round in a dream, boring the pants off your pony. Do try and think what you're aiming for and practise energetically for short spells. Think of yourselves as teachers and then see how you rate. I see Alice as a bit too demanding, Rupert as droning on and on, putting everyone to sleep, and Lizzie so uptight about it all she makes her pupils feel that they'll never make it."

"What about Harry?" asked Rupert.

"I haven't decided about him yet."

"David." Paul, who had been waiting for his chance, braced himself to speak. "I suppose you couldn't give us *all* some extra lessons, could you? I know our ponies aren't really difficult, but we would like to improve."

"Yes, so would Netti." Lizzie spoke up for her sister. "And I'm sure the Rookes would love to have some lessons too."

"What about training us for this new cup?

I don't mean that we should *enter*, I know we're not good enough for this year, but it would give us something to *work for*," said Lynne in very diplomatic tones. She'd discussed the whole matter with her mother.

David looked around at their serious faces. "You mean that you're not content with a rally once a week?" he asked.

"No. Four rallies in the Easter holidays don't get you anywhere," complained Rupert.

"The Cranford Vale have a week's camp in the summer and three-day courses as well as the ordinary rallies," added Lizzie, who'd seen Jennifer Blacker's fixture card.

"We'll never be as good as them, but I'm sure we'd improve with training," observed Lynne.

"If we're going to train for this cup we'd need a cross-country course and a dressage arena," David pointed out. "Who's going to do all the work?"

"We would," answered Paul in a determined voice. "You and Dad could tell us what to do and I know James would help if it was cross-country, and he's very strong."

"Yes, we'd all help," agreed Lizzie, and Hanif and Alice made assenting noises.

"We might do something on Coppice Hill, I suppose," said David thoughtfully.

"It's a bit rough and steep up there, isn't it?" Paul sounded dubious.

"That's the whole point. You can't do cross-country on the flat. Look, leave it with me. I'll talk it over with Mrs Rooke and if we decide to go ahead she'll telephone you all. O.K.?"

"Yes," Paul nodded, trying to hide his disappointment. He couldn't see Mrs Rooke agreeing.

"And thank you very much for today," said Lizzie.

"Yes, it's been a great help."

"Thanks a lot."

"Pleasure," said David. "You go on, I'll follow slowly."

Hanif collected his rucksack. The Wheelers and Alice said goodbye to Paul and Lynne and then the four of them clattered away down the lane.

"I wish Paul and Lynne hadn't brought up this cup business again," said Hanif. "I was going to ask if we could come again for another lesson, but now I'm sure he'll be put off by the thought of dressage arenas and cross-country jumps."

"I thought he rather liked the idea of cross-country. His face brightened at the thought of Coppice Hill, wherever that may be," said Alice.

Rupert stood in his stirrups and pointed over the hedge with his whip. "It's that hill, over there, with the round wood on the top. It's never ploughed. Too rough or too steep, I suppose."

Hanif looked across the flat, orderly fields, shaded in different greens by their various crops, to the rising hills. "That one?" he asked, pointing in horror. "You'll never see me or Jupe again if we have to go up there."

CHAPTER FOUR

Coppice Hill

It was Sarah Rooke who telephoned the pony club members.

"Message from David," she told them. "He's willing to start training for next year's Area Cup and there will be cross-country sessions at Garland Farm on Monday, Tuesday and Wednesday. Ten-thirty till about one. Bring your lunch. Do you want to come? If you do, you have to come to all of them."

"Yes," answered Alice, firmly silencing her qualms and fears and the knowledge that Saffron wasn't ready to jump. "Yes, that's terrific. I'll be there."

Lizzie, who answered the Wheeler's telephone, said yes without even consulting the others.

"Well, I suppose it'll be all right," said Rupert when she told him. "David did say Rosie would be able to do cross-country with her peculiarly set-on head, and I suppose by some miracle she may discover how to take off."

Hanif was taken aback when Sarah told him that it was cross-country. "Are you sure he meant you to ask me?" he asked. "Because he told me that Jupiter wasn't ready to jump yet."

"You're definitely on the list," answered Sarah, checking. "Perhaps you don't have to do the jumps. I don't know, you'll just have to make up your mind."

"Well," said Hanif doubtfully. "I suppose you'd better include me in."

On Monday morning Alice and Hanif met in the lane outside Shawbury. They had crossed the river and the Waterford road and were trotting up the bridle path to Four Cross, when they saw Lesley Rooke coming from the direction of Woodbury. They waited for her at the crossroads.

"Hullo," they said. And Alice asked, "Isn't your sister coming?"

"She's gone on ahead with Tina Spencer. Mummy thought Tina might be useful putting up jumps."

"It was good of your sister to telephone everyone," said Hanif.

"Oh yes, well the Great Sarah has such a perfect telephone manner no one else can touch her," sneered Lesley.

Embarrassed by the viciousness in her voice, Hanif and Alice were pleased to see James waiting for them at the fruit farm gate.

"Jennifer's not coming," he told them gloomily. "She says it's pointless to train if David's not going to let us enter for the Cup and next year she'll be too old. She's right, of course. It's pointless for me too. I'll be fourteen next March, but my mother nagged me into coming. She has this idea you must have an interest; she even groomed Ferdie for me this morning. My sister Nina's potty about ballet so she's all right, but I'm not potty about anything."

"But you're a good rider and Ferdie's so lovely," said Alice, shocked. James's heavy, solemn face brightened at the compliment. "We never do anything new," he complained," and pottering over cavaletti for ever isn't much fun. I might enjoy it if we jumped something decent for a change—hedges and banks and streams."

"Do you think we will?" asked Hanif in horror.

"No, not in this pony club," answered James.

"You can't expect people to give up the time to make grand jumps," Lesley told him briskly. "The Cranford Vale raised a lot of money from a barbecue to pay for their cross-country course and they've got two or three keen fathers who built it. There aren't enough of us to hold a barbecue and none of the parents take much interest."

Alice and Hanif both had nervous flutterings and gnawing sensations in their stomachs as they rode up the Garland Farm lane, and the sight of Mr Roberts, helped by Paul and Lynne, loading poles, drums, and flags into the Land Rover did nothing to calm them.

James groaned loudly. "I knew it. I wish I'd taken Jennifer's advice. It's going to be the same old scene."

"Except that it's all going to Coppice Hill," Paul told him.

"Look at Chess. Isn't he beautiful?" Sarah appeared from the cattle yard leading Chess, his white parts showing pink skin through the damp hair, his mane half plaited. "We've been practising for the turnout."

"*You* won't do any good in that," said Lesley scathingly. "Your tack's too old and you're hopeless at plaiting."

"Lynne's teaching me to plait and I'll persuade Mummy to buy me some new tack before next Easter," Sarah snapped back.

"Tina can go in the Land Rover with David and steady these poles," decided Paul.

"I'd rather bike along with the rest of you," said Tina, feeling suddenly shy.

"You can't bike along the track to Coppice Hill. It's deep mud. The tractors have been churning it up all winter and we drove the cattle along it last week when we put them out on the hills."

"Tina can ride Berry and I'll go with David," offered Lynne. "I can ride round the farm any day."

"Oh thanks," Tina's thin, freckled face lit up. "Are you sure?"

"David said we were to start and he'd catch up with us, but the Wheelers aren't here yet," complained Paul.

"If they've any sense they'll go straight to Coppice Hill." Lynne told him. "It's much nearer for them to go along the sunken lane from Kidlake, but if they turn up here I'll send them on."

Paul mounted and led the way along the muddy track, the single wire of an electric fence separating them from the pale green of young oats. Saffron and Jupiter jogged impatiently on Banjo's tail. Lesley rode with James, but they didn't speak to each other, and behind them, Sarah shrieked with annoyance as Chess's immaculately white patches were splashed with liquid mud.

Netti and Lizzie were waiting in the sunken lane.

"We've lost Rupert."

"He forgot his lunch so he went back for it, ages ago," they explained.

"He'll turn up," said James.

"But he's so vague," Lizzie looked down the lane with a worried expression. "I think I'd better go and look for him."

"Oh, don't be pathetic," snapped Lesley. "He can't possibly lose himself between Kidlake and here."

"You don't know Rupert." Netti giggled. "He's probably half-way to the Woodbury Riding School by now, I don't suppose he listened when we told him we were going to Coppice Hill."

"Here's the Land Rover," said Paul, dismounting and tugging at the slip rails that led from the lane into the rough pasture at the foot of the hill. "Get out of the way, Tina. David will want to drive in."

"Morning all," said David, opening the Land Rover door to inspect the nine riders and ponies. "Who's missing, Rupert?"

"Yes, he forgot his lunch."

"Well, we're going to begin by schooling, so perhaps some of you could mark out a school with the smaller drums. The flattest place you can find. Along the hedge, I should think."

"The short sides will be up and down hill," complained Paul.

"Only slightly. It won't matter for the sort of schooling we're going to do."

James, groaning at the prospect of more schooling, insisted on pacing out the distances and the correct placing of the oil drums. Hanif, delighted at even a temporary reprieve from the horrors of the hill, helped him willingly. As they remounted, a mud-bespattered Rupert came galloping up the track.

"Sorry," he said, dropping his rucksack beside the others. "I went up to the farm by mistake."

"Well, now you're all here, form up the ride and start walking round the school," said David. "Then I'll tell you what we're going to do."

James took the lead and the others followed him, grading themselves according to size. David settled himself on his shooting stick, and Tina, who'd given Berry back to Lynne, perched herself on the front bumper of the Land Rover and waited to see if she was needed.

"I decided on a cross-country course—it's going to be a sort of introduction to cross-country riding—" said David, "because most of your ponies aren't ready for show-jumping, which requires a fairly high degree of schooling. Cross-country, riding up and down hill and over rough going, popping over natural fences, is good for young horses. It muscles them up and improves their balance. Because you have plenty of space you don't have to ask for instant obedience and you don't need collection, or at least not until the fences become large and complicated. By choosing cross-country, I reckon we can improve every one of these ponies far more than if we had stayed in the paddock, schooling and jumping on the flat. Any questions?"

"Why do we have to school? Why not get going with the cross-country right away?" asked James.

"Because I have to make sure that you're all riding properly and that the ponies are going well. It's no fun riding an out-of-control pony downhill, so we've got to get them all going forward and on the bit before we begin. So, start riding forward now. I want to see them all over-tracking: that is, taking such a long energetic step with their hindlegs that the hoof comes down on or in front of the hoofprint left by the fore-foot." He paused and watched them.

"Rajah and Rosie aren't overtracking, nor is Stardust, nor Chess, nor Banjo. Three of you are jogging. Only Ferdinand and Tristram are walking properly. Come on— legs. One at a time. Try and feel the pony's stride and then fit your legs in to ask him for a longer step. We don't want a hurried walk, but we do want an energetic one."

When the lively ponies had been persuaded to settle down and everyone was overtracking in a determined manner, David told them to trot and they were soon circling and changing the rein and sepentining, with angry roars directed at those who let their ponies look the wrong way.

"It is tremendously important that a cross-country pony looks where he is going," said David when he had halted them for a rest. "I know that some of the show-jumpers look the wrong way on corners, but you'll generally find they're beaten by the ones who are correctly bent when it comes to jumping off against the clock. The trouble is that you all use your outside reins to hold the ponies out on corners and circles. You mustn't. You're *making* them look the wrong way."

"But if I don't, Ra just cuts in," protested Lizzie.

"So does Berry."

"All right, we'll try a new exercise. Divide into two rides. James leads the bigger ponies, Netti the small ones. James, your lot are to make a circle in the other half of the school, I don't want to be trampled on. The rest of you watch."

When they were all circling at the walk, David told them to make the circle gradually smaller using only their outside reins and legs. "That's the idea," he said. "All right, that's small enough. Now I want you to make it bigger, gradually, using only the inside rein and leg. No outside hands, just the inside aids. See if you can do it."

To their surprise all the riders found they could, that by turning the ponies heads inwards and using the inside leg they could make the circles large again. David propped himself against the Land Rover and had his two rides circling in the two halves of the school. They tried at the walk and trot and were soon all patting their ponies enthusiastically.

"Now we're going to canter," said David. "Not a school canter but a cross-country one. It's rather faster and freer. You sit forward, your weight in your stirrups and just above your saddle. You use the lower leg to keep the pony going with impulsion and on the bit. Your reins are shorter and your arms more extended. Don't worry, it's quite easy," he added as some of the riders began to put themselves in strange positions. "Just pull up your stirrups a couple of holes, more if you ride very long, and we'll try it out at the trot."

"I shall probably end up in Woodbury," Hanif told Alice as they stopped to alter their stirrups. "See you tomorrow morning, same time."

"I'm going to turn Rosie uphill if she tries anything," decided Rupert.

"The trouble about that is you have to come down again," Hanif pointed out.

"I'll dismount and lead her," said Rupert.

David insisted on a very energetic trot. "Now that you're riding short you can't use your seats as a driving aid, and that's a disadvantage," he told them. "But you will be able to stay balanced and with your ponies up and down hill, over rough ground and over fences, which you can't do if you're riding long and sitting deep. It's a different sort of riding, but we still want the ponies full of impulsion and going on the bit. You've got to use what leg you've got left harder, but no kicking, Lesley."

When he had them all trotting round in a very energetic manner, he told them to stand in their stirrups and pretend they were riding at the cross-country canter.

"James, not as high as that. Sharpen the angles of your heels, knees and hips, then you'll come closer to the saddle."

"Lizzie, you're looking down, stiffening your elbows and resting your hands on the pony's neck. Your weight must be over your stirrups. No pony can jump with the rider's weight on his neck."

"Lesley, that's much better, but stop kicking. If she won't obey your legs, use your whip. If you kick you'll always have to kick. You've got to teach your pony to obey a proper leg aid."

"Stop messing about at the back. Sit closer to your saddles. Sharpen up those angles."

Lynne and Sarah were tipping about and giggling help-lessly as they tried to stand in their stirrups. Paul was crouched over Banjo's neck and looked as though he were riding the final stages of a flat race.

"Rising trot," ordered David. "Paul, you're going ahead of your pony. Straighten up your back and push him on ahead of you. This is something you could all think about," he shouted. "You should always have the feeling that two-thirds of your pony is in front of you and only one third behind. I'm sure that Paul, Lizzie, Rupert and Lesley feel the opposite. They've only got one third in front and two thirds trailing behind. But I want you all to try to recognise the feeling, because it's one way of telling if a pony is going well."

"Prepare to canter on. James, we want a brisk pace. Make the school bigger by going outside the drums and anyone who finds he's catching the horse in front, go wide and pass on the outside. Remember, sit forward and ride forward. Canter on."

Hanif had expected to be run away with at once, but, to his surprise, Jupiter seemed quite content with the pace that James had set. They thundered round the school with David shouting at Lizzie to look up, to study the trees or the sky, instead of always the ground. At Lesley to chase the pony in front of her. At several people to sharpen the angles of their heels, knees and hips, and at everyone to use his or her legs.

The ponies were beginning to puff, when he called to James to change the rein, trotting at X and starting off on the other leg. Several people got angry yells because they let their ponies stumble into the trot, or kicked them into a canter.

"We don't want messy transitions," roared David. "Ride them, you've got legs."

Soon they were all flying round on the other rein, chasing each other energetically. The ponies were glad when the order came to walk.

"All right," said David. "I think you've all got the idea.

You can have a rest. Get off the ponies and give their backs a rest too."

"That was great," said Rupert, patting Rosie's sweaty neck quite lovingly. "It's the best she's ever gone for me."

"I'm still here, I can't believe it," observed Hanif. "Oh Jupe, you were a marvel of good behaviour."

"Saffy went quite well too," said Alice. "I think he likes my cross-country seat, especially at the canter."

Then everyone began to complain about his or her aching legs, but they were very cheerful and even James's solemn face wore a smile, while Lesley unbent enough to tell Alice that Stardust was a lot faster than she had thought.

After a few minutes, David interrupted the chatter. "I was pleased with the riders of the bigger ponies," he said. "They were all working hard, but the four of you at the back weren't doing so well. As I've said before, just because you've got nice easy ponies you think you can sit there having an easy time, but you can't. You're still passive riders. You can walk, trot and canter and stop more or less when you want to, but you don't influence the *way* your pony walks, trots or canters. If you're going to be any good you must start using your legs and your brains." He eased himself off his shooting stick and stood up. "Now, we're going on to the next stage and I'll need some help with the flags."

"Ferdie doesn't mind flags, where do you want them put?" asked James.

"On the hillside in the next field. I'll drive through and show you. Can someone take down the slip rails, please?"

In the second field the hill rose much more steeply, and the flat space along the floor of the valley was narrower.

"He's not really going to make us go up there, is he?" asked Hanif, gazing up at the coppice on the crest and giving an apprehensive shudder.

"From the look of the flags, we've only got to go up half way," Rupert observed, as they watched James press two red flags on canes into the ground at points along the hillside, while Lizzie, who had lent Rajah to Tina to ride round, drove along the valley with David and put up two lower flags, opposite James's.

"Now," said David, when they had all gathered round the Land Rover, "it's fairly obvious what we're going to do. You start, one at a time, from here. Ride along the valley to the first flag, turn uphill, ride straight for the next flag halfway up, go outside it, no cutting of corners, turn left and carry on along the hillside towards number three, outside that, turn downhill and ride straight for number four where you halt. Then you *walk* back here. The rest of the time you ride at a steady trot, and I mean a *steady trot*. We all know what the ponies will want to do, they'll dawdle uphill, hurry downhill, cut the corners and charge back here to their friends. But the riders are to be in charge, not the ponies. Any questions?"

"Supposing you can't keep the same steady trot?" asked Hanif.

"You can, if you use your legs," answered David. "Ride well forward in the saddle uphill, if you keep your weight off your pony's loins you make it easier for him. Keep him going nicely along the top and use your legs like hell coming down. If you're having difficulty in keeping the pony's hindlegs under him, you can sit close to the saddle and use your seat too, but don't start leaning back or hanging on to the reins or you'll give yourself a rough time. You come down riding the pony forward and sitting with the jumping seat, so that when we start *jumping* downhill there'll be no problems."

"Do we really have to trot coming down?" asked Lesley.

"Yes."

"Supposing we simply *can't* stop?" inquired Hanif.

"You'll have to circle, but make up your mind that you're going to ride forward and use your legs and you *will* stop. Right, we'll change the order of the ride for this. James first, then Lizzie, Netti, Paul, Rupert, Sarah, Alice, Lesley, Lynne and finally Harry."

"Would it be O.K. if I loaned Tristram to Tina and he went twice? He's quite fit," asked Netti.

"No. I'm not worried about the pony, but I can't have Tina riding up and downhill when I haven't seen her in the school. If anyone can lend her a pony tomorrow, she can join in the schooling and we'll see how she goes."

"Ollie might lend Hobbit," suggested Lizzie. "He's a bit small, but Tina's very light."

"You'd have to bribe him," said Rupert.

"He might agree if we said he could help David with the jumps."

"It's a brilliant idea. I'll persuade him," Netti told Tina, as James set off along the valley at the steadiest of trots. Soon Ferdie, confronted by the hill began to slow down, but David produced a loudhailer and the valley echoed with his cries of 'legs!'. Horse and rider made an elegant pair as they crossed the hillside, but they slowed to a very cautious trot as they turned downhill.

"Legs! Keep him going. Look up!" David was shouting as they came down and halted just past the flag.

"All right, not bad," was his verdict.

"Not bad! I thought it was brilliant," said Sarah.

"It was the first time I've trotted down a hill as steep as that," said James, patting Ferdinand and looking quite pleased with himself.

The others were watching Lizzie. She had had to work hard to keep Rajah trotting up the hill, but she was going well along the top. David told Netti to start and, as the little grey tackled the uphill, Lizzie and Rajah turned round the third flag and came to a dead halt, both peering at the slope before them with horrified expressions.

"Legs, I said keep trotting!" roared David.. "Look up! Get going!"

Lizzie urged Rajah into a reluctant trot, but his wise chestnut face wore a very disapproving expression as he slid thankfully to a halt beside the final flag.

"Not bad for the first time," said David, signalling to Paul to start. Netti was enjoying herself as she turned downhill. She used her legs feverishly and felt Tristram's hindlegs go further under him. He stayed balanced and halted close to the flag.

"Good," said David.

"It was lovely," Netti told the others. "Using the legs really worked. Only now they feel ready to drop off."

Paul was much less controlled. As he came round the third flag Banjo broke into a canter. He hauled him hastily back to a walk. Then he got him trotting, but missed the flag and halted almost in the hedge.

"Rotten," shouted David. "You see, you're not in control."

Rosie had left the other ponies reluctantly and weaved an uncertain path along the valley. The uphill was an effort for her. She began by cantering and then slowed to a puffing walk.

"Legs!" yelled David.

Rupert got her going along the hillside, but when she saw the downhill slope she came to an abrupt halt. Urged on by Rupert's legs and David's yells, she was persuaded to slip and slither down at a sprawling trot. Then she saw the other ponies and decided on a short cut, charging back to them at a canter, with a surprised Rupert pulling ineffectually on the reins.

"Take her straight back to the top flag," ordered David. "And this time be ready for her—right rein and left leg— and halt beside the final flag."

As Rosie came down for the second time and halted only a few yards from the flag, Sarah appeared at the top of the slope.

"Come on, faster. Why are you walking?" roared David as Chess picked his way down cautiously. "Legs!"

Saffron had started well, but, coming along the hillside, the feel of great open spaces seemed to go to his head. He trotted faster and faster and when Alice tried to control him he began stargazing. They came round the third flag, broke into a canter, whirled past Chess, and Saffron, ignoring Alice's attempts to make him circle, careered into the group of waiting ponies. With a furious squeal, Berry

72

lashed out at him. One of her hoofs thudded against his chest.

David swore. "Is he all right? Bring him over here and let me see."

Alice had dismounted.

"His chest's a bit cut, but it doesn't look very deep," she answered as she led Saffron over.

"Paul, could you get the first aid kit from the Land Rover?" asked David as he inspected the wound. "Better give it a quick bathe and a puff or two of wound powder. Has the pony had a permanent anti-tet?"

"I don't know," answered Alice, taking the bathing bowl from Paul.

"Well you *must* find out, and quickly. Telephone his owner the moment you get home and, if he hasn't had a permanent one, the vet will have to come out and give him the ordinary one. It has to be done today because tetanus is a killer and, as I expect you all know, it's in the earth, so a kick with a muddy hoof can easily transmit the germ. And it doesn't need a serious wound, any little cut or scratch will do. That's why it's important that all your ponies should have the permanent anti-tet with boosters as necessary, and so should all of you. Right, Sarah, get back up that hill and come down at a *trot*. You're the boss, not the pony."

Lesley had stopped and waited when she saw the confusion ahead, but as Sarah rode uphill for her second attempt, she came round the red flag and began to walk down. Despite David's ferocious roars she made no attempt to trot, and, when she halted neatly at the final flag, he said, "Straight back, and this time trot. And look ahead, not down at the ground."

Chess was still disapproving, but slightly less cautious at his second attempt. Lesley came down at a grudging tight-reined trot. Then it was Alice. Saffron seemed none the worse for his kick.

"Now get him on the bit before you come round the flag. You've got a difficult pony so I don't mind if you stop or circle. Get him on the bit and ride forward. If you don't keep pushing him on you'll lose him. I know it sounds silly but it's the truth."

Alice, determined not to be galloped back to the other ponies, took a firm hold on her right rein with the result that Saffron began to come down sideways, almost at the full pass.

"Ride straight," roared David. "It's dangerous to come down sideways. He could cross his legs and fall. Use your legs and keep him straight."

Alice straightened him hastily and Saffron immediately broke into a canter and swept down the hill, but this time Alice managed to circle away to the right.

"Take him back and this time come down at the walk," shouted David.

Lynne had appeared. She came down the hill at a trot, but it became faster and faster as Berry lost her balance. As the trot became a canter Lynne's crash cap flew off and she was laughing and giving excited shrieks as they whirled round and stopped dead among the other ponies.

"Very bad. You didn't even attempt to use your legs," said David. "Take her back and come down properly."

Hanif had set off steadily, and the steepness of the uphill had kept Jupiter going at a sober pace, but along the top he had increased his speed despite endless half-halts, Hanif knew he was losing control and viewed the flag ahead with feelings of impending doom. "Steady boy. Whoa, Jupe, steady," he said as he turned the corner. Jupiter saw the other ponies and Hanif the full horror of the slope.

"Half-halt, legs," roared David as Jupiter broke into a canter, but Hanif felt as though his legs were made of some soft substance, cotton wool, he thought, as Jupiter snatched the reins from him and thundered down the hill.

"Circle," shouted David.

Hanif tried. Right rein, left leg, he told himself. He must at least prevent Jupe from galloping into the other ponies and getting kicked. With Jupiter fighting to turn left and Hanif struggling to turn him to the right, they stayed on a straight course, racing towards the thick, overgrown hedge which fenced the field from the lane. At the very last moment they pony realized he had to stop. He threw back his weight, his hoofs skidded, Hanif shot over his head and landed in a thicket of thorn and bramble.

"Are you all right?" asked David.

Rupert went after Jupiter, who trotted away, reins dangling. Alice hurried to the hedge.

"Are you hurt, Harry?"

"No, I don't think so. Just spiked and pierced," answered Hanif, trying to disentangle himself from clutching brambles as he emerged backwards from the hedge.

"Your face is bleeding."

"Where?"

Alice pointed and Hanif dabbed at his cheek with his handkerchief. "It's not much," he said, inspecting the blood, "and I've no beauty to lose."

"One disgracefully bad pony." Rupert appeared towing Jupiter from Rosie.

"It was lack of legs," said David. "You stopped using them when you saw the hill. You should have made a half-halt and used your legs in the interest of self-preservation. Up you go again and keep his hindlegs under him."

Hanif trotted up the hill feeling heavy-hearted and weak-legged. He knew he couldn't do it and, sure enough, Jupiter was off the moment he pointed him downhill, only this time he agreed to circle and they avoided crashing into the hedge.

"All right, you wait here a minute. I want to send the others round again. Are you ready, James? Same steady trot. Unless there's a hold-up, you all start when the pony ahead of you is halfway up the hill. Alice, you'd better walk down."

Nearly everyone was much better at the second attempt.

Alice, who walked halfway down and then lost control when she tried a trot, was sent back. But Lynne, who again whirled down giving squeaks of excitement, got an angry roar of, "You're not trying."

"James, you take Harry's pony, and Lizzie, let's see you

on Berry. And, while they're sorting themselves out, the rest of you can go round again. Alice, you lead."

The ponies were settling down. They were no longer excited by the feeling of space. They set off soberly, and soon the hillside was covered in ponies all moving at the same steady trot and not attempting to overtake each other.

"Good," David was shouting. "Well done. That was much better," as rider after rider came down the hill and halted at the flag.

James and Lizzie had had a ride along the valley to try out their strange mounts.

"He's strong and very gassy," James told David.

"Berry's got terribly rough paces," complained Lizzie.

"Yes, she's a real old-fashioned harness pony," agreed David. "She really picks her feet up and you see an awful lot of her knees. It's not the right action for a riding pony, but that doesn't mean she has to run away downhill. Are you two ready? Off you go then and all the others can follow."

Hanif watched James carefully. He was older, stronger and more experienced, so he didn't mind learning from him, and he felt pleased to see how well Jupiter was going. David was roaring "Legs!" and "Half-halt!" at intervals. When they turned downhill, Jupiter made a determined effort to take control but when he did begin to canter, James turned him uphill again and took him back to the flag. Suddenly Jupiter gave in and decided to behave. He trotted down smoothly and made a very elegant halt.

"Terrific," said David.

"He's not easy." James rode over, patting Jupiter. "Shall I take him round again? Would Harry like to try Ferdie? He's much easier."

"He's a bit big for Harry," said David, watching Berry. "Well done, Lizzie, but do remember to look up when you halt. I know, we'll try Harry on Stardust. I'd like to see her with another rider. The rest of you keep going round."

They were nearly all delighted to go round again. They had decided that they enjoyed riding downhill. Only Hanif, using his legs frantically to keep Stardust going, almost wished himself back on Jupiter. But he managed to keep her trotting down the hill and to halt at the flag, while Jupiter, who had stopped rolling his eyes and arguing, was pretending to be an obedient and well-schooled pony.

"Back on your own nags," said David, "and everyone but Lynne and Harry can ride the course the other way round. You will halt at the far flag and then *walk* back here. Anyone who comes charging back out of control will be expelled from the course."

"But that hill's steeper."

"Much steeper," they began to complain, looking at the slope suspiciously.

"Yes, it is a bit, but now you've learned to ride downhill you can ride down *any* hill. You don't have to start measuring gradients. Plenty of leg, look where you're going and halt at the flag. Lead on, James."

Some people crept down the distant hill, some went too fast, but they all managed it, and the second time round it began to seem easy. Alice had discovered that if she began by walking she could then push Saffron forward into a trot when she had him going well and this worked much better than beginning fast and losing control.

Then it was Hanif's and Lynne's turn. They both set off with very determined expressions on their faces. Hanif was in the lead and he felt much more confident than before. He knew now that he could do the hill and Jupiter could do it. It's just a matter of legs, he told himself, gritting his teeth as he fought to keep Jupiter balanced. It worked. He didn't halt absolutely at the flag, but he halted.

"Well done," shouted David. "Go round once more."

Lynne, rather indignant that Lizzie had controlled her pony so easily, concentrated this time and found that she too could make Berry behave if she tried. She felt quite pleased with herself as she followed Hanif round for another try.

When they came back they found the other pony club members all dismounted and gossiping.

"That's all for today," said David. "Tomorrow morning, here at the same time."

"Thank you very much," they said.

"Yes, it was terrific."

"Great."

"The best rally ever."

"Except for the inconvenience of damaged legs," said Rupert. "Mine have never ached so much in my life."

"It's the first time in your life that you've used them," retorted David, twisting himself into the Land Rover.

"Would you like Banjo, Tina?" asked Paul. "I'll go with David and do the slip rails."

The ponies were weary and were quite happy to walk back to the farm on a loose reins while their riders discussed the morning.

"It was far more fun than an ordinary rally," said James, "and we actually learned something new."

"The ponies enjoyed it, which was nice," remarked Lizzie. "At least I'm sure Ra prefers cross-country to ordinary schooling. David says he's to have a worm dose and then I'm to increase his oats and nuts. Do you think Mummy'll have a fit at the expense?"

"Two, probably," said Rupert.

"No, she won't," argued Netti. "She oughtn't to anyway. Parents are always wanting you to take things seriously, so now we're doing it they ought to be pleased and take notice of what David says."

"I've been giving Stardust huge feeds since last Wednesday," Lesley told Lizzie. "I think it's beginning to have an effect. She wouldn't have trotted up that hill in the Christmas holidays."

When James saw all the other pony club members watering their ponies and tying them up with feeds, before settling down to eat their own lunches in one of the empty barns, he felt rather sad that he couldn't stay.

"I'll bring mine tomorrow," he said, waving goodbye as he rode away down the lane.

"Tina, will you come home with us and try Hobbit?" asked Lizzie. "We've decided to tell Ollie that it'll be a huge advantage to have a ready-schooled cross-country pony next year, when he's old enough to go on the course."

"I'd love to try him," answered Tina, "but I have a feeling David will take one look at me and say I'm not good enough."

"You know, it's very odd," said Hanif, sitting down on Alice's straw bale. "If you have bikes or cars you can give one set of instructions to *all* the owners, but with ponies that wouldn't work at all. David looks round and says that this one mustn't wear a pelham, but that one can. Some need dropped nosebands and others don't. Jupe mustn't have oats, Rajah and Stardust must have more. Even the riding instructions are different for different people."

"Except for legs," said Alice ruefully. "We *all* get yelled at to use them."

"It does seem to work though," observed Tina. "I've watched Mr Foster and all the working pupils teaching at the riding school. They don't get as excited as David. They go on and on about heels down and straight backs and hands low, but nothing ever seems to change. I learned a lot watching today because when the riders did the right thing the ponies *did* change. It was quite exciting."

"You wait till you're at the receiving end of David's roars," Rupert told her, "you won't find it so exciting then. Does anyone know what happens to overworked legs? Do they wither away?"

"No, of course not," Lesley sounded cross at such absurdity. "If you use muscles, they develop. They wither when you *don't* use them."

"You mean we're all going to end up with huge thick legs, really brawny ones, like blacksmiths' arms?"

"No, she doesn't. Don't tease," Lizzie told her brother.

"The Cranford Vale people all have quite nice legs," said Sarah, inspecting her own, "and they must use them or they wouldn't win everything."

The Robertses came into the barn to ask if Tina had put Banjo away in the cattle yard and found his water and feed.

"Yes, everything was fine," answered Tina, "and he drank two buckets of water."

"I asked David if he'd like us to start building the cross-country course this afternoon," Paul went on, his face serious, "but he said he was too whacked to think about tomorrow. I don't know how we're ever going to get those jumps built."

"I hope we haven't tired him out too much," said Lizzie, looking anxious.

"Mum says it's good for him to have an interest, and we won't do him any harm so long as we don't ride over him," Lynne told her in comfortable tones.

CHAPTER FIVE

We'll Never Do It

Except for Tina, all the pony club members were much more confidant and light-hearted when they rode to Garland Farm on the second morning of the course. Tina had tried Hobbit out on Monday afternoon and liked him very much. He was a little, dark brown Dartmoor, handy and willing, who raced round the Wheelers' messy jumps with ease.

"He's lovely," Tina had said, patting him afterwards with a smile on her thin freckled face. "It's very kind of Ollie to lend him to me, and of you to arrange everything."

"He only has two faults," Lizzie answered. "One is that he hates cantering on the near fore—Ollie can never get him on it—and the other is that he didn't grow when we did. It was so lovely when Rupert had Tristram and Hobbit was mine. We felt that we were quite good riders, and we did fairly well at the pony club, but now, with Rosie and Ra, we feel right out of everything. We used to be the equals of James and Jennifer when they had their little ponies, but now we're not in the same class at all."

"Of course, if you've *never* had a pony of your own, you long to have one so much you don't really care how hopeless it is," Tina had said, as she unbuckled Hobbit's cardboard-stiff bridle and threw his green encrusted bit in the bucket of water, "but I suppose once you've had a good one you feel differently."

"Yes, I do love Ra, but I can't help feeling envious when I see everyone else whirling over jumps so easily, and Rupert minds even more," Lizzie had agreed sadly.

When Tina arrived back at Kidlake at nine the next morning, Oliver was grooming Hobbit unwillingly.

"Thank goodness," he said, handing her his dandy

brush, "I thought you were never coming. I've picked out his hoofs and groomed a quarter of him."

"Which quarter?" asked Tina, looking from Oliver's round, cheeky face to the mud-caked pony.

"Near fore," answered Oliver. "The front is much nicer to groom than the back, except for the head. I hate grooming heads, they're all corners."

"He's the laziest boy on earth," said Lizzie, who was dodging Rajah's angry nips as she groomed his stomach.

Tina had taken off her anorak and was brushing energetically. She was used to grooming dozens of ponies to earn one ride at Mr Foster's. It was a real treat to be getting one ready for herself, she thought.

"Well, you *must* help David with the jumps and flags and things," Netti told Oliver in an elder-sisterly voice. "If you start being silly or showing-off we won't take you again."

"I might not want to go again," countered Oliver. "And I might come home if it's boring."

"Has anyone seen my bridle?" demanded Rupert, appearing dramatically at the back door. "It's completely vanished. I've looked everywhere, and now I'm going to be late again and this time David will be furious."

"It's probably hanging up in the tackroom. You know how hopeless you are at looking," Netti told him.

Lizzie stopped grooming and stood with an anxious expression on her face, trying to cast her mind back to the evening before.

"You cleaned it while you were watching television, don't you remember? Mummy was cross when you spilled metal polish on the rug."

"Yes, but where is it *now*?"

"Rupert and Rosie are both a bit dozey, Ra and Liz are both in a tiz," chanted Oliver.

The Rookes' separate arrangements didn't go according to plan. Lesley had made her way to the field early, cleaned her tack as Stardust munched her way contentedly through her extra large feed, and then started grooming. But Sarah, who had cleaned her tack at home the night before, persuaded her mother to drive her to the field and, grooming briskly, found herself ready to start at the same moment as her sister.

"Aren't you waiting for Tina?" asked Lesley as they approached the gate together.

"Of course not. You *know* she's borrowing Hobbit from the Wheelers. She's gone over to Kidlake to groom him."

"I can't remember every little detail about what your friends are doing," snapped Lesley.

"Who cares," said Sarah, fastening the gate. "By the way, Mum's coming to watch tomorrow. She's going to leave Janet and Mrs Cox in charge of the Ds and come to Coppice Hill."

"That'll ruin everything." Lesley's voice was bitter with anger. "She'll interfere. She'll keep telling David what a wonderful little rider The Great Sarah is and how he should put *her* on all the sticky ponies."

"She won't. Why are you always so horrible, so cross and jealous?"

"Because I'm sick and tired of hearing your praises all day. Because you're Mummy's nasty, slimy little pet," shouted Lesley, her anger getting the better of her.

"It's not my fault. I can't help it. I didn't *ask* to be Mum's favourite," Sarah shouted back.

They rode on in angry silence. Sarah took a sideways glance at her sister's face and thought, it's no wonder Mum likes me best when she's so ugly and cross and boring; it's her own fault.

Lesley escaped from her seething indignation into a dream world. She began to imagine a great triumph. Sarah had made a complete mess of the cross-country jumps, then it was her turn. She rode brilliantly, whirling downhill, clearing everything. "Well done," shouted David through the loudhailer, then he turned to her mother and added, "That's the horsewoman of your family, Mrs Rooke."

Sarah took another look at her sister. Oh let her sulk, she thought. I don't care. Soon I'll be with Lynne and Netti and

83

Tina and I like them a million times better than Lesley.

Alice and Hanif had ridden over to Garland Farm with short stirrups and their cross-country seats. They arrived with aching legs, but a feeling of accomplishment for there was do doubt that their ponies went better when ridden in this manner. Saffron hadn't stargazed, Jupiter hadn't pulled and they had both gone with pricked ears and contented expressions.

David was already in the yard, leaning against the Land Rover. He had spread a large sheet of paper on the bonnet and seemed to be going through details of a plan with Mr Roberts.

"What about the anti-tet?" he asked Alice.

"It was O.K.. I rang Mr Crankshaw and he'd been done."

"Good. Bring him over here and let me have a look at the wound. Oh yes, that's healing nicely. Now do keep away from Berry, all of you, she's in a very mare-ish mood. If everybody's here, you can go on, I'll follow in a minute or two."

"He really is planning a cross-country course, isn't he?" James asked Paul as they set off along the farm track.

"Yes, we're to help Dad with the jumps after lunch," answered Paul, "but I don't think they're going to be much—mostly baling string and poles, though they have looked out a plastic sheet for the water."

"Water? To jump?" asked Hanif in horrified tones.

"Yes, and a ditch."

"Chess can't bear black plastic," moaned Sarah. "He's got a phobia. When we went as a junior team to the Cranford Vale hunter trials he refused three times. Afterwards Mum got all sorts of people to try to get him over, but they couldn't; he just won't go near it. It's a phobia, everyone said so."

"David will know what to do." Alice tried to comfort them. "After all, we couldn't ride downhill until he told us how."

"I'm not at all sure I can do it today," observed Hanif gloomily. "Yesterday might have been a fluke, or just that Jupe was too worn out to keep up the argument."

84

The Wheelers and Tina came trotting along the lane from Kidlake at the same moment as the Land Rover appeared, and James and Paul dismounted to take down the slip rails.

"Will you put them up again when I'm through?" asked David. "Drop the top rail at the right-hand end. I want you all to jump in over them. Don't make a great fuss about it, just pop over. James first, large and lively ponies in the front, and Lynne, keep Berry well away from everyone. All right?"

He drove through and waited. The riders milled about in the lane, arguing.

"Give me some room, I want a run," demanded James.

Oliver who had appeared on a bicycle, flung it in the hedge and asked what was going on.

Ferdie popped over neatly, Jupiter shot after him, hurled himself over and set off at a gallop across the field, but finding that Ferdie was standing calmly by the Land Rover and that Hanif had turned him uphill, he slowed down. Saffron charged over, head in air. Rosie refused dead, her nose almost touching the ground on the far side.

"Go back and take another lead," shouted David, clearing the way for Rajah who came over in slow motion. Stardust trotted up and refused. Tristram passed her and flew over. Banjo took it neatly and was followed by Chess, Hobbit and Berry. Rosie refused again and so did Stardust, with a disappointed Lesley kicking frantically.

"Hold it," David shouted to them. "Alice and Harry, you jump back into the lane and give them a lead. Lesley," he went on, grabbing the loudhailer, "don't *kick*. Use your whip to get the pony going before you start jumping, then sit still and use your legs properly—invisibly. Nothing could jump with you throwing yourself about like that."

Oliver, who had used the lull in the jumping to come through, approached David. "I'm supposed to be helping you," he said.

"Great, I need it. As soon as those two ponies have jumped back will you see if you can find a pole or branch to act as a ground line. Put it about two feet in front of the slip rail. Rosie wants some help in finding her take-off."

Hanif was looking at the slip rails doubtfully. There was a grass verge to land on and then the lane. It was all slightly downhill. "Go on, don't make a great thing about it. Just pop over," David shouted to him.

Jupiter made an unnecessarily large jump, but, as there was no where to gallop to, he stopped of his own accord. Alice trotted and popped without any stargazing this time. They decided that Hanif should give Rupert a lead and Alice, Lesley. The two girls went back a long way down the lane to give Lesley a chance to get Stardust going.

"Wait, wait! you've got to have a ground line," Oliver was shouting at his brother. With loud crackings and splinterings he pulled a rotten branch off a tree and dragged it along the lane.

"Will this do?" he shouted at David.

"Yes, fine. A good two feet in front."

Hanif turned Jupiter at the fence and bounded over, but Rosie did another of her head-down refusals.

"Follow the girls," shouted David, as Alice and Lesley came cantering up the lane and both flew over easily. Rosie refused again.

"Right, on to the school, all of you. She won't like it when she finds she's on her own," said David. "Come on, Oliver, leave her."

Rosie neighed indignantly as they all jogged on across the field, and then, deciding that she would have to jump, she heaved herself over from a standstill and galloped after the other ponies, giving a series of unseating-looking bucks. Rupert arrived at the school laughing.

"I don't know how you stayed on," said Alice. "It looked horrible."

"He's got such long legs he never falls off," Oliver told her.

"He's like the sugar tongs in the poem," added Netti. "'His legs are so long and so aptly constructed': It's a great help."

"Form up the ride, the same order as yesterday," said David. "And we want everyone riding with long stirrups, please. Do remember that you now have two distinct seats —and keep them distinct. Whatever you do, don't ride short unless you're sitting forward. Sitting at the back of the saddle with short stirrups is always a disaster. You can't influence the pony's hindlegs and your weight is too far back, you're behind the pony's movement.

"Lynne, you'd better go last, we don't want Tina's pony kicked. Now, an energetic walk. Make sure they're over-tracking."

They walked and trotted and circled. They made circles larger and smaller. Except for Rosie, they leg-yielded then they serpentined with encouraging shouts from David, who said that they were all getting the idea at last. There were groans when everyone but Lynne had to cross their stirrups, and they practised halting from the trot. Rosie and Saffron were allowed to make very slow transitions through the walks but the others were expected to manage with only two or three steps of walking.

"Sit up. Take your weight back a little. Sit deep. Use your legs," roared David. "Go on riding forward until you've actually halted. We want their hindlegs under them, not trailing behind. They must stand at attention, not straggle all over the place."

Everyone was relieved when they were told to have a rest and shorten their stirrups for cantering.

"Do you think legs *ever* get used to it?" asked Rupert, flexing his ruefully when the cantering was over.

"At least with two seats you spread the aches," observed Alice. "Knees upwards for schooling and knees downwards for cross-country."

"Are you all right, Tina?" asked Lizzie. "It's a bit hard on you. We've worked up to this stage gradually."

"I'm fine. I do a lot of bareback riding, taking the ponies back to their fields, and Hobbit's lovely and easy to ride."

"Right, now I'm going on into the next field and Oliver's going to put the slip rails up again for you to jump in," said

David. "*Don't* ride on each other's tails. *Don't* get excited and *do* sit still. I'd rather see the odd stop, the occasional refusal, than people riding like maniacs at tiny jumps. Ponies don't need to be 'got over', they're quite capable of jumping small fences. Your job is to organize the correct pace, have the pony balanced and on the bit and, if you've walked the course and know what sort of fence lies ahead, indicate that knowledge to him. But if you're waving you're arms and legs about, you can't indicate anything, and the pony can't concentrate on jumping if you're giving him thumping great kicks in the ribs. So don't be a hindrance. Sit still and help."

Oliver was very efficient with the slip rails and even found an old broken rail to act as a ground line for Rosie. As soon as he shouted that it was ready, James set off at a steady canter and flew over the high end. Hanif and Alice jumped in the middle, Rupert rode at the low end and everyone cheered when Rosie jumped. The ponies seemed to be inspirng each other. Tristram and Stardust took it fast and sailed over and all the little ponies followed in fine style.

"Now we're going to do the hill the easy way, at the trot, twice," said David. "Off you go James. And as soon as one pony is half way up the hill the next one can start."

For most people the downhill had suddenly become easy; only Hanif, Alice, Rupert and Lynne still had to work hard to keep their ponies under control. Tina went down very cautiously the first time, but at her second attempt she managed to keep trotting and David sent her round a third time on her own.

Then they went round the other way. Alice and Hanif hadn't tried the steep hill before, but as everyone else could do it they were filled with a grim determination not to be beaten, and since their ponies, who were enjoying themselves, had become far more cooperative, they managed it quite easily.

"Good. Well done, everyone, especially Tina," said David when they had all been round twice. "Now I want you to go the easy way at the canter. You all know what to do. Ride forward. Legs. Look where you're going and halt at the flag."

"Doesn't James look brilliant," said Netti as horse and rider crossed the hillside. "He looks like a competitor at Badminton."

"Very competent," agreed Rupert. "Harry doesn't look too bad either."

"They all look better at the canter," agreed Tina as Alice reached the second flag.

"I am about to spoil the pretty picture," said Rupert, turning Rosie and setting off in pursuit of Rajah.

The ponies were used to the hillside and the feeling of open spaces and they knew the routine so they were content to canter in order. They didn't attempt to overtake or race, and one by one the riders came back smiling and patting their mounts.

David had arranged for James and Alice to go with him in the Land Rover, and the moment Lynne and Berry returned he announced that the riders should dismount to give the ponies' backs a rest while he organized the jumps. He drove up the hill slantwise and stopped at mid-point between each pair of flags to deposit drums and poles. Soon there were three jumps, low ones with drums on their sides on the two hills and a larger one midway along the top. Rupert was relieved to see that they all had ground lines and everyone, even the boldest among them, was pleased to see that the downhill jump was so small.

"Right," said David, when everyone had remounted and Oliver, who was being very attentive, had handed him the loudhailer. "Now we're going to include the jumps this time and, once again, don't fuss. Start at the canter, get your weight well forward for the uphill jump, canter along the top and don't forget to use the half-halt to draw your pony's attention to the fact that there is now a jump there. He doesn't know. When you come to the third flag, slow up to a trot, then ride the pony forward over the jump. I don't mind whether you trot or canter the last bit, provided you halt at the flat. Any questions?"

"Must we trot at the third flag?" asked James.

"It depends on how effective your half-halts are," answered David. "The important thing is that your pony must be balanced and under control so that you can be pushing him *forward* as you come to the fence. If you're hanging on to his head and trying to slow him up he can't jump. Most of the ponies here would need to trot a couple of strides and then push on."

"If we give them their heads over the jump they can race off the moment they land," objected Lesley. "I don't see how we're supposed to keep control."

"You don't 'give them their heads', or at least you shouldn't once you've passed the beginner stage of jumping. You've all got firm seats, you can jump, now you're expected to learn how to jump well and how to be active riders and *help* your ponies. I've explained about approaching with impulsion, sitting still, using your legs quietly so that you don't disturb him. Now your hands should 'follow him'. That is, you keep a light contact with the pony's mouth and as he extends his neck over the fence you keep that contact but give him the freedom he needs by extending your arms, slowly, and with quiet movement of the elbows. Then, as he lands, your elbows slide back and you still have contact. But of course it isn't the reins which keep him balanced, it's your legs and seat which will do the hard work. All right, James, off you go."

James made it look easy, and Hanif, who had set off with a very anxious expression, managed to persuade Jupiter to trot to within three strides of the jump, then he cantered, but remained more or less in control and managed to halt a couple of yards from the flag. Alice brought Saffron to a walk at the third flag and then pushed him forward as they approached the jump. Rosie refused the uphill fence, she seemed to think it was an impossible feat to jump at the same time as climbing a hill. David shouted to Rupert, telling him to by-pass the jump and go on. They took the middle fence quite happily, but at the sight of the downhill one, Rosie's eyes bulged with horror and she stopped again. Rupert forced her on and she crept over, one leg at a time, knocking down the pole.

Oliver, complaining loudly, ran up the hill to restore the jump just in time for Lizzie, who took it cautiously and got a roar from David for looking down. Lesley had produced enough impulsion for the uphill and kept going well along the top, but when she saw the jump down she was overcome by nerves and took it from a walk. Netti went round very well. She and Tristram seemed to be full of confidence, but the other small ponies all lacked impulsion, heaving themselves over the uphill jump with difficulty and creeping downhill too carefully.

"You must get them going with more energy and impulsion," David told their riders. "Ponies don't enjoy things that are an effort to them and, by going slowly, you're making the uphill jump an effort. We want a bit more dash from you. Let's put every slow pony behind a fast one and see if we can't inspire them a bit."

When the riders tried to sort themselves out they found that there were only four fast ponies, so Lesley and Paul attached themselves to James, Lizzie and Lynne to Alice, Tina and Sarah to Netti. Rupert followed Hanif and everyone refused to follow Rupert in case he knocked down the jump again. But Rosie *was* inspired by Jupiter's example and she followed him boldly over all three jumps.

"Well done all of you," said David when the last of the smiling riders and blowing ponies had returned. "You've obviously got the hang of it now."

"Even dozey Rosie," said Oliver, patting her. "Silly old pop eyes."

"Now you can jump both slip rails. But be sensible, steady down in between them and keep off each other's tails. Wait for me in the lane."

Delighted at the thought of more jumps, they set off in a long string, the slower ponies still following their leaders. This time most people were jumping the middle of the rails between the fields. Only Rupert and Tina took the lowest point, while Hanif, Alice and Paul followed James over the high end. But into the lane they were more cautious and jumped the middle.

"Mr Roberts wants all the help you can give him with course-building this afternoon," said David, when he caught up with them. "And tomorrow's the pony club rally, but I thought we'd carry on out here on the cross-country. Janet Green is going to take the younger ones in the paddock and Julia's going to give me a hand getting you over the water. All right? Can I rely on you to help Mr Roberts?"

"Yes," they answered. "We've brought our lunches."

"We'll take the ponies home and then come back here," said Lizzie.

"What time?" asked Netti.

"About an hour," said Paul, "Or an hour and a bit."

Shouting 'thank you' to David, the Wheelers and Tina clattered off down the lane. Oliver grabbed his bicycle, and shouting, "See you later!" followed.

The others ate lunch peacefully, exhausted by the morning's efforts. They were beginning to revive when Mr Roberts appeared in the yard carrying a bag of tools, and followed by Lynne and Paul laden with garden forks and spades.

"Black plastic sheet," said Mr Roberts, consulting his list. "Put that lot in the Land Rover, Paul, and fetch the sheet out of the barn. It's the one under the chaff-cutter. The rest of you come and help me with the stuff from the tractor shed. We're going to need at least a dozen fencing stakes."

They loaded the stakes, an enormous mallet, an iron bar with a sharp point for making holes, several buckets and a reel of binder twine into the Land Rover and then drove into Long Meadow to collect more poles. Then, with Sarah, Lynne and Lesley sitting in the front and everyone else crouched perilously on top of the poles, they bumped slowly along the track to Coppice Hill.

Through the slip rails they turned left and stopped beside a water trough which stood close to the hedge.

"Three poles, the plastic sheet and the buckets come off here," said Mr Roberts. "Just leave them in a pile beside the trough. We'll come back and sort it out later."

He stopped again halfway up the hill, at a little group of trees. One large, ancient elm had fallen at some time and its trunk lay sprawled across the hillside. They all got out to inspect it.

"Who can saw?" asked Mr Roberts, producing two saws from his tool bag. "David wants the middle trimmed up a bit. These branches taken off close to the trunk and no pointed or jagged bits left that could harm the ponies. He wants the boughs on the ends left alone, says they make it 'more inviting'."

"It doesn't look very inviting to me," complained Hanif.

"No, it's so solid, *and* uphill," Lesley agreed.

"Well, we can't knock it down, that's one thing," said Paul.

"I'll saw if someone will show me how," offered Alice.

"Don't you know?" they asked, shocked.

"No, it's not the sort of thing you learn in a modern flat in big cities abroad."

"Well, I'll need some diggers at the next fence—that's the ditch," said Mr Roberts. "David went round on his own yesterday evening and made us a plan."

"I'll saw," offered Hanif. "I do woodwork at school, so I can show Alice."

"Well, don't cut yourselves."

"There's nothing to it," said Hanif as the Land Rover went on up the hill, "you just saw. I have to do woodwork because my stepfather disapproves of people who are only good at normal lessons. He says I'll turn into a swot."

"Well I suppose it *is* useful to be able to make things." Alice chose a thin straggly bough and started work. "I don't know how to do anything useful. Aunt Margaret says she'll teach me to cook."

They sawed. The angles were awkward, the branches

scratched them and when the sun came out the day was suddenly hot. They stopped for a rest and took off their anoraks. Then they sawed again until they heard voices and the four Wheelers and Tina appeared, puffing up the hill.

"The bikes are all bust up and we had to walk the whole way," complained Oliver, collapsing on the short, cowslip-studded turf.

"What are you doing?" asked Netti.

"Sawing," answered Alice.

"We can see that."

"We're making this tree trunk jumpable. It's part of David's course," Hanif told them.

"It's wide."

"And jolly solid."

"Are we going to jump it uphill?"

"I hope so," answered Hanif. "Are any of you good at sawing? My arms are aching."

Lizzie and Netti took over.

"You need a chain saw," said Rupert, collapsing on the grass beside Oliver, "then it would be done in a second."

"And a bulldozer to dig a ditch, I suppose," suggested Hanif.

"That's not a ditch they're digging," said Rupert with conviction. "It's a communal grave for pony club members who expire from too much exercise."

"I think I'll go and see if they need help," decided Tina. "It's no use having seven people for two saws."

Oliver followed her. Alice was looking at the view, over Garland Farm and Four Cross to Woodbury and the river. And, beyond the river, to the beechwoods, coloured purple by the millions of unopened buds. "We're on top of the world," she said to Hanif.

"Not bad is it," he answered, turning to look as he threaded the sawn-off branches among the ones they had been told to leave at either end. "I wish I could fix Jupe up with a hang glider and we could both drift gently home."

"Here, you two take over again," demanded Netti. "My arms are completely worn out. Are yours, Lizzie?"

When the sawing was done they all walked on slowly to the ditch. Paul and Sarah, Tina and James were all digging or shovelling energetically.

"Not very impressive," said Rupert, looking at it critically. "I expected it to be several feet deep, but you've only managed a few inches."

"See if you can do any better," answered James, handing him a fork.

"It's all stones and very hard work," Sarah told him.

"And anyway, it's meant to be shallow, only six inches deep, because it's *introducing* the ponies to ditches," Paul added defensively. "David said he didn't want them all falling in and frightening themselves into fits."

"Quite right," said Hanif, taking Sarah's spade. "We don't want the riders falling in either—but why are we pilling the earth on the far side like this?"

"Some idea of Dad's," answered Paul. "And he's coming back to rivet the ditch when he's finished knocking posts in over there."

Assisted by Oliver and Lesley, Mr Roberts had taken down a section of the wire fence between the two fields and was knocking in four posts to make a frame. "We're going to fill this up with brushwood and greenery," he explained. "So while I'm nailing these lengths of timber across, some of you can go collecting branches in the wood. No yew or we'll be losing the cattle. It only takes the smallest bit of yew to kill an animal, and dead yew's even more lethal than when it's green. But you'll find plenty of box and laurel."

The Wheelers, Lynne and Tina all decided that they wanted to branch collect, and set off armed with the saws and some secateurs. Alice joined the digging party. James and Paul were taking the ditch very seriously and insisting on straight edges, and Mr Roberts was pleased when he arrived with Lesley, both of them carrying tools.

"Fine," he said. "Just the job. I'm going to put this pole along the take-off side and fix it there with a couple of short posts knocked into the ditch. Otherwise, if the ponies start refusing and messing about, the edge will crumble away

95

and you won't have a take-off. Now, we want something for the far side so they know it's a jump. By rights it should be a brush fence, but I spotted a fallen tree in the little copse over there, just a small one, and it's been lying there a good while so it won't be heavy. Will you go and see if you can fetch it over, while Lesley and I get on with this?"

James didn't think much of the log. "Far too small," he complained. "Ferdie will trip over it."

"It would do under a pole," suggested Alice.

"Help heave," said James. "It weighs a ton."

Mr Roberts was delighted with the log, and when it was embedded in the bank of earth they had dug out, it looked quite impressive.

"It's terrifying," said Hanif, standing back to inspect the fence. "You can't tell that it's not a real ditch; I'm sure they'll all refuse."

"It does look awfully wide," agreed Alice, joining him. "I think they'll all fall in."

"Right, back to the little copse," said Mr Roberts, producing his plan.

As they climbed through the wire fence, the greenery collecting party appeared on the edge of the wood, dragging branches and shrieking cheerfully.

"Three poles and baling string," said Mr Roberts, observing that his helpers had all begun to wish themselves in the wood. "David's marked the trees we're to tie the poles to with an X in chalk."

They found the marked trees. The first two pairs made an angle jump, the third pair were on the very edge of the coppice, and as the hill fell away steeply at that point, you seemed to be jumping right out into space.

"Ugh, it's horrible," said Alice.

"Do you think David would notice if we moved it back a bit?" asked Hanif.

"Yes, of course he would. Don't be so *wet*. Your pony's a first class jumper, but you never stop moaning," James told him irritably.

"It's called Horizon Fence on the plan," said Paul. "How high, Dad?"

"About two feet six. Tie the baling string round the tree at about three foot and then make a loop for the pole," instructed Mr Roberts.

"I don't suppose we'll ever get this far," Alice comforted Hanif when James wasn't listening. "I can't see many of us getting over the ditch."

They walked back to the Land Rover. The wood party were filling the frame with branches and giving cries of horror at the height of the jump.

"That's great," James told them. "Don't squash it down too much, we want one decent-sized fence."

"Well, none of *us* are going to get over that," said Rupert, squashing hard.

"Squash it down to start with," suggested Sarah. "We can always make it higher later."

"At least it's on the flat," observed Hanif.

"Now, down to the gate in the corner there," said Mr Roberts, pointing to the far end of the field where a five-barred gate led to the sunken lane. "Anyone want to ride down?"

James, Rupert and Lesley made for the Land Rover. Everyone else began to run down the hill, pretending to be nervous riders on badly behaved, runaway ponies. Only Alice proceeded at a collected pace, roaring, "Legs!" and "Look up!" in a David-like manner. Lynne jumped the pole on the drums and then fell, lying in a giggling heap, until Hanif announced that it was tetanus and he was about to inject her, when she made an instant recovery.

The Land Rover party were behaving much more soberly. Mr Roberts and James were tying a pole across the gateway while Rupert, who had insisted on a turn with the mallet, was narrowly missing Lesley with every blow he took at a reluctant post.

"I suppose it's a bounce fence," he said gloomily, "but with the second pole on the edge of a drop into the lane, Rosie's bound to fall on her nose."

"Look what you're doing!" Lesley shrieked at him angrily. "You only just missed my hand that time. Oh, Mr Roberts, do come and knock this one in. Rupert's quite hopeless."

Mr Roberts knocked in the two posts with a few effortless strokes. "Right, you can tie the second pole on. Two feet high, David says."

"There's not enough room to land on the bank," objected Rupert.

"It is a bit tricky," James admitted. "Not much room for manoeuvre if you've got a big one like Ferdie; the little ponies will be all right."

"We seem to have lost the rest of our gang," said Mr Roberts as the four of them climbed back into the Land Rover.

"They're over by the water trough," Lesley told him. "I can hear my sister's voice. I expect they're tired of working and are just fooling around."

But when they drove into the schooling field they found great activity going on; everyone seemed to be dragging logs and boughs and tree trunks from the hedges and woods.

"We're building a stick heap," shouted Oliver to Rupert.

"A logpile," Netti corrected him.

"We thought we'd show some initiative and give David a surprise," explained Hanif. "Please will you add it to the plan, Mr Roberts? We're building it between the water and the tree trunk."

"I'll wait till I've seen the final result," answered Mr Roberts unenthusiastically. "We could do with a couple more helpers down here. Paul, come and give me a hand with this sheet," he called. "And we need another digger."

Lizzie came running and offered to be the fourth digger.

"It's easier here than on top of the hill," James told her. "Far less stones."

It's been churned to mud by the cattle coming to drink," said Lesley. "If you'll loosen, Lizzie, I'll shovel."

They scraped and shovelled energetically. Ten feet by

98

five, Mr Roberts had ordered, and with the earth piled at either end, but as there was a natural dip in the field, they didn't have to dig very deep. Mr Roberts and Paul shook out the plastic sheet, folded it to a suitable size, and they all fitted into the hollow. They wound the spare ends round two heavy poles to hold it on the landing and take-off sides and weighed it down with earth at either end. Then they grabbed buckets and began to fling water in it from the trough, wondering if it would hold. It seemed to take an incredible number of bucketsful to even cover the sheet. Mr Roberts left them to it and went to inspect the log jump. Alice and Netti were trying to build the untidy heap into an orderly-looking jump with the largest logs at the bottom.

"Not bad, is it?" asked Alice.

"Not *bad*? It's brilliant," Nettie told her.

"I'll knock in a couple of posts and put a pole across to make it solid," said Mr Roberts, "otherwise the ponies'll start dragging their legs through it, and you'll spend half the morning building it up."

They helped Mr Roberts with the posts and pole, but everyone else had lost interest in the log pile and drifted down to the water.

"It's horrible. Chess simply won't go near it, I know he won't," wailed Sarah.

"Well, at least you won't shoot into it head first," said Hanif. "I'm convinced that will be my fate."

"And mine," agreed Rupert. "I can just see Rosie coming to one of her shuddering halts."

"I hope the sheet's watertight," said Paul. "It's going to be a bit of a disaster if it all drains away in the night."

"I think it would be quite a good idea to *start* with it empty," said Lizzie. "Less wet for falling into and we could fill it up later."

CHAPTER SIX

Fainthearts and Lionhearts

"I decided that I'd rather help David than ride in the rally," Oliver explained to the other pony club members when they met at the water on Wednesday morning.

"It's lost about three inches in the night," said James, intent on the jump. "If you wouldn't mind holding Ferdie for a couple of minutes, Alice, I'll fill it up."

"I can't stand that Janet Green," Oliver went on. "She must be the most boring instructor that ever existed. You spend at *least* half the rally touching your toes. *And* she only gives about two for turnout."

"That's generous," Netti told him, "considering that Hobbit's always caked in mud and you never clean your tack or your boots."

"Julia always gives me at *least* five," replied Oliver haughtily. "Anyway, it means that Tina can have Hobbit and I'll find out whether he can jump ditches and water."

"We're all going to find that out. The moment of truth is here," said Hanif gloomily. "I've brought some dry clothes."

As the Land Rover bumped into the field, they saw that Mrs Rooke, looking severe and wearing a brown macintosh and matching hat, despite the sunshine, was sitting beside David. Several people remembered that Sarah and Lesley were there just in time to choke back their groans.

"Good morning, all," said David, coming to a halt beside the water. "That looks very wet. I expect we shall have a mighty splash or two this afternoon."

"Chess won't go near it. I've tried to lead him up, but he won't move a step. I'm never going to get over." Sarah sounded indignant.

"Perhaps Sarah could have Lesley's pony for the water,"

suggested Mrs Rooke. "It's rather hard on her to have a pony with a real phobia about black plastic, and Lesley doesn't really care about jumping."

"Well, let's deal with the problems as we come to them," said David. "We'll begin by schooling."

The schooling went well that morning. The ponies were all becoming more supple and energetic and the riders, feeling the improvement, felt they were getting somewhere and cheerfully tried harder still. Rosie was allowed to join in the leg-yielding for the first time and seemed to understand it immediately. Rupert said that she had been watching the other ponies, but David insisted that it was Rupert who had been watching and was therefore able to explain clearly what he wanted.

They cantered a lot. David told them to make the school bigger by going wide, outside the markers, and then to increase their speed along the long sides and slow up on the short ones. He was soon shouting, "Go on, gallop!" as they hurtled along the long sides and, "Steady!" at some people who were failing to slow up for the short ones. The ponies enjoyed it tremendously; the fast ones enjoyed showing off their speed and the slow ones were enlivened by the company. When the time came to halt they all pulled up with pricked ears and shining eyes.

"Very good." said David. "Do you all begin to see that it's a lively but controllable pony we're trying to produce by our schooling? We don't want a meek, dreary animal creeping round, and we don't want a sullen animal that's been mastered by force. Obedience must be something that the pony agrees to willingly and cheerfully; there must be nothing slavish about it."

He turned back towards the Land Rover. "Right then, off you go along the valley. The people who want to jump the slip rails at full height go first. The Land Rover party will lower them for the rest of you."

James set off steadily, followed by Hanif, Alice, Netti and Paul. The Rookes and Lizzie dithered.

"Wait till we've put it down and then jump at the high

end," David told them as he watched the first five ponies fly over.

Oliver managed to make the lowered rails a little higher by adding a broken rail as a cross pole and all the ponies jumped confidently.

"Twice round the easy way at the canter," said David when everyone had arrived in the second field, "and either half-halt or trot before the downhill jump. Keep your distances and if anything goes wrong ahead of you, stop."

They set off, a long string of riders all enjoying themselves; it had become so easy and the ponies had become partners instead of opponents.

David had struggled up on to the Land Rover bonnet and was sitting beside Oliver, loudhailer in hand. Mrs Rooke stood a little apart, watching in amazement.

"I can't get over it," she said as pony after pony popped over the downhill jump and halted beside the flag. "What have you done to them, David? I know Sarah, James and Netti were quite good little riders, but the *rest* of them! I can't imagine how you've done it, I really can't."

"It shows there was nothing wrong with them. They were quite willing to work at it when they had someone to tell them what to do." David picked up the loudhailer to roar "Legs!" at Lynne. "I must say I'm quite pleased with them."

"I should think so," said Mrs Rooke. "They all look as though they'd been riding cross-country for years and even that dreadful pony the Wheelers bought for Rupert is going in the right direction for a change."

"Round the harder way, once," David told James as the last pony halted at the flag. "And Lizzie, do remember to look up."

"I never thought you'd teach that mutton-fisted little Harry Franklin to ride; when I saw him that first morning at the rally my heart failed, but look at him now!" said Mrs Rooke, her magnified eyes full of admiration.

"Well done," David told the pony club members as Tina, who had been the last one to go, joined the group. "You've all got good cross-country seats and you all know how to jump downhill. And I'm pleased with the ponies too; the idle ones are going with a lot more impulsion, the wild ones have calmed down, and they're all on the bit most of the time. They also seem quite a lot fitter than when we started."

The pony club members looked at each other. It was something to have satisfied David, they thought, patting their ponies self-consciously.

"Now you can all jump the slip rail and wait for me by the tree trunk. Full height for everyone this time, so will those who are doubtful take a good lead."

Inspired by leads and encouraged by the fact that they were heading homewards, the ponies jumped willingly. Only Rosie, going last, almost refused and then made an enormous leap.

"There's nothing to tree trunks," said David, catching up with his ride. "They're solid, straightforward and natural, ponies understand them. This one is slightly uphill, so you make sure that you have plenty of impulsion."

Only Rupert was worried by the tree trunk, everyone else was longing to get at it. They rode fast and with determination and the ponies sailed over. Rosie made one of her huge leaps.

"Over the logpile and then over the tree trunk again," shouted David.

The ponies were less certain about the logpile. Even Ferdinand and Saffron took large careful leaps over it. Banjo made one of his stag jumps, high into the air, Stardust refused, so did Berry, Chess and Rajah. Only Jupiter and Tristram seemed completely unconcerned.

"Form up the ride again," said David. "Will the ponies that have got over give leads. Now come on, it's not a big jump and I think it's the riders who are being faint-hearted."

When they got going again, the ponies' courage rose and they followed their leaders over. Then all the refusers were sent round on their own.

"Now for the ditch," said David, struggling back into the Land Rover. By the time he had driven up the hill the riders were gathered round the ditch, all looking anxious and slightly green.

"Do any of the ponies jump ditches?" he asked. "James?"

"Ferdies done them in riding club competitions with my mother, but he generally had a stop or even two; they're definitely not his strong point."

"Anyone else?" asked David.

"Only those little ones at the side of the road," said Netti "but Tristram jumps most things."

"I have a feeling a Crankshaw pony living at Waterford farm won't be too bothered about ditches or water, so we'll send Alice first, then James and Harry and Netti, Paul and Lizzie. After that we'll see," David decided. "Now it's wide but not high, and what height there is is on the far side, so obviously you take off as near to the ditch as you can, which means you come fairly fast and with a light contact—a giving hand. *Don't* jump it as though it were a stile or a gate, *don't* stand back, jump it as you would a triple."

Alice wasn't very happy about her position as leader, but she gritted her teeth and tried to convince Saffron that she knew all about jumping ditches and to her surprise it worked. He jumped it easily. Behind her Ferdinand made a last minute run out, but Jupiter thundered on and jumped, without hesitating. Tristram followed him, Banjo stopped, looked, and then jumped, unseating Paul, who clung round his neck, but managed to get back into the saddle on the far side. Rajah refused, peering down into the ditch with a disapproving expression.

"Clear the course," ordered David. "We'll now have the people who haven't tried, but with leads. James, you don't need a lead, just be ready for him this time and keep him straight."

Lesley followed Alice, but at rather a half-hearted pace, and then slithered nervously on the edge of the ditch.

"Take her away," shouted David as Jupiter thundered

up with Rosie on his tail. A great cheer went up as she followed him over.

"I don't think she saw the ditch," said Rupert, patting her profusely. "I think she thought it was just another log with some earth lying about."

The fact that Rosie was over encouraged several people who had been certain that they would never make it, and though Chess, Berry and Hobbit refused, they all three had a look and then went over at their second attempts. Rupert offered Lizzie a lead in a very lordly manner and, much to his amazement, Rosie again jumped the ditch easily. Rajah followed.

Only Stardust was left, she was still cantering up slowly with her ears back and obviously had no intention of jumping.

"Go on, Lesley. Wake her up, get her over," called Mrs Rooke in exasperated tones. "Give her a good whack, don't just sit there, kick."

"You'd better put Sarah up," she told David: "she's the one with the drive. We'll be here all night if we wait for Lesley to get the pony over."

"This little mare is a bit faint-hearted, she lacks self-confidence," said David, limping forward to give Stardust a consoling pat. "I don't think kicking and whacking are the answer. Ponies are so very different; old Jupiter is a real lionheart, prepared to take on anything, but Stardust's at the opposite end of the scale; she's a bit of a softie and you'll get most out of her by building up her confidence and encouraging her."

Hanif was patting Jupiter's liver chestnut neck. "Jupe the Lionheart," he announced, pleased with the compliment.

"I think Saffron's quite lionhearted too," said Alice.

"Yes," David agreed, "but he's the sort of pony which needs a partner, he has to like and trust his rider. Jupiter would cart anyone over anything; he relies on himself."

"That is perfectly true," said Hanif, remembering the Brunstock show.

"What about Ra?" asked Lizzie.

105

"He's cautious by nature. If he was a person he would insure everything. He disapproves of taking risks."

"And Chess?"

"Like so many small ponies which have belonged to little children, he doesn't have much respect for his rider. He thinks *he* knows best and he likes to take a look at the jumps before he attempts them; you've got to convince him you're grown-up.

"Now I want you to form up the ride again. All go down and start over the logpile, then the tree trunk and then the ditch. Alice, I want you and Lesley at the back."

Everyone but Lesley was delighted to be jumping a piece of the course. They jogged down the hill arguing about leads. Lesley patted Startdust. The furious anger she'd felt at her mother's interference had cooled when David had told her she was wrong. And of course he was right, it was no use kicking and hitting a pony or person who lacked confidence. She patted Stardust again. "You're just as good as the rest of them. Don't worry, just copy Saffron."

James and Ferdinand came racing up the hill looking very pleased with themselves as they sailed over the ditch. David shouted, "Go on, over the brush, keep going."

He roared the same message at the other riders as they jumped the ditch and one by one they went on, swooping over the brush with ease.

The later riders could see what was happening. "If Stardust refuses, let's go on and jump the brush," Alice suggested to Lesley as they set off. But this time Stardust's blood was up; she was excited as she chased Saffron and the flying ponies ahead, and followed them over the ditch and then the brush without thought of refusing.

The riders all patted their ponies delightedly.

"I never thought Rosie would jump as high as that," Rupert told everyone who would listen.

"It's at least three feet to the top leaf," said Sarah, who had dismounted and was measuring the fence against herself.

"Angles," said David, leaving the Land Rover on the

106

edge of the trees and limping towards the two jumps. "The most important thing is to *look* where you want to go. Your head is very heavy and, as you know, the rider's weight is an aid, so by turning your head and shoulders in the direction you want to go you give the pony a clear signal. If you look straight ahead or down at the ground when you want to turn, you're giving the pony a totally incorrect signal; it's your fault if he doesn't get over the second fence. Point him at the first fence, but *look at* and *think about* the second one. O.K.? Start slowly, but with impulsion. If you go too fast the pony won't have time to adjust his stride and you may have a refusal. As all our ponies are novices we're not going to cut corners or go the shortest way; that comes later. So pop over the first, ride at the second, circle left and come back here."

With all the riders staring rigidly in the correct direction, the ponies found the little jumps perfectly simple and only Berry ran out of the second one.

"Now for the horizon," said David when Lynne was over at her second attempt. "Ours is very small and easy, but you can see that if you came galloping at some great hairy brush fence set on the hill like that, your pony might easily think, 'Good grief there's nowhere to land,' and you'd have a last-minute refusal. The secret of jumping all tricky fences is to approach slowly but with impulsion. And that's why they have them in competition courses; they want to test the pony's training. Unschooled horses can only maintain impulsion by going fast. So pop over, look right, circle the coppice and come back here. If you look straight down the hill you'll probably find yourself going there."

James and Alice jumped it easily. Hanif, looking right with desperate concentration, found it worked; Jupiter made no attempt to run away down the hill. Rosie and Stardust refused, but both jumped at their second try. The little ponies popped over eagerly, wondering what all the fuss was about. Then David sent them all back with instructions to jump the brush, angle and horizon fences one after the other. Everyone was pleased, their worries and fears had all vanished—it was fun and the ponies, enjoying it too, didn't need much riding.

"Down to the gate into the lane," said David, making his way back to the Land Rover.

They rode down on loose reins, chattering. Oliver walked proudly beside Hobbit.

"'Isn't he going *well*?" he asked Tina. "I never thought he'd do the big ones like the ditch and the brush."

"He's great," agreed Tina, "so brave; he's another lionheart. I'm having a lovely time, Ollie, thanks to you. I've learned more about riding in these three days than in my whole life."

"David's good, isn't he? I can't wait to get into his ride."

"Now," said David, gathering them round the gateway, "this is a test of the pony's cleverness and agility and, of course, impulsion. Think about the second fence and look the way you want to turn in the lane, and go slowly so that the pony has a chance to see what he's got to do. O.K., James. This time we'll turn left on landing. Don't follow too closely as some people are bound to get stuck."

Ferninand, looking very serious, jumped it perfectly. Rajah and Banjo followed him carefully. Jupiter flung himself over the first one, landed too near the second and had to turn round before he could jump down into the lane.

"That'll teach him to look before he leaps," shouted David. "Combinations are very good for over-confident ponies."

Saffron went over neatly, but Rosie over-jumped the first one, refused the second, then changed her mind and decided she could jump it from a standstill, but hit the pole so hard with her hindlegs that she broke the baling string.

"Oh, dozy Rosie, you make more work than all the others put together," complained Oliver, hurrying to repair the damage.

Then Tristram led the small ponies over and they all found it quite easy because they could fit in so many strides. Last of all Stardust jumped in and then spent several minutes teetering on the bank before she summoned the courage to jump down into the lane, which she did from a standstill.

"Now you can come back," David shouted through the loudhailer. "You'll need some impulsion to get up the bank. Go a bit further up the lane so that you've room to get going. Then keep as near to the left hand hedge as you can so you give yourself the maximum turning space, and don't take your pony by surprise."

Ferdinand *was* rather surprised, but he climbed over somehow, and the other ponies following knew they had to jump. Rajah heaved himself over with a great grunt, Banjo did one of his stage-like springs, vertically into the air. Berry and Chess gave their riders uncomfortable, slow motion jumps and Rosie climbed over the pole one leg at a time. Saffron jumped it well; Stardust followed without refusing and Hobbit, coming last, flew over in the neatest possible manner.

"We'll do it into the lane again," said David, "but this time I want you to turn the opposite way to the pony in front of you. James, you'll go to the right, so if you're next, Lizzie, you'll turn left, Paul right and so on, all down the line. Does everyone understand? I want to see that you're in charge, not the ponies."

Only Rosie went the wrong way; she made such an awkward jump that Rupert was in no position to steer. Sarah and Lynne were giving shrieks of dismay as they jumped, but managed to turn their separate ways. Then they all leapt back into the field in fine style, finding that the bank was perfectly easy if you had enough impulsion.

"A volunteer to give Rosie one more lead," said David, and chose Lizzie from all the shouted offers.

"Now lunch," he said when the Wheelers returned. "You can jump both slip rails on the way in, but don't go mad. James, will you hold everyone up in the lane until the last one's over."

"What a morning!" said Hanif, settling contentedly to his lunch, when all the ponies had been watered, fed and tied up in the barn, out of kicking distance of each other.

"I'm glad it's only us and all that dreary D lot have gone home," remarked Oliver, munching pork pie.

"You're a dreary D yourself," Paul told him. He and Lynne had persuaded their mother to let them eat their lunch in the barn with the other pony club members.

"I may be a D, but I'm not dreary," Oliver told him fiercely.

"Mummy thinks we've improved out of all recognition," announced Sarah, who had been collecting her lunch from Mrs Rooke's car. "*She* thinks we're quite good enough to go in for the Area Cup and she's going to persuade David to relent and let us enter. She's gone home now, but she's going to ring him tonight when he's had a rest."

"It'll be too late," said Lizzie. "The entries will have closed!"

"That's what I said, but being an efficient secretary she entered a team at the very beginning of the holidays, before David decided we would disgrace him."

"Oh *no*," groaned Hanif, his contentment vanishing. "We don't want to spoil everything with teams and prizes and having to win."

"There's no need to get worked up," Rupert told him. "O.K., she's entered a team, but that's only five people; you don't have to be in it."

"He's one of the best at cross-country," James pointed out.

"But not much good at dressage," added Sarah quickly.

"He'd be good for turn-out though," observed Lynne. "Jupiter always looks lovely and his tack is practically new."

"Thank you," said Hanif, "but I don't want to be in it. I renounce any claim I may have."

"Mummy wants Jennifer to be in it," Sarah told them.

"Why? She isn't on the course," protested Paul. "She thought she was too good."

"Well, that's the point isn't it?" said James. "She's the best rider in the Woodbury and she knows it."

"My mother will want James, Jennifer, the Great Sarah,

Netti and a Roberts," Lesley told Alice. "She settled it months ago; I expect she'll get her own way."

Lynne had produced a quiz book. "We'd better practise," she said, "just in case."

"It's not fair to ask questions out of that book. Both you and Sarah know all the answers by heart," Paul objected.

"Oh come on, it's not a competition, it's just for fun," Sarah told him. "Will you quiz us, James?"

"It's not my idea of fun," said Rupert, retreating to a distant straw bale.

James swallowed down a sandwich and opened the book obediently.

"Name two plants which are poisonous to horses," he demanded.

"Yew."

"Deadly Nightshade."

"Privet."

"Rhodedendrons."

"Ivy," they shouted all at once.

"Spaghetti," said Rupert. Sarah gave him a withering look. "Let's go over there in the corner," she suggested to her team mates. "And James, you must ask us each a question in turn and give us marks for a correct or semi-correct answer."

"What do the following initials stand for?" asked James. "B.H.S."

"Beastly. Horrible. Stinking!" shouted Oliver.

"Oh, shut up. Can't you understand that we want to have a good team for a change?" snapped Sarah. "We want to beat the Cranford Vale even if you don't."

"Leave them alone, Ollie. It's not fair to spoil their practice!" Lizzie told him.

"Jokes are only funny once," Rupert added. "It's boring to go on and on."

"I *wasn't* going on and on," objected Oliver.

The team soon grew tired of their question master. James was very slow and deliberate and insisted looking up all the answers in the back of the book though Lynne and

111

Sarah knew they had given the correct ones. They began to discuss what they should call themselves. Sarah and Lynne wanted to be The Woodbury Wonders, Netti said it sounded a bit boastful and she thought they ought to wait until they had done something wonderful before they gave themselves a name like that.

"We could have T shirts with it printed on the front," suggested Lynne.

"Well, if Jennifer's going to be in the team we'd better wait and ask her what she thinks," said James, "but I think we should just be the Woodbury, or Woodbury P.C."

"I knew all this talk of teams would spoil the atmosphere," Hanif complained to Alice as they bridled their ponies. "They are going to divide us into two lots."

"It's only Sarah," Alice told him. "I'm sure Netti and James and the Robertses aren't like that."

"Teams can ruin people's natures," said Hanif gloomily.

Some of the pony club members were still tacking up when David drove the Land Rover into the yard.

"Come on, get moving," he told them. "Julia will be waiting at Coppice Hill and we've got to get you all over that water before dark."

"I know I'm *never* going to get over it," wailed Sarah. "Not even if we stay there all night."

"Where are my dry clothes?" demanded Hanif, looking round.

"You left them under the hedge by the water jump," Alice reminded him.

They were all rather silent as they rode down the farm track. Quite a few people had hollow-feeling stomachs and weak legs at the thought of the water, and these feelings grew worse when they found Julia waiting for them, armed with a lunge rein and lungeing whip.

"We'll warm up by jumping the slip rail into the second field and then doing the hill the easy way," said David. "Do it well, because I want to show Julia how you've come on. Let the slow ponies chase a fast one and don't forget to halt at the final flag. Off you go, James."

They felt much more on their own, starting from the first field and with no David and main group of ponies waiting below in the valley, but they all enjoyed the feeling of being alone with their ponies and the long string of ponies and riders looked very impressive as it snaked up and down the hill in a controlled manner.

"I'm stunned," said Julia when they had all come back. "Truthfully. I never thought you could improve that much in three days, even with David cursing you. They'll all go straight over the water, won't they?" she asked. "You won't need me and my gear."

"Yes we will. I'm told we have one confirmed hater of black plastic among the ponies and several of the riders have made up their minds to refuse."

"The water's gone down two inches," reported James. "Shall I fill it up?"

"*No!*" the other pony club members shrieked at him.

"No," agreed David. "There's plenty there for our purpose, but I would like a pole over the centre. The long one, resting on a couple of drums on their sides. James, give Julia a hand."

"That makes it worse," complained Netti.

"*Much* worse," agreed Lynne.

"It makes it easier for the ponies," David told them. "They realise it's a jump and don't fall in and it protects my plastic sheet from the ones that want to wade through. Now, has anyone a pony that's jumped water?"

"Well Ferdie *has*, but he doesn't like it much," answered James. "He generally has a stop or two with my mother at the riding club."

"Let's try Alice in the lead then," said David. "Come at a brisk pace, Alice, but the important thing is to increase your speed during the last few strides. Some riders start too fast and run out of steam as they get there, that's fatal. Harry, you're second, James third. Then anyone else who feels they *might* make it. We deal with the difficult ones later."

Alice cantered a circle and approached briskly. Saffron

saw the jump, pricked his ears, lengthened his stride and flew over effortlessly. Everyone cheered, he made it look so easy. Hanif had turned and was riding in pursuit. Jupiter made an enormous leap, far higher and wider than was necessary, but it was a smooth jump and Hanif sat tight. James followed grim-faced. He rode in a very determined manner but, at the very last moment, Ferdinand's heart failed, he braked violently, skidded to a halt on the very brink, head down, almost tipping in. James went on, landing with a loud splash on the far side, the bottom half of him in the water.

There were cries of horror which turned to laughter as James crawled out and then stood looking ruefully at his dripping jodhs.

"Oh Ferdie, you brute," he said and then began to laugh too.

"You can have my spare jodhs," offered Hanif. "They are stretch ones."

"I'm all right, I'll soon dry out."

"You won't, you know." Julia, who'd caught Ferdinand, took a closer look. "You're sopping and you won't do your mother's beautiful saddle any good."

"O.K.," James agreed, "I'd better see if I can get into them."

The two boys went off together, Hanif to retrieve his clothes from their hiding place in the hedge, James to find a bush he could change behind.

David shouted, "Next!" at the riders, none of whom felt the least desire to be next in the water but Lizzie, always obliging, stirred Rajah into a canter. He approached as slowly as possible, a highly disapproving expression on his long chestnut face, and with obviously no intention of jumping.

Lizzie let him inspect the water, he sniffed it suspiciously and then gave a loud snort.

"Take him away," said David. "He knows all about it, you showed it to him this morning; he's just putting on an act. Anyone else want a go?"

Lesley rode up flapping her legs, but not throwing her heart over. Paul came fast but let Banjo run out at the last moment.

"I think Tristram would do it, but could we have a lead?" asked Netti. "All this falling off and refusing has unnerved us."

David called for Alice. "Put them over the log pile and then circle round and over the water," he instructed.

"Hurry up, Harry! We need you," called Julia.

Harry came trotting back. "Everything's a bit tight," he said, giggling, "but he's got into the jodhs and the socks."

"I'll need a leg-up," complained James, following at a stiff-legged walk. "I can't bend my knees."

Alice and Netti leapt the log pile, swept round and sailed over the water with no problems at all.

"It looks so easy when they do it," wailed Lynne.

"It *is* easy," David told her. "The difficulties are all in the minds of the riders and ponies. All right, Harry and James. And be ready for him this time, James."

"I will," James shouted back, as, brandishing his whip, they rode at the log pile. And, though Ferdinand made a large and apprehensive-looking jump and James, determined not to go over his head again, got left behind, they reached the far bank safely.

"Do it once more," shouted David. "Paul, you follow them."

This time James and Ferdinand jumped well, but Banjo made another of his last-minute run-outs.

"Very bad," shouted David. "Anyone can be taken by surprise, but to let a pony run out twice to the same side is bad riding. You must tell him with reins and legs before you start that he's not going to do it; turn him into the hedge, have a dead refusal. You see if they come up to a fence with a run-out in mind they don't make any plans for jumping, they don't think about the take-off, so you don't have a hope of getting over. Come once more on your own, Paul, and *make* him do a dead refusal."

While Paul was trying to convince Banjo that he wasn't

going to run out again, David asked Julia and Oliver to make a wing. They placed a large oil drum on the non-hedge side of the water and rested one end of a pole on it and the other on a small drum.

"Don't think that a wing will do your work for you," said David, "it won't, but it may help a bit. Right, Alice, give him another lead."

This time Banjo refused and then, before Paul could turn him away, he made an enormous leap from a standstill. Paul shot out of the saddle, clung round the pony's neck, and then fell off on the far side, just clear of the water.

The riders of the other small ponies became even more glum.

"I don't think we're ever going to do it," said Tina. "It's too wide for little ponies."

"If Banjo won't, Berry hasn't a hope," agreed Lynne.

"I always knew it was a waste of time even *trying* with Chess," complained Sarah. "Why doesn't David let us go round the whole course on our own? That would be much more fun."

"If there's a lead going, I will be the next sacrificial victim," offered Rupert suddenly.

"Good. We'll have Netti and James, just to make sure their ponies are really happy about it, then Harry and Rupert, then Alice and Paul."

Tristram was obviously perfectly happy, but Ferdinand was still jumping carefully. Then Harry and Rupert, who'd warmed up over the log pile, came in fast and Rosie didn't seem to notice the water. Chasing Jupiter, she sailed over as though it was only the pole she had to jump. Everyone cheered and clapped.

Flinging himself off, Rupert hugged her enthusiastically and then began to beg bread and pony nuts from anyone who had some left in his or her pocket. "Do you think she actually saw the water?" he asked David anxiously.

"Yes, I expect she jumped streams as foal, followed her dam over; she doesn't understand what all the fuss is about. Now where's Paul? James, you can give him another lead

116

and then we'll start using the Irish method on the rest of them."

"Can Lesley and I have one more lead?" asked Lizzie, who was rather annoyed that her brother and sister were over.

"Yes, O.K., but neither of you looked very hopeful," said David, watching Paul. Banjo made another enormous leap, but this time Paul was ready for him and stayed on. Then Lesley and Lizzie came with their leads but, though they both looked very determined and, kicking and whacking with a windmill of arms and legs, tried to make their ponies jump from a standstill, they couldn't get over.

"What *are* you supposed to do when your pony just *won't* jump?" asked Lizzie despondently.

"I'm going to show you one method, which seems to work well over ditches and water," answered David, as Julia passed the lunge rein through one ring of Rajah's snaffle and buckled it to the other.

"Try and see it from the pony's point of view," he went on, raising his voice and talking to all the members. "There's this horrible jump and you have to decide how to get over it, where to take off and how high and how wide you ought to jump. If you get it wrong you can fall, bang your legs, drown. Bad enough without a rider, but when you've got one of them, all your troubles are doubled. They whack you and kick you when you're trying to work out the take-off, their weight tips all over the place, unbalancing you when you're dithering on the brink, trying to get up the courage for an enormous leap, and, if you finally make the enormous leap, they go and fall off. Now we're going to try without riders. Cross your stirrups, Lizzie."

"I want you to lead him up to it," Julia told Lizzie, "then I'll tow him over it from the far side. Be ready to stand clear when he jumps."

"*If* he jumps," Lizzie corrected her.

Rajah dithered and teetered for several minutes while Julia pulled gently and Lizzie and David made encouraging noises.

"Jump over yourself, Lizzie, or wade through. Show him that even humans can do it," called David.

Lizzie scrambled and hopped across, trying to keep her leaking boot out of the water, and then called Rajah from the far side. His dithering increased, but his eyes had stopped rolling with obstinacy.

"He's going," said David and everyone began to shout encouraging remarks. Suddenly Rajah made a huge leap and found himself being praised and patted and rewarded from a scoop of oats on the far side.

Lizzie led him back for a second attempt and this time he only dithered for a moment, and the third time he didn't dither at all.

"Now Lesley," said David.

Stardust made less fuss than Rajah, and Hobbit, who went next, made no fuss at all. Berry was more difficult. Always inclined to kick, she lashed out angrily at anyone who went near her and kept charging into the wing rather than face the water. Julia gave the lunge rein to Lizzie, with instructions to move back quickly if Berry show signs of coming over, and, taking the lunge whip, stood outside the wing and kept the pony straight. Furious, Berry sulked. She stood, ears back, with a mulish expression, and refused to budge. Julia began to tap her on the quarters with the lunge whip, Lynne shook the scoop of oats invitingly on the far side. Berry stood and sulked, but the annoying tapping of the whip went on and the oats became more tempting; suddenly she gave in and jumped with the greatest of ease. At her second attempt she went over with no trouble at all. Lynne was amazed and delighted.

"Now, let's have those four ponies over, mounted," said David. "The rest of you can give them leads. Make a sort of hunt of it; we want them to enjoy themselves. Then we'll deal with Master Chess."

The ten ponies were soon racing over the logpile and the water. Pony after pony flew over happily. Only Berry misbehaved, jumping the wing, but when Lynne had been roared at for not keeping her straight, she tried again and this time jumped it easily.

"I never thought Stardust would take to it so quickly," Lesley told Alice as they dismounted and fed their ponies on handfuls of pony nuts and bread. And her warm glow of triumph was increased by the sight of her sister watching with a dismal face as piebald Chess stood stockstill at the end of the lunge rein and refused to move one step nearer the water.

"Do you know if he's ever been lunged?" asked David.

"Yes, I think so. We tried him out once at a pony club rally and he seemed to know all about it," answered Sarah.

"Great," said Julia. "I'll get him going first then." She took Chess away from the water and soon had him trotting round on the lunge rein and looking like a well-behaved pony. Then, gradually she moved the circle nearer the jump and still kept him going forward. It wasn't until she actually pointed him at the water that he stopped, and refused to budge.

"See if you can lead him forward, Sarah."

"He won't do it, I know he won't. It's just a waste of time," moaned Sarah, as Oliver tried to tempt Chess nearer with oats.

Julia gave the lunge rein to Lizzie and managed to persuade Chess to within a few strides of the water by tapping him on the hindquarters, but then he stuck again, and he still wasn't within dithering distance.

"Does he kick other ponies?" asked David.

"No, never."

"Good. Lesley, you ride Stardust alongside him. Better go on the hedge side. Sarah, you lead Chess and try to walk them both up to the edge of the jump."

Chess was persuaded to take another couple of steps, but then he stood rock-like again. Sarah was wailing that it was useless, and, except for those who were helping, everyone had lost interest and started to talk of other things. James was trying to dry his jodhs and socks by flapping them in the wind. Netti took one sock and waved it aloft on her whip.

119

"Lesley, go back a bit, take a short run then trot past Chess and pop over, O.K.? Sarah you keep Chess standing straight and make sure he watches."

Stardust popped over neatly and Chess, taken by surprise, moved forward without meaning to. Julia was tapping him with the whip again, Oliver was shaking the oats, David and Lizzie were making encouraging noises; he began to dither.

"Round again, Leslie," called David.

Stardust pushed past him and jumped over. "Go on boy!" everyone shouted, "Go on."

Suddenly Chess reared up, plunged into the water, knocking down the centre pole and waded out on the far side. Everyone cheered and he began to wolf down huge mouthfuls of oats as though they were his just reward.

"Keep some for next time, Ollie," said Julia, fishing in the water the the pole.

"And mind my plastic sheet. This is not a water splash but a jump," David told Chess, as Sarah and Lesley went back for a second try.

This time Chess jumped properly and made another greedy rush for the oats. Then they towed him over without Stardust, and finally Sarah mounted, and Stardust, Berry and Hobbit were all told to give him a lead and to go round twice without stopping.

Sarah hardly knew whether to be pleased that she had a pony which now jumped black plastic and water, or annoyed that David had proved her wrong, but Tina and Lynne were both so loud in praise of their ponies and of David's Irish method, that she didn't have to say anything at all.

David, who seemed suddenly anxious to get away, called for quiet. "That's all for today," he said, "and tomorrow I'm going to hospital for a check-up. I think all the ponies should have a rest; we've worked them quite hard. Would any of you like to do a very, very basic dressage test and go round the whole course individually on Friday?"

"A *dressage* test?" asked some voices in horror, but

others were already shouting, "Go round the whole course? Yes, *please.*"

"Same time then," said David, climbing into the passenger seat of the Land Rover. "Will you drive, Julia? I'm whacked."

"Thank you!" the pony club members shouted after them. "Thank you, David. Thank you, Julia."

CHAPTER SEVEN

Clear The Course

On Friday morning, Alice and Hanif, trotting down the track from Four Cross, found Sarah waiting for them on the road.

"Hullo," she said. I thought I'd wait and tell you the news. My mother's determined to get a team to the Area Cup. She and Mrs Blacker were plotting all day yesterday and Julia agrees that we're good enough. They've got the rules and some copies of the dressage test and some new quiz books and they're all going to work on David today."

"Poor David," said Hanif. "I really do pity him. All this stupid fuss about teams."

"I hope everything was all right at the hospital and they didn't say we had been wearing him out too much. Has anyone heard?" asked Alice.

"Yes, Mummy telephoned to ask last night. He said they were pleased with him and said he was to carry on and do a bit more each day."

James was waiting for them at his gate. "I've got your clothes," he told Hanif. "My mother *would* wash and iron them. I kept telling her that I'd only worn them for two hours, but she's got a phobia about dirty socks. It's great about the team, isn't it Sarah? I read the whole of the Pony Club Manual last night, in case I have to go in for the Quiz, but I'd rather not. I'm not as good as the rest of you at answering questions. I'd rather do the other sections. Is Jennifer coming today?"

"Yes, I think so. But I don't think Mummy's dared to tell David yet."

They found Mrs Rooke already in the field at Coppice Hill, unloading biscuit tin dressage markers from her car, and making a cross and reluctant Oliver arrange them round the school.

122

"He's doing it all wrong," James pointed out immediately. "He's jumbled all the quarter markers up. K should be on this side. Ollie!" he shouted.

"Go and sort them out," said Mrs Rooke. "Here's a copy of the test. I've brought one for each of you, but of course only the team have to learn it by heart. David's going to have it commanded this morning."

The pony club members read their dressage tests through gloomily. "You and I will lose three points straight away for not having snaffles," Alice pointed out to Hanif.

"That's not many, look what I'll lose when Jupe refuses to halt."

"Oh dear, there's a serpentine," wailed Lizzie.

"Do we really have to?" asked Rupert, "I'll never remember all this."

"You don't have to remember it, it's going to be commanded," Lesley snapped at him. "Someone stands at A and shouts the next movement just before you get to the marker where it begins."

By the time David arrived, the prospective team members had arranged the arena properly; James had even paced out all the distances. But the people who had never ridden a test before had worked themselves into a panic and, without even answering his 'Good morning all', they crowded round him asking questions.

"Must we do it?"

"What happens if your pony won't stand?"

"How do you know where four metres from the centre line is, when there's no line?"

"There's no marker for G."

"How big is a twenty metre circle?"

"We're going to begin by schooling," David shouted them down. "Will you all walk round on the old track, outside the markers, please."

As soon as the ponies were going well and on the bit, David started practising the various movements in the test. As they trotted round, everyone was called in turn to trot down the centre line and halt at X. The boys saluted by taking off their caps, the girls by putting their reins in one hand, dropping the other at their sides and bowing in the direction of the imaginary judge. They rode at the ordinary trot, at the sitting trot. Individually they made the smaller serpentine, half-circling about three yards on either side of where the centre line would be if there was one. They cantered and circled, they changed the rein and went through all the movements again. They practised halting and saluting all round the school and then walking on a long rein.

"There you are," said Daivd as they walked round him. "There's nothing to panic about; there's nothing in the test, except the salute, which we haven't done every day this week. Any questions?"

"Is it true you can't wear a martingale?" asked Alice, who had been told to take hers off by Sarah.

"In competitions, yes," answered David. "And you're not allowed to carry a whip, and the use of voice loses you points, so you can't talk to your pony. But none of that applies this morning; we're having a rough and ready practice in a very rough and ready arena. By the way, though you can practise the various *parts* of a test as often as you like, riding the whole test straight through should be done very rarely. You don't want the pony to learn the test. If they do, they begin to 'anticipate' and start the movements before you tell them to. Now I'm going to be the judge and I want someone to command; we'll use the loudhailer. Here, you, Lizzie," he went on quickly as Mrs Rooke began to say what a fine voice Sarah had. "You have to watch the rider and call out the instructions well before the marker at which the movement begins. Will the people who've ridden in dressage tests before come first, please."

James had ridden in several so he agreed to go first. Netti and Sarah, who had been in junior teams, offered to go second and third. Alice said she'd go fourth, if no one else wanted to, and Hanif said he would follow Alice. Gradually everyone found a place in the order.

"It's going to take quite a time," David told them, "about

five minutes each, so the people who aren't going early should dismount and give their ponies a rest, then start warming up again about ten minutes before they're due in."

Lizzie was good at commanding and James seemed very efficient at riding the test. Everyone except Netti, who was preparing to go in next, watched admiringly as James and Ferdinand entered at a steady trot and halted squarely at X. James saluted elegantly, David bowed back—he had no hat to take off—and horse and rider moved off at a trot round the arena. They serpentined, they cantered, circled at the canter, trotted and then, changing the rein at the walk, rode the serpentine and the cantering movements again, going round to the right. Finally they trotted down the centre, halting this time at the non-existent letter G, which James found by looking out of the corner of his eye for M.

"Well done," said David. "That wasn't at all bad. Your transitions are your weak point. You started cantering late on both reins. Try giving the aids a bit earlier. And the transitions back to trot were rather unbalanced, you need to put his hindlegs under him with a half-halt before you actually slow down. Then you could do with a bit more impulsion in the serpentines. You're inclined to put him to sleep and aim at neatness, but I want to see impulsion, hindlegs really working, back swinging. You won't do your jumping any good if you put your horse to sleep when you're schooling. But, as I say, it wasn't too bad at all."

Netti was ready, and Lizzie commanded her sister to 'Enter at ordinary trot sitting or rising'. Tristram moved well and, like Ferdinand, he had a good head-carriage. Netti kept calm and was able to think ahead and so be accurate.

"Good," said David when she bowed at the end. "That was another nice one. Your serpentines have come on a lot, but you're still cantering too fast on the circles. Try to sit down more and use the half-halt to slow him up."

Chess was next. He was too small and sturdy, too short-striding and thick-necked, to perform an elegant test, but it was obedient and neat and Mrs Rooke clapped loudly as he

125

came to the final halt. "Every movement carried out precisely at the marker, nothing slipshod there," she announced.

"She wasn't in the same class as James and Netti." Lesley's bitter voice was equally loud.

"Little ponies can't really be judged against the bigger ones," said David calmly. "We all know that short strides and lack of presence will tell against them in a real competition, but at home we judge people on how well they've done with a particular pony."

"Like tack inspections," suggested Lizzie, who hated quarrels. "In your own pony club it doesn't matter if your tack's ancient, it's just judged on cleaness, but if you go against other clubs you've got to have good tack as well."

"Exactly," said David. "Come on, Alice."

Alice, suddenly overcome with nerves, made a very wavering entrance until David called to her that she must look at a point over the judge's head and not down at X. She made a crooked halt and a very hurried bow.

"Take your time, there's no rush," David told her.

Gradually as they trotted round, she and Saffron settled down, and though the pony sometimes escaped from her in the transitions and came off the bit, everyone could see that when he was on the bit he was calm, supple and occasionally a look of grace and distinction came over him, which set him apart from the other ponies.

"He bends beautifully," remarked Lizzie, eyeing his serpentine enviously, "and his steps are much more spaced out than Chess's"

"Yes, he has good cadence and a lot of potential," agreed David.

Hanif, in a ferment of worry, had thoroughly upset Jupiter. Instead of riding in quietly, he had found himself engaged in a pitched battle over halting and standing. When Oliver, who had appointed himself collecting steward, called him in, Jupiter bounced round C and entered, swinging his quarters and fighting for his head. Hanif forced him to a halt, but he refused to stand and twirled round and round.

"What's the matter with you?" asked David. "Why are you getting uptight, Harry? You've been doing all these movements perfectly well for days and now you go and work the pair of you into this ridiculous state. Take him away and calm him down. Walk on a loose rein and relax. You can try again after Lesley. And stop thinking you've got to *prove* something"

"Lesley, you look ready. Can you come now?"

Stardust's performance was an eye-opener to the other pony members. They had all be too intent on schooling their own ponies to see how other people were progressing and it was only at jumping that they had sometimes had the opportunity to watch each other. Now to see the pretty part-bred Arab trot into the arena was a great surprise. She no longer looked depressed and overbent. No longer weighed down by the pelham, her head had come up, better feeding had put a sparkle into her eyes and more of a shine on her chestnut coat, schooling had brought her hindlegs under her and given her impulsion. She looked quite different and certainly the most distinguished of the performers so far. She had a very long, slow stride, her cadence at the trot was even more pronounced that Saffron's, she stayed on the bit, and Lesley, like Sarah, was very accurate about carrying out movements exactly at the markers.

"Well done," said David when she came to her final halt. "That was very good. Here, I've made you some notes, small criticisms. The general impression was very good. Your walk is still your weakest point, it lacks impulsion; you'll have to try and improve it out hacking."

"Now, has Harry calmed down?"

"Has Jupe calmed down, you mean."

"No I don't. Jupe didn't even know we were planning to do individual dressage tests until Harry went tense and indicated that there was something unpleasant ahead."

"Well, I've decided not to care. I'm not going to try at all."

"Great, let's get started."

Except for David, Alice and Lizzie, no one watched Hanif's performance, they were all too stunned by Stardust. Lynne, Netti and Tina had all rushed to pat the pony, who looked very pleased at the unaccustumed admiration.

"She may not be much good at cross-country, but she's absolutely brilliant at dressage," said Netti.

"Brilliant," agreed Lynne. "Even better than Sea King."

"Oh, far better than him. She's up to Cranford Vale standard," said Netti.

"And far far better than anyone I've seen at the riding school," added Tina.

"Thank you." Lesley dismounted. "I didn't think I liked dressage tests before, but now I think they're good fun, and Stardust enjoyed it too. I think she likes people watching her."

"Why didn't Mrs Rooke clap Lesley?" Oliver asked Paul in a loud and indignant voice. "She was streets better than Sarah."

In the arena Jupiter was still bouncing a bit, but the fact that Hanif had given up trying to make him perform the movements exactly at the markers was helping.

"Don't halt," called David as he came down the centre at the end. "Carry on round and go through the whole test again. Now you've a rough idea how long he's going to take to obey your relaxed aids, try giving them a bit earlier and see if that makes it more accurate. Don't fuss him, just experiment calmly."

After Hanif came Rupert, and his was a very different performance. Rosie drifted round vaguely and neither of them seemed to be bothering much about markers. But they kept calm; Rosie only left the arena once, and she managed to do every movement in her own time.

"What a mess, just like Rupert," complained Mrs Rooke.

"Well done," David told Rupert. "That wasn't a bad test for a youngster and you didn't try to get hold of her which was sensible. Keep going like that and you'll find she'll improve gradually."

Paul's test was neat and accurate, but Banjo, like Chess, didn't really use his hindlegs and his small pony stride was a disadvantage. Lynne and Berry started well but when it came to the canter, the roan pony went back to her old habit of trotting faster and faster. Lynne, shrieking with horror, lost her way and, despite Lizzie's firm commands, continued in a state of confusion for the rest of the test.

"Terrible," she shrieked cheerfully halting at X. "We were awful. Much the worst."

Hobbit followed her into the arena, a serious expression on his dark-brown Dartmoor dish-face. Tina, looking pale beneath her freckles and concentrating grimly, managed quite well until Hobbit went on the wrong leg and she stayed on it for the whole of the canter movement, including the circle.

"Did you realise you were on the wrong leg?" asked David when she halted. "Because you should have corrected it. Leading off on an incorrect leg loses you a few points, but carrying out a whole movement on it means that you haven't done what was asked for, and as there were two movements, you would have lost twenty points."

"Sorry," said Tina.

"Don't be, you're here to learn. It was a nice test otherwise."

Lizzie was the last to go. She had been riding in while Netti commanded Tina and as she trotted into the arena, the watchers realised that they were in for another surprise. Rajah wasn't light and elegant, he didn't have the poetical appearance of Stardust, but he was energetic and on the bit, his long stride was cadenced, his back swung and he was bending correctly on all his corners, serpentines and circles as he plodded round with pricked ears and a learned expression.

"Well done, Lizzie, you only looked down twice and the old horse has improved out of all recognition." David turned to address the others. "I hope you've all learned something by watching each other," he said. "It's quite interesting to see how some of the ponies have come on;

they've all improved, but some had more hidden potential than others."

"My word, yes," said Mrs Rooke in a cross voice. "It's certainly confused things."

"We have an hour and a half for lunch," said David. "So only small feeds please, or they won't feel like galloping round the cross-country this afternoon."

After lunch the Land Rover party left for Coppice Hill before the ponies. Mrs Roberts had joined Mrs Rooke and Oliver, and when the riders reached the field they found the mothers had been hard at work, helping Oliver drag poles and drums from the two unwanted hillside jumps and build a new fence in the valley. The slip rails had been strenthened with extra cross poles and made to look more formidable, but otherwise the course was as before.

"I have the plan here," said David, "if anyone wants to look at it. These poles and drums are the first fence, then slip rail, water, logpile, tree trunk, ditch, brush, angle, horizon, then the little downhill jump and the gateway into the lane. This is where you've got to be careful. If you do get out of control down the hill, circle and stop *before* jumping into the lane. The gateway jump must be taken slowly, O.K.? Then you canter along the lane, jump back into the field over the slip rails and the Land Rover will be the finish. It'll be parked between the ditch and the brush. Oliver will be the starter, Mrs Rooke will steward the gateway jump and Mrs Roberts the water."

"I've got the best position," interrupted Mrs Roberts, laughing merrily, "but I'll fish you out quick."

"If you have three refusals at a jump, go on to the next and we'll sort you out afterwards. Any questions?"

"Do circles count as refusals?" asked Sarah.

"Normally, yes, but today isn't a competition; there are no prizes to be won."

"Do you want us to go fast?" asked James.

"A fair hunting pace, as they say; that's a hand gallop or a fast canter. This is an experiment, you have to find out what pace suits your pony. If the small ones start too fast they won't have the puff to get over the water, much less up the hill. And as I have already said, the gateway jump must be taken slowly. Now, we'll leave James and Harry down here and the rest of you come up the hill with me; you'll get a better view of what's going on. Remember, starter, when the first pony comes down the hill you can start the next one, but never more than two ponies on the course at once. And if anyone is in trouble we all wave our red flags. Our white ones signal that all is well again."

"Don't worry, I'll keep things under control down here," said Oliver.

From their vantage point on the hill, the other pony club members watched James start. He jumped the first two easily and then made the long journey to the water at a good cross-country canter. They saw him half-halt before he reached the water and then sit down and ride.

"He didn't mean to go in again," commented David as Ferdinand made a careful jump and turned uphill for the logpile. It was then that two figures, one mounted and one on foot, appeared at the lane slip rails.

"Who the hell . . ." began David.

"It's Mrs Blacker and Jennifer," said Sarah. "They mentioned that they might come and watch."

"I thought she asked Mummy if she could join in," said Lesley maliciously.

David turned his attention back to James who, riding hard at the ditch, was obviously prepared to foil last-minute attempts to run out. As he landed safely everyone shouted encouraging remarks.

"Those idiots are still on the course," complained David. He picked up the loudhailer and, waiting until James was over the brush, he shouted, "Clear the course, please. Wave at them, will you, Lesley?" he asked, looking down angrily at his useless arm. "They don't seem to understand I'm yelling at *them*. They can't both be deaf."

Everyone began to wave, for James was over the horizon fence and heading for the downhill one at a steady canter.

131

At last Mrs Roberts realized what was wrong and ran across to the Blackers.

Below in the valley, Hanif started. James hopped neatly over the gateway jumps. Mrs Blacker stood arguing with Mrs Roberts in the middle of the course and Jennifer, unused to popping over jumps with short runs, refused the slip rails.

"Clear the course!" David gave an angry roar through the loudhailer. Hanif, who was coming fast because he had decided to let Jupiter have his own way over the easy jumps at the beginning of the course and then steady him down later, shouted too, scattering the mothers. James coming along the lane yelled indignantly at Jennifer to get out of his way. He pushed past her and jumped into the field as Hanif sailed confidently over the water. Jennifer took James's lead, jumped into the field and went to stand with her mother and Mrs Roberts.

"I hope Mum's giving them hell," said Paul as James came galloping up the hill to finish.

"Great," he said, dismounting and loosening Ferdinand's girths. "Really great."

"The course rode well, did it?" asked David, his eyes concentrating on Hanif, who trotted through the trees, popped over the angle jump, and then angled the horizon jump too, so that he didn't land pointing straight downhill.

Oliver started Alice. She was looking forward to her ride; she felt completely at home with Saffron now, and having jumped everything but the first jump, she had no qualms about the course. She was filled with happiness as she galloped along the valley; sailing over the jumps. She felt that Saffron was a partner; she was steadying him and sending him on, but he was agreeing with the arrangements, he wasn't having to be controlled.

Oliver started Rosie with encouraging shouts of "Go it, Dozey!" and was very disgruntled when she refused dead at the first jump. He longed for Rupert to be a hero brother and do well, but as usual it would be bossy old Netti who did the best of the Wheelers. "Oh go on, you stupid twit," he muttered angrily, and at the second try she did.

132

Rupert got going on the long gallop across the second field and Rosie jumped the water easily. She was suspicious of the logpile and made a large slow motion jump. After the tree trunk, Rupert slowed her up. "You've got to keep some breath for the ditch," he told her. She jumped it well, but then Rupert was so busy shouting and waving to the other pony club members that he almost ran out of the brush.

"Concentrate!" roared David after his departing figure. But he still managed to lose himself in the trees and had to circle before he could take the horizon fence.

"That's another refusal," said Sarah who was keeping the scores.

Lizzie started; she made certain that Rajah was alert and ready for a new jump. He jumped the first two easily and galloped on towards the water. When I'm over that I'll start to enjoy myself, thought Lizzie.

Rupert was having trouble at the gateway. He had forgotten to look the way he wanted to go, so Rosie had gone straight on and almost collapsed on her nose in the hedge across the lane, but Rupert sat tight and the pony recovered somehow.

"We're O.K., don't worry," Rupert shouted in reply to Mrs Rooke's inquiries, and, sorting themselves out, they galloped away.

Rajah had slowed to an obstinate refusal at the water. Lizzie, uncharacteristically severe, gave him a whack with her whip. "You've jumped it dozens of times, you're just being stupid," she told him crossly. At the second attempt he jumped it easily and thundered on, taking the logpile and tree trunk with no trouble at all.

"Old Ra's beginning to look like a cross-country horse," observed James, as the pony cleared the ditch and went on with pricked ears and a wise expression towards the brush.

"Except for Rosie, they've all looked good," said Alice, who was sitting on the ground with Saffron cropping the turf beside her.

"And she's coming home like a veteran," announced Hanif, as she appeared over the slip rails.

"The trouble is that nearly all the good people have gone; the disasters are about to start," said Lynne.

"There are still Netti and Paul to go," James pointed out. "They ought to go round clear."

"But now we have my sister, she's bound to make a mess of it," said Sarah as Lesley cantered along the valley. Stardust cleared the first two, but objected to jumping the water on her own and slowed to a suspicious halt. Lesley didn't start hitting and kicking: she let her have a look, gave her a pat and tried to sound confident as she said, "You'll do it easily." Then she took her away and got her going before she rode at it again. This time Stardust agreed to jump.

"Well done, dear," shrieked Mrs Roberts, as Lesley galloped on.

"Here's Lizzie coming home. She's done very well," said Tina.

"Lesley's being a bit slow over the downhill jumps, but she's doing them all," said Lynne. "Netti's starting. It's nearly time for us to go down."

Netti had complete confidence in Tristram, she knew that he would take her round; all she had to do was to sit tight and remember the course, he would do the rest. She loved jumping him and cross-country was her favourite, she thought, as she galloped over the fields, clearing jump after jump.

Paul was slower, but equally clear. He had to take the hill slowly because Banjo was clearly running out of breath, but he was very neat and quick over the angle jumps and in the gateway.

"He wouldn't be much use for racing, he jumps too big," said David, when Banjo had arrived, puffing, at the Land Rover. "All these huge stag-like jumps he makes take it out of him and slow him up. He's a Puissance horse by nature. He'd love to go on jumping one enormous fence all evening."

"Which of them would you choose for racing?" asked Hanif.

"Well, yours would be all right for the big fences, and

Saffron has the right ideas, but if I wanted a hurdler I'd take Rosie." Rupert began to express amazement that anyone should want Rosie for anything, but then Lynne, who had refused twice at the water, stopped again at the ditch.

"A *short* run!" roared David.

All the pony club members began to make encouraging noises and Berry went over at her second try. She cantered boldly at the brush and then trotted carefully over the angle, horizon and downhill jumps. Sarah and Chess set off along the valley and Tina waited all alone at the start. Her teeth were chattering and her legs were shaking. She had never ridden round a course before. She's never ridden in anything, not handy pony or even egg and spoon; she had never realised that you felt like this. It was awful.

Sarah hadn't approached the water with much confidence. She'd kicked for all she was worth and shouted, "Go on, Chess!" to hide her feelings, and for a brief second she thought he was going. But then he stopped, and she went on, very slowly, over his lowered head and into the water. She climbed out quickly and began to scream at Chess, telling him what a perfectly beastly and ghastly pony he was. "I hate you," she shrieked, stamping her foot angrily, while Mrs Roberts and Mrs Blacker tried to remove her dripping anorak.

"We'd better send down a lead," said David, looking round. "You go, Lesley, he'll follow his stable companion. Then, if she jumps it, let her go on alone."

Lesley didn't like to argue, so she went reluctantly, knowing that Sarah wouldn't be at all pleased to see her.

"Poor Tina," said Paul. "This'll put her right off. But look, here's Lynne. Come on Lynne, gallop."

"What do you want?" Sarah, whose anorak had been forcibly removed by Mrs Roberts, shouted at her sister.

"David says I'm to give you a lead. He says Chess will follow Stardust."

The sisters glared at each other angrily. "Oh, all right," said Sarah, remounting, "but I bet all that happens is that you refuse too."

Stardust didn't refuse, she jumped in fine style, and Chess followed her. Mrs Robert's cheer was echoed by the watchers on the hill. Sarah went on alone.

"Now Hobby, a clear round, please," said Oliver, patting his pony's neck. "Are you ready? On your marks. Go."

Tina's legs recovered before she reached the first fence and she forget her teeth. The slip rails loomed up, friendly and familiar, and the long canter to the water settled her and Hobbit down. She rode hard at the water, hoping to disguise a slight faint-heartedness, and Hobbit, with a small pony's cleverness, knew that she wasn't happy about it, and jumped the wing.

"Do I have to go back?" Tina shouted to Mrs Roberts.

"No, dear, you go on. That'll do," Mrs Roberts shouted back, for she believed in a comfortable life.

"It doesn't count. She'll be eliminated if she goes on," objected Jennifer.

"Oh goodness, it's only for a bit of fun, and I expect poor Tina was a bit put off by Sarah's splash. Well, that's the last one round then. They *have* done well. David must be pleased with them."

"No, Jennifer's going last," said Mrs Blacker. "Mrs Rooke says David won't mind. Go on, darling, down to the start. We mustn't keep everyone waiting."

Jennifer ignored Oliver, who told her she couldn't start until Tina was halfway down the hill. She simply rode through his flags and started. Muttering angrily, Oliver took down his flags and started up the hill, intending to complain to David.

Jennifer was riding down the valley at a slow canter, sitting in her saddle, and not looking in the least like a cross-country rider thought Hanif, who had watched her start. Tina had stopped at the ditch, mainly because Hobbit was out of breath. The Wheelers all made encouraging noises, but David said, "Don't hurry him, let him get his second wind."

As soon as he had got his breath, Hobbit went on willingly and then shouts from the water drew everyone's attention to Jennifer. Sea King was dithering on the brink, Jennifer was shouting, both mothers shooing.

"I didn't know *she* was going round," said Lizzie as Sea King got over and turned up hill.

"Nor did I," said David in a cold, angry voice. "Well, she's nothing to do with us, so we'll go down and have all those who stopped at the water over again. Rupert, I think you should do the gateway jump properly."

The pony club members mounted. Jennifer seemed to be having trouble at the logpile. Oliver, puffing from his climb up the hill, stumped over to the Land Rover and complained, "That Jennifer Blacker wouldn't listen to me. She started herself, though I told her that she had to wait until Tina was down from the trees."

"Some people have no manners," David spoke quietly but his pale face was set in hard angry lines and his blue eyes flashed with annoyance. "But don't worry, I'll be having a word with Miss Blacker presently."

"I don't think David's very pleased at Jennifer turning up like this," said Lizzie in a worried voice.

"I'm sure he isn't. He looks absolutely furious," agreed Rupert.

"Oh dear, I hope he doesn't explode and spoil the last day, when it's all been so lovely," moaned Lizzie, who hated rows.

"You can't blame him. It is awful cheek just turning up and going round without asking." Netti sounded indignant.

Jennifer was crashing about in the trees and cursing Sea King. The two older Wheelers, Alice, Hanif and Lesley stayed to watch. Everyone else was making for the water.

"Do you think we ought to help her?" asked Lizzie.

Sea King appeared suddenly, making a huge leap over the horizon fence, pecking and then setting off down hill at a canter.

"Whoa," yelled Jennifer, pulling him sideways, "Whoa."

"That looks dangerous."

"David gave a terrible roar when I tried going down sideways," said Alice, "He seemed to think that Saffy was about to cross his legs and fall."

Jennifer straightened up as she came to the downhill jump, but it was too late for Sea King to take off. He crashed through, scattering poles and drums, which rolled away down the hillside. Jennifer was round his neck, but she quickly regained her seat. She was going far too fast, but she seemed to decide to take a chance on the gateway jump.

"Circle!" shouted Hanif.

"She probably thinks that pole is all there is," said Lesley. Lizzie shut her eyes as the pony flung himself at the jump. There was a crack and a thud and the sound of splintering wood as pony and rider disappeared from sight. Without a word the five of them cantered down the hill. As they came to the gateway they could see the pony scrambling to his feet, pulling back to get free from the entangling hedge. The baling string holding the second pole had snapped. They slid carefully down into the lane.

"Are you all right, Jennifer?"

"No, of course I'm not. He fell on me and I'm all tangled up in this hedge."

Lizzie flung her reins to Rupert.

Sea King had obviously been going too fast to stop. He had hit the second pole, catapulted across the lane and crashed into the hedge with its strengthener of post and wire. Alice gave her reins to Hanif and ran to help Lizzie, who was clearing the chunks of broken thorn, splintered post and rusty wire, so that they could inspect Jennifer.

"Do you think you've broken anything?" asked Lizzie.

"How do I know? Where's King?" Jennifer sat up suddenly. "Haven't you got him? Well go and catch him, you fools."

"His bridle's here," said Alice, disentangling it from post and wire.

"The Land Rover's coming," announced Lesley in relieved tones, " and the mothers are there with David."

"Better get the ponies out of the way," said Lizzie.

"We're a bit redundant here. We'd better go after the pony," said Hanif as Mrs Blacker and Mrs Rooke emerged from the front of the Land Rover, and Mrs Roberts from the back. David followd them slowly.

With Alice carrying Sea King's bridle, they set off at canter along the soft centre of the lane. Then they heard the thud of hoofs behind them and found Lesley cantering in pursuit.

"David sent me after you," she told them, when they slowed down and let her catch up. "He said you were too new to know the way or the Roberts's telephone number or anything, and that I'd better come and help."

"Great," said Hanif. "We're simply following hoofprints."

"And there's been nowhere for him to turn off so far," added Alice as they cantered on again.

The track wound upwards, round the side of Coppice Hill, and as the ponies began to puff they all slowed to a trot. They reached the ridge where the woods ended and looked out across the green humped Downs, which stretched away for miles until they met the distant line of the sky.

"I hope he doesn't get out there. We'll never catch him," observed Alice. The chalk track widened, became grassy and they cantered on again. There were no hoofprints to follow any more, except on occasionally muddy sections of the track and then there were dozens, leading in all directions.

They began to grow anxious.

"He wouldn't have come as far as this, would he?"

"We must have missed him."

"Could he have got into the woods?"

They came to a crossroads. Four white tracks met and then wheeled away over the green hills, into space and sky.

"Shall we each take a track and ride a short way along it, looking for signs?" suggested Alice.

"All right, for five minutes, and then turn back. We don't want to lose each other, it's pretty vast up here," said Hanif.

He and Alice took the tracks that led along the ridge in opposite directions. Lesley took the one that led straight ahead and down into a hollow. Soon, long before five minutes was up, she was shouting, "Harry! Alice!"

They heard her and turning their ponies galloped back. They couldn't take short cuts for the wide tracks were fenced. They met at the crossroads and trotted down the hard chalk of Lesley's track. She was waiting for them.

"Look, my eyes aren't much good, but surely that's him, down there by the farm?" Their eyes followed the direction of her pointing finger and they both saw a weary-looking pony plodding along a beaten chalk track which led to the farm buildings.

"Oh *poor* Sea King, he's looking for help and a stable," said Alice.

"I don't think we're going to have much trouble in catching him," added Hanif as they set off at a brisk trot. They rode down into the hollow and then along the farm lane. When they drew close to the plodding bay pony they walked and called his name.

"Sea King," they called, "King." He stopped and turned and whinnied. He made no difficulties when Alice dismounted and approached him with the bridle, in fact his sorrowful expression brightened a little.

"Poor old boy, he is feeling sorry for himself," said Hanif.

"I'm not surprised, look at that." Lesley pointed to a triangular gash in his chest. "It's still bleeding."

"And look at his legs," added Hanif in a shocked voice. "They're cut to pieces."

"Blood everywhere," agreed Alice, who, now that the bridle was on, had begun a thorough inspection. "But I can't see anything that's likely to prove fatal."

"And the blood's not gushing out in torrents," observed Hanif, who had crouched down to get a better look at the inside of Sea King's legs. "The chest's the worst wound."

"Yes, but I don't think it's deep. It's a sort of horrid flap," said Alice, taking a closer look. "Do you think we can walk him home?"

"It'll take ages. What do you think, Lesley?" asked Hanif.

"I think we should go on to the farm and telephone for a box—well, David's is only a cattle truck, but the Roberts's must be home by now and they could send it."

"That sounds sensible. Two of us had better telephone and one stay with King."

"One of the telephoners had better be Lesley, as she knows telephone numbers and where we are," said Alice.

"And the other had better be me, if you don't mind," said Hanif, "because if Saffron goes, Jupe will start his twirling and that won't be much fun for Sea King."

So Alice found herself waiting in the lane, holding two ponies with quite different ideas. Sea King wanted to stand with drooping head, resting his legs in turn until he was rescued, while Saffron was hungry and insisted on grazing the sweet spring grass along the verges of the lane. In the end, Alice took off Saffron's pelham, and attached one complete length of rein to his noseband, then, each time he ran out of grass, she persuaded the poor stiff invalid to walk a few steps nearer the farm. She occupied herself picking choice morsels of grass for King, because she knew that if she did nothing she would begin to think gloomy thoughts. The course was over, it had been lovely, but like all lovely things it had come to an end. Soon the holidays would end and Saffron would go back to Mr Crankshaw. That didn't bear thinking about. She picked more and more grass for King.

The farm seemed deserted. There was a house, but it was surrounded by piles of bricks and window frames. A concrete mixer stood idle. There were no curtains at the windows.

"Anyone about?" shouted Hanif, as they headed for the farm buildings. "Anyone at home." But silence reigned everywhere until they heard grunting coming from one huge building which looked more like a village hall than a pig-sty. The door was locked, but they found a window open and from their ponies' backs they were able to peer in.

Hundreds and hundreds of pigs stood in tiny pens, row upon row of tiny prisons. They were big pigs, it didn't look as though they could even turn round.

"It's horrible."

"And there's no one here."

"Someone must come to feed them."

"I expect it's done automatically. There's a sort of droning noise."

"Let's go, we're wasting our time."

"We'll have to walk him all the way home then," said Hanif.

"No, look, there's a way out to the road down there. I'll go on ahead," decided Lesley. "I'll hope to find a telephone, but if not I'll go all the way to Garland Farm and send them to meet you."

"But how do *we* know where to go?"

"There's only one road at this end of the Downs. You just follow the signpost to Kidlake."

"That's a long way round. Wouldn't it be better to go back the way we came?"

"That track's too rough for trailers and boxes. They always get stuck. I'll tell them you'll be on the road," she called back as she trotted through the farm gate.

It was a horrible journey. Poor Sea King had stiffened up while he was standing and could scarcely hobble along. They felt very mean forcing him to walk, but Hanif explained to him that they would never be found unless they reached the road. The movement seeemed to do him good and he gradually unstiffened, but he still looked very sorry for himself and walked with a hanging head.

Hanif was in a continual panic convinced that he had misunderstood Lesley's instructions, that they were on the wrong road and would shortly come to a signpost with no mention of Kidlake on it.

Alice pointed out that so far there had only been *one* road to take and that, anyway, David and the Roberts's must know the pig farm when they lived so near. Then she went back to consoling Sea King with encouraging words and promises of horse boxes, vets, deep-bedded stables and bran mashes.

They had come at last to a signpost, which offered Coombe Lentworth, Kidlake or The Downs, and Hanif had just given a small cheer on seeing the telephone box from which Lesley must have telephoned, when a large cattle truck came slowly along the road.

"It's them!" shouted Alice.

Mr Roberts was driving, and Paul, Lynne and Sarah were sitting beside him. They jumped out as the box stopped and gathered round Sea King, giving cries of horror at his wounds.

"I'll turn the box before we load him," said Mr Roberts and drove on to the crossroads.

"Is Jennifer all right?" asked Alice.

"She doesn't seem too bad," answered Paul.

"Her arm hurts so her mother's taken her to hospital for a check-up," explained Sarah.

"Mum thought she was making a bit of a fuss," said Lynne. "Still, better to be safe than sorry."

"Let's get those headcollars on," said Mr Roberts, coming back. "Lynne, you take the Blacker pony. Paul, give me hand with this ramp. We'll load the fit ponies first, and put the partitions between them. Come on, Alice, let's have yours first."

Saffron and Jupiter seemed pleased at the idea of a lift and made no difficulties. Sea King hurried up the ramp after them, as though afraid of being left behind.

"He'll live," said Mr Roberts, looking at him critically.

"Poor Jupe must be starving, I only gave him half his feed at lunchtime," observed Hanif suddenly as they left the Downs and drove into Kidlake.

"Well, you can give him the rest in a minute," Sarah's voice was bossy. "David wants to see us all in his house before we go home. He's in a terrible mood. He really blew Mrs Blacker up. When he found that Jennifer wasn't seriously hurt, he got into the most terrible rage, and he was quite rude to Mummy, too."

"I don't blame him," said Alice.

"What does he want us for?" asked Hanif suspiciously.

"To tell us about the Area Cup, of course."

"Then he doesn't need me, I'm not going in any team," objected Hanif.

"Yes he does. He want you *all* in there as soon as you've settled your ponies," said Mr Roberts firmly.

"What about Lesley?" asked Alice as they bumped down the lane to Garland Farm.

"She should be here by now, if she found the short cut through the wood. Now get a move on, we want those ponies watered and fed and you indoors quickly."

"There's tea in David's kitchen," Lynne added encouragingly, "and Mum's made two huge cakes."

CHAPTER EIGHT

Dress Rehearsal

Though it had been modernized, David's kitchen had kept its old-fashioned look. Long and low-ceilinged, furnished with an old wooden dresser and table, it was now full of people. The wheelback chairs, the basket chairs and the window seats were all occupied. Handed mugs of tea and huges slices of cake by Mrs Roberts, Alice and Hanif joined Rupert and Oliver who were sitting on the floor, their backs against the dresser.

Alice waved to Lesley. "It was a good idea of yours," she said. "They came quite quickly. We'd only just reached the proper road, so it saved poor King several miles."

Mrs Rooke was counting heads. "Twelve," she announced triumphantly, and David, who was sitting in one of the basket chairs, said, "Right, I'll begin. First of all I'm sorry that our course ended in confusion. As you know, this was caused by the bad manners and stupidity of someone who shouldn't have been there; she had refused to attend on the two earlier days. And it's only by sheer luck that neither pony or rider were seriously hurt." He did not look at Mrs Rooke, who seemed busy, studying a sheaf of printed details.

"Now, you will all remember that when Mrs Rooke mentioned the Area Cup at the beginning of the holidays I refused to consider entering a team. Since then you've all worked so hard and improved so much, some of you almost miraculously so, that, yesterday, I changed my mind. Then, as it seemed rather a shame only to enter five of you and I knew it was going to be very difficult to decide which five, I spoke to the organizers and they've agreed to let us enter *two* teams, and also an individual should we have anyone left over. This means that you can all go."

Nearly everyone was pleased.

"Oh *good!*"

"Terrific."

"It'll be much more fun if we all go."

Only Rupert and Hanif took the news gloomily. Rupert put up his hand and asked, "Can I be the individual, because then I won't let anyone down?"

"I think it ought to be me," argued Hanif. "I hate being in teams and my dressage is terrible."

"No, me. I'm the least experienced of you all," said Tina. "I've never ridden in anything, not even a gymkhana event, in my whole life."

"Can Netti and I and Lynne go with James?" asked Sarah.

"Yes, Lynne's brilliant at turnout and the quiz," agreed Netti.

"But you'll need someone to take Jennifer's place," Mrs Rooke pointed out. "We must choose the best out of all the others to make up a really good A team."

"What on earth is Sarah doing in an A team?" asked Lesley disagreeably. "Half the people on the course are better than she is."

"Well at least I . . ." Sarah began to shriek an angry retort, but David sat up in his chair and interrupted her. "In this branch, the District Commissioner chooses the teams," he said in a very firm voice. He brandished a sheet of paper. "And I've been working on the possible combinations. First of all, as the individual has to compete in all four sections, it can't be Rupert. I don't feel that Rosie's dressage is up to a public performance at present. I think it should be Tina. She and Hobbit are both good all-rounders, and I agree with her view that she is the least experienced of you all. I don't propose to have an A and a B team. I haven't seen you ride in competitions so I don't know how you react under pressure. We'll just have two teams and you can call yourselves what you like. In one I've put Alice, Lizzie, Lesley, Harry and Rupert. Rupert will stand down for the dressage, Lesley for the cross-country. I

146

don't think Stardust should be asked to go round a strange cross-country until she's developed more self-confidence. I don't know which members of the team should enter for the quiz or the turnout, perhaps you can tell me, or we can consult Julia." He paused for a moment.

"Now, in the other team we have James, Netti, Sarah, Lynne and Paul. I don't think Berry is going well enough for either the dressage or the cross-country, but as Lynne tells me she'll be quite happy to do the quiz and turnout that doesn't matter. Any comments?"

"I still think it would be better to try and pick one really good team," said James. "We want the Woodbury to win for a change and that's not going to happen if you divide us into two more or less equal lots."

"I'm not aiming to win this year," David answered. "This is more of a trial run, a school, and it'll be a better school if both teams are in with a chance. Now would you like to get into your groups and sort out the quiz and turnout. We've paper and biros here. Tina, you come and have a look at the rules."

"Which first?" asked Hanif, who had the paper and pen.

"Turnout," said Lesley. "Who has reasonable tack?"

"Harry's is lovely and mine's bearable," answered Alice.

"Mine's just about bearable, I suppose," Lesley went on, "and then we'd better have you Lizzie. At lease Ra will be well groomed."

Lizzie gave a moan of dismay. "My bridle's so ancient, you simply can't get it to look nice, and my stirrups are awful plated things and half the plating has come off."

"Well, they only count the marks of the best three," Alice reminded her soothingly.

"Quiz?" asked Hanif.

"Not me," said Rupert. "I have absolutely no idea how many pounds of hay a pony should eat, or how many nails there are in a shoe."

"But you must be in something else," Hanif told him. "You can't just go in the cross-country."

"I don't see why not. If I survive that I shall have done my

147

duty for the honour of the Woodbury pony club," argued Rupert.

"Oh, wait a minute. If Rosie had Ra's saddle with my leathers and girth, but your irons, we could make up quite a respectable set of tack," said Lizzie. "Then you could be in the turnout and that would make two things."

"Turnout?" Rupert's face was full of horror. "But you know I'm hopeless at grooming and tack cleaning."

"I'll help you and so will Ollie," said Lizzie. "Don't you think that's a good idea?" she appealed to her other team mates.

"So Alice and I go in everything. Lizzie's not in the turnout, Rupert's not in the quiz or the dressage, and Lesley's not in the cross-country," announced Hanif, reading from his list. "Is that settled? Shall I give this to David? I must say I think it's crazy putting me in the dressage. I'm just as bad as Rupert."

"Only three scores count," Alice reminded him.

"I'll have a nice restful day," said Rupert contentedly.

"No you won't, you'll have to help the rest of us," Lesley told him. "Holding ponies, tying on numbers, fetching and carrying."

As David studied Hanif's list, Mrs Rooke read it over his shoulder.

"If Lesley's not going in the cross-country, why not try Sarah on Stardust?" she suggested, "She's a really game little rider. I'm sure she'd get the pony round and then we wouldn't have the problem of Chess and black plastic."

"No, they won't let them ride more than one pony, and anyway Stardust is really going well, her dressage is good. We don't want to upset her with a change of rider." Mrs Rooke was silenced.

"Come on, James, where's your list?" David went on. "I've promised to telephone the secretary with names before seven."

"Our list's easy, we've done that," answered James, handing it over. "I'm not going in the quiz, Paul's not going in the turnout, and Lynne's out of the other two. It's a name for the team that's holding us up."

"Woodbury Wonders," shouted Sarah. "It must be, James."

"Yes, come on, James," agreed the rest of the team.

"It doesn't matter, names are only for fun," David told them. "Now, tomorrow's a day off. All the ponies and I suspect, most of the riders, need a rest. Then on Sunday I want to do some *real* water. I'll fix it up with Mr Crankshaw over at Waterford farm—we'll splash about in the ford. We also need a flat field to do the test once more and I'm hoping he may be able to provide that too."

Alice looked at Hanif. "Your arena's lovely," she said, "all marked out and everything, and very near Waterford farm if you go through the woods."

"Yes, it's not bad." Hanif sounded doubtful.

"Would your stepfather mind eleven pones?" asked David. "We are rather an invasion."

"I don't know, shall I ask and ring you up?" suggested Hanif.

"We'll have to think about transport too," said David in a suddenly exhausted voice.

"You have a rest and think about that tomorrow," said Mrs Roberts, beginning to wash up the mugs piled on the sink.

Everyone was talking again. Mrs Rooke clapped her hands. "Time to go home," she announced. "Sunday morning, ten o'clock, just inside the Waterford Farm gate. We'll let you know if there's any change."

"Thank you, David," they said, crowding round him. "The cross-country was lovely."

"Really terrific."

"It was the most exciting day I've ever had."

Lizzie offered her services to Mrs Roberts, "Can I help you wash up?"

"No, I think it would be better if you got off home," said Mrs Roberts, looking anxiously at David. "I think he's in pain so the sooner we leave him alone for a bit of peace the better. See if you can get them moving dear."

"If they're going to be The Wonders, supposing we're the Washouts?" Rupert suggested to Hanif. "We don't want to compete."

"I do," said Lesley fiercely as they left David's house. "I'd love to show my mother that her little darling isn't such a wonder after all."

"Yes, let's be The Washouts," said Lizzie. "It's much better to sound useless and then do well, than the other way round."

Saturday wasn't much of a rest for the humans. Aunt Margaret had gone to a dog show so Alice decided to walk into Woodbury with her stirrup leathers and two keepers that were flapping on her bridle, and persuade the shoe mender to stitch them up while she waited.

Hanif, who hadn't told his parents much about the course and had been very careful never to mention the Area Cup, found himself compelled to ask if it would be all right for eleven people to use the dressage arena on Sunday and, while he was in the middle of explaining that David would be in charge, Lesley telephoned and said. "Look, we've got to have a quiz practice if we're not to make complete fools of ourselves. The "Wonders" are having theirs here, and anyway, the Wheelers have persuaded Julia to pull Rosie's mane and tail, so they want us to go over there. Alice's Aunt Margaret is at a dog show and my mother wants to coach Sarah's lot, so do you think your parents could do something?"

"I don't know, I'll ask," answered Hanif. "How many people need collecting?"

"You, me and Alice," snapped Lesley impatiently.

"What on earth was all that about?" asked Mr Franklin.

"I'm afraid it's another request—transport this time," explained Hanif. "It's this team thing I'm in. They want to have a quiz session over at Kidlake and no one has any transport."

"A team?" Mr Franklin's face lit up. "You never told us this was in the offing."

150

"I didn't know until last night. We thought that at the most there'd be one team, but now David's decided to send two."

"Well of course we must get you to this practice. We can't have you letting the side down. What time do they want their transport?"

Hanif checked with Lesley, who said that if they could be there at about two, Julia would stay and do the quizzing.

Hanif was overcome with gratitude when his stepfather insisted on changing his plans and arranging for a golfing friend to collect *him* so that Mrs Franklin could have the car for the pony club use, but he was less pleased when he had to explain precisely what he would be doing and the exact purpose of the Area Cup.

"You mean that you will be performing in all four sections, and that some of the others will only be in two or three?" asked Mr Franklin, beginning to glow with pride."

"Yes, but I'm not much good at dressage. I hope they won't have to count my score. Anyway, can I ring David and tell him that we can use our field tomorrow."

"Both teams are coming, that'll be quite a crowd." Mr Franklin sounded pleased. "I think I'll telephone your Mr Lumley myself; make sure I know exactly what he wants. I seem to remember putting down white lines at pony club camp. Do you have a copy of the test with the exact measurements?"

The Wheelers were in rather a state about Julia's visit. They all agreed that the saddle room must be tidied up in her honour and Netti said that they must also weed the yard.

Leaving the yard to the others, Lizzie threw out enormous numbers of ancient rags, old saddle soap tins, gruesome-looking bottles, which had long lost their labels and lengths of rotting rope. Then she swept out several inches of dirt, dust, dead leaves and cobwebs and cleaned the window so that there was far more light. By the time she had put the tack back on its brackets and the halters on their hooks she was worn out, but justly proud of her efforts. She emerged into the sunlight to see how the others were doing. Oliver's broom lay abandoned and there was no sign of him. Netti had weeded two square yards of the cobblestones, producing a huge pile of grass, groundsel and dandelions, but the cleared space made the rest of the stableyard look much worse in comparison. Rupert had found a pot of blue paint and was dreamingly painting Rosie's stable door.

"Oh Netti, do stop weeding and take those weeds to the bonfire," wailed Lizzie. "Julia will be here in ten minutes and it all looks so awful. Rupert, it's no use starting to paint, the ponies will get wet paint all over them, and we *must* start grooming and tack cleaning for Tuesday."

But everything turned out much better than Lizzie expected. Mrs Wheeler had cooked a delicious lunch. Mr Wheeler was in a good mood and opened two bottles of wine. Julia, who was doing design at college, was able to talk about illustrating with Mrs Wheeler and architecture with Mr Wheeler so there were no long pauses or awful silences.

The arrival of Mrs Franklin driving Hanif, Alice, Lesley and Tina, who had decided that as Hobbit was a Wheeler she'd better join the Washout's practice, broke up the luncheon party. Netti departed on a creaking bicycle to the Robertses, who had agreed to give her a lift to the Rookes. Julia carried an armful of books and a folder of questions out to the saddle room.

"Supposing we talk about horsey things in general while I pull the mane and tail," suggested Julia, "and then I'll try the quiz questions on you afterwards. I don't think they'll be terribly difficult ones as the whole point of the Area Cup is to encourage the people who don't get into teams normally."

"Us, in fact," said Rupert, putting a halter on Rosie, who had been moved into Tristam's box to avoid the wet paint.

"The Wonders know all the quiz book answers by heart. Do you think we ought to get hold of some copies and learn them too?" asked Alice.

"Obviously, the more you know the better, but I think the setters of questions will probably try to think up one or two original ones."

With Oliver, Tina and Rupert as well as the four who were in the quiz team packed into the loosebox, it was a tremendous squash, but Lizzie sat in the manger and Oliver and Hanif and Alice astride the partition. Lesley said she must stand beside Julia as she wanted to watch, and then she would pull Stardust's mane herself.

"Initials," said Julia. "Someone is bound to get 'what do these initials stand for? BHS. BSJA. BFSS. NH. RSPCA!"

They all shouted out the answers at once. British Field Sports Society was the only one no one knew. They went through the name of the Chairman of the pony club, the whereabouts of its headquarters, and the names of their own district commissioner and secretary. They listed the names of the grooming tools, the names of the tools used in shoeing and what they all looked like and were used for. They went through the markings a pony could possess, from races and blazes to eel stripes and ermine marks. Then points of the horse from ergots and chestnuts to stifles and gaskins and hamstrings. By the time Rosie's mane was pulled, most peoples' heads were reeling with the weight of so much knowledge. Rosie seemed to enjoy the mane part, but when it came to pulling her tail her co-operation ceased. She kicked out angrily and Rupert had to try to divert her attention with pony nuts and conversation, while Julia, standing well to one side, pulled away at the tail hairs.

Afterwards they all sat on upturned buckets in the yard and Julia went through her list of questions, quizzing everyone in turn. Lesley and Tina were the best on stable management, but Alice knew most about foreign breeds and was good on horses in history and in books. Hanif was very vague on questions about how many pounds of hay or nuts or anything else should be given to his pony—he always answered in scoops and haynets, which Julia said was useless—but he knew what FEI stood for and he was a lot better than Rupert. No one knew much about racing and Julia said they must memorize the names of the classic races. The fact that the Derby was for three-year-old colts and was run at Epsom. The Oaks was for fillies. The names of the horses who had last won these races and, of course, the Grand National. "There's bound to be at least one question on racing," she said as she handed out books.

"Thank you," they shouted after her as she mounted her moped and rode away. "Thank you, Julia. Thank you very much."

"Look at Rosie," said Rupert, leading her out into the yard. "Doesn't she look *civilized*. No longer a country bumpkin, but a slick show pony."

"That's going too far," objected Lesley. "But she does look a lot better."

They met at Waterford Farm on Sunday morning and found themselves lined up in a water meadow and minutely inspected. Julia advised on manes and tails and even snipped at a few on the spot. The rules of the competition banned plaiting, so there was no way of disguising messy manes. David inspected the tack and grooming. Several people were told to polish up their buckles, and to get the grease off saddle flaps or the inside of their reins while dusty rumps and muddy briskets abounded.

Chess was found to have a risen clench, which would go against him in the turnout, but Mrs Rooke said she would send for the blacksmith first thing on Monday morning.

David grumbled about muddy and unpolished boots and Mrs Rooke threw both teams into confusion by asking about riding jackets and gloves. "Polo necks for the cross-country, white shirts and pony club ties for the quiz, riding jackets for the dressage and the turnout," she announced firmly.

"But I'm only an individual," objected Tina. "Won't my anorak do?"

"I've outgrown my jacket. Lizzie's got it," protested Rupert. "Can't I wear my polo neck for the turnout too?"

"My jacket will do for the turnout, but as it's miles too small I can't possibly wear it for dressage," added Alice.

"Honestly, Mrs Rooke, I can't move my arms in it, and Aunt Margaret's in no mood to buy me another."

"We could pass jackets round for the dressage," suggested Hanif, who owned everything, even gloves. "You can have mine, Alice, but that's no good for turnout if we all go in together."

"Now let me deal with this, Harry," said Mrs Rooke sharply. "When I've made a note of what everyone needs I will go home and see what we have in our secondhand shop. Netti, your boots are all to pieces. I'd better see what I can find for you. Lizzie's crash cap is green with age. I'll make a note of your size. Alice, if there's a jacket to fit you, you can swop it for your old one, so your aunt won't have to worry about the expense, and I'm sure there's one that Tina can borrow just for the day."

"Now we're going to do everything the wrong way round." said David when the inspection was over. "We're going to do our jumping and messing about in the river *before* we go on to Harry's field for dressage. It's not a procedure I'd recommend, it's just convenient this morning. Alice and Harry, can you lead the way through the ford, please."

The river caused very little trouble. Saffron and Jupiter knew it so well that they were prepared to go backwards and forwards, encouraging the other ponies, and few made any fuss. Ferdinand insisted on trotting across at a very high cadenced trot which splashed everyone. Stardust teetered on the brink timidly and then decided to follow the others. Chess said he didn't mind *water*, it was black plastic he couldn't stand, and Berry caused the only uproar by trying to lie down. However, Paul raced to his sister's rescue and walloped Berry on the quarters until she changed her mind.

When all the ponies were splashing about happily and obviously enjoying themselves, Julia, assisted by James, who seemed to be the only rider with non-leaking boots, placed the two cavaletti David had brought on either bank so that whichever direction you came from, you jumped the first one into the water and the second one out on to dry land. The ponies, who knew now that the water was shallow and the bottom hard gravel, all enjoyed this too. "Right," said David. "Harry's going to guide you through the woods to his house. I'm going round by the road. See you there."

Mr Franklin had worked on the dressage arena until darkness fell on Saturday night. The pony club members were suitably impressed. They admired the white lines round the outside and up the centre and the fact that they now had an X at which to halt. James paced out the distances and announced that they were absolutely correct. But it was Hanif's jumps they really envied.

"Six real showjumps," said Netti. "Oh, Harry, you are lucky. Do you think David will let us jump them?"

"No. My stepfather suggested it, but David said we'd got to concentrate on dressage today. You'll all have to come again another day and try them."

"The arena's exactly what we need though," said James, looking pleased. "It'll give us a really good dress rehearsal. Double our chances of doing well."

"Please note that it belongs to a Woodbury Washout who is sharing it willingly with the Wonders," announced Rupert loudly. "*We* do not have the dog-in-the-manger attitude that is sometimes noticeable among members of other teams."

"What's been going on then?" Alice asked Lizzie.

"Oh, it's mostly Sarah. She didn't want Netti to let me use her quiz book. She seems to want to beat us more than all the other pony clubs."

"We'll have the people who live a long way off first," announced David as soon as he had parked the Land Rover at C. "That means that Harry, Alice and the Rookes can water and feed their ponies now. We won't want them until this afternoon. Now, no whips, martingales or voices, please. We'll have James first as he looks as though he's been riding in. Julia, will you come and write for me? I brought some dressage sheets so that we can give them my comments to digest."

156

The dressage was rather dull and took ages because David sent people back for coming in crooked and made them repeat unbalanced transitions, over-large circles and shapeless serpentines until they got them right. The pony club members drifted away to try on the collection of jackets, boots, caps and even gloves that Mrs Rooke had produced.

Alice was delighted with her riding jacket and wanted to go home and fetch her old one at once, to cement the swop. The only one which fitted Tina was a rather revolting ginger colour, which didn't go well with her reddish hair, but everyone agreed that when she had her crash cap on it made her look very smart. And they all felt that they looked much better riders when they wore jackets instead of anoraks.

Hanif was horrified when at lunch time his mother carried out a dish of Samoosas to the Land Rover and his stepfather followed her, bearing an assortment of drinks. But David seemed very cheerful and pleased with everything. He congratulated Mr Franklin on the dressage arena and Mrs Franklin on her cooking, and Julia said that the pony club had become much more fun for the junior instructors since Mrs Smythe gave up being D.C.

CHAPTER NINE

We'll Persuade Them Somehow

"It all seems very highly organized," Hanif told the occupants of the Garland Farm cattle truck as they led their ponies down the ramp. "Alice and I got here first of the Woodburys, the posh horsebox arrived a few minutes ago and there's still no sign of James. My stepfather and Julia have gone to get the numbers and find out if the programme is running to time. You've never seen so many highly-polished ponies in your life."

"What are the jumps like?" asked Rupert.

"I don't know. The cross-country's miles away. You can't see any of it from here."

"The turnout's being judged in the farmyard and the quiz in the house," said Alice. "The dressage has just started and it's in that field over there."

"Ollie, can you find the water brush? Rosie's sat on her tail and completely ruined it in spite of the tail bandage," wailed Lizzie.

"Here you are, but I'm helping Tina," Oliver replied ungraciously and hurried away to the hired horsebox which had brought Netti, Tina and the Rookes.

"Rupert, do come and help," wailed Lizzie.

"What with?" asked Rupert. "You're dealing with the tail and the rest of her looks perfect."

"You could give the tack a final polish or pick out her hoofs."

"You polished the tack the whole way over here. It *can't* need any more polishing. And her hoofs have been oiled so, if I pick them out, you'll be screaming at me for having an oily white shirt."

"Oh dear, I forgot they'd need picking out after the horsebox."

"I'll do it," offered Paul. "I'm not in the turnout and I haven't changed yet."

"James has arrived," announced Hanif, "so all the riders are here. Only David's missing."

"Mrs Rooke's driving him. As he's not really needed for the turnout and quiz she was planning to start a bit late," explained Paul. "Mum and Dad reckon the dressage and cross-country will be quite enough for someone in his state."

"The cardboard ones are to be worn on the backs for turnout, quiz and dressage," said Mr Franklin, handing out numbers. "There are real cross-country ones for this afternoon and they'll be in the back of the car."

Julia appeared. "'For the turnout, the ponies are to be tacked-up, but they're shown dismounted. You lead them in, stirrups run up, reins over the head. It's all running to time at the moment, so would the humans get dressed, please. Don't forget your crash caps and gloves.

"Rupert, your shirt's hanging out and your tie's crooked," snapped Lesley as the Washout team assembled.

"Here, you tuck the shirt in, I'll deal with the tie," said Mr Roberts, who had just finished brushing and polishing Lynne.

"I think we all look incredibly smart," said Hanif, looking round.

"Almost unrecognisable," agreed Alice. "Look at James! I don't know whether his boots or Ferdie's coat shine the most."

"Some of Chess's white bits are still sticky," moaned Sarah.

"You and Berry look perfect, absolutely brilliant," Netti told Lynne. "If only Sarah or I were as good as you and James we'd be bound to win."

"One of the team that's being judged now has a risen clench," Oliver reported with pleasure.

"But have you seen that team over by the scoreboard?" asked Tina. "They've got *black* jackets and *buttonholes.*"

"*Too* got up," said Julia firmly. "They don't look like

pony club members. Come on! The collecting steward is waving at us."

The turnout judges were very thorough and very slow. One judge inspected the pony, a second the tack, while the third peered critically at the riders. Then they all wrote their marks on efficient-looking forms attached to clipboards before moving on to the next pony. It was very dull standing in line and waiting for them. The ponies became restive and would rub their spotless bridles against their elegant owners, who became bad-tempered and afflicted with aching legs.

The Woodbury Wonders were inspected first, and as soon as the ordeal was over they hurried out, talking excitedly.

"All three judges said 'Excellent'," James told his mother. "But I couldn't see what marks they were writing down."

"I was told I'd left saddle soap in my noseband buckle," observed Netti ruefully, "and the grooming judge made tiresome noises about Tristam's brisket. I really had body-brushed it for hours."

"They said I was 'Excellent' too." Lynne was all smiles. "The tack judge said I had kept my saddle beautifully."

Sarah wasn't so happy. "One of them said I ought to have scrubbed Chess's white bits harder and the other one complained my reins were stiff. I thought they were beastly judges."

"Look, will you tie the ponies up and start thinking about the quiz," ordered Julia. "They want you at the house as soon as you can make it. You're going against the South Barset team and they've done their turnout."

"Are the Washouts against the ghastly team with black coats and fancy browbands?" asked Oliver. "They're next in the turnout."

"I expect so."

Mr Roberts and Mrs Morgan chivvied the the Wonders back to the horseboxes, while Mr Franklin and Julia waited for the Washouts, who came out of the judging area giggling.

"They said the Woodbury had some exceptionally good boys," explained Rupert. "I nearly said it was all Lizzie and Mrs Morgan and that only Harry actually did any work, but I managed to control myself. What did they say to you, Alice?"

"Oh, they asked if Saffy was Connemara and if he was my own. They seemed quite pleased, but they didn't go into raptures."

"The tack judge talked to me very slowly; she thought I didn't understand English," said Hanif in an offended voice, "but she admired my saddle. What about you, Lesley?"

"One of them asked me if Stardust was part-bred Arab. Silly question; it's obvious, isn't it? I don't think they were terribly impressed by my tack."

"Well, put the ponies away and get ready for the quiz," said Julia. "I'll go in with the first lot."

Though James wasn't in the quiz, he had collected his team together and led them towards the house, making encouraging remarks in an attempt to keep up their spirits.

"The South Barsets look very old and brainy. They'll beat us easily," moaned Netti.

"Nonsense, you girls are all brilliant, you know *everything*," James told her firmly.

The quiz didn't seem to take nearly as long as the turn-out, and by the time the Washouts had swopped bridles for headcollars, tied their ponies to horseboxes and the trailer, taken off their jackets, caps and gloves, tied on each others numbers and wandered over to the house, The Wonders were emerging.

"What was it like?"

"How did you do?"

"Where the questions hideous?" they all asked at once.

"They were terribly good, quite as brainy as they looked."

"Yes, they were brilliant. They knew who wrote the books about Mr Jorrocks, which we didn't," added Netti.

"We lost by two marks and one was my fault I forgot the St Leger," said Lynne sadly.

161

"It doesn't matter whether you win or lose, it's your *score* which counts," Julia told her, "and you clocked up a high one compared with some of the earlier teams. You all did very well."

"I got the question about blacksmiths' tools," said Paul, who was looking quite pleased with himself.

"Wonders, go and tack-up for dressage," ordered Julia. "And The Washouts had better come in and get their bearings. I can see the Frogmorton lot approaching."

The two teams filed into the dining room of the farmhouse and took their seats at opposite ends of the table. The question master and scorer were sitting in the centre of one side, and, facing them, the audience on rows of chairs, filled the rest of the room.

Hanif was pleased to see that the Frogmorton team, still wearing black coats and buttonholes, looked very young and nervous and were shaking worse than he was.

The question master, who was fat, red-faced and jolly, seemed to be trying hard to put the contestants at their ease. He made a lot of jokes as he announced the teams and explained the rules. Then they were off. Lesley had the first question. It was on the correct fitting of the saddle and seemed suspiciously easy, but she answered it well. Then Alice was asked about martingales, Hanif about the aids and position of the pony when circling, and Lizzie to explain the natural and artificial aids.

The Frogmortons were less certain over the fitting of the bridle; they were good at bits, but confused about the halt and forgot several reasons why a pony might refuse. So it went on, questions about feeding and points of the horse, questions on lameness and first aid. Questions on racing and horse trials, polo and show-jumping, questions on horsey writers and painters. They had no time to think how they were doing, they were completely absorbed with question and answer, or waiting, lynx-like, to pounce on anything unanswered by the other side.

When it was over and they burst out into the sunshine again, they found David, Mrs Rooke, most of the parents and the mounted Wonders all waiting to hear how they had done.

"We weren't bad," said Lesley. "We managed to answer one or two of their questions which may be a help."

"We did *much* better than I expected," added Lizzie.

"Lizzie knew all about horsey painters," said Oliver with pride.

"And Harry answered a horrible question on polo, which the girl on the other side had to pass."

"Which of our teams has done best so far?" asked Sarah.

"The Wonders did best in the turnout, the Washouts in the quiz," Julia answered.

"But the dressage carries more weight than either of them, so let's start riding in," said David. "Come and find me in the collecting ring as soon as you're ready. Harry, will you ride round and round the horsebox park at the walk and trot, just exercising and keeping Jupiter very calm, until I send someone to fetch you. Don't start practising bits of the test or you'll upset him."

Mr Franklin had already tacked up Jupiter, and, carrying Hanif's crash cap, was coming to meet them. When he had seen Hanif off on his first circuit of the horsebox park, he helped Alice with Saffron, which was just as well for her hands had suddenly become weak and unable to pull up girths or fasten buckles. It was worse when she was mounted, for her legs had become weak too, and an excited Saffron, stiff-backed and star-gazing, jogged over to David.

"It's having no martingale," wailed Alice.

"You managed without one on Sunday," David reminded her. "Calm down, put him on a circle and don't trot until you've got his head down at the walk. I'll sort you out as soon as I've got the first four going."

James, looking solid, straight and not at all nervous, was riding round outside the arena, waiting to be called in. As the judge, sitting in a car at C, honked the horn, James broke into a steady trot and entered at A.

"I can't bear to look," said Mrs Morgan, who seemed

much more nervous than James. "Tell me how he's doing, Alice."

Alice watched as she circled. "A good halt," she said, "and he's standing there for hours, making sure the judge has noticed. Now he's proceeding at a nice steady trot. He's remembered to sit. The first loop of his serpentine looks a bit flat to me. The second one's better, and the third. He cantered a bit late, but it was a very smooth transition and he's on the right leg. I think you can look, Mrs Morgan, he's doing very well."

"Well done, that was good," said David, as James came out, patting Ferdinand and looking pleased.

"Good luck, Netti," shouted the Woodbury supporters as she rode into the roped enclosure and began to walk round.

"Go and see how Harry's doing. I'll want both of you over here in about five to ten minutes," David told Alice as Mrs Rooke came hurrying towards him with the urgent look of a sheep that has lost its lamb.

"David, Chess is having an attack of temperament. He suddenly refuses to stand. I don't know what can have got into him. He's never behaved like this before, and the poor child's working herself up into a state."

"Send them over here," said David calmly. "Yes, Paul, what's the matter with you?"

"I've forgotten the test and lost my copy," announced Paul in a voice of quiet despair.

"Well, cheer up and watch Netti, she's just beginning. Now, Sarah, what's your trouble?"

"He keeps swinging his quarters about and he won't stand."

"Well, calm yourself down, hold the reins in one hand and pat his neck. If the rider gets tensed up she's bound to affect her pony."

"Yes, I know. I wish you'd tell Mummy to go away, she's making me worse."

Alice found Hanif cowering behind a very large horse-box.

"I'm hiding from my stepfather," he explained. "He's

164

found the scoreboard and worked out exactly how many marks the Washouts need to take the lead."

"What a waste of time," said Alice briskly. "I heard David telling Mrs Rooke that everything depended on the cross-country. It's got a possible total of two hundred marks."

"Yes, you're right *and* it's possible to get them all too," said Hanif, cheering up. "No one ever gets a hundred per cent for dressage, do they?"

"I suppose Olympic gold medallists might, but no one else. Let's go over there and school near Lizzie and Lesley. They're halfway to the collecting ring."

Lizzie and Rajah seemed to be going very well in their steady, plodding way.

"Ra seems to go better when he's a bit excited," Lizzie told them happily. "It gives him more impulsion. Did you see how Netti was doing?"

"No, David sent me away just as she was starting. We ought to trot round a bit, Harry. Come on, let's circle."

Lesley rode across to the arena feeling quite surprised at her own confidence and calmness. She was glad that she didn't have to go in the cross-country. She knew that she'd only have made a fool of herself and given her mother and Sarah a chance to crow, but she was actually looking forward to the dressage and she knew that Stardust was going to enjoy it too.

"Don't try and do the best test of your life," said David when she joined him in the collecting ring. "Just aim for a reasonably good one. She's going beautifully. Her carriage and cadence are improving every day."

"How have the others done?" asked Lesley, who wasn't used to compliments.

"Not badly. James and Netti were good. Sarah started badly, but did quite a neat test once she settled. Paul forgot his, but the judge sorted him out. He won't have lost too many marks."

They watched Paul halt neatly at the end of his test. "Right, he's finished," said David. "Now, you know what

165

to do? Walk round outside the arena until she's ready. The judge will toot the car horn at you."

Paul, shamefaced, tried to creep away unnoticed, but David called him over. "That wasn't at all bad for your first try in public," he told him. "Plenty of people forget their tests. The great thing is to keep your head and not go completely to pieces. You won't have lost many marks."

Alice, Hanif and Lizzie had all arrived in the collecting ring and were trying to watch Lesley while riding their ponies in. Mrs Roberts handed round barley sugar and made comforting noises. David made Alice and Hanif trot circles, but seemed to be watching Lesley most of the time.

Stardust seemed pleased to be in the arena, showing off her paces to a judge without the bother of keeping up with a ride, or the worry of jumps. She halted elegantly, head high, neck arched and on the bit and then trotted on with a cadence that none of the other Woodbury ponies possessed. Her serpentines flowed, fluent and supple, her canter was slow but full of impulsion, her ears were pricked and her expression contented throughout.

David looked more and more pleased as the test went on, and Mrs Rooke and Sarah, standing beside him, were obviously impressed.

"What a pity Lesley's so useless at cross-country and showjumping," said Mrs Rooke as her daughter came to a final halt. "Dressage alone doesn't get you anywhere."

"Oh I don't know about that. There's Olympic dressage, plenty of riding club dressage and even a pony club inter-branch dressage. Perhaps we'll have her representing the Woodbury at Stoneleigh next year." David laughed; he seemed rather pleased at the prospect. "Now, Alice, keep calm, sit very light in the sitting trot and if he tries to get his head up, keep squeezing that inside rein."

Alice nodded. She felt nervous, but no longer weak. She made Saffron overbend a little as she walked round the outside, then she tried leg yielding. He was giving his back, relaxing his jaw. The judge tooted at her. Slowly, she thought, very, very slowly, there's tons of time.

166

He was on the bit when she entered at A, but she lost him a little as he came to a halt, she squeezed the rein and put him back on the bit before she saluted. As she trotted round she could feel Saffron gradually settling down and relaxing. He seemed to recognise the familiar markers and to begin to feel at home. By the time she turned him into the serpentine he was going well and she was able to concentrate on making the right-sized loops.

Then they cantered, and she was so pleased with him for staying on the bit that she nearly told him what a clever pony he was, but choked the words back just in time. The circle seemed all right but her transition down to trot went wrong, his back went stiff, his head began to go up and she had risen at the the trot when she should have been sitting. But he relaxed when they were walking and she was able to keep him on the bit as they began trotting again, and now he was going round to his best side and everything became easier. At last she was turning down the centre. G seemed very close to the judge, this time she looked at her and smiled when she saluted.

"You clever boy," she told Saffron as she rode out and was allowed to speak again. The Woodbury people rushed up to pat him. "Well done," they said, "he didn't stargaze at all."

Lesley gave her a small smile. "David said you were doing well. Now we've got to keep our fingers crossed for Lizzie, because Harry's going to make a complete mess of it, he's practically in hysterics. David's trying to talk some sense into him."

Alice led Saffron across the collecting ring. David was leaning on his shooting stick and saying, "I don't give a damn what sort of cricket score you knock up. Lizzie will do a reasonable test so you don't matter, but you're going in, and that's an order."

"It's not so bad once you've started," Alice told Hanif, "and by the end I was quite enjoying myself, honestly."

"Just keep your head and stop fussing about scores," added David. "Will you ride round with him, Alice? I want to watch Lizzie."

167

"Now *he's* furious with me," moaned Hanif as Alice mounted and David limped away.

"No he isn't," said Alice as they walked off, side by side. "Don't you remember when he was furious with Mrs Blacker, he went pale with hard steely eyes and set lips, he's not a bit like that now. Anyway, Sarah panicked before she went in and Paul forgot his test. I expect you get used to this sort of thing if you're a team trainer. Do you want to give Jupe a trot?"

Except for looking down, Lizzie was doing well. She was being very accurate and Rajah was moving with plenty of impulsion and remaining steadily on the bit. His long plodding stride was more cadenced that Ferdinand's but lacked the lightness of Stardust's.

"He goes like a German horse and Stardust more like a French horse," observed David to no one in particular. "Both good in their way."

"Well done, Lizzie," he said as she came out. "I'm going to buy you a collar with upward pointing spikes on it before your next test, but, apart from looking down, you rode that really well."

Alice rode right up to the entrance with Hanif. "Good luck," she said. "It'll soon be over. Lovely cross-country this afternoon."

"Lizzie's done well so you can regard it as a school," said David. "Try and keep him calm, never mind about doing the movements at markers."

As Hanif rode round, Mr Franklin appeared with an expensive-looking camera. "I must keep out of sight," he told Lizzie and Alice. "Can I hide between your ponies?"

The judge tooted her car horn and, to all the Woodbury supporters' horror, Jupiter immediately broke into a sideways canter and bounced his way towards A. But Harry suddenly decided not to enter, he turned the pony and rode him all the way round outside the arena on the other rein. Gradually they settled into a trot, and this time, when they reached A, they entered. Jupiter *was* trotting, but he was bounding along far too full of life and not under control at all. It was obvious that Hanif was going to have a battle on his hands if he tried to halt at X. He didn't try, he went on, slowing down gently and halted at G. He took off his cap, but Jupiter was impatient to be off so the cap went on again very quickly, and they bustled on. The serpentine was performed at a very brisk pace and then Jupiter bounced eagerly into a canter and circled far too fast. However, to the anxious watchers' great surprise, he consented to come back to a trot and then a walk as he changed the rein. Going round the other way, Hanif eased him into a very gentle trot and managed his second serpentine at a much more controlled pace. The second canter and circle were better too and finally he trotted down the centre and halted quite obediently at G.

"One huge sigh of relief all round," said David. "And it's a good sign if you finish going better than you started. He's not an easy pony, but I think we're making an impression."

"You certainly are," agreed Mr Franklin, emerging from his hiding place. "A couple of weeks ago he would have left the arena at full gallop and disappeared into the carpark. I'll just get a photograph as they come out."

Hanif was patting Jupiter and looking at David, trying to tell from his expression whether he had done well enough.

"Yes, you did all right," David told him. "You used your legs and your brains. No instructor can ask for more. We'll get the old horse sorted out in the end. These things take time."

"If everyone's finished, can we have lunch?" asked Rupert.

"Yes, small drinks and feeds for ponies and riders taking part in the cross-country." David looked at his watch. "There's an hour and a half to digest."

"We've lost Tina," said Lizzie, looking round with a worried expression.

"No, it's just that the individuals are doing each section in a bunch at the end, but Julia and Oliver are looking after her. As soon as you've eaten we'll walk the cross-country," David went on. "Or at least you will. Mr Franklin's going to drive me from fence to fence."

Lynne and Lesley were the happiest people at lunch as they had both finished for the day and felt that they had done well. Hanif was much more cheerful now that the dressage was over, but Rupert's gloom increased minute by minute. Sarah had seen a plan of the course and said there were two waters and a ditch, as well as a quarry, and they were all bound to have black plastic.

Mr Franklin and Mrs Rooke had got together over the marks and kept rushing to the scoreboard to see if the dressage results were out yet. It seemed that the Frogmorton had won the turnout, and the East Tulworth the quiz, but by very small margins. The Washouts had tied second in the quiz, while The Wonders were a very close third in the turnout, but as their combined marks were good they'd moved up to second place overall, while the Washouts were tying third with several other teams. The Cranford Vale hadn't entered, to everyone's surprise.

"We're nine points ahead of you," Sarah told the Washouts, when she had seen her mother's score sheet.

"The whole thing is wide open," Mr Franklin told her firmly. "Nine points is nothing at this stage. We'll have much more idea where we stand once the dressage marks are out, but as David says the final results depend heavily on the cross-country."

"I wish you'd all shut up about the cross-country, it's putting me off my lunch," complained Rupert.

"Now concentrate," said David when they were all assembled at the start. "No chattering about other things. Lynne and Lesley, you'd better come in the car, I don't want you distracting the riders. Mr Roberts is going to walk round with you and make sure that you notice the yellow direction arrows and work out a sensible approach, I'll wait for you at each fence. Now, this is the start. Don't start before you're told. See you at fence number one."

It was a straight run to the first fence, a brush, built out in the middle of a field.

"It's a bit low. Ours will trip over it," James told Hanif in a dissatisfied voice. But everyone else was pleased with it.

170

"Always ride carefully at first fences," David told them. "Your pony may not realise that this is a cross-country course. He may be thinking of his stable companion or his next feed, so make absolutely sure he's concentrating. And, as this fence is stuck out in the middle of a field, make quite sure he doesn't surprise you by running out. O.K.?"

Number two was straight ahead, rustic rails with cross poles, and this was set in an actual fence.

"Nice and easy, none of your ponies should mind that," said David. "But you are still going away from home and stable companions, so ride at it."

In the next field there was a yellow direction arrow.

"Everyone see that?" asked Mr Roberts, "and do you all know that it's there to help you? It doesn't matter which side you go of it, or anything like that. You *must* always jump between the flags on the fences, of course, and leave the red on your right and the white on your left."

"Number three's the quarry," announced Sarah as they obeyed the arrow and turned right. They came to a grassy hollow surrounded by thorn bushes. A low but very stout pole was followed by a slope. The pony club members looked at it doubtfully.

"No problem," said David. "You just pop over. It's exactly what you've been doing on Coppice Hill for the last week. Come up slowly, or half-halt if you can, pop over and start looking for the next fence."

A yellow arrow pointed into a thicket of thorn bushes and the pony club members ran down to look. A large tree trunk, on a bend in the path, was hidden by thorn bushes until you were almost upon it.

"It's a good jump," said David when he caught up with them. "A test of impulsion. You all ought to do it all right. Come round the bend slowly but with plenty of energy, make sure your pony knows there's something exciting ahead. Now go back to number three and make sure you know where to look for four as you jump it."

Number five was a rustic gate built into the next fence, and then they had to swing right-handed towards a spinney.

171

"Don't cut the corner," said Mr Roberts as they approached. "Always walk the way you mean to ride. If you head for the direction arrow and *then* turn, that'll bring you in to the fence at a good angle."

David was waiting by the post and rails into the narrow wood.

"The fence is easy," he told them, "but ponies don't like jumping into woods. They don't like jumping into the dark, so you'll have to ride twice as hard as usual. This spinney's not particularly dark as there aren't many leaves on the trees yet, but don't take chances."

Another post and rails took them into a ploughed field and a direction arrow sent them left, along the headland beside the spinney.

"Keep on the headland," said Mr Roberts. "The plough's very holding and will tire the ponies."

The spinney ended at a brook and there was a ford with a gravelled bottom to cross.

"It's not nearly as wide as the Vole," remarked Lizzie cheerfully. "I don't think Ra will mind that."

"It's numbered eight." David, who had crossed by a narrow plank bridge, pointed out from the other side, "So it counts as a fence and dithering on the brink will go down as a refusal."

On the far side of the brook, number nine was a bank with a pole on top.

"No problem as long as you have plenty of impulsion and look where you're going," said David. "People looking down into the ford could have a stop, Lizzie please note, and it could be difficult for the little ponies if they've run out of steam."

Mr Franklin had had to leave the car on the other side of the brook and he fussed round David who insisted on limping all the way to number ten. It was a grid, and the pony club members, who had gone on ahead, didn't like it very much.

"They're jolly short distances for a big one like Ferdie," complained James, pacing them out.

172

"It's a double bounce, isn't it? Just land and take off," observed Paul.

"It's where Rosie falls flat on her nose. She's never done three jumps in a row before," said Rupert gloomily.

"At least they're good solid telegraph poles and wired to these great lumps of tree trunk: they're not going to break or fall down," announced Hanif approvingly.

"The secret of success is to look at the last one," said David, hobbling up. "Look at it and ride for it. Ignore the other two. If you do run out you have to re-take them all— it's numbered as one jump, you see. But you won't have any trouble if you come at a slow canter with plenty of impulsion, a feel on both reins, and look at the last one."

After the grid, the course turned left-handed and they were on their way home. Number eleven was a steep, muddy slide down to the brook, which they then had to wade across, before jumping out over a tree trunk on the far bank, which was numbered twelve.

The pony club members looked down the slide despondently.

"Ugh, the ponies aren't going to like that."

"Ra will be horrified."

"The slide's nothing," said David firmly, "but don't let them dither because it counts as a fence. The problem is how to explain to the ponies that you don't expect them to jump the brook *and* the tree trunk all in one. If you ride straight at the water they'll think that's what you want, and as it's too wide for them they'll refuse. So you go down the slide, *slant* them at the water. Make it quite clear you're not interested in getting across, then, when you're *in* the water, show them the jump on the far side. Do you understand what I'm getting at? It's important, because this is where a misunderstanding between horse and rider could arise."

The pony club members made their plans and then went on to fence thirteen while Mr Franklin and Mr Roberts helped David over an even narrower plank bridge and back to the car.

Thirteen was a ditch with a pole above. It was quite a

deep ditch and by the time David reached them the pony club members were all gazing into the bottom of it with fearful faces.

"Rule number one," said David. "Never look into the bottom of a ditch. It's the width that matters, not the depth."

"We'll never jump that."

"Of course you will. We've been practising for this."

"Our ditch was brown and shallow, not deep and green with water in the bottom."

"It's on the way home and with the pole over the top the ponies will take off the right distance away. They won't even know there's a ditch there, unless you're all shaking and quaking so much they begin to think there's something wrong. Just ride at the pole, look up, and throw your hearts over."

Lynne began to say that she was glad she hadn't got to ride round such an awful course, but her father told her to keep quiet.

"I like it," announced Alice. "Well, so far."

"I don't like that grid much, nor the second river jump," said James. "They're a bit trappy for Ferdie. He likes the sort of course where you can gallop on a bit."

"So does Jupe, but *I* like a bit of trappiness to slow him down."

"Your wish is granted," Alice told Hanif as they came to the lambing pen. "You couldn't have anything much more trappy than that."

James groaned. "This is the end."

The pen was an oblong, built of straw bales, with a wattle jump in at one end and then a sharp right turn out over more wattles.

"You can see the problem," said David. "The larger ponies and the tearaways will jump in and then go straight on over the straw bales and be eliminated for taking the wrong course. You've got to slow right down to nothing, pop in, reins, legs, weight and eyes all turning him to the right as you land. If you jump in on the left it'll give you a bit more room. Small ponies are a bit suspicious of pens and inclined to stop. You drive on hard. Harry, you're the most likely to come to grief here."

"I'll creep and pop," promised Hanif, pacing out the distance.

The last fence was a length of dry stone wall which had been built into the field fence.

"No problem," said David, "unless anyone has a very tired pony. Now you go for the finish. Between those two flags over there. If you forget it you'll be eliminated, so, when you land over the last, don't think, 'hurrah, I've done it'. Think 'finish!'"

"Finish, finish," said Paul, pushing Sarah.

"Rupert, are you listening?" asked Netti.

"What?" he asked.

"The finish!" they all shouted at him. "You *must* go through it. You'll be elminiated if you don't."

"Look, over there." They marched him towards the flags.

David was waiting for them at the finish. "The bigger ponies will have no trouble about getting round in the time, but the little ones will have to keep going. They can't afford refusals, as they'll be clocking up time faults. You're allowed three refusals at each fence, as it's a novice event. If you lose count consult the jump judges. And be polite to them and all stewards. You can be eliminated for rudeness to officials, and the fact that you're excited or upset is no defence. The supporters must *not* shout advice or instructions to the riders as that can get them eliminated too. It's an easy course to find your way round, so you shouldn't get lost, but don't forget the finish."

David looked at his watch. "They're due to start in ten minutes, so we'd better get tacked up and think about a practice jump."

They met Tina and Oliver in the horsebox park. Tina said that her turnout marks were awful—the worst in the Woodbury—her quiz questions had been lovely, except for one, and Hobbit had gone on the wrong leg in the dressage.

David drove over to give Julia some advice about things she was to be sure to tell Tina as they walked the cross-country, then he stationed himself beside the practice jump, a rustic pole on oil drums and waited for the Woodbury riders who were pulling on their polo-neck sweaters and then tying on each other's huge back and front numbers.

Jupiter was so delighted to see a jump at last that he flung himself over as though it was a four-foot triple, but Hanif found that he didn't mind that sort of behaviour any more. He just laughed and took him round again, until after three jumps and a good deal of cantering about, Jupiter settled down.

Rosie, in a vague mood, looking around her and at the other ponies, forgot to take off and, tripping over the jump, nearly landed on her nose, but, as Rupert said, this seemed to do her good, as she then jumped much more carefully than usual.

Alice, pleased to have her martingale on again, was feeling quite cheerful about everything but the lambing pen. She kept rehearsing how she would jump it in her mind, but with Saffron feeling so calm and confident beneath her, she couldn't be too worried.

Lizzie was anxious, so much seemed to depend on her doing a good round, and David kept roaring at her to look up.

"Except for the first two and the last they're all fences where looking ahead is *essential*," he told her.

"I really will try terribly hard," promised Lizzie.

The Wonders, on their more seasoned ponies, didn't have to do so much warming up, and when they had all had a couple of practise jumps, Berry and Stardust were left in the charge of the horsebox driver and the whole Woodbury part moved up to the collecting ring.

The scene had changed. There were spectators and jump judges beside the fences, more spectators and mounted runners hurrying about in between.

Lesley and Lynne, who had stayed to watch the early competitors, came running to meet their teams. "The

Brackenhurst did very well, they had three clears, and the first two from the South Barset went well, but the one's who's coming in now has had masses of refusals and the last one to go has been ages in the quarry."

"Shush," said Lizzie, "You mustn't sound so *pleased*."

"Why on earth not?" snapped Lesley.

"Because we don't want people being pleased when we fall in the water," answered Rupert.

David had Mrs Morgan and Mr Roberts checking girths. Mrs Roberts was handing out barley sugar to non-riders. James had gone to the start, Netti circled, waiting for her call. The last of the South Barsets had fallen off at the grid. There was a delay until the pony was caught.

At last Ferdinand was on his way. He started fast and made the first two fences look easy, then he vanished down the slope into the quarry. He reappeared, heading for the rustic gate, jumped that and disappeared again into the spinney.

Mr Franklin had produced a pair of binoculars and, standing on the seat of his car with the roof open, was trying to give a running commentary.

"Ah, here he is, out of the ford and up the bank. He's steadied for the grid, one, two, three." But then Netti started, and with two of them on the course, no one knew where to look. Sarah was called to the start. David told Paul not to canter Banjo round and round, he had more than enough work ahead of him. Mr Franklin announced that James was through the lambing pen and Netti just coming up the bank.

Lizzie and Rupert were walking round together, reciting, "Look up!" and, "Finish!" to each other.

James galloped through the finish and then rode over to David, his solemn face suddenly transformed by a huge smile.

"It was great," he said breathlessly as he patted Ferdinand. "I didn't have any trouble that I know of. He was brilliant over the streams and that pen thing. I don't think he even noticed the ditch."

"Well done, you looked very good from here," David told him.

"How's Netti doing?" asked James as his mother rushed up with a handful of pony nuts.

"Terribly well, but Sarah's being rather slow. Get off, darling, and loosen his girths."

"Netti's over the pen, but Sarah's stopped at the spinney. Ah, it's all right, she's over this time," announced Mr Franklin.

Paul was looking grim, he *had* to be clear.

"Don't go mad, you can't do more than you can," David told him.

Netti came galloping in. "Oh, he was brilliant!" she shrieked, dismounting and patting Tristram excitedly. "He was really brilliant and I enjoyed every minute. The jumps are lovely, Lizzie, Rupert, I promise you. The jumps are really gorgeous."

Mr Franklin was making disapproving noises. "Silly girl, she's turned round on top of the slide, but Paul's going very well. That little black of his has a surprising turn of speed."

The starter was calling Hanif.

"Keep calm, you've a few minutes' wait yet," David told him. "Sarah's taking her time and Paul's not going to keep that speed up for long."

As Sarah rode in, Hanif started out. He let Jupiter gallop on over the first two fences and then slowed him right down for the quarry. Mr Franklin took his eyes off his stepson for a moment and announced that Paul was safely over the grid, then he went back to Hanif. "Harry's going great guns," he told David. "I hope the pony's not running away. No, he's steadied him for the spinney, he's in. And Paul's over the ditch, coming up to the lambing pen, but the pony's slowed down a lot. Oh dear, he's stopped." A groan went up from the Wonders.

"Harry's over the grid," shouted Mr Franklin excitedly, "and Paul's got going again."

David had sent Mr Robert's to pull up Alice's girths.

"Get them up another hole if you can. That's the sort of pony which loses weight on a long gallop."

Paul came in slowly, he seemed very cast down. "He just couldn't go any faster. I suppose I'll have time faults as well as a refusal."

"Jump off, loosen his girths and turn his head to the wind," said David, looking at the blowing pony. "He went as fast as he could."

Mrs Roberts arrived with barley sugar and a handful of oats.

"Harry's managed to slow down for the lambing pen, he's gone to the left and he's trotting. He's done it," shouted Mr Franklin, sounding like a radio commentator who's just seen a vital goal scored in the World Cup. "He's only got to do the wall and he's home!"

No one heard how Alice was doing because Mr Franklin left his post and rushed to the finish to welcome Hanif home, but she was enjoying herself. She loved the feeling of galloping over the grass, looking for the next fence. There seemed to be lots of time and plenty of space between them. She felt clear-headed and happy. Saffron felt happy too. A pop, he seemed to agree, when he saw the way into the quarry. Now where? He followed her gaze.

He didn't mind the spinney; the ford he took as a matter of course, the grid carefully and neatly. The slide and the brook he summed up quickly. I know how to do that, he told her. He didn't notice the ditch. He let her slow him right down for the pen, he popped in and then, realising what was wanted, turned and jumped out. They galloped for the stone wall and the finish.

Mr Franklin, suddenly remembering Hanif's team mates, rushed back to watch. He was in time to announce that Lizzie, who had started well, had stopped at the spinney, but was over at the second attempt and that Alice was finishing very fast indeed.

"Good luck and don't forget the finish," David told Rupert as he took a suspicious glance at his girths.

"Lizzie's done the grid," shouted Mr Franklin

179

"Any trouble, Alice?" asked David, as Rupert set off towards the first fence.

"No, it was lovely. He jumped every one perfectly." She gave Saffron a handful of pony nuts.

"Lizzie's over the second brook, heading for the ditch," reported Mr Franklin.

"How's Rupert doing?" asked Hanif. "Lizzie had a stop," he told Alice.

"I've lost him, he must still be in the quarry," answered Mr Franklin. "No, there he is. He's over the rustic gate. He's cut the corner a bit. He's giving her a very short run, but he's done it."

"I don't suppose we'll ever see him again. Knowing Rupert, he'll forget to turn left," said Lesley.

"Lizzie's crawling up to the pen. She's in, and she's out. Now she's really galloping."

"We can see her. Tell us how Rupert's doing."

"He's over the brook, approaching the grid."

"Rosie'll never do it," said Netti, standing in her stirrups and trying to see.

"She's having a try," reported Mr Franklin. "Heavens! Something went wrong over the last one, she practically stood on her head. How that boy stayed on . . ."

"He always does. His legs are so long and so aptly constructed," Netti chanted triumphantly.

"Touch wood," shrieked Lynne.

Lizzie came galloping in as Rupert disappeared down the slide, and the first of the Frogmorton team started.

"Oh, that was fantastic!" said Lizzie, dismounting. "I never thought he'd go so well, but I'm afraid I've let the Washouts down though, because I did have one stop. He insisted on a good look before he would jump into the spinney."

"You did very well," David told her. "*I* didn't expect a clear round from old Safety First at his first outing."

"Rupert's doing brilliantly so far," Netti told her sister.

"He's over the ditch, no trouble there. He's going pretty fast. I hope he remembers to slow up for the pen. Too fast, he's in, but he's not going to turn, he's going straight on.

180

No, he's refused. Well, he's collided with the straw bales. He's turned and he's out," shouted Mr Franklin.

The pony club members were all climbing back on their ponies to see Rupert finish.

"Isn't Rosie going fast."

"I didn't know she could gallop like that."

"Good old Rupert," shouted Oliver as his brother jumped the last.

"Will him to go through the finish," shrieked Netti.

Rosie went through the flags so fast that it was some way before Rupert could pull up, then he dismounted and led her back, looking round vaguely for David.

"That was terrific," he said, "I did just about everything wrong, but it was still terrific. I wish we could come back tomorrow and have another go."

"Did you have any refusals?" asked Lesley impatiently.

"Dozens, I should think. I got lost in the quarry. We hit the last pole of the grid a fearful clonk, but I think it stayed up. Then we went down the slide too fast and practically fell in the river. We took that pen thing too fast as well and she refused the straw bales, which was a bit of luck really as we weren't meant to jump them. While she was stationary I managed to haul her round and point her at the wattles and she was terribly pleased to see an easy way out. Poor old Rosie," he went on, patting her, "I'm afraid you had a lot of frights."

"But how many refusals did you have?" asked Lesley in an exasperated voice.

"Did you circle or turn round in the quarry?" asked Lizzie.

"I don't think so, I just got lost and wandered about in the bushes. And in the pen we sort of collided with the bales, I don't think I turned round."

"You'll have to wait and see what the judges say," David told Lesley. "He didn't have any time faults. You did well," he told Rupert, "and Rosie's got the makings of a good cross-country pony. She needs experience and a bit more education. Now you'd better all water and feed while we're waiting for the results."

181

"Hold it," said Oliver. "Julia sent me to tell you that one of the Froggie ponies isn't going. It's gone lame, so she's persuaded the collecting steward to put Tina in the space. They went dashing off for a practice jump, but they're back now."

"Oh we must stay and watch Hobby," said Lizzie.

"I think Tina's going to mess things up," Oliver sounded gloomy. "Her teeth keep chattering and she's gone pale grey with fright."

"I'll go and see if I can cheer her up," said David, limping off towards the start.

The pony club members turned their attention back to the course. The Frogmorton team had taken off their black jackets and donned polo-necks like everyone else, but their elegant little ponies didn't seem at home on the cross-country. The first one had gone so slowly that the second one caught up with it and they came through the finish together. Then the third one set off and Tina took her place at the start. Julia checked her girths. David said, "Take it steady. Just try to get round."

Tina could only nod miserably, as she tried to control her chattering teeth.

"You'll be all right once you get going," David told her. "I can remember feeling ghastly before my first race."

Tina set off with fumbling hands and weak legs, her mind was taken up with how awful she felt. Hobbit knew his stable companions were all in the collecting ring, *he* didn't want to leave them and go out in to the unknown, and sensing that his rider also disliked the expedition, he went slowly and without his usual zest. He came to a stop at the first fence.

"I knew it," groaned Oliver.

"Oh go on, Tina, don't be feeble," said Sarah.

"Legs!" added Alice.

Tina suddenly woke up to the horror of her situation. She might not even get over the first fence. Ollie would never forgive her. She shook herself into action and gave the surprised Hobbit a whack.

"Short run and legs," she told herself. Hobbit, finding that she did want to go after all, decided to oblige. He jumped the brush and cantered on towards the crossed rails. By the time they reached the quarry Tina had forgotten herself and was concentrating on the course. Flying in and out of the spinney, a sensation of pleasure began to creep over pony and rider. Hobbit forded the brook willingly, jumped the grid neatly and then they caught up with the third Frogmorton pony, dithering with horror at the top of the slide.

"Clear the course," shouted the jump judge. "Stand to the side, number thirty-four. Let the next pony through."

"Get out of the way and I'll give you a lead," shouted Tina. Hobbit slid down carefully, splashed through the brook, jumped the pole and galloped for the ditch.

Oliver gave cries of triumph as Hobbit reappeared, leading the Frogmorton pony home.

"She's clocked up a few time faults, I'm afraid," said David, looking at his watch. "But they may let her off some of them if the other pony held her up."

The Wheelers all rushed to congratulate Hobbit, and a few minutes later the mothers began to emerge from the course.

"I've been watching by that horrible slide." Mrs Franklin was wearing green jeans and short yellow gumboots instead of her usual sari. "I am very proud of you, Hanif. You have done so well. Both our teams are doing very well."

Mrs Wheeler was looking at her children with new eyes. "I never knew that you were all so accomplished," she said. "You've been telling me for years that Rupert was the most hopeless tack-cleaner on earth, yet he's got seventy-five marks for turnout. You told me that Rosie and Ra couldn't jump and then I find you flying round the most terrifying-looking course."

Mrs Spencer had rushed to hug Tina. "You were great," she told her. "I nearly died when you refused the first one, but after that you got going and you were fantastic. The way you yelled at the little Frogmorton girl on top of that terrifying slide. Oh, Tina," she hugged her again, "I never realised that when I joined you to the pony club it would lead to this."

"No," agreed Tina, who was rather embarrassed by all the hugging, "and it wouldn't have come to this if Ollie hadn't lent me Hobbit."

"You must be proud of your elder daughter," Mr Franklin told Mrs Rooke as they hurried back to the collecting ring area, carrying the latest scores, "To come out top in the dressage, that really is something."

"Oh yes, well, Lesley's a specialist by nature, but Sarah has a more balanced character. She's a real all-rounder. I expect you noticed that not many of the younger children took part in all four events."

Lesley's won the dressage!" Hanif shouted the good news as his stepfather handed a carefully-marked score sheet to David, who had been sat down in the car and was being given coffee by Mrs Roberts.

"Well done, Lesley."

"David said you were good."

"Will she get a rosette?"

Then, to Alice's amazement, her Aunt Margaret appeared.

"You have done well," she said, smiling her thin smile. "I had no idea you could do dressage and cross-country."

"I had no idea you were coming," answered Alice.

"Well, it hadn't occured to me, but then Clare suddenly arrived. She's home from Turkey. I think she's finished with her latest boyfriend, and she wanted to come. She said it would remind her of *her* pony club days—not that she ever attempted a dressage test. Ah, here she comes. She stopped to get your score."

"Hullo, Alice. Your lot are doing terribly well. You've acquired eight hundred and thirty five marks without counting the cross-country," said Clare, who had Uncle Peter's rather square figure, Aunt Margaret's decided manner, combined with a much more cheerful expression. "You're lying second and the other Woodbury team are only ten behind you. And doesn't Sandra Crankshaw's

Saffy look *different?* He used to have a dreadful skinny neck and charge about with his ears in Sandra's face. I can't imagine how you've persuaded him to do dressage."

All the other Woodbury members were pressed round David.

"How are we doing?"

"Did Lesley really win the dressage?"

"Yes, with a hundred and eighteen points. Three ahead of her nearest rival. But the rest of you haven't done too badly. James and Netti—a hundred and six. Lizzie, a hundred and four. Alice, a hundred and three. Harry, ninety-eight. Well, you can all see for yourselves in a moment."

"But how are we doing in the whole competition?" asked James impatiently.

"It all depends on the cross-country. There are six teams more or less level-pegging at the moment. It looks to me as though the one with three clear rounds will win."

"But both our teams are in the first six," added Mr Franklin proudly. "And the other six are right out of it."

"Go and put the ponies away," said David when they had all had a look at the score sheet. "It's bound to take some time to sort out the cross-country scores and do the final adding up."

The ponies knew they had done well. They accepted their owners praise and cossetting graciously, feeling that it was theirs by right. Ferdinand and Jupiter looked very superior in their dark blue, fishnet sweat rugs. The cattle truck ponies were all wearing rugs of some sort. Lesley was bandaging Stardust's legs. Alice had no rug, but she brushed out Saffron's saddle mark and gave him an enormous feed. She was feeling desperately sad. She knew this was really the end of the holidays. The course was over, soon she'd start school. Saffron would be sent back. Supposing Mr Crankshaw sold him? She loved him so much, she thought, swallowing tears. She'd never love another pony so much, even if they could find one to hire next holidays. Hanif was calling her, his mother had made

185

far too much tea. He pleaded with her to come and help him eat it. She went over, trying to force a cheerful smile on her face.

They were still eating when Oliver came running. "David says there are rosettes to six places so he thinks both teams will get them. You're all to come up looking tidy, wearing jackets and crash caps," he told them.

"I needn't bother, need I?" asked Tina, who had already put her borrowed jacket in Mrs Rooke's car.

"He said 'everyone'," answered Oliver, "so I expect you'd better."

They all walked up together.

"If only we'd had one of the Washouts in our team, we'd have had a really good chance of winning," complained James, who had borrowed his mother's score sheet and studied everybody's marks. "If we'd had you, Alice, we'd certainly have won, and with Lesley too, we'd have been streets ahead of all the other teams."

"But it wouldn't have been so much fun, because the rest of us would have been nowhere," Lizzie pointed out.

Mrs Rooke bustled round inspecting them. "Rupert, your shirt's out, your tie's crooked and you can't wear your cap on the back of your head like that," she snapped. "Paul, there's orange juice on your face. Do up your jacket buttons, Alice."

David was sitting in the Franklin's car, and, as they gathered round, he asked, "Do the boys all know they have to take off their crash caps if they're given rosettes? The girls only have to say thank you and smile."

"Rupert, did you hear," demanded Netti. "You take your cap off."

Oliver rushed up. "They've taken down the scoreboard and they're adding the cross-country marks," he announced, and rushed away again.

A moment later he reappeared, waving his arms excitedly. "They've given Rupert a clear. You've six hundred cross-country points."

The Washouts looked at each other and hope grew.

186

"Great!"

"Fantastic!"

"That means you didn't turn your back, then." Lesley looked at Rupert accusingly.

"It means they've beaten us," moaned Sarah.

"We knew that. We both had two clears and one dodgy round, but they were already fifteen points ahead." No one listened to James.

Lynne, Paul and Sarah raced after Oliver. David had climbed out of the car and the others walked beside him as he headed slowly towards the table that had been set up for the rosettes.

Mrs Franklin appeared with a picnic chair. "Will you sit down, please," she said, offering it to David.

"No, I'm all right. I've been sitting in the car." David waved her away.

"Persuade him to sit, Hanif. He must, he is exhausted."

Hanif opened the chair. "It's no good, David. She's a terrible bully. You'd better surrender with dignity because she'll win in the end."

"Put it round to the side then," said David with a sigh. "I don't want to sit bang in the middle, looking like a presiding judge."

With David sitting, most of the Woodbury members collapsed on the ground around him and tried to wait patiently for the final results. They didn't have to wait long. Suddenly Mr Franklin and Mrs Rooke detached themselves from the crowd round the scoreboard and hurried over. Mr Franklin was trying hard not to look too pleased.

"First and third," he told David quietly. "They've labelled your lot Woodbury A," he added, turning to Hanif, "so don't be thrown into confusion when they call you."

The Washouts gave no shout of triumph, partly because they didn't quite believe they had won, and partly because they didn't want to crow over the defeated Wonders.

Then Oliver rushed over and broke the tension by shouting, "Tina's sixth in the Junior Individual. You are," he repeated, seeing the blank look on Tina's face. "You're sixth *and* you get a rosette, I asked the secretary."

"Oh Ollie, you shouldn't bother officials..." Lizzie began but they shushed her as the Area Representative began to speak.

"She was a famous showjumper when she was young," Paul told the others. "I've got a photograph of her in one of my books."

She was telling them what they already knew, that the Area Cup was a new idea especially to encourage pony clubs which couldn't produce teams of the standard required for the main interbranch events, and to bring on the younger members. Then she thanked the organizers, congratulated them on their efficiency, and came at last to the winning teams.

"First, Woodbury A. Second, East Tulworth. Third, Woodbury B. Fourth, Brackenhurst. Fifth, South Barset. Sixth, Northdown."

Walking forward in a row, the five Washouts *had* to believe that they had won. This was no dream.

"Congratulations," said Jill Donaldson five times as she handed them their red rosettes and, "Many Congratulations," as she held out the large silver cup. "You must all be very proud that The Woodbury will be the first name on it."

Lesley and Lizzie took the cup, the boys' hands were too full of crash caps and rosettes to carry any more. Everyone clapped and the photographer told them to hold it high. Then, as the East Tulworth were called in, they rushed out and Lizzie handed it straight to David.

"You really won it," she said. "None of us would have come anywhere at all without you."

David looked from the cup to Lizzie and then smiled. "Well, let's say it was a combined effort," he suggested. "I couldn't have done it without five people prepared to put up with my roars of rage and really work. Here, come on, clap the Wonders, all of you, I can't."

James and Netti came back carrying their yellow rosettes and trying to stifle feelings of disappointment and envy, but

Lynne and Paul, who were truly delighted, rushed to show theirs to their parents. Sarah gave hers a look of disgust and stuffed it in her pocket.

The senior individuals had been given their rosettes. The juniors were called forward and Tina took her place at the end of the line. She came back smiling. "The first thing I've ever won, but it's yours, Ollie. They go with the pony."

Oliver looked at the rosette in horror. "Why did it have to be pink? Ugh, it's a colour I can't stand. You keep it, Tina. I'll wait until next year and try to win one myself."

The Area Representative was explaining that so many people had tied first in the quiz, turnout and cross-country sections that it was impossible to award special rosettes, but in the dressage two riders had been outstanding: Lesley Rooke of the Woodbury and Amanda Goddard of the East Tulworth, and would they come forward for their rosettes.

Everyone but Sarah clapped enthusiastically, and Netti and Lynne shocked by this unsisterly attitude, each took one of Sarah's hands and clapped them for her.

Lesley came back looking rather dazed, and took the large red and white rosette with *Special* across the centre to show David.

Mrs Rooke swept up bossily. "You look all in, David. I've sent Mr Franklin to fetch my car and I'll take you home at once."

"Oh, I'm O.K.," said David, struggling to his feet. "I've enjoyed it and there's nothing like a little success to drive away the aches and pains. Well done, all of you," he told the pony club members. "I'm very pleased with the way you all went." He looked round at their faces, "Don't you think, Mrs Rooke, that there's something about our pony club? They look much nicer than anyone else's."

"They performed better today, and that's what counts," snapped Mrs Rooke opening the car door.

Alice's relations reappeared. "Congratulations Alice. We're bursting with pride," said Clare. "If only I'd done something like this in my pony club days, but teams and cups and red rosettes seemed an unattainable dream. I've been telling Mum that she must get a move on and arrange to buy Saffy from old Crankshaw. I imagine he's what you want most in the world?"

"Oh yes, the only thing really. But it's difficult about money," explained Alice sadly.

"The Trustees have to wait until probate is granted...," Aunt Margaret began in her dreary voice, which almost welcomed the fact that nothing could be done.

"Oh, don't be dotty, Mum. You and Dad could easily lend Alice the money until that happens and, if you don't do something quickly the Crankshaws will hear how much Saffy's improved and ask twice as much," said Clare, who had learned how to manage her mother. "You'd be mad not to fix the whole thing up tonight."

"I'll discuss it with Daddy."

Hearing the unenthusiastic note in her Aunt's voice, Alice's fragile hopes collapsed, but then her cousin smiled at her. "Don't worry, we'll persuade them somehow," whispered Clare.

"Hold it everyone." Mr Franklin had produced a large bottle of cider and was pouring it into the cup. "Before we go home we must all drink to the future of the Woodbury Pony Club. You take the cup round, Harry, David first."

"To the Woodbury, remembering that a pony club is only as good as its members," said David and drank.

"But that's not true," objected James, "except for Alice and Harry and Tina, we've all been members for years and it's always been a pathetic pony club, really boring and hopeless; everyone said so."

"Right," agreed Rupert. "I'll drink to the new and transformed Woodbury," he grabbed the cup and drank greedily.

"If only the Cranford Vale had been here to see," moaned Netti, "you know how they despise us, they'll go round telling everyone that the standard must have been absolutely ghastly if the Woodbury won."

"Drink," ordered Hanif, offering her the cup. "And stop *worrying*. Now we've got David to teach us we're all going to become fantastically good riders and amaze the world."

PONY CLUB CHALLENGE

CONTENTS

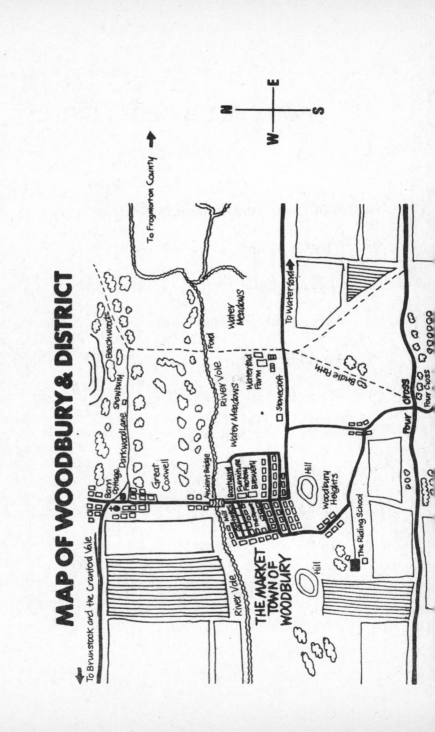

MAP OF WOODBURY & DISTRICT

To Brunstock and the Cranford Vale

To Frogmorton County

To Waterford

N E S W

Beechwoods

Watery Meadows

Ford

River Vole

Waterford Farm

Stonecroft

Old Bridle Path

Snowburn

Darkwood Lane

Great Coxwell

Barn Cottage

Ancient Bridge

Hill

Backyard

Furniture Factory

Brewery

Four Cross

Hill

Woodbury Heights

THE MARKET TOWN OF WOODBURY

Hill

River Vole

The Riding School

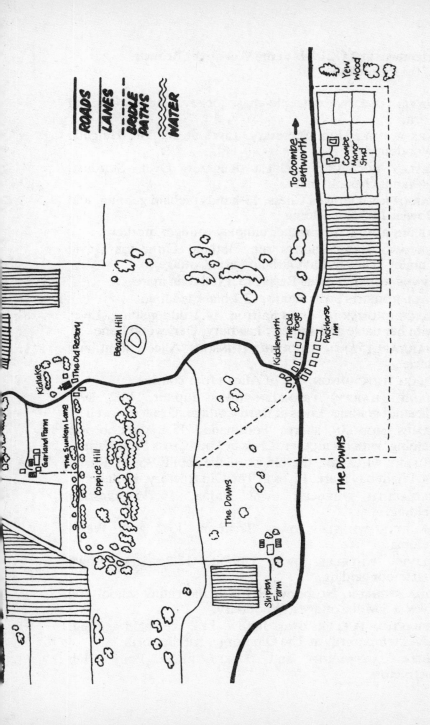

Members and Officials of the Woodbury Branch of the Pony Club

DAVID LUMLEY, ex steeple-chase jockey. Lives at Garland Farm.

MRS ROOKE, Hon. Secretary. Lives at 20, The Heights, Woodbury.

LESLEY ROOKE, her eldest daughter. Owns Stardust, 14-hands chestnut mare.

SARAH ROOKE owns Chess, 13-hands piebald gelding, and Bowie, 13.3 bay gelding.

JULIAN ROOKE their rather unhorsy younger brother.

MR AND MRS ROBERTS run Garland Farm for David Lumley. They live at Garland Farm Cottage.

LYNNE ROBERTS owns Berry, 13.1 red roan mare.

PAUL ROBERTS owns Banjo, 12.2 black gelding.

ALICE DRUMMOND owns Saffron, 14.1 dun gelding. Lives with her uncle and aunt at Shawbury, Darkwood Lane.

MARGARET AND PETER HUTCHINSON, Alice's aunt and uncle.

CLARE HUTCHINSON, one of Alice's four cousins.

HANIF (HARRY) FRANKLIN owns Jupiter, 14.2 liver chestnut gelding. Lives at Barn Cottage, Great Coxwell.

JAMES MORGAN shares Ferdinand, 15.1 dark brown gelding, with his mother. Lives at Four Cross Fruit Farm.

RUPERT WHEELER, the eldest of the family, owns Rosie, 14.1 light bay mare. Lives at The Old Rectory, Kidlake.

ELIZABETH WHEELER owns Rajah, 14.1½ chestnut gelding.

ANNETTE WHEELER owns Tristram, 13.2 grey Welsh gelding.

OLIVER WHEELER owns Hobbit, 12.2 dark brown Dartmoor gelding.

TINA SPENCER. No pony. Helps at the riding school and lives at 5 Mill Cottages, Woodbury.

SEBASTION FULLER, owns Jigsaw, 14.2 skewbald gelding. Lives temporarily at The Old Forge, Kiddleworth.

JULIA CARTWRIGHT and JANET GREEN. Pony Club instructors.

CHAPTER ONE

Will David Be Disappointed?

Alice Drummond waved goodbye to Mr Crankshaw and rode her dun pony, Saffron, down the track to the river. It was the first day of the summer holidays; she had made the long journey home from school the day before.

Home, thought Alice. Well, since her parents' death, Aunt Margaret and Uncle Peter were always telling her that she must look upon Shawbury as her home. But then, even when her parents were alive, she had never had a proper one—a house full of brothers and sisters, dogs, kittens and rabbits, where you've lived for as long as you can remember. Her father had worked for a multi-national company so they had moved about the world living in smart company flats in Rio de Janeiro, Washington and Mexico City. She hadn't had a brother or sister, there were just the three of them, and she had never had a pet, not even a hamster, until Saffron. He had become hers after that miraculous day last holidays when the Woodbury Pony Club had won the Area Cup. She had ridden Saffron, hired for the holidays, but afterwards Clare, the youngest of her four grown-up cousins and her only real friend among them, had persuaded Aunt Margaret to buy him. He'd spent the term turned out on his ex-owner's farm and was now fat and sleek from the rich grass of the water meadows.

The pony club fixture list was a bit of a disappointment, thought Alice, splashing through the ford. She had hoped that David Lumley, their instructor and District Commissioner, who had been a famous steeplechase jockey until a crashing fall had left him disabled, would run another course. In her wildest dreams she had even imagined a camp, but there were only working rallies, a

195

picnic ride and a test day on the fixture card. As she took the silent, leafy path through the beechwoods, she wondered whether David was all right; she did hope that they hadn't worn him out last holidays. Then she thought about Harry Franklin and wondered if he would still want to ride with her. That was the worst of going to boarding school, you didn't see people for ages and they changed. She conjured up Harry's brown face, dark eyes and curly, blue-black hair. He was bound to be older and taller, but she'd telephone him as soon as she had settled Saffron and see if the rest of him was the same.

Alice heard her aunt's champion springer spaniels barking in their kennels and saw the red-brick, gabled house through the trees. Last holidays it had seemed a dismal, dripping place, but now, on a hot summer's day, the house and garden looked deliciously shady and cool.

The Rookes were cleaning tack in the old conservatory attached to their tall, red Victorian house on Woodbury Heights. Neither Mr Rooke, who was a solicitor, or Mrs Rooke, who was the pony club secretary, cared about plants or gardening, so the conservatory had long ago become a general dumping ground for unwanted objects and a tack room.

Generally, Lesley and Sarah, who hated doing anything together, managed to stagger their tack cleaning, but as their school had only broken up that day, there had been very little time to prepare for the first rally of the holidays.

"You could have cleaned yours on Monday, you didn't have anything like the amount of homework I had," complained Lesley, glaring at her younger sister through thick-lensed glasses as she waited impatiently for the metal polish.

"Well, I didn't." Sarah shook the can with deliberate slowness and then applied the polish to her cloth with irritating precision. She was much prettier than her sister, with a narrow face, mouse-brown hair cut in a fringe and she didn't have to wear glasses, but her mouth was rather small and thin-lipped. "Anyway, you're lucky that Julian's not cleaning tack too," Sarah went on. "If Tina hadn't cleaned his there would have been three of us sharing; *that* wouldn't have pleased you."

"Tina won't go on cleaning it now she's not riding Chess, and I can't see Mummy making Julian do anything, so you'll have two sets to clean and two ponies to look after," Lesley told her sister. "If the great Sarah's such a brilliant rider she has to have two ponies at her disposal, she can jolly well see to them. *I'm* not going to help out," she added spitefully. She hated Sarah for being their mother's favourite.

"You're jealous. It's not my fault if the only thing *you're* good at is dreary old dressage. Anyway, Tina *may* go on helping. Just because Mummy's put Julian down for every rally it doesn't mean he'll go, and if he doesn't Tina can have Chess."

"You can't expect her to bike up here and do all the work on the chance of a ride."

"I don't see why not," Sarah retorted. "That's what she does at the riding school."

"Well, if she's fool enough to let you use her, that's her business, but don't think you'll get *me* doing extra work so that Mummy's pet can be in *all* the teams," sneered Lesley.

"No one's asked you. And I know what you're afraid of," Sarah snapped back. "You thought you were the only person who could do dressage, but now I've got a decently schooled pony like Bowie you're terrified I'll beat you at that too."

At the Old Rectory at Kidlake, the Wheelers were having a family flap. It was getting dark, there was no light in the tack room and, when they had moved all the tack and cleaning materials into the kitchen, they found they were low on saddle soap and that the tin of metal polish wadding had had its lid left off and had dried up.

"Ra's tail is full of burrs, his mane needs pulling and this

197

tack's filthy," moaned Lizzie, the second eldest of the Wheelers, as she dismantled her saddle.

"I've found this old tin of metal polish, it was dried up too, but I've added a bit of water," said Netti, inspecting the result critically. "There's just enough for badges; the stirrups and bits will have to stay tarnished. Come on, hand your badges over; you know how the Old Rooke goes on and on if they're dirty."

"Oh, she goes on about *everything*," complained Oliver, the youngest of the Wheelers, who had the same pink and white complexion, the same pale, straw-coloured hair as his brother and sisters, but a rounder, cheekier face. "She's a real pain."

"Still, she does a lot of work for the pony club," Lizzie, who wore her flaxen hair in one thick plait, pointed out. "I know David's much nicer and a terribly good instructor, but I don't suppose he'd do the boring things like collecting subscriptions and sending out fixture cards."

"I wish Julia would be secretary as well as junior instructor," grumbled Oliver. *"She's* really nice."

Rupert's pink and white face, which was long and dreamy, appeared round the kitchen door. "Has anyone seen my boots?" he asked.

"But I thought it was your bridle you were looking for." A note of irritation crept into Lizzie's usually patient voice.

"No, I've found that. It's been hanging on a tree by the field gate; it's been rained on and it's hideously stiff," Rupert explained. "I've got all my tack now. It's just my boots."

"You'll have to use neat's-foot oil," Lizzie told him as she looked at the cardboard-stiff bridle. "We're running out of saddle soap. And you must do something about the drop noseband, it belongs to Harry Franklin," she reminded him.

"Harry won't mind, but his stepfather's terrible fussy," added Netti. "Can I have your badge, Rupert? I don't want too many sniffy remarks on Wheeler's turnout from the Old Rooke."

"One thing is, we haven't got far to go," said Oliver, dipping Hobbit's green encrusted bit into the bucket of water.

"Yes, but that makes it even worse when we're always last or late," lamented Lizzie, scrubbing hard at a greasy saddleflap. "Do you think that David will be very disappointed when he finds we haven't done much schooling in the term? Do you think he expects the ponies to have improved?" she asked anxiously.

"He'll get a very nasty shock if he expects anything so unlikely," answered Rupert, swamping his bridle and the kitchen floor with neat's foot oil. "Rosie's so fat she can scarcely waddle, and I'm quite sure she's forgotten everything she learned last holidays, including how to take off."

"Oh, we won't be anything like as hopeless as we were last holidays," Lizzie told her brother. "David's instruction changed us completely. Don't you remember everyone's amazement when we all whizzed round the cross-country at the Area Cup? Even Julia said it was a miracle. No, I'm just afraid he may be disappointed that we haven't schooled the ponies since then."

"Perhaps our lack of improvement will make him run another course," suggested Netti. "Working rallies and a picnic ride aren't going to help much."

"I don't see why we can't have a camp—all the other pony clubs do," complained Oliver. "Except for boring inspections, they have a terrific time at the Cranford Vale camp and, on the last night, no one, not even the juniors, goes to bed until two in the morning."

Tina Spencer sat on the bench in Woodbury's only launderette and watched the sheets, towels and her best white riding shirt spinning round. It was a job she took over in the holidays to help her mother, who worked long hours at *Fanny's Food and Wine Bar* in Cross Street.

Tina was feeling rather dreary about the rally. After all the fun and excitement of having the dark brown

Dartmoor, Hobbit, to ride in the Easter holidays and then of competing in the Area Cup, it was difficult to go back to being a "dismounted member", a pony-less person; hanging about, watching other people ride. Still, anything was better than sitting alone in the flat with nothing much to do, and Lynne Roberts, who was always generous, would probably let her have a short ride on Berry. You're getting spoiled, she told herself, you'll soon be as bad as Sarah. You had such a lovely term with Chess to ride every weekend and practically every evening; you can't expect the holidays to be like that too. But she couldn't help feeling envious of Sarah; she was *so* lucky. To be given a lovely second pony like Bowie before you had really outgrown your first, and to be allowed to keep Chess as well. It was true she was to share the stout little piebald with her younger brother, Julian, but he didn't ride much. Not that I'd swop Mum for Mrs Rooke, she thought. Not for a second. She smiled as she visualized the tall, grim, rather old-fashioned-looking figure, in her drab clothes, and the magnified eyes glaring from behind thick glasses, and then her own mother, wild-haired, bright and laughing, dressed in a colourful shirt and jeans—centuries younger. She and Mum were more like sisters, people said, than mother and daughter. Anyway, she wasn't missing anything as special as a camp. She *would* have felt hard done by if she had had to watch the others ride away for a wonderful week in tents. And there would have been no hope of hiring a pony on Mum's wages; they just kept the two of them and paid the rent of the flat in the little street of crooked cottages near the river. The River Vole, meandered slowly along the north side of Woodbury, an old market town famous for its square of Elizabethan houses and its ancient stone bridge.

At Four Cross Fruit Farm, James Morgan, who was large and solid for his age, which was fourteen, was feeling cross and ungrateful.

"But there's no point in making all this fuss about a few

miserable working rallies," he told his mother. "If we had a pony club show, or I was going to be in an interbranch team, there might be some point in you grooming Ferdie up to the nines and me spending hours polishing the tack. I thought things were going to be better now that David was in charge, but all he's arranged are these feeble working rallies and a pathetic picnic ride. The Cranford Vale are having a camp and a show *and* a barbecue. I can hear all the other pony clubs pitying us again."

"I'm sure David's doing his best," said Mrs Morgan. "He wrote to all the parents asking them either to come on the committee or to help in other ways, but the trouble is that everyone's so busy. And you must remember he's disabled and make allowances."

"This boy I know at school, Seb Fuller, is probably coming to live near Woodbury," James went on. His parents split up some time ago and now they're selling their house. He's very fed up. He's got his own pony and belongs to the Frogmorton but everyone there has told him what a hopeless, piddling little pony club we are."

"You beat the Frogmorton hollow in the Area Cup," protested Mrs Morgan. "Our teams were first and third, and they weren't placed at all."

"But the Area Cup is only for hopeless people, anyway," James snapped at her. "The people who are good enough for real interbranch teams aren't *allowed* to enter. The Cranford Vale didn't bother."

"That's not true. The Cup is for junior teams and the Woodbury's a young pony club; you have to give David time to build it up. And being so small makes it very friendly. How would you like to go to a huge rally where no one spoke to you?"

"I wouldn't mind if they had decent cross-country events and, anyway, all the big branches have camps where you *get* to know people."

"You're being over-critical, you know very well you had a wonderful time last holidays."

"And you might say thank you to Mum for all the days she's spent tack-cleaning and grooming so that you can be the shiniest member of the Woodbury," James's elder sister Nina told him, and then put on the headphones of her walkabout radio to escape his answer.

"Stand, Jupe." Hanif Franklin made another dab at Jupiter's mud-caked, liver-chestnut stomach and then continued the argument with his mother. "Don't you understand? She may not want to ride everywhere with me these holidays. At Easter she was sad and lonely, but now she has plenty of *English* friends."

"Of course she has friends, but you are the one who lives very near and it is natural that you should ride over to Garland Farm together," said Mrs Franklin, who was wearing her pink sari.

"It's no use, Jupe," said Hanif, dodging a cowkick and then a crocodile snap, "all this ancient mud *has* to come off. I've given in to you for far too long, but now I'm more frightened of Mrs Rooke's glares and David's piercing blue eyes than I am of you."

"The brush is too stiff, you are hurting him," protested Mrs Franklin. "Why do you not wash it off?"

"The Pony Club Manual says you remove mud with a *dandy*-brush," argued Hanif, "but Jupe thinks that's nothing less than torture, so I am using a body-brush and my hand. There, now don't lie down in a muddy part of the field tonight or you'll have to go through all that agony again tomorrow," he lectured the powerful liver-chestnut pony.

"And now you have finished grooming you will ring Alice?" asked Mrs Franklin. "I think she will be very hurt if you do not and it is the cheap time."

"Oh, don't bully, Mum," answered Hanif, putting his grooming tools away in their box. His stepfather was a great believer in tidiness. "If Alice wants me around she'll get in touch."

"I think you are being proud," said Mrs Franklin, but at

that moment the telephone began to ring and Hanif raced towards the back door without answering.

"Are you going to the rally tomorrow?" Alice asked.

"Of course, I was going to ring you," Hanif lied. "We'd better start early. Jupe is disgracefully fat."

"So's Saffy, even his skinny neck. I don't think he'll be *able* to stargaze."

"Jupe still twirls, but at a slower speed."

"Nine o'clock, here then?" asked Alice, who had observed Aunt Margaret hovering in the hall and thinking of her telephone bill.

"Great," said Hanif. He put the receiver back and stood feeling pleased. Alice was still a friend. He was fond of the other Woodbury members, but, like his stepfather, they all seemed very English. Alice was different. With her brownish skin, rich golden hair and dark blue eyes, she could be Scandinavian, he told himself. He approved of her straight nose, big mouth and decided expression, and then she'd lived abroad and travelled a lot, as he had. And having no parents at all was far worse than having to cope with a stepfather.

At Garland Farm, Lynne and Paul Roberts looked despondently at the broken-down jumps in Long Meadow. Living in the cottage and with their father running the farm for David Lumley, they felt a certain responsibility for the success of the pony club rallies, and no one else seemed to be doing anything about this one.

"I know my practising hasn't exactly improved them," said Lynne, straightening the pig trough which filled in under a heavy pole on two oil drums, "but they never were very exciting jumps. I did hope we'd have one or two new ones for the summer."

"Dad and David have no time for the pony club," sighed Paul, who was small and dark with a neat, serious face and grey eyes. "First it was the hay, now it's the barley. Then it'll be the wheat and then they'll start ploughing. Since David got his specially adapted tractor he's only interested in farming."

"Well, it is his work now," Lynne pointed out. "The pony club's only his hobby." She was a year older than Paul, much larger and quite different. Her wavy, light-brown hair stuck out from her plump, cheerful face and when she laughed, which was most of the time, her hazel-coloured eyes disappeared into the plumpness and became slits. "Anyway, now we've got a student to help Dad, David won't be so busy."

"Dad says Gary'll never make a farmer," said Paul as he kicked a broken straw bale into the hedge. "Give us a hand with this pole, Lynne, it's one of the green ones and still weighs a ton. Then I'd better fetch some tools and mend the cavaletti you and Berry broke, David's sure to want it tomorrow."

CHAPTER TWO

The Challenge

They hadn't changed, thought Alice contentedly as she watched the pony club members gathering in the farmyard, shadowed by the great Dutch barns. Harry had dismounted to stop Jupiter's twirling, and was rumpling his curly, blue-black hair as he listened to Netti's account of his dropped noseband's life since it had been loaned to Rupert. Paul and Lynne were discussing the urgent need for new jumps with Julia Cartwright, the junior instructor with a pony-tail hairstyle and a nice smile. Tina Spencer, small reddish-haired and freckled, was stroking Oliver's Hobbit and telling a worried-looking Lizzie that she didn't mind being the only dismounted member.

Then Rupert Wheeler, his blue shirt hanging out of his breeches, his cap on the back of his head and his long legs encased in a pair of hastily washed and very smeary boots, rode up and, sitting loosely on light bay, mealy-nosed Rosie, began to tease James.

"Must you be quite so clean and shiny?" he asked. "You make the rest of us look even worse than we are. Couldn't you rub a little mud on your stirrups or let Ferdie have a few mouthfuls of hedge?"

"I don't think we need worry, he's *so* shiny he'll dazzle the instructors," decided Netti. "One look at James and they won't see the rest of us, they'll be blinking for the next ten minutes."

"It's my mother," explained James, his heavy face staying solemn. "She's got a thing about washing and grooming and polishing, so it's all done for me; it's a bit embarrassing really."

"I wish my mother was like that, but no such luck," complained Oliver. "I'd love to get up and find my pony groomed, my tack shining, and even stingy Janet Green giving me ten for inspection."

"Julia says that so many new members are joining that we may have to have three rides next week," Paul told them. "She's going to take the D-plus lot and Janet the real Ds."

"Great," said Oliver. "I've had enough of being lumped in a ride with people of six."

James groaned. "We don't want any more younger ones, we want some older people with good horses so that we can make up some decent teams."

"Here's Mrs Rooke, quite late for her," said Lynne, who was longing for someone to remark on the shining state of Berry's red-roan coat.

"And the rest of the Rookery coming up the lane behind her," announced Rupert, standing in his stirrups. "They're actually riding together!"

"Bowie's a bit silly in traffic," Tina told him, "so Mrs Rooke said Lesley had to ride outside him. I do it when I ride Chess, but Julian's not experienced enough."

They all gathered round to inspect Bowie.

"He's lovely, Sarah. You are lucky."

"Terribly well-bred and good-looking."

"He's a bit spindly-legged. Does he jump?"

"Of course he jumps. You don't think we'd go and buy a pony that couldn't jump, do you? We're not that stupid. He's won a lot."

"He's been bought so that she can be in the Woodbury showjumping team," sneered Lesley, who hated the way her mother pushed Sarah forward.

"Here's David," said Alice, as he drove his specially adapted Land Rover into the yard.

"Good morning, all," said David, opening the Land Rover door to get a better look at the waiting riders. "Those ponies have put on a lot of weight."

He looked the same, thought Alice, except that his tanned face made him seem healthier. Dressed in jeans and a blue checked shirt, his thin, wiry body was still broken and twisted, his useless arm hung limply at his side. But his hair was nice—brown, thick and vaguely curly—and his bright blue eyes looked out of a face that was drawn and seemed older than the rest of him. He isn't any better, thought Alice sadly. Though everyone had said last holidays that he wasn't going to improve, she *had* hoped for a miracle on his behalf.

David was looking at the milling ponies. "Could we have the D ride in the paddock, please," he called. "Oliver, you lead the way."

"Tina, will you be my assistant?" asked Julia. "I've got one or two tricky ones I'd like you to ride."

Tina ran off delightedly, and as the Ds moved out of the way, everyone else mounted and rode into Long Meadow.

"He hasn't even noticed Bowie," complained Sarah.

"Oh yes he has. Those piercing blue eyes notice everything," Hanif told her. "He's reserving judgement until he's seen you in action."

Sarah forced her way into the line of ponies, behind Jupiter and ahead of the two older Wheelers and her sister. Lizzie was too polite to object, but Rupert said, "Here, stop shoving."

"*I'm* not going at the back with the little ponies any more," Sarah told him firmly.

"Your pony may be bigger than Tristram but he's still smaller than Stardust and Ra," Rupert said accusingly.

"Can I have your attention, please?" David had parked the Land Rover in the centre of the school, climbed down, settled himself on his shooting stick and was studying each rider and pony in turn.

"First of all, we'll run through the schooling we did last holidays and see how much of it has stuck. The ponies are all looking very well, though on the fat side. The ones which haven't been ridden at all during the term will be very unfit, and we must be careful not to overdo them. No galloping for at least a week and then only for a very short distance. And watch out for girth galls. These string-type nylon girths are a great help, but it's a good idea to bathe

207

the girth area with salt and water or dab on surgical spirit—they both act as a preventative. You can also pull each foreleg out in turn after you've girthed up. This ensures that there are no folds of skin trapped under the girth."

Alice, who was the only member who hadn't ridden at all during the holidays, asked, "Can I stop and check Saffy's girth? He's terribly fat and podgy."

"Yes, come into the centre. Now, are the rest of you overtracking? I know it's a warm day but that's no reason for riding without impulsion. Remember that when you're on your pony you ride *forward* the whole time. If your legs need a rest, stop and get off. Beginners should be passive riders, but you're past that stage. You have to ride *every* stride."

There was a good deal of leaning over and peering down to make sure that the ponies' hind hoofs were at least stepping up to the print left by the forefoot on the same side.

Then they trotted, circling and serpentining with David giving angry roars at those who let their ponies look the wrong way. Alice was pleased with Saffron. He hadn't forgotten anything he had learned at Easter, and it seemed much easier to keep him on the bit and prevent him stargazing. She took a quick look back at Hanif. He seemed quite cool and calm, and Jupiter was trotting steadily and making no attempt to run away, as he had at the first rally last holidays.

We've stayed improved, thought Alice triumphantly, as they changed the rein and serpentined again. What David used to call "the lunatic ponies" are behaving quite normally.

But when David called them to a halt and lined them up in the centre of the school he didn't seem very satisfied.

"I know I mustn't work you too hard, that you and the ponies are unfit," he began, "but when you're riding at the sitting trot very few of you are sitting deep enough. Remember that to produce impulsion you have to influence the hindlegs. At the slower paces you sit deep, drive the hindlegs under the body. Sarah, you are trying to pull your pony's nose in with the reins because you think that makes him *look* right, but you're actually *preventing* him using his hindlegs and coming on the bit. Would you pedal a bicycle with the brakes on?" He turned to look at the second half of the ride. "If you want to go on riding like beginners, fine, sit on top of your saddles and kick away. But, if you want to progress and become active riders, able to influence and school your ponies, you have to learn to give the correct aids and to sit deep."

He turned back to James. "Come over here and demonstrate, please, James. I think you're riding a bit short for schooling," David went on. "It's more than likely that you've grown. Has that occurred to you? Have you checked your stirrup lengths lately?"

"No," James admitted, hanging his legs down. "You're right, I have grown. I think they'd better go down two."

All the other riders began to check their stirrup lengths guiltily and there was a good deal of letting down.

"Now," said David. "We want a rider who is tall above the saddle and tall below, sitting in the centre of the saddle, not the back, and not with the stirrups so long that he or she tips forward with a weak 'fork' seat." He made James demonstrate both the incorrect seats and then the right one again. "Now, Netti and Paul, you come and show us, please."

Netti, sitting tall and elegant on grey, Welsh Tristram, was told, "Good, you've got it." But Paul was criticized for sitting on top of his saddle and told to lower his knees, straighten his back and grow.

"Right, cross your stirrups," said David, turning back to the ride, "and we'll try to give you the correct feeling."

"Oh, David, must I?" wailed Lynne. "You know what Berry's trot is like."

"You can go round a couple of times," David told her. "Hold on to the pommel of the saddle, pull yourself down, try to relax and sit deep."

They trotted on slowly. Lizzie, struggling to influence sturdy, dark chestnut Rajah, was told that she was trying *too* hard, that her knees were too low and she was sitting with a fork seat.

"If you feel weak and ineffectual you're not sitting correctly," David told them. "You should feel tall, proud and in control. I'm trying to teach you to recognize the right feeling for yourselves. A good rider isn't someone who needs an instructor bawling at him or her the whole time, it's someone who's learned to see and feel and so knows what he or she is doing. Relax, Harry, hold on to the pommel. Go on, experiment, don't just sit there grinning and bearing it. I think you're still gripping. Relax, let the forces of gravity hold you down."

Alice was pleased. Last holidays she hadn't been allowed to sit to the trot, because whenever she did, Saffron had stiffened his back and stargazed, but now he was jogging along with his head quite low and didn't feel in the least worried.

David was roaring at Sarah to sit deep, but, like Paul, she had discovered that it was comfortable if you kept your knees high and gripped hard, and she wasn't going to try any other position, whatever David said.

Rupert's long legs were dangling satisfactorily. "Good!" David shouted to him. "You've got the idea. Sitting correctly won't have an immediate effect on your mare, because she's young, she's got to develop the right muscles, but in time it will."

He looked along the line of riders. James and Netti were good. Lesley had the pretty, light chestnut, Stardust, going well. "Good, you've got the little mare really working," he called to her. Lynne was flopping about and giggling. Paul was sitting comfortably, but uselessly, on top of black Banjo, who's sweet-itch was as bad as ever. He ignored them—it was no use wasting breath on people who wouldn't listen—and called the ride to a walk.

"Give the ponies a pat, but don't take back your stirrups. We're going to do some leg-yielding next, and I want you sitting deep."

Everyone groaned. "Remember it's the first day of the holidays, David; show some pity," protested Hanif.

"Yes, and some of us haven't ridden for three months," added Alice.

"I'm about to launch the Society for the Protection of Pony Club Members," announced Rupert. "The SPPCM will only permit riding without stirrups for one minute per rally, and there will be inspectors with stopwatches at all rallies to make sure the rule is enforced."

"Good idea," agreed Paul. "And there'll have to be at least an hour's showjumping."

"Compulsory cross-country," shrieked Netti.

"Trotting races," demanded Lynne.

"The DCs and Instructors would soon resign," observed Hanif. "They don't enjoy teaching unless they torture us a bit."

"I'm not torturing, I'm stretching you," David told him. "It's an effort to use muscles you've never used before, and most people won't make the effort unless someone roars insults at them. Once you've been shown what you *can* do, then it's up to you whether you make use of the knowledge or not. Now we're going to divide into two rides." He limped over to the Land Rover. "We'll have James, Alice, Harry, Rupert and Lizzie in one, and Lesley will lead the other. Two circles, each using half the school, please."

"He said *I* was to lead," Lesley snapped at her sister.

"I'm not deaf and there's no need to push and shove," Sarah snarled back.

"Yes there is, with you about," answered Lesley, taking the lead.

"We'll begin by making the circles smaller using only your outside aids," said David. "*Outside* rein and leg," he repeated. "Any fool can make a circle smaller by pulling on the inside rein. Good, that's small enough. Now make

211

them larger, using the *inside* aids. Ask the pony to move away from your inside leg. Very gradually, Paul, I don't want to see your aids. Sit straight, Lizzie." David was looking from one circle to the other. "O.K. Now do it again, slowly. Good. You've all remembered that. Now, can you remember leg-yielding?"

"Yes, of course we can."

"We practised on the way here."

"Even Rosie's remembered it," said Rupert proudly. "Look at this!"

David was limping about the centre of the school, trying to watch both rides at once. "Look up, Lizzie. Sarah, use gentle aids. *Explain* what you want; don't be impatient with that pony, he may not have leg-yielded before."

"He jolly well ought to know how; he cost enough and he's supposed to be well-schooled," stormed Sarah, giving the bay pony a sharp kick.

"Right, James's lot can stop and have a rest," said David. "You keep going, Lesley."

James's ride dismounted gratefully. Rupert, pretending that his legs wouldn't hold him, collapsed to the ground.

"Weakling," said Hanif, prodding him with his whip.

"You've got the longest legs, you ought to find it easy," Alice told him.

"But Rosie's the youngest and least educated pony; even David admits that," Rupert pointed out.

"I wish we could get on and do something new," grumbled James. "I hate going over and over the things we know already."

"That's because Ferdie's well-schooled," Lizzie told him. "The rest of us are teaching our ponies as we go along; we're bound to take longer."

"Bowie *looks* well-schooled, but he doesn't seem very happy," observed Alice, who was watching the other ride.

"He'd better be good," said Rupert. "They are expecting to decorate every room in the Rookery with his rosettes."

"His ears keep flashing back, but perhaps he prefers jumping," suggested Hanif.

"He'd be too well-bred for us," said Lizzie. "I'm sure he couldn't sleep out in the winter."

"No, he looks too flimsy and fragile, the sort of pony that would melt in the sun or be washed away by the rain," agreed Rupert.

"Stardust's looking *very* supple," observed Lizzie, watching the pretty, white-socked chestnut admiringly. "I wish Ra went like that."

"And Lynne's not trying at all," said Alice disapprovingly. "I'm sure Berry could leg-yield a bit."

But David's cries of, "Sit up, feel the inside rein, turn her head in a little. Now, push the quarters out, but keep going on the same circle," were given in vain. Giggling and shrieking, Lynne charged about the centre of the school.

"All right, take back your stirrups and pull them up for jumping," said David wearily. "Next time everyone who's mastered leg-yielding can go on to shoulder-in."

"At last," said Paul, pulling up his stirrups.

"*I* wish we could start shoulder-in today," snapped Lesley, who didn't really like jumping.

"We're going to do some cantering before we jump," David told them. "As you know, I don't believe in slowing the canter too soon. Some of our ponies are too green, and not many of our riders are sitting deep enough for a school canter. If we try to force it, you'll all be holding the ponies back with the reins and they'll go behind the bit. So we'll stick with the cross-country canter for the moment; in your stirrups, riding forward, lots of impulsion."

They cantered fairly sedately at first, until David called to James to enlarge the school and then go fast down the long sides and slowly along the short ones. They flew round, most of the riders and ponies enjoying themselves, though Bowie was becoming excited, and Sarah was yelling, "Steady, Bowie, steady!" in a far from calming voice.

"Ride forward," David shouted to her. "Remember that you can only control lively ponies by riding forward.

213

Come on, Sarah, use your legs, put him on the bit. You're not on Chess now."

"I know I'm not on Chess. I'd be dead stupid if I didn't," said Sarah as loudly as she dared. David pretended not to hear.

After the cantering, they trotted over the cavaletti five or six times and then they started jumping. "Straight round the course," said David. "Keep going smoothly, circle if you get out of control."

"I wish we could have the jumps six inches higher," grumbled James as he warmed up. Circling Ferdie, he set off on a neat, controlled round. Hanif, who was next, also went clear, but Jupiter rushed round treating the fences with contempt; taking off anywhere, he made huge careless leaps.

"Disgraceful," said Hanif, riding back with a crestfallen expression. "He's so arrogant, he thinks he knows everything about showjumping and totally ignores me."

"Yes, he's the sort who breaks your neck over a two foot fence," agreed David. And your schooling has to progress a stage further before you can control him. Showjumping demands a better balanced, more obedient horse than the basic cross-country stage we reached at Easter. But even when he's schooled you'll have to pick large, solid, well-built courses for Jupiter. These very bold horses despise small, flimsy jumps."

Saffron was flying round happily. The three feet fences suited him and Alice. Netti followed her, jumping round with equal ease. Banjo was next. He knew the fences well and jumped them all with his straight up and down, stag-like leaps. They were quite an effort for a pony of his size, but Paul knew exactly how to ride him. He was followed by sober, serious Rajah who peered at each fence cautiously, and Lizzie had to ride hard to get her clear round. Rupert rammed his crash cap on hard and, getting Rosie going at a brisk pace, followed his sister. Mealy nose poked out, and her large toad eyes full of alarm, Rosie took off too late and crashed through the first jump.

"Sorry, that was ony the practice jump," announced Rupert, circling.

"If some kind person would put it up, I'll start again."

"Make sure she's 'listening' to you *before* you start," called David. "Impulsion on its own is not enough. Luckily it was a good heavy pole," he went on, as Lizzie and Netti ran to restore the jump.

Rosie, rather shaken by her crash, concentrated carefully and jumped a clear round at her second attempt. Rupert rode back patting her enthusiastically. "That reminded her how to take off," he announced triumphantly.

"She's coming on," agreed David. "She jumps off her forehand, but that's due to her conformation so we can't change it. Still, there've been quite a few famous horses who jumped the same way, though they're never very comfortable rides. Luckily, sticking on isn't one of your problems."

"'His legs are so long and so aptly constructed,'" quoted Netti.

David looked round at the remaining riders. "Sarah, do you want to go at this height or a bit lower?" he asked.

"I don't want them any *lower*," snapped Sarah in a rude voice. "Bowie's a *good* jumper; he's won masses of rosettes."

"That doesn't stop you jumping low fences until you've got the feel of him," David pointed out mildly. "Off you go then."

Sarah, used to sturdy, sleepy Chess, gave Bowie a sharp kick, and the thin-skinned little bay laid back his ears resentfully. As she turned him for the first jump, Sarah kicked again and this time the pony stopped dead and began to run backwards, napping towards the other ponies.

"Oh, come on, Sarah, give him a whack." Mrs Rooke, wearing a beige dress, came hurrying from the paddock where she had been watching Julian. Sarah whacked Bowie hard. He retaliated with a half rear, swung round,

215

reared again and then ran backwards even faster, as Sarah's kicks thudded against his ribs.

"Stop kicking!" David roared at her. Then he limped over and spoke quietly. "Look, Sarah, I've told you dozens of times that good riders don't kick and that you should teach your pony to obey a light, invisible aid. When you had Chess you wouldn't listen and now you've bought a sensitive, well-schooled pony who's used to being given light aids. He's been schooled by a good rider and he's far too sensitive to be ridden by a beginner. If you won't change your ways you're going to ruin him. He won't stand for whacking and kicking and general roughness. If you go on like this you'll have a battle on your hands, and he'll win."

Sarah sat sullen and silent. David turned to the other members. "Could we have those jumps down about six inches, please," he asked. "I can't help," he added with an angry look at his limp arm.

"Now, Lesley," David went on when the jumps were ready. "I know Stardust *can* do the three feet fences, but she doesn't really enjoy them, so I'd rather see her racing round a lower course and building up her confidence. She's the opposite of Jupiter."

Lesley cantered Stardust round. She was going very smoothly and calmly.

"Don't put her to sleep," called David, "we want a bit more life. Try cantering faster and slower as we did round the school."

"You all canter these circles before you start," David turned back to the other members, "and it *looks* very professional, but I sometimes wonder if you have any idea what you're doing. You ought to be checking that your pony's wide awake, full of impulsion, supple, obedient, on the bit, and not resisting you in any way. You certainly shouldn't be calming him down to the point where his hindlegs are trailing behind him, as Lesley was. Nor should you canter round and round with a wrong bend as Paul does."

Lesley had woken Stardust up and they started full of energy. David called to Sarah, who was cantering a circle, to follow her sister and to sit still and try and *learn* from her pony. Bowie, seeing his stable companion ahead, set off willingly, and Sarah sat still and let him carry her round.

"Good," shouted David. "That was well-ridden, Lesley. Sarah, we've got to get you using your legs correctly on the flat, then you won't have any problems jumping. You see, you have to use your legs quietly and every stride on a sensitive pony, you must never surprise him with a great kick out of the blue. Do you understand?"

"Yes," Sarah scowled as she rode away. "I *hate* sensitive ponies," she told Paul and Netti.

"But David." Mrs Rooke had hurried forward.

"Half a sec, we haven't had Lynne round the jumps yet," said David, waving his good arm.

Lynne kicked Berry into an uncontrolled canter. She got over the first fence, jumped the corner of the second, ran out of the third. Laughing cheerfully, Lynne circled away from the fence and then ran out again. "Berry hates the tyres, she *really* hates them. I always have a job to get her over," she told David with a giggle.

"Well *don't* circle her away from the fence. When she runs out stop her dead and turn her back into the jump. It's bad riding to run out. Now, try again and this time have a dead refusal. Then, when she finds she's not going to be allowed to run out, she might *begin* to think about jumping. She might make plans to take off." David spoke in a patient, bored voice. He'd told Lynne so often before. Why bother to repeat himself, if she was too pigheaded to listen?

Lynne tried again, holding Berry into the fence. The roan pony refused.

"Good, now a short run, left rein, right leg. Keep her straight and she should go," said David.

Berry did go, with a large unseating leap. Lynne lost both stirrups and her crash cap, but she was still laughing as she rode on round the course. As soon as they turned for home and the other ponies, Berry began to jump willingly—the height was no problem to her.

"She ought to have had a clear, we practise round these jumps enough," said Paul critically. "But Berry's not much of a jumper. Luckily Lynne doesn't mind; she likes grooming and that sort of thing."

Mrs Rooke had gained David's attention. "He's a good pony, a first-class jumper. He's won over sixty rosettes—I saw them with my own eyes. Surely we can get him going better than this?" She protested, "I expected to see Sarah flying round a big course, not jumping two-feet-six with Lesley and Lynne."

"Get her riding correctly and she will fly round," answered David. "You've bought a good pony and she must learn to ride him. She can't go on flapping and tugging like a gymkhana kid, he's a sensitive, thin-skinned pony and he's not going to stand for rough aids. She'll have real trouble if she doesn't improve her riding."

"You mean she should just sit there quietly?" asked Mrs Rooke. "But that's not Sarah, she's always been such a live wire, always got the stickiest ponies over. I'm sure Bowie's only trying it on. New ponies do, don't they? I expect, as you say, they've got to get used to each other, and it's wiser to keep the jumps low for a day or two."

David sighed as he turned away. "Now I want to talk to you about the next three weeks of the holidays," he said, looking at the pony club members. "So could you all come a bit nearer, please."

"We've been invited, no, it was more of a challenge, to take part in a competition," he went on as they gathered round, "but I wanted to see how the ponies were going before I gave my O.K. Having seen them, *I'm* quite happy about it, but the final decision is up to you as you'll have to give a lot of time to practice and training."

"Decision about what?" asked James, as David paused.

"Shush, he's coming to it," said Lizzie.

"It's a junior Tetrathlon competition," David went on. "The Cranford Vale Pony Club are running it and they said, rather condescendingly, that we could enter as many teams as we liked and gain some experience. They're inviting all the pony clubs in Area Ten.

"Tetrathlon?" The pony club members looked at each other.

"You run, ride, shoot and swim," David told them. "The teams are to be of either boys or girls, you're not supposed to mix the sexes. The shooting is fairly elementary. You use air pistols, and the Woodbury Rifle Club say they can find me an instructor. The riding phase is a mile-long cross-country, no fence over three feet. The swimming is up to the individual, as many lengths as he or she can do in three minutes. The running is across country, fifteen hundred metres—that's less than a mile."

"What's the age limit?" asked James.

"Under fifteen," answered David. "I know you'll all enjoy the cross-country riding," he went on. "Shooting, well you're either a good shot or you're not. The question is whether you're prepared to train for the running and swimming. I can't do much about that."

"And can they all swim?" asked Mrs Rooke.

"I hate cross-country runs," groaned Hanif.

"Rupert always gets lost when he does them at school," said Lizzie.

"I wish it was showjumping," grumbled Paul.

"Or a junior one day event," added James.

"I'd be willing," said Netti, "If anyone else wants to make up a team."

"*Can't* we do the Prince Philip?" whined Sarah.

"Not this year," David answered patiently. "Janet Green's going to start training a team for next year in the autumn. As for the main interbranch competitions, you're simply not good enough, but when you're all sixteen and the owners of large horses we'll see what we can do."

219

"Does it mean lots of cross-country riding practices?" asked Alice.

"Yes, I'll fit in as many as I can."

"That would make even running worthwhile," said Alice, looking at Hanif who seemed depressed.

"I wouldn't mind shooting and I'm not bad at swimming." James's voice suddenly became enthusiastic. "And there's a boy at my school who's coming to live over here; I think he'd join the Woodbury if there was something like this to go in for. He's quite a good rider, he's got his own pony, and he's a brilliant swimmer. If Seb joined we'd have quite a decent boys' team."

"And we've got a *very* good girls' team," said Mrs Rooke. "Sarah, Netti, Alice and one other. It's either three or four to a team."

"Then, if we could find Tina a pony we could have two girls' teams," suggested Alice.

"And we've got four boys already, without this Seb," said Paul, who saw himself being pushed into a very junior team with Oliver and Julian.

"We won't begin by deciding the teams," said David. "The first question is who wants to do it? The second, *can* you do it, or are any of you going away for holidays?"

"Not till September," answered James.

"Not at all, our parents are too broke," announced Rupert.

"My aunt offered to send me somewhere, but I said I'd rather stay here and ride Saffy," explained Alice. "I'd like to do it, David, only I've never tried shooting."

"Nor have we," said Lizzie.

"All right," said David. "We'll put it this way. Hands up everyone who would like to start training, with an escape clause that you can opt out at the end of a week if you hate it."

James, Netti and Alice put their hands up at once. The Rookes, getting an angry glare from their mother, added theirs. The older Wheelers looked at each other and raised theirs doubtfully. Lynne said, "We'd better, Paul, if everyone else is doing it."

"It's all right for you," Paul told her grumpily. "You're good at swimming." But he put his hand up.

Alice felt rather sad that Hanif had waited until last and then raised his hand with such obvious reluctance.

"Is it because you hate going in teams?" she asked, as Mrs Rooke counted the hands officiously.

"No," Hanif shook his head.

"Of course, they're sure to beat us easily," said James. "The Cranford Vale are good at everything and they've probably been training for years."

"Years," agreed David cheerfully. "They're a large and very well-run pony club, but that's no reason for us to put off starting *our* training any longer, is it?"

"No, and who cares if we're beaten," demanded Netti, "so long as we're all brilliant at cross-country."

"Have you put Tina down?" Alice asked Mrs Rooke.

"Look out, Cranford Vale, here we come," said Rupert, who had dismounted and was flexing his muscles and jogging on the spot.

"And when do we start the training?" enquired James.

"As soon as I've got my barley in," answered David. "There's a mounted rally next week, anyway, and as soon as I've found a shooting instructor and got hold of some pistols I'll let you know. Meanwhile, you are all to start swimming and running."

CHAPTER THREE

"I Hate Him!"

"There's a new jump." Paul was greeting everyone with the news when they met the following week. "A proper bank, sleeper-faced and quite high. Dad and Gary, our farm pupil, made it. Well, David helped too; he had the bulldozer fitted to his tractor."

"Sleeper-faced—you mean like the one at Badminton?" asked Lizzie, looking anxious.

"Yes, not as big, but it looks really horrible," answered Lynne. "Berry'll never jump it, not in a million years."

"Rosie might do a natural one, but I should think she'll fall straight on her nose at the sight of a *sleeper-faced* one," said Rupert despondently.

"Yes, it does look a bit stark and new," admitted Paul. "I don't think any of them are going to like it much."

"A bank? Oh, great." James was delighted. "I've never jumped one. Have you, Seb?" He turned to the slim boy riding a skewbald of about 14.2 who had arrived with him.

Seb shook his head. "No, never had the chance."

"Oh, by the way, this is Seb Fuller," James introduced his friend proudly. "He's living at Kiddleworth, up on the downs."

"Only for the holidays," Seb told them, looking down at his pony's half-white, half-chestnut mane. "My father's rented a cottage."

"You are lucky," said Alice. "Masses of lovely rides right on your doorstep."

"It's all right, I suppose. But I'd much rather have stayed where we were." Seb's voice was full of sadness and no one knew what to say. An embarrassed silence fell.

Netti broke it. "What's your pony called?"

"Jigsaw."

"I like his chestnut head and his star."

This time James broke the silence. "Has anyone done any tetrathlon training?" he asked.

The Wheelers looked at each other guiltily.

"We made a resolution to run round our fields every morning, but we haven't kept it up," admitted Lizzie in a worried voice.

"We've been swimming once, but we were too long, and my mother got fed up of sitting in Woodbury pool car park, so she's refused to take us again," added Rupert.

"My stepfather is having a keep-fit craze. He's made me go jogging with him three mornings *before* breakfast," said Hanif with a shudder.

"Poor old Harry. Still, it'll sound terribly virtuous if David asks. What about you, Alice?"

"I've run through the wood to the ford and back twice. And I persuaded my aunt to drop me at the pool while she shopped, so I've had one swim."

"I've had two swims," James told them. "And I've run whenever I've had to go down the orchards with a message for my father, but I don't think that really counts."

"We haven't done much either," Paul admitted. "Lynne keeps making excuses, and I hate running on my own."

"I hate running—full stop," said Rupert. "I don't think David's going to be very pleased with our lack of keenness."

"No, he was a bit sharp with *us*," agreed Lynne. "He said he'd kept his side of the bargain—buying pistols, finding the lady from the rifle club and building the bank—but we weren't keeping ours. Mum took us swimming on Sunday to calm him down a bit."

"Here are the Rookes," said Paul, mounting. "David said I was to take you to Coppice Hill as soon as everyone had come."

"Hang on, I think it's only Lesley," said Hanif, standing in his stirrups. "No, it's O.K., the others are trailing along behind."

"I expect there's been a lot of pecking and cawing in the Rookery," said Rupert with relish.

"Hello, Tina. What are you doing on Chess?" asked Netti.

"Sarah's lending him to me for the cross-country. Aren't I lucky?" said Tina, smiling all over her thin, freckled face. "Julian didn't want to ride."

"David won't let him train for the Tetrathlon, and he was longing to shoot, so he's furious and wouldn't come," Sarah told them.

"Quite right too," said James. "There are enough of us as it is, we don't want a lot of D ride people holding things up."

"Hear, hear," said Paul, setting off down the farm track.

The bank had been built in the second of the valley fields, and they were all standing round it giving cries of horror when David, tooting the Land Rover horn, drove over to collect them.

"Come on, schooling first," he said.

"It looks ghastly, are we going to get over it?" asked Alice.

"Of course you are. Harry's the only one who's going to have any trouble, answered David. "He has to persuade Jupiter not to jump the whole thing." Then he saw Seb. "Hallo, you must be Sebastian Fuller. Welcome to the Woodbury."

"Thanks," answered Seb, gazing down at Jigsaw's mane.

Alice was studying Seb from a safe distance. He was quite nice-looking, she thought. Tall and slim with brown hair and brown eyes, a normal sort of nose and a very wide mouth, but he didn't look at all happy. He's wishing he wasn't here, she thought. He doesn't like the Woodbury at all.

David waited impatiently while his ride formed up.

"You'd better follow me, Seb," advised James, as he started to walk round the school.

"You go next." Alice held Saffron back to let Hanif go ahead of her. "I was first of us last time." The Wheelers allowed Sarah to go ahead of them without a murmur, while, at the back of the ride, Tina and Lynne argued about who should go last.

Except for James, the pony club members were all wondering how well Seb rode and whether Jigsaw was better schooled than the Woodbury ponies. So, as they trotted round, circling and serpentining, they were too busy trying to catch sly glimpses of the newcomer to concentrate properly, and David's roars about wrong bends grew fiercer and fiercer.

He's not all that superior, thought Alice. In fact, he fits in rather well. He's about the same standard as James, and though *he* was miles ahead of the rest of us at the beginning of last holidays, we've all been catching up. And, though Jigsaw's well-schooled and well-behaved, his dressage isn't exceptional—he doesn't suddenly look elegantly poetic like Stardust does.

When all the ponies were going well and most of the riders were using their legs to his satisfaction, David called the ride to a halt and announced that they would try shoulder-in.

"This, as you know, is a suppling exercise," he began, "and it's one of those exercises which you go on using for the rest of your pony's life. Some movements are used simply to teach the pony to obey the legs. The turn on the forehand and leg-yielding, for instance, show him that the rider's legs can mean 'move sideways' or 'take a longer stride with your hindleg', that they don't always mean 'go faster'. *And*, once the lesson is learned, these movements can be given up. But I'm sure you've all seen the international showjumping riders using shoulder-in to supple their horses before they go into the ring and, done correctly, it is a very valuable exercise. O.K?"

He looked round at the members' faces.

"Yes, so far," answered Hanif cautiously.

"Right. We'll begin by carrying out the movement along the hedge side of the school. As you come round the corner you will increase your cornering aids so that the pony remains in the slightly bent position. But then, by feeling the outside rein, by sitting deep and using the upper leg, and by looking where you want to go, you will guide him down the school track in that bent position. Do you understand?"

The pony club members were moving their arms and legs, trying to work out the aids and looking puzzled.

"This is one of those moments when it would save hours of talking if I could get on a pony and *show* you," said David bitterly. "But let's have a try and see what happens. Remember, it's not leg-yielding. You're bending the pony as though he was circling and riding down the track in that position. Don't ask for too much bend and, once you've got one, concentrate on looking where you want to go and on the pony's inside hindleg, which will be doing all the work."

David began to limp towards the corner of the school. "We'll try the best of the leg-yielders first," he said. "James, Lizzie, Lesley, Alice and Netti. Lead on at the walk, James. Along the short side, allow a couple of lengths between you. Now, as you come round the corner *hold* that bend."

The first attempt wasn't very successful. David was roaring at James to *bend* Ferdie; at Lizzie to sit up and look where she was going; at Alice, Lesley and Netti to sit deep and *ride* their ponies instead of drifting about the middle of the school.

"All right. Circle, half the school, and we'll try again," he said. "Lizzie, you're *not* helping your pony by looking back and down. Remember that looking where you want to go is an *aid*; it tells him something. You're giving mad aids to the wretched animal. Lesley, Alice and Netti, you don't just sit there and let your ponies come into the centre of the school, you explain that you want them to go on down the track. *Show* them what you want with your right rein, take the hand a little sideways, *lead* them down the track with it. O.K., try again."

This time the riders had more idea of what they wanted and began to convey it to the ponies. They all stayed on the track and kept their bends for a few strides. "Good, well done. Pat him," David was shouting. All right, I think you've got it. Ride on and try once more."

He turned back to the watching riders. "They are all doing it a bit. Can you see it? Have you got the idea?"

"It's penetrating slowly," answered Hanif.

"Don't ask for too much bend and don't go on for too long," David told them. "If your pony does a couple of steps, pat him and let him walk on."

The first seven riders were looking pleased with themselves and patting their ponies enthusiastically, when David called them into the centre for a rest and sent the other seven on their way.

"You're not going to like it, Rupert, it does killing things to your legs," James told him as they passed.

"Yes," agreed Alice, dismounting gratefully. "I remember from last holidays, dressage kills your legs above the knee and cross-country kills them below."

Sarah was leading the second ride and as she came round the corner she turned Bowie's head in and held him in position so firmly that he stopped dead.

"Keep going!" shouted David, as the pony rolled his eyes and backed into the hedge. "Ride on, Sarah, don't lose your impulsion." But Sarah would only battle with the pony, shouting, "Bowie!" in an angry voice as the other riders piled up round her.

"Clear the course," said Hanif.

"Don't mind me," remarked Seb in a sarcastic voice, as Bowie backed into Jigsaw.

"Sarah, *will* you circle and join on behind," roared David ferociously, at last having some effect.

They tried again with Hanif leading. He was persuading Jupiter to bend, but the pony was jogging to avoid having to take an energetic stride with his inside hindleg. Jigsaw was bending too, but he was moving without impulsion, and Seb was roared at for looking down. Rosie's first reaction was to open her mouth and charge off to escape from the whole problem, but Rupert stopped her, circled and tried again. Chess was merely bending his neck, Berry was trotting about the centre of the school, and Paul was tying himself in knots, drawing up his legs and leaning to one side as he tried to force Banjo into the correct position.

"Halt," called David. "Come in to the centre, all of you. You're so awful I'll have to look at you one at a time. You start, Harry. Seb, allow about six lengths before you follow. Sarah, you go last, but don't get on Berry's tail."

Jupiter jogged again. "Try a half-halt and then straight into shoulder-in," suggested David. "Seb, you've got the bend, but no impulsion. Sit deep, get his inside leg working. Rupert, that's not bad. Pat her. Remember it's difficult for Rosie and don't go on too long. Sit deep, Tina, you're only bending his neck. Lynne, did you hear what I said about using the outside hand? Of course if you just give the aids to turn, she comes into the centre. Give the aids for *shoulder-in*. Take your right hand to the right. Sit up, Paul, you're making it impossible for yourself."

Sarah, scowling ferociously, came last. "The most important thing is to maintain your impulsion," David told her. "So keep going at all costs and just ask for a little bend. It's no use losing your temper with the pony. Try to explain more clearly. It's the rider's fault if the pony doesn't understand."

When everyone had produced some slight bend, the whole ride formed up and tried on the other rein. Most of the older members were doing quite well. Ferdinand, Rajah, Stardust, Saffron and Tristram all received shouts of "Well *done*." Jupiter, Jigsaw and Rosie were all, "Much better." Only the last four collected roars of disapproval.

"Right," said David when he had called them to a halt. "I think you all know what you're *supposed* to be doing, but it's obvious to me that only the riders who are sitting deep are getting results. I know it seems boringly fussy to go on

228

and on about how you should sit, but an incorrect seat will hold you back all through your riding career and make it very difficult for you to school horses successfully. But, if you do take the trouble to get it right, everything else will begin to fall into place." He looked at Sarah and the Robertses as he finished, but Sarah scowled and Lynne giggled in reply.

"Now, I've bad news for you," David went on, turning to the other end of the ride. Though we've been explaining shoulder-in to the ponies at the walk, it is normally ridden at the sitting trot."

"At the trot?" James sounded disbelieving.

"Oh David, we can't, we'll never do it at the trot," objected Lizzie.

"Where's the SPPCM inspector?" demanded Rupert, looking round wildly. "They're never there when you need them."

"It's all a question of sitting deep," said David. "Lead on, James. The last four can wait and then try at the walk, but the rest of you prepare to trot on. Trot on, and sitting trot as you come into the corner."

At the first attempt the whole ride failed and found themselves being carried across the school. But they rode on round, and the second time, sitting down grimly and struggling to use their hands independently, they all managed a few steps.

"Change the rein," called David, "and try again. Sit deep, ride those ponies. Half-halt, Harry," he roared as they came to the corner. "Good Lesley. And Alice. Yes, Netti. Some of you *are* getting the idea."

When he had called the trotting ride into the centre and sent the walkers out for another try, David, who seemed to have lost interest in the walkers, said, "I want you to do a little shoulder-in every time you ride. Out hacking, anywhere. Just a few steps and then lots of praise and patting so that the ponies enjoy it."

"At the walk or trot?" asked James.

"The walk for the moment, then we'll see how the

trotting goes at the next rally. Now, shorten your stirrups, please."

"Saffron looked quite different when you were shoulder-inning," Hanif told Alice as they pulled up their leathers. "He suddenly became powerful and really rather handsome. I could see what David means by impulsion.

"It *felt* gorgeous for about ten seconds," answered Alice. "I began to feel that advanced dressage might be almost as exciting as jumping, if you rode really well."

"It couldn't be as exciting as cross-country," objected Hanif.

"Yes it could, there's much more to dressage than just whizzing over things," snapped Lesley.

"Whizzing over things becomes immensely complicated if you've got a pony like Jupe," argued Hanif.

"A lot depends on your pony," said Rupert. "Stardust likes dressage and is good at it, but Rosie-of-the-trailing-hocks will never be good at it, according to David, and I ought to take up hurdling."

"Stop chattering and form up the ride," said David.

They cantered round with their cross-country seats until all the ponies had settled down and were going well, and then David announced that they would do the hill a couple of times.

"I want to make sure that Jigsaw and Bowie know how to come down," he explained. "I haven't brought the flags, so we'll have to put some oil drums round as markers. Could I have a volunteer to come round with me in the Land Rover, please. And, while we're doing that, the rest of you can explain the object of the hill to Seb."

Lizzie and Alice found pony holders and both went with David. Lizzie took down the slip rails into the second field, and Alice collected four drums that had been left under the hedge.

"There's nothing to it," James told Seb as they jogged into the second field to inspect the bank. "You ride along the valley, turn uphill when you get to that drum they've just dropped, go outside the one they're about to drop, keep going along the hillside round the next drum, straight down, and halt beside the final drum."

"You're supposed to keep the same pace the whole way," Hanif added. "That's the problem. The first time I did it I ended up in the hedge."

"What pace?" asked Seb.

"It depends on David's mood," Rupert told him.

"No it doesn't. We began at the trot and ended up at the canter, with jumps," Hanif explained.

"You have to sit forward and use your legs," added Lesley.

"Have we *all* got to jump the bank?" asked Tina, looking at its stout sleeper-faced sides in horror. "It looks much too solid for the little ponies."

"You'll be all right," Rupert comforted her. "Little ponies are born knowing how to jump natural fences. Harry and I are going to be the ones in trouble."

"It doesn't look a very natural jump to me," said Tina, turning slightly green.

David sent the ponies up and down the hillside at a trot first, with Bowie following Stardust, and Jigsaw behind Netti. Sarah seemed nervous and held Bowie on a tight rein despite David's roars. Seb, wearing a very determined expression, used his legs as directed and managed to halt only a few feet past the drum.

"It was steeper than I expected," he said as he joined the other riders in the valley. "It gives you a bit of a shock."

"You get used to it," Hanif told him. "On the last day of the course last holidays we were all cantering down from the very top."

"Round twice at the canter," said David. "But be sensible, stop if anything goes wrong."

The ponies and riders enjoyed flying round the hillside, and the pony club members began to feel much braver now that their blood was up.

"Can we do the bank, David?" they asked, gathering round the Land Rover. "Please, David."

"No, never begin with a new fence, that's asking for trouble. Warm up over the old and familiar," said David. "If you want the sort of pony that jumps new fences first go, you have to introduce them carefully. When I'm through the slip rails will someone put them up, please? You can jump them, the old stickheap and the uphill log. You go first, Harry, James second and Sarah third; after that I don't mind."

Except that Sarah had to circle Bowie, who got going too fast after the slip rails, no one had any trouble. And when they all jogged back across the field, chattering cheerfully, Alice noticed that there was an occasional smile on Seb's sad face.

"Why can't we have a more natural-looking bank?" complained Sarah. "I hate those horrible straight sides; it's like a box."

"What happens if we fall off sideways?" asked Rupert cheerfully.

"Or try to jump the whole thing."

"Shut up, you're putting me off." Tina dropped her reins and put her fingers in her ears.

"Get into a tidy line and I'll explain," said David, climbing down from the Land Rover. "The first thing to remember is that a bank is two jumps. Number one is up, number two is down. So, as in all combinations, grids ecetera, you ride for the last fence. You think about the down, you look over the bank, beyond the bank to wherever the next fence is. What you don't do is to let the pony dwell, or stop, on the top. Straight on, straight off. Apart from that it's like any other jump. Approach with impulsion and don't let them run out. Any questions?"

The pony club members looked at each other doubtfully.

"Supposing I get stuck on top?" asked Rupert.

"You use your legs, and if that doesn't work I give you advance permission to yell, whack or kick," answered David. "You look where you want to go, but never down. There *is* one other thing," he went on. "If you go to

232

Ireland and jump natural banks you take them slowly. Partly because they can crumble under your weight, but mainly because there may be a sleeping pig or, worse still, a harrow, lying on the landing side." David settled himself on his shooting stick. "Right, James, are you going to show them the way?"

"O.K., but I don't think Ferdie's done one before." James circled and came up to the bank briskly. Ferdie jumped up easily, but then stopped dead and looked with horror at the drop.

"Legs," yelled David. "Go on, get off." And with a wild flurry of arms and legs they did.

"Well done. Go again and this time come straight off."

Ferdie, knowing what to expect this time, banked neatly. Hanif was circling, ready to go next.

"Now steady. You've walked the course, Jupiter hasn't. You have to tell him, with a half-halt, that there's a problem ahead. Don't just sit there and let him race into trouble."

"Steady, Jupe, look before you leap," said Hanif soothingly, and slowed the powerful pony to a trot. Jupiter took an enormous leap up, braked when he saw what lay ahead, summed up the problem in a moment and jumped down. Alice followed. Saffron slowed down, took a careful look at the bank, then he jumped up neatly, trotted across the top and popped down with no trouble at all. Alice patted him gratefully as Lizzie set off. She rode Rajah in a very determined manner, but he insisted on slowing up and inspecting the bank from a standstill. Lizzie, exasperated by this caution, said, "Oh Ra, don't be so stupid!" and gave him a whack. The sturdy chestnut promptly heaved himself up on the bank with a very unseating jump. Lizzie lost both stirrups and clung round his neck. Rajah saw that he was surrounded by drops and stood snorting with disapproval. "Oh, come on, Ra." Lizzie brandished her whip and they lurched down; she was still stirrupless.

"Well done," shouted David.

233

Nettie followed her sister, and grey Tristram seemed to know exactly what to do and jumped on and off with brisk efficiency.

"If she can do it, so can we," said Seb, leaving the dithering group of waiting riders. "Come on, Jigsaw." The skewbald set off at a brisk canter, but at the last moment he saw that the jump was more complicated than he had thought and refused, sliding right into the sleepers. Seb shot up his neck, half landing on the bank, and then heaved himself back into the saddle. "None of that," he said and, landing Jigsaw a couple of hard whacks, he turned and rode him at the bank again, kicking vigorously. Jigsaw refused.

"Hold it," said David, as Seb swung round for a third attempt. "It's a new fence, he may never have seen one before; you should have let him have a look the first time he stopped. I think he's uncertain, rather than obstinate, so let's give him a lead. You follow James. Then we'll have Harry and Lizzie. Netti, you give your brother a lead. Lesley, follow Alice. Don't follow too close," he added as they found their pairs.

Ferdie jumped the bank perfectly, but Jigsaw, who followed him up, then stood teetering on the brink while David roared at Seb to look up and use his legs. Suddenly Jigsaw found the nerve to jump off and then, delighted by his own bravery, he galloped across the field, celebrating with a series of bucks. Jupiter jumped confidently and well, Rajah soberly, but without any fuss. Lesley gave Stardust a lead, but the Araby little chestnut lost heart at the last moment and refused. Lesley let her inspect the jump, then took her back quietly and tried again. This time Stardust heaved herself up in slow motion, walked across the top and heaved herself down on the far side.

"Too slow, try and bustle her up a bit next time," shouted David and turned to watch Tristram, who whipped over in copybook manner, and Rosie, who approached with large goggling eyes, leapt on boldly, looked round her in horror, turned and jumped down the way she had come up.

"Steer, and look where you *want* to go," David shouted at Rupert.

"At least it was original. Can I have another lead?" asked Rupert, ramming his cap on harder.

"Rosie really is the stupidest pony in the Woodbury Pony Club," said Netti in a forgiving voice. "I only hope Rupert finishes schooling her before I grow out of Tristram and have to take her on."

"I thought it was quite bright of her," shouted Rupert, circling. "She knew *this* side was safe. O.K., Seb, I'm ready." This time Rupert was prepared, he stopped Rosie turning and steered her firmly across the bank. She looked down with goggling eyes and then, deciding to follow Jigsaw, flung herself recklessly from the top.

"Terrific," shouted Rupert, as he rode back patting her. "Does anyone want a lead?"

"Yes, please, but what does it feel like?" asked Tina apprehensively. "It looks enormous from down here on Chess."

"It's good fun, rather like going on a switchback at a fair." Rupert looked at David, shouted, "Can we go next?" and was waved on.

Rosie, proud of her new accomplishment, flew over with a pair of dramatic leaps, but Chess refused.

"One more go and then I'll put some one else up," David threatened Tina. "Someone give Paul a lead."

Banjo's usual stag-like leap landed him on the bank and he had plenty of room to trot across and pop down on the far side.

"Well done," shouted David, and several people clapped.

"There, Banjo's done it first go; you're miles bigger and you made all that stupid fuss," Lizzie reproached Rajah.

"I think he'd have done it without a lead," said Paul, jumping off and patting the little black proudly. "Go on, Lynne, it's great. You'll love it."

"I'll give you a lead," offered Alice.

But Berry ran out, and Lynne, laughing helplessly, circled. "I'm not going to jump that in a million years," she shrieked, "Berry really hates it."

"You're not going to jump it in a million years because you're riding badly," roared David. "Why won't you listen . . ." Then he decided he was wasting his breath and turned to Sarah. "Do you want a lead? Can we have everyone again. The three who haven't done it take leads. Don't jump on each other's tails."

The ponies who had already jumped were racing over with evident pleasure, but Chess, ridden without much enthusiasm by Tina, refused. Berry ran out. Bowie, going last and following Netti, approached the fence cautiously. Sarah attacked him with a flurry of legs and whip, and the flustered pony leapt on to the bank at an angle and, slithering across, almost plunged over the side.

"Bowie!" shrieked Sarah, "Bowie!" as he teetered, scrabbling with his hoofs and fighting to get his balance.

"Sit *still*" roared David and then, as the pony found a firm foothold and stood trembling, he told her to calm him down.

"Talk to him, Sarah, pat him and then show him where he's supposed to be jumping down," said David quietly. But Sarah threw herself off. "I hate him," she stormed. "He's a stupid, clumsy, screwy pony; he's useless at cross-country."

"Sarah, Sarah," Mrs Rooke joined in. "You know that's not true, just think how many rosettes the pony has won."

"I expect it was all lies. It's not my fault if you were cheated; anyone can see he's useless at cross-country," Sarah screamed back.

David sighed. "This is when it really gets me," he said, looking down at his limp arm and lame leg. "Oh for the days when one could get up on a horse and prove one's point. Lizzie, could you get the lunge rein from the back of the Land Rover. James, hop up on the bank and buckle it on the snaffle ring. Sarah, cross your stirrups and put a knot in your reins, we're going to tow the pony down."

Lizzie towed, James led Bowie to the edge and made encouraging noises, Netti and Alice held out handfuls of pony nuts. Bowie, allowed to consider the matter calmly, decided that the drop wasn't as bad as he had feared, and jumped down nimbly. The waiting pony club members all made a fuss of him.

"Any volunteers to put the two refusers and Bowie over?" asked David.

"Yes, I'll try Chess," offered Paul.

"No, I want to put Chess over," screamed Sarah, jumping down from the bank and snatching her pony from Tina.

"Can I have a go on Berry?" asked Netti.

"And I wouldn't mind trying Bowie," said Alice.

"Alice recklessly sticking her neck out," teased Rupert.

"Alice the Amazon," added Hanif.

"I'd like to have a go on him," said James, "but I'm much too big."

"Leads, please. Netti and Berry first," decided David.

Netti was absolutely determined not to let Berry run out, and the pony, having tried a couple of swerves and found that this new rider had her firmly between hand and leg, suddenly gave in and followed Banjo over with no trouble at all.

Everyone cheered. "Well *done*, Netti."

David had sent Lesley to give Chess a lead. And Sarah, on her metal, for she had to show everyone that she could get a sensible pony over, rode like a whirlwind and Chess heaved himself up and down in Stardust's wake. No one cheered Sarah.

Then Alice, who had been riding round getting the feel of Bowie, asked, "Can I try without a lead first? He seems a very willing pony, not a bit obstinate. I like him."

"Right you are," agreed David, "but take him slowly and ride *straight*. Look where you *want* to go."

Alice rode at a slow canter, but, as they drew close, Bowie pricked his ears and accelerated of his own accord, and she only had to sit tight as he leapt lightly on and off with an air of complete confidence.

"He's clever," said Alice, riding back. "He was convinced he knew how to do it this time. He practically told me to shut up and leave it to him."

"I don't know what to make of this," worried Mrs Rooke. "Sarah's such a good little rider. She's always done so well in the past. Do you think we've let her stay on dear old Chess too long, David? Perhaps we should have made the break last year."

"I don't think that would have helped," answered David. "If Sarah wants to move up in the competition world she'll have to change her style, but I have a feeling that she'd rather have another year as a carefree gymkhana kid. It's a pity, you've got a good little pony there.

"Now," he turned back to the pony club members. "We'll jump it once from the opposite direction. Make sure your ponies know what you intend. Tell them, don't take them by surprise."

"Do you hear that?" Rupert leaned forward and whispered the instructions into Rosie's ears.

"And, as we've overrun our allotted time," added David, "any one who refuses or runs out will just have to end on a bad note, there will be *no* second tries."

Sarah was demanding a lead from Netti, Lynne had arranged to follow Paul. Tina was left holding Bowie as the long line of riders snaked round the field and then came cantering at the bank. Bursting with confidence and proud of their new skill, the ponies followed each other, leaping on and off with ease.

"Good," David was shouting, "Good." And he added, "Well *done*, Lynne," as Berry, coming last, hopped neatly over.

Tina watched them sadly. You had your chance and you bungled it, she told herself. You were the only person who didn't jump the bank. And now it looked as though Sarah meant to ride Chess home. I suppose Lesley will lead Bowie and I'll go in the car with Mrs Rooke, she thought drearily as she led him towards the group of triumphant, blowing ponies. Then she stopped. "Stand," she told Bowie as she mounted. "I'm going to give up being gutless, *I'm* going to ride you home."

"And now we've to pay for our glorious bank-jumping," Rupert was moaning. "Back here on Friday for this revolting running."

"It'll do you good," Lesley snapped at him. "You'll know how Rosie feels when *she* has to gallop uphill."

"I know already, she hates it as much as I do," Rupert answered, "but at least she's got four legs."

"Don't forget that we begin with shooting," said Alice, "and that could be fun."

CHAPTER FOUR

Guns Are Dangerous

It felt very odd, thought Alice, to be going to Garland Farm by car, without a pony and clutching a bag of swimming things. Mrs Franklin, who was driving them, wasn't wearing a sari but a pink blouse and a fashionable denim skirt and looked like all the other pony club mothers. Well, she thought, all of them except for Mrs Rooke, whose clothes were always very old-fashioned and dull; worse than Aunt Margaret's. Alice was wearing shorts, ready for the running. Harry was dressed in jeans, but as his holdall looked even fatter than hers she decided that he was carrying his running clothes.

"It's going to be exciting finding out who's good at other things," she said, turning to talk to him in the back. "We only know each other as riders."

"You mean it may change the whole peck order of the pony club, that Lizzie or Lynne will suddenly become our leader instead of James?" suggested Hanif.

"No, nothing as dramatic as that, because I expect James is good at other things too. I guess he's a good all-rounder."

"Yes, he looks irritatingly pleased with himself like all good all-rounders," agreed Hanif, a jealous note creeping into his voice.

"I think James is a very nice boy; he is kind and sensible," said Mrs Franklin reprovingly. "You should not be jealous of him. He is older than you, so of course he is better at sport."

"Yes, Mum, but I do *hate* all this competition, this picking of teams; it makes people like the Rookes worse than ever."

240

Mrs Halford, of the Woodbury Rifle Club, was plump, brisk and confident with short, grey hair, and dressed in greenish trousers and a pale yellow anorak. She had arrived early and, as the pony club members drifted into the farmyard, they found her bustling about with string and targets, turning the half-empty Dutch barn into a firing range.

David, sitting on his shooting stick and watching helplessly, called to them. "James, Seb, can you come and move these bales for Mrs Halford? Alice and Harry, you take over the reel of string and fix it to divide the watchers from the shooters."

"Why don't we shoot outside, it'd be far less trouble?" commented James.

"Because of the breeze," answered Mrs Halford briskly. "The air pistol pellet has a low muzzle velocity and is badly affected by wind and rain. Grab the other end of this measure, would you? You pony club juniors have to stand seven metres from the targets, which will be pinned to those frames. We will fire towards the stack of straw bales; they'll absorb the pellets, while a wall would cause them to ricochet." She turned to Paul and Lynne who'd appeared carrying two small card tables, "Put them up opposite the targets, please, and with the far side exactly on the seven metre line."

She inspected Hanif and Alice's string barrier. "Good. That'll keep the general public out of the firing line."

Hanif laughed, "There are only about two mums."

"And Ollie and Julian, looking for trouble because David won't let *them* shoot," added Rupert, who was inspecting the arrangements suspiciously.

"*And* all the competitors waiting their turns," said Mrs Halford. "It'll be a long-drawn-out business with only two pistols, and it's impossible to shoot well if your concentration is broken by people chattering round you."

By the time the range was ready, with the targets pinned to their frames and the two pistols lying on their tables, each with a box of pellets beside it, everyone had arrived—including Tina, who said she hoped it was all right if she trained, though she had no pony to ride in the actual competition.

"Of course," David answered, getting to his feet. "Will everyone sit down and stop talking, please," he shouted to be heard above the chatter. "Now," he went on when they were silent and seated. "I want to introduce Mrs Halford, a member of the Woodbury Rifle Club who's very kindly giving up her time to come and help us. She's an expert shot and shoots regularly in competitions so she does know what she's talking about. As I know nothing about the correct drill I want you all to listen very carefully, so, when we practise without her, we'll know exactly what to do. Guns, even air pistols, are dangerous, so we must be very careful and take this section of the tetrathlon seriously. Right, Mrs Halford, over to you," he added and, limping to the nearest straw bale, sat down.

"The first thing I want to talk about is the legal position," began – Mrs Halford briskly. "The laws connected with air pistols. First of all it is illegal for anyone to carry a *loaded* pistol in a public place or on private land unless you have permission. If you are over fourteen but under seventeen you may not buy a pistol or ammunition. You may be loaned one, but you must only carry it about firmly shut in a box or gun cover.

"If you are under fourteen, and I believe that most of you are, you may not even be loaned a pistol, but you *can* shoot as a member of an approved club or at home or at a friend's house, provided you are being supervised by someone over twenty-one. It's important to remember these points as none of us wants trouble with the police.

"Now we come to safety. First of all, never, never point a gun at anyone. Doesn't matter if it's unloaded, these pistols aren't toys and you mustn't play with them. Never leave a loaded gun unattended even for a second, someone else may pick it up and not realize it's loaded. A younger brother or sister might play with it and press the trigger. When you are pointing a gun always do so down

242

the range or in a safe direction. When you carry a gun about in your hand it must be unloaded and pointed at the ground. When you are taking it from place to place it *must* be carried in a bag or box. Now, any questions?"

"It'll be years and years before I can have my own pistol then," said Oliver in disgusted tones. "I call that really mean."

"Oh, I don't know, the authorities don't mind you shooting, but they don't think you're old enough to have the worry and responsibility of a pistol. That's not mean, surely?" asked Mrs Halford. "Now, let's begin. Has anyone shot before?"

"Yes," James and Seb leapt to their feet and hurried forward to take up the pistols. They loaded and then, taking his pistol in two hands, James crouched, looking like an American cop on the television.

"No, no," said Mrs Halford, hurrying over. "This is a competition, you have to fire from an erect standing position. You are not allowed to support the pistol-holding hand or arm. Stand up straight, feet apart, extend your arm. Turn your shoulder towards the target. That's better. Now, look along your arm and *squeeze* the trigger." James fired, and Seb, who had copied his position, fired a moment or two later, just as James was starting forward to inspect his target. Mrs Halford grabbed him quickly.

"There, now you can see how accidents happen," she told him, and, turning to the watching pony club members said, "To avoid this we must have a very strict firing drill. It may sound rather absurd to do everything on an order when you're merely practising, but from the safety point of view it's essential, and if you practise the correct drill at home you won't have any trouble remembering it when you take part in competitions. The orders are: "Load. Are you ready? Stand by. Fire." You have four seconds in which to fire, then I will say, "Stop. Reload. Are you ready? Stand by. Fire." all over again. In your competition you have two series of five shots; two targets and you fire five shots at each of them. So, after five shots, I shall say, "Guns down. Change targets." And then you all go forward *together* to look at your scores and there is no danger." She looked at David. "It is very important that some one is appointed to give the orders whenever they practise."

"Yes, I can see that," he agreed. "We don't want anyone shot in the back."

When James and Seb had fired, they collected their targets and Mrs Halford called for the next two. "This morning I want to run straight through, letting you shoot one target each," she explained, "and then, with the second one, I'll give you more individual instruction."

Paul and Sarah had rushed forward eagerly and, while they were being put in the correct positions, everyone else crowded round James and Seb to see how they had scored. David, who had produced a rule book, read out: "Ten for a Bull, eight for an Inner, six for a Magpie, four for an Outer and two for anywhere on the target outside the outer circle. Then, for the purpose of the tetrathlon you multiply your score by ten, so the two targets are worth a thousand points."

James was looking modestly pleased. "Two Inners, two Outers and a Magpie," he told David. "Not too bad for a first go."

"Three hundred," announced Julian, peering through his large, dark-framed spectacles. "Shall I add yours, Seb?"

"Done it, a hundred and sixty," answered Seb in dissatisfied tones.

"I wish we *were* allowed to use two hands," complained Oliver, watching Paul.

"Oh, I think they look lovely standing like that with their left hands in their pockets," argued Lynne. "Trouble is my shorts don't have any pockets."

"Nor do mine. Next time we'll have to wear special shooting clothes," said Alice.

"Tetrathlons seem to need an awful lot of clothes," observed Lizzie.

As Mrs Halford was only showing them how to stand and how to hold a pistol, and most people had already discovered this by watching the others, she got through the impatient queue quite quickly. Especially as no one wasted any time, but darted forward the moment a pistol was put down.

"I got a bull," announced Hanif, brandishing his target proudly at Alice.

"You've done better than me," said James.

"Let's see," demanded Julian, "I'm keeping the scores. Three-twenty. You're the best so far," he added, writing it down.

"I bet my dozy brother's got nought," said Oliver sadly, as Rupert came over and Lesley and Lynne took up the pistols.

"An eight, three fours and a two. Terrific, Rupe." Oliver patted his brother proudly. "I didn't expect you to get any on the target at all."

"I probably won't next time," said Rupert, collapsing on a straw bale.

"Sarah only got three shots on. She's the worst so far," Julian announced, "but I don't suppose girls are much good at shooting."

"Julian!" exclaimed Netti in shocked horror. "You male chauvinist pig."

"I don't suppose Sarah's ever tried shooting before," Hanif told him, "and all the boys except Paul have."

"I've beaten you, Paul," Lynne shrieked excitedly. "At least I think I have. I got all five on."

"Not by much," Paul told her as he inspected her target.

"Oh, come on, Lesley, let me see yours—everyone else has," protested Julian, as his sister folded her target carefully and put it in her pocket. "Please."

"I wish you wouldn't all go on and on about who's beaten whom," complained Hanif. "It's not important, and my stepfather says that the whole point of a tetrathlon is that you compete against your *own* score and not against other people."

"They'll calm down when they've done the running and swimming and find how the picture keeps changing," David told him. "I want to start the running when we're halfway through the second series, so, as you finish shooting, will you get into your running gear and come to the start in Long Meadow?" he asked. Then, struggling to his feet, he added, "I'm going to organize stopwatches and mothers."

"Want any help?" asked Oliver.

Alice was quite pleased with her shooting for, though her total wasn't high, all her shots had scored, and she found herself trying to comfort Lizzie whose aim seemed very wild and only two of whose shots had found the target.

"You're too tense, that's your problem, dear," said Mrs Halford. "Try a few deep breaths before you start, and rolling your shoulders round will help to relax your shooting arm. Don't worry, you'll do better next time."

Tina was tense too and, gripping the pistol tightly, pressed instead of squeezing the trigger, which counteracted her careful aim. But Netti, cheerfully confident, hit a Bull and an Inner, and then, finding that she had equalled James's score, pursued Julian round the barn with her target, saying she was going to make him eat it.

They began the second round, and Seb, who was preparing to redeem himself by an enormous score, was furious when Mrs Halford announced that they would practise "dry firing": going through the drill and motions of firing, but without loading the pistol. "Simply blazing away won't improve you, dear," she told him. "We have to correct your stance and then your trigger control."

He was even more enraged when she called for Lizzie to pair him and then made everyone watch while they went through the drill and she explained their faults. But when, finally, she allowed them some ammunition, they found they *were* far better; Seb produced a much more respectable score, and Lizzie put every shot on the target.

James and Hanif didn't have to go through the indignity of a dry shoot, nor did Lesley and Netti who were called next, but Paul and Sarah who followed them were full of faults of stance and grip. Oliver appeared in the middle of their sorting out session.

"David's going spare, he wants some runners. Haven't *any* of you finished *yet*?" he demanded.

"Oh, we forgot all about running; this is just getting interesting," said Hanif, collecting his holdall. "Lizzie, you're ready dressed, can you go and calm David while I persuade the others to change?"

David had stationed himself just inside the Long Meadow gateway which was decorated with two cardboard notices announcing START and FINISH. He was sitting impatiently in the Land Rover with a row of stopwatches in front of him. "Here's the map," he said, showing it to each of the runners as they appeared. "It's quite easy, just a square. Down this field, vault or climb over the gate in the left-hand corner, along the headland of the next one, keeping off my wheat. Through the slip rails straight on across a grass field until you come to a pond and a turning flag. Go outside the flag, and Mrs Rooke is there to make sure you do. Turn left along the hedge, over a gate into a stubble field straight to the copse in the corner. We've flagged the path through the copse, and Mrs Roberts is there to see no one gets lost. Then you turn for home and come back across two stubble fields and into the paddock. You can see the flags, and this gateway is the finish."

"I'm positive that's more than fifteen hundred metres," complained Seb.

"It may be," agreed David. "I'm incapable of pacing a course out so I had to guess. But even if you measure properly it's difficult to work out a correct bogey time, because you have to allow for hills, gates and slip rails to slow the runners down. Anyway, it'll do for a start. The important thing is to get you all running."

"How long are we supposed to take?" asked James, who was limbering up by running on the spot.

"The good runners should do it in five minutes, forty seconds," answered David. "If they take a longer or shorter time you blame the course. Right, I'm supposed to send you at one minute intervals, but since Oliver and I are both new to the job, I think we'll just have two on the course to start with. So James and then Lizzie please. James's starting time will be zero plus one, Lizzie's zero plus two, and then you write their finishing times in when I yell them out," David told Oliver. "O.K., James? On your marks. Go."

As James ran swiftly down Long Meadow, Paul and Sarah appeared in shorts and track shoes.

"How did you get on?" Hanif asked.

"Much better second time," Paul answered. "Mrs Halford said I'd be all right with a bit of practise."

"I hate her," said Sarah with a scowl. "She's so bossy. I'm sure we'd get on better if we were just left to practise on our own."

"No you wouldn't, dear, you'd just blaze away." Seb tried to imitate Mrs Halford's brisk, high voice.

Lizzie giggled. "I think she's good though, *I* wouldn't have got any better on my own."

"Ten seconds to go, Lizzie," called David. And then, as she raced away, long legs eating up the ground in long strides, and her flaxen plait flying, "You're next, Harry, then Seb, but I'm going to allow two minutes before I start you. They'll be zero four and zero five, Oliver."

"Yes, I've got it."

Netti was the next of the shooters to appear.

"How are things going in the barn?" David asked her.

"Great, Mrs Halford seems quite pleased with us; everyone's improving. But Lesley's the star." She looked at Sarah. "Your sister's brilliant, her two cards came to some terrific score. Julian's furious that a girl has beaten all the boys."

"There's still Rupert to go; I hope he beats her," said Sarah spitefully. "When Lesley wins things she becomes more hateful than ever."

"I expect her glasses give her an unfair advantage. They probably magnify the target," suggested Paul. "I shouldn't think they're allowed in proper competitions."

"Oh yes they are," David told him.

"Does anyone know the course?" asked Netti, changing the conversation as they watched Hanif start.

"If you come up here, you can see almost the whole course and the poor devils panting their way round," Seb told her from his perch on the five-barred gate. "James has disappeared into the wood, Lizzie's approaching the pond."

"And you're wanted at the start," said David. "Oliver, can you give Netti the map."

"Thanks." Netti threw herself down on the grass to study it. "Shooting's fun but exhausting. Good luck, Seb."

"Hinge end," said Paul to Sarah as they both climbed on the gate. "We don't want a rocket from David."

"Come on, James, faster," called Sarah.

"He's had it, he's getting slower and slower," said Paul.

"What's his time like, David?" asked Netti, getting up to look.

"On the slow side, he's not going to get his thousand points," answered David.

"He's practically walking." Sarah sounded shocked. "We're not going to do very well if even James can't get round in the time."

"Seven-fifty," David told Oliver, as James jogged wearily through the gateway and collapsed by the hedge. "Come on, Netti, you can work his score out; deduct one because he started at zero one. Then deduct the bogey time—five forty. Multiply what's left by three, subtract the answer from a thousand and you've got his score."

"Not so fast. You're being mean, David. You're trying to muddle me."

James got up. "It seemed like miles," he complained, "that last field nearly killed me. What did I get, Netti?"

"Wait, I'm still struggling . . ."

"You see, you do need Julian and his calculator. They say boys are better at maths than girls," teased David.

"No we don't, come and check this, Sarah. He was seventy seconds over. That's two hundred and ten points, which from the thousand leaves seven hundred and ninety. Agreed?"

"Lizzie's coming quite fast," Paul announced from the gate. "She doesn't look as blown as James."

"She's like Rupert, she's got long legs for her size," said Netti. "Come on, Lizzie," she shouted. "You're doing brilliantly, keep it up."

Lizzie finished fast and then stood, bent double, trying to get her breath.

"Eight ten," said David. "And she started at zero two." Everyone began to work out her score.

"You only lost ninety points, Lizzie. Brilliant," Netti told her.

"I'm starting you in twenty seconds, Sarah," called David.

"Harry's in sight," announced Paul from the gate. "He looks fast too."

"You're next, Paul," called David, as Sarah started. "Then Netti, at one minute intervals."

"Shall I take over the scoring?" asked James.

"Yes, fine, but could you round up Lesley first? Tell her she's due to start in three minutes."

Hanif's time was even faster than Lizzie's and he also beat Seb, who was three seconds slower than James. Sarah and Paul had slow times which annoyed them. They scowled at their scores and eyed the stopwatches suspiciously.

"Be reasonable," David told them. "People of eleven *can't* run as fast as people of thirteen, who are normally taller as well as physically stronger."

"You mean we haven't a hope of winning then," snapped Sarah. "In that case, why go to all this bother?"

"And it's under *fifteen*," Paul pointed out, "which

means that half the competitors will be older than James. It's not fair to lump all the age groups together like that."

"In three years' time you'll be the older ones," said David, one eye on the stopwatch, for Netti was racing towards the finish. "You'll be pleased then that you started training young, and the Woodbury will have some cracking teams."

"Anyway, we don't expect to win," Hanif told Sarah.

"No, we're entering for fun," agreed Lizzie.

"I want to jump a superb cross-country round," decided Alice, "I don't mind much about anything else."

"How did you do in the shooting?" asked Sarah suspiciously.

"Quite well, much better the second time, but I wasn't brilliant like your sister."

"I was *very* nearly brilliant," said Rupert, knotting his broken shoelaces. "Blazeaway said my trouble was lack of concentration, and that I must try to visualize a button for ten seconds at a time. I forgot to ask what sort of button."

"Well done, Netti."

"You finished full of running."

"You're much the best of the younger people," Oliver, who was looking over James's elbow, told her proudly.

"I think I started too slowly, I didn't want to run out of steam at the end," gasped Netti, "but I could have gone faster."

"Rupert, on your marks," called David. "Haven't you got those shoelaces organized yet?"

"Sorry, they're a bit rotten."

"Well, buy some new ones before next time. Are you ready, or shall I send Alice?"

"I'm ready," Rupert jogged on the spot. "Prepare to be broken, Woodbury records. Here I come."

"He's got long enough legs," said Paul, as they watched him run down the meadow, "he ought to be the fastest of us all."

"Yes, over a short distance," agreed Seb, "but he looks more like a sprinter than a cross-country runner."

Lesley finished at a steady pace. Her time was the same as Netti's, and Sarah was quick to point out the difference in age.

"You ought to have beaten Nettie by miles," she told her sister contemptuously. "You're *much* older than she is."

"But Netti's tall for her age," objected Lizzie quickly.

"And I couldn't see a thing, my glasses kept misting up," complained Lesley, producing a handkerchief and polishing the lenses.

"Oh, you've always got some excuse," snapped Sarah.

As Alice set off in pursuit of Rupert, Mrs Halford, Lynne and Tina appeared in the field.

"All finished," said Mrs Halford briskly. "We've locked the pistols in the tack room, Lynne showed where you keep them, and here's the key."

"Oh thanks." David put down the stopwatch and took the key. "It was very good of you to come and give them such a splendid introduction to shooting; we're all most grateful."

"That's all right, I enjoyed it. And they all worked hard. Can I give you a ring about next week, either Monday or Tuesday? Goodbye." She waved to the pony club members as she bustled away.

"Thank you," they called after her, "Thank you very much."

"Are either of you ready?" David looked at Tina and Lynne.

"No, some bit of my shoe's digging into me," complained Lynne, sitting down and removing her track shoe to investigate.

"I'm ready, but I haven't a clue where I'm supposed to go," answered Tina. Oliver held the map under her nose, and everyone else explained the course at once.

"For goodness sake let her look at the map in peace." David sounded irritable. "And are the rest of you ready for the swimming session? We must be in the cars and off to Woodbury the moment Lynne has run, and anyone who's not there, with swimming gear, will be left behind."

"We'll wait till Rupert comes in and then we'd better collect up our stuff," Lizzie told Netti as they watched Tina sprinting down the field.

"Too fast," said Oliver. "She'll never keep that pace up."

"Alice is going well," announced Seb, who had returned to his perch on the gate. "She's coming up to the pond. I can't see Rupert, he must be in the wood. Alice will be closing up on him if he doesn't appear soon. That's funny, there's still no sign of him."

Netti groaned. "Oh Rupert, what *have* you done now?" She asked as she joined Seb on the gate.

"How long has he been, David?" asked James.

"Over four minutes, he should be out in the middle of the stubble. Have you sorted that shoe out, Lynne?" asked David. "Hurry up, you've thirty seconds to go."

"David, shall I go and look for him?" asked Lizzie anxiously.

"No, he'll turn up. Mrs Roberts is in the wood, so if he's sprained his ankle she'll wave her red flag for help. On your marks, Lynne. Go."

"Isn't there any sign of him, Netti?" asked Oliver. "He's going to have the worst time of everyone at this rate."

"Alice is out of the wood and coming home at a cracking pace," said Seb. "But there's no sign . . . Oh, wait a minute, someone's chasing Alice. It can't be Sarah, no, I mean Tina, can it?"

"No, too tall and that's Rupert's red and white shirt," Netti told him. "He looks all right, Lizzie, he's following Alice home."

Oliver sighed. He minded Rupert's failures more than Rupert did. He had a feeling that elder brothers ought to be heroes, people you could look up to and admire.

"He's caught up with Alice, but he's not trying to pass, he's running beside her and *talking*. What a nutcase." Seb sounded disapproving. "Tina's slowed up a lot, but she's nearly at the wood."

Rupert and Alice came through the finish, running stride for stride.

"Alice has tied with Lesley, fifth, three points behind Seb," announced James.

"You ought to have sprinted the last bit," Nettie told her, "you're not half as blown as I was. But I suppose my silly brother distracted you."

"Yes, he did a bit," Alice admitted. "He was saying mad things and trying to make me laugh."

"How long *did* Rupert take?" Sarah asked David.

"I don't know, I didn't bother to take his time since he wasn't trying." David's voice was cold.

"I was trying to start with, David. Honestly." Rupert assumed a conciliatory voice. "But I took the wrong path in the wood, and by the time Mrs Roberts had explained where I was supposed to go and we'd had a chat, Alice was in sight, so I let her go on ahead."

"The wood was flagged, the way through was obvious, and no one else went wrong." David was not to be appeased. "You simply don't bother to concentrate."

"Oh, but I was concentrating, that was the whole trouble," Rupert explained eagerly. "I was doing exactly as Mrs Halford suggested and trying to visualize a button for ten seconds; that's why I didn't see the flags."

David gave him an angry glare and turned to watch a very tired Tina jogging home.

"We'd better collect our swimming things," said Lizzie. "Come on, Rupert, David says anyone who isn't ready will be left behind."

"He's furious." Rupert looked back at David with a puzzled expression.

"Well, of course he is," said Hanif. "What do you expect when you fool about?"

"You think you're hilariously funny, but you're not, you're a stupid oaf," snapped Lesley.

"Everyone's glaring at me," moaned Rupert.

254

"And if you don't shut up and be sensible, Lizzie and I will probably kill you in a minute," Netti told him in a suddenly savage voice.

The Woodbury pool was a new one—in fact, there were two pools. Dropped at the entrance by the mothers, who then drove away to park the cars, David limped to the spectator seats by the deep pool, while the pony club members went to change. When they reappeared, the younger members, shrieking and giggling, made a wild dash for the shallow pool with its wave-making machine and were soon queueing up to whiz down the shute. Seb, sinister in goggles, plunged into the deep pool. Lizzie wandered disconsolately from the coffee bar to the changing cabins looking for Rupert, who had already vanished, and only Alice, Hanif, Lesley and James found David and asked what was happening next.

"As the pool's fairly empty I suggest you all go in together and we see how many lengths you can do in three minutes. I've brought a stopwatch," said David. "I've been studying the rules and it all seems very free and easy. You can swim any stroke you like, change it as often as you like, start *in* the water or dive in. The only thing you have to remember is to touch the side of the bath every time you turn."

"How do we know when the three minutes are up?" asked Hanif.

"Well, officially a whistle is blown, but we haven't brought one so the mothers and I will wave at you. Can you collect the other three older ones, that's two Wheelers and Seb?"

"Here, can you look after these," Lesley handed her mother her spectacles. "And have you seen Lizzie? We want her in the first heat."

"Why not have Sarah? She's a good little swimmer, I'm sure she'd hold her own with the big ones."

James collected Seb, Alice found Lizzie, and they decided to begin without Rupert.

"Is it really only three minutes?" Seb asked David.

"Yes, as you're juniors. The seniors do four," David answered. "Start when I drop my arm. The mothers are going to count the lengths."

"I'm starting in the water," said Hanif, rather shamefaced. "I'm useless at swimming."

"It won't be a proper trial because the other people are going to get in the way," complained James.

"How warm is the water?" Alice asked Hanif.

"You should get in and get wet first," Seb told her. "David. Is it O.K. if I make tumble turns?"

"Yes, provided you touch the side of the bath with some part of your body."

"How many points do we get for each length?" asked Lesley.

"That depends on the length of the pool," Seb told her.

"I know *that*," Lesley snapped at him.

"Look, stop talking and let's get going," called David impatiently. "Are you ready?"

They lined up, plunged in, and then ploughed up and down avoiding the other swimmers as best they could. Seb shot ahead at once, his powerful crawl sliced through the water, and his professional-looking tumble turns increased his lead with each length. Seb, far ahead, and Hanif, trailing behind, had to swim on their own, but the other four, evenly matched, raced neck and neck. They were flagging and looking hopefully for waving mothers before the three minutes were up.

"Seb, you were terrific," said Alice, climbing out. "How many lengths did you do?"

"Almost three and a half, but I was baulked once," answered Seb.

"I had an actual collision," said Lizzie, rubbing her arm.

"How did we do?" asked James, trying to see the scores which Mrs Rooke was writing down.

"It's highly complicated," said David. "You score four points per metre up to fifty metres, and then six points up to two hundred metres when it goes back to four points.

So, as it's a fifty metre pool, the first length is worth two hundred points; the second, third and fourth, three hundred points each. Which means that Seb gets a grand score of nine hundred and fifty, the two and a half length people get six hundred and fifty, and Harry's length and a half earns three hundred and fifty. We haven't counted odd metres."

"You're swimming does let you down," said Mrs Rooke, glaring at Hanif. "You'll have to do something about that."

"But he's one of the best at shooting, running and riding," protested Alice. "You can't expect him to be brilliant at all four."

"Not brilliant," snapped Mrs Rooke, "but he's letting himself down with a poor performance like that."

"Alice, Harry, could you go and round up the rest of them, please? I'd like to see what they can do in the time." asked David. "And as for improving *your* scores, I should think if you keep on swimming slightly longer distances than you've managed today, you're bound to do better. It's no use setting yourselves unrealistic targets."

"Oh, do we *have* to?" moaned Lynne, when Alice told her that David wanted her for a practice.

"Coming, just one more go," answered Tina who was queueing for the shute.

"Must we?" asked Paul indignantly as Hanif dragged him out of the wave pool. "I'm training here."

Lizzie rescued Rupert, who had managed to lock his numbered armlet in his locker and couldn't remember which it was, by pointing out that his was the one above hers.

"You're more trouble than all the rest put together, Rupert," snapped Mrs Rooke when the reason for his lateness had been explained to her.

"Don't worry," Rupert told her soothingly. "It's all under control; everything has been sorted out."

"Oh come on." David sounded exasperated. "You're now holding up the second heat as well as the first."

Rupert missed David's sign and started late, but being older, he soon overhauled Tina and Paul, then he passed Sarah, swam stroke for stroke with Netti and, gradually drawing ahead of her, caught up with Lynne. He didn't manage to shake off Lynne until he was into his third length. As he reached the two and a half mark, the mothers began to wave that time was up, but Rupert swam on, oblivious of their signals.

"Tina and Paul were on three fifty," said David, when the rest of them emerged dripping from the pool. "Netti, you were five hundred, Lynne was five sixty. Remember that once you've completed the first length, every metre is worth six points and really go for them." He turned to the three mothers. "I'm whacked. Shall we go and have a coffee and leave them to practise on their own?"

Later, the mothers began to round up the pony club members. Mrs Roberts collected the Wheelers and her own children and, saying that David was exhausted and must be taken home at once, sent them off to change.

David was limping round telling everyone that the next cross-country practice was on Saturday at 9.30 a.m., but when he found Tina he said, "Look, I particularly want you to come. I'm being given a pony, a staid and elderly fourteen-two. A friend of mine thinks I'll be able to hack him round the farm. There's not much hope of that at present, but as he jumps and has carried a whole family of children through their pony club years, he might do for the Tetrathlon, so I want you to try him. O.K.?"

"Me, really?" asked Tina, surprised. "Oh, I'd love to try him, but I don't suppose I'll be good enough for a fourteen-two and I'm not much use at any of the non-riding tetrathlon things."

"District Commissioners have to take the long view," said David. "If I get you all practising now, when you *are* larger and older you may be some use. Anyway, it's always good to have a spare pony, and if you'll ride him on Saturday I shall see how he goes."

The Land Rover party left, and Mrs Rooke collected up

Lesley and Sarah. Mrs Franklin persuaded Hanif, who was struggling grimly up and down the pool in a vain attempt to increase his speed, that he'd taken enough exercise for one morning and it was time to go. Especially as she had promised an English lesson to a Pakistani friend.

"What did you think of it, Seb?" asked James.

"It was O.K." Seb's voice lacked enthusiasm. "The shooting took so long and we didn't get nearly enough practise. Twelve people and two pistols just isn't on."

"But it was the first time most of us had shot, and as no one knew the drill, it was bound to take ages," Alice pointed out.

"And we're such a small pony club I don't suppose we can afford more than two pistols," added Hanif.

"I'm going to ask my father to buy me one so that I can practise at home," said Seb in a determined voice. "A boy at school's got a really modern German one, far better than those second-hand jobs David's bought. I'm sure a good pistol makes a huge difference to your score."

"Except that Lesley got a cracking score with one of David's 'second-hand jobs'," observed Alice.

CHAPTER FIVE

You're Jealous

It was Saturday, and Tina felt very nervous climbing up on to blue roan Vulcan. Nervous and hurt, for Paul and Lynne had deserted her, mounting their ponies and riding away down the farm track to Coppice Hill. She'd been afraid that Vulcan would go mad when he found himself alone, but he'd only given her a couple of impatient nudges, as though telling her to hurry up, and now Alice and Harry had arrived and were waiting for her in the lane.

"You do look grand," said Alice, as Tina rode out of David's stableyard. "I've never seen you on a big pony before."

"I've never ridden one. He feels terribly high and wide," answered Tina, a worried expression on her freckled face.

"I had to do it the other way round," said Alice. "When I lived abroad there never seemed to be any ponies, so children rode fifteen-hand horses. When I came back and rode twelve-two ponies it felt very peculiar. They bobbed and scuttled and had such short necks; I kept expecting to shoot over their heads."

"I thought David's doctors told him he'd never be able to ride again, so why is he buying a pony?" asked Hanif.

"I don't think he's buying Vulcan, he's a present from a friend whose children have outgrown him or something; he said a spare pony might come in useful," explained Tina.

"It doesn't seem fair," said Paul for the second time as he, Lynne and the two Rookes rode down the farm track to the sunken lane. His small, serious face wore a sulky expression and his grey eyes were dark and brooding.

"I suppose he picked Tina because she hasn't a pony of her own," suggested Sarah.

"But he knows us *much* better than Tina, and we *live* here."

"And he knows that if one of us had Vulcan we'd have loaned Tina a pony." Lynne, whose usually laughing face was red and cross, supported her brother. "Mum and Dad think it's a shame too, when they've done so much for him."

"I expect he's tired of your giggling and fooling about," Lesley told her unsympathetically. "Neither you nor Paul ever try very hard, and now you're jealous."

"Oh, what a horrible thing to say." Lynne sounded very upset. "We do try, don't we Paul?"

"Don't pay any attention to her, she's always like that, really spiteful," said Sarah. "Come on, let's leave her behind," she added, kicking Bowie into a canter.

"My father's buying me a pistol," Seb announced as he joined the group of pony club members waiting by the slip rails. "He said he'd do his best to get one today."

"Great," said Netti, "that means more turns for everyone."

"And I'm going to practise like hell. I'm going to get really good," vowed Seb. "You can come up and have a go if you like, James. We're living in this cottage at Kiddleworth now. It's a bit of a mess, my father cooks, I wash up, but we're not much good at housework."

"We might get the whole of the senior boys' team practising regularly," suggested James, his face brightening.

"Oh, don't be mean, you can't just have the boys, Seb. That would make you a real chauvinist pig," objected Netti.

"And you have to have someone over twenty-one there to supervise," Lizzie reminded him.

"My father'll be there at the weekend."

"I agree with Netti, no discrimination on grounds of sex," announced Hanif. "We are all equal; my mother's very hot on that, she's just joined a society to raise the standing of women in Pakistan."

"Here's David," said Alice as the Land Rover turned into the lane. "Shall I take down the slip rails?"

"If you want," Paul, who usually took them down, answered in a sulky voice. "I'm not going to."

"Good morning, all," said David, stopping the Land Rover in the lane while he counted them. "Did anyone do any running or swimming yesterday?"

"My stepfather bullied me into jogging with him," answered Hanif.

"I went swimming, but the pool was rather full so I couldn't work out my times," explained Tina. "I did quite a lot of lengths though, with rests in between."

"No one else?" asked David as the other pony club members looked at each other guiltily and shook their heads.

"Oh dear, I did *mean* to run," moaned Lizzie, "but other things kept happening and then we *had* to tack clean."

"I meant to go to Woodbury pool," said Alice, "but Harry was out and it seemed rather dreary to go on my own. I'll call you next time Tina," she added as they followed the Land Rover into the field.

"I'll be in next time," objected Hanif.

"Well then, we can all three go together," said Alice.

"I want to concentrate on the shooting this weekend," Seb told James. "We can swim and run on Monday."

"Form up the ride," called David as he climbed out of the Land Rover.

Lynne and Paul watched enviously as Netti drew back to let Tina go ahead of her, and the tall blue roan took his place behind Rosie. They were the only people left on little ponies.

Of course, Tristram was only a tiny bit taller than Berry, Lynne admitted to herself unwillingly, but he was such a super pony, well-schooled and a good jumper, that he had always counted as a big one. While Berry—well, everyone said that she was really a harness pony. That hadn't mattered when the whole pony club had been useless, but now, if there were going to be teams and everyone was getting good at dressage and jumping, she and Paul were going to be left behind.

Paul felt himself burning and seething with indignation as he rode round, but he didn't try to sort it out, to put it clearly into thoughts and words. He let himself be taken over by rage, his mind repeating the same thought again and again, *It isn't fair. It isn't fair.*

"Come on, let's have some impulsion," said David, settling himself on his shooting stick. "Get those ponies at the back overtracking."

They rode the usual circles and serpentines. They practised shoulder-in at the walk and then attempted it at the trot. Only Sarah, Lynne, Tina and Paul failed completely. David, roaring ferociously, said that it was because they didn't sit deep and really *use* their legs, and then sent them back to practising at the walk.

"Now," he said, calling the ride to a halt just as all the riders felt they were about to collapse with exhaustion. "In this Tetrathlon cross-country, and I take it we are still entering, though no one seems to be training for the rest of it with much enthusiasm, you have to open and shut a gate and take down a slip rail. We are going to practise both of them." He went on, ignoring Hanif's cries of horror. "But, before we do so, I want to make sure that you all know the correct way to rein back."

"That puts me right out of it," said Rupert in a mournful voice. "Rosie's totally useless at gates."

"The slip rail puts me out." Hanif sounded even gloomier. "Jupe will never stand for me to mount when he's excited."

"Shsh!" Lesley glared at them. "Some of us want to hear what David's saying."

" . . . not an exercise you want to practise too often, generally one is better employed teaching the pony to go forward, but, as it's necessary for practical reasons like

263

gate-opening the pony must learn it," said David. He looked along the ride. "I need a demonstration pony."

"Ferdie's not bad, my mother taught him," offered James.

"Right. Well, you walk round half the school while I explain what you're going to demonstrate," David told him and turned to the rest of the members. "It sounds dotty, but the rein-back must be ridden as a forward movement. You remember that I'm always yelling at you to ride *forward* into your halts? Well, you ride the rein-back in the same way. Your legs ask him to move forward, your hands tell him no. Prepare to halt, James. Good. Now rein back, four steps and walk on. Good."

David turned to face the line of riders. "The pony stayed on the bit, his head was in the correct position, he was straight and calm. His only mistake was taking one more step than I asked for. O.K., James, when you're ready, halt and rein back again. This time I want everyone to watch Ferdie's legs and tell me what *time* he reins back in."

The pony club members watched carefully as Ferdinand, a serious expression on his dark brown face, reined back sedately.

"Two time," shouted Sarah as soon as she had seen the first step.

"More or less two time," agreed Hanif cautiously.

"Right," said David. "He moved his diagonally opposite legs in pairs, which gives the movement it's elegant, fluid look. Reining back in four time, that is, one leg at a time, is horrible to watch and incorrect. Give Ferdie a pat, James, and do try to look up. Who'd like to try next?"

Seb and Hanif hesitated, so Alice rode forward on Saffron. She halted carefully, for though he seemed to have given up stargazing, he sometimes went above the bit. Then she used her legs again, asking him to back. Saffron's head went up, his mouth opened, he laid back his ears.

"Don't upset him," said David. "We know he's had problems. But once a pony's head is up, it's more difficult for him to back as he's thrown his weight on to his hindlegs. So you ride forward and halt again, Alice. Try saying 'Back' in a long-drawn-out voice. Good. One step is plenty to start with. Pat him and ride forward." David turned back to the watching riders. "Don't be too demanding," he told them. "If something is difficult for your pony, be content with very little at first: one step, then, when he's giving you that willingly, ask for two."

Seb who tried next, was inclined to pull on the reins.

"No, don't use force," David told him. "Your hands are only to give him a signal; they're explaining, not *making* him go back. It is difficult for an unschooled horse to grasp what you mean—your legs say forward, your hands say no—but once you've taught him, once he understands, he'll remember the aids for the rest of his life. So, take your time and use your brains rather than your strength."

Seb's second attempt was better, though Jigsaw backed grudgingly and without impulsion. Then Hanif bounced round on Jupiter, who refused to stand still for a second, twirling frantically every time Hanif mentioned the word "Back".

"Relax, Harry," called David. "It's always the same with you. You're the one who goes stiff and gets worked-up, then you pass it on to the pony. It must be you, because Jupiter didn't know he was going to be asked to do anything new. Ride him round until he calms down. Come on, Lizzie, let's see what you can do."

To everyone's surprise, Rajah, wearing his wise expression, reined back soberly and correctly. Lizzie patted him delightedly as David shouted, "Good! Well done, Lizzie. *And* you looked up."

Stardust was good too, though she hadn't quite enough impulsion, and David made Lesley ride on at a trot before she halted for a second try. Then it was Rupert's turn. "Rosie's hopeless," he said, riding up to David. "She's convinced that it's totally impossible for her to go backwards, and we've wasted hours trying to teach her to open gates. I'll be a terrible disgrace to any tetrathlon team, you'll have to leave me out."

"I realize it's difficult for her," David answered calmly. "She's so very long between the hip and hock, which isn't exactly helpful when you want your hindlegs under you. Still, we should be able to produce a step or two. Have a try, let me see what happens."

"Nil," said Rupert, walking on and then halting. He used his legs and declaimed, "Back, back, back," in soothing tones. Nothing happened. Rupert's face turned red, Rosie's wore an obstinate expression. Then suddenly, as his legs became more insistent, she opened her mouth as far as the dropped noseband would allow, and charged forward.

"O.K., she's resisting you," agreed David. "Either she doesn't understand the aids or she's objecting because the movement is so difficult for her. To make it absolutely plain, take her over and face that overgrown hedge." He pointed to a section of the hedge which hadn't been layered and was about twelve feet high.

"Never use a gate or a low fence," he added, turning to the other pony club members, "because you'll find yourself jumping it from a standstill, or stuck on top. Keep trying, Rupert. Be kind but determined, and no pulling on the reins as that's counter productive." David looked across the school to Hanif, "Are you calm?"

"Not really, but I'm less uncalm," answered Hanif.

"Well, that's something. Let's see you have another go."

This time Jupiter reined back, but he took five or six rapid steps before Hanif could stop him.

"O.K., pat him. But it should be a controlled movement, one step at a time. The last thing we want to do is to teach ponies to run back, for they can then use it as a defence or disobedience against their riders. In future, ask for only one or two steps and then try to ride forward. But you'll have to give very light and tactful aids, he's not an easy pony."

"She's taken one step," shouted Rupert from the hedge, "but though I made a terrific fuss of her, she's now forgotten the aids again."

"Ride round a bit in between," David shouted back. "Who's next?" Netti and Tristram reined back perfectly and were followed by Sarah and Bowie.

"Yours is a super little pony," said Seb, looking at Tristram admiringly. "He does everything. Doesn't having him make you a bit swell-headed?"

"No," Netti laughed. "He was Rupert's before he was mine. Once, Rupert could do everything, but look what's happened to him now he owns Rosie."

David was telling Sarah that Bowie was one of those ponies which ought not to practise reining back at all—he had already discovered that it could be used as a defence. But as it was essential for gate opening, he just wanted to see her take one or two controlled steps.

"Now, very, very gently," he reminded her, "the lightest possible aids. You can always increase them. And I shouldn't be able to see them, it should look as though it's all done by magic."

Sarah scowled. "Oh come on, Bowie," she said impatiently.

"You're confusing the pony," David told her patiently. "You must say what you mean, which is 'Back'."

"Back!" shouted Sarah in a cross voice, and Bowie ran back several steps in an equally abrupt manner.

"O.K. it wouldn't do for a dressage test, but if you keep him calm you should manage a gate," David told her, and then turned to Rupert who was calling him from the hedge.

"Look David, she can do two steps. Back," Rupert went on, applying the aids carefully. But Rosie stood obstinately, a baffled look in her large, toad eyes. "Sorry, I really thought she *had* got it this time," added Rupert in a mortified voice.

"Keep trying," said David and smiled one of his rare smiles at Tina, who rode into the centre of the school feeling cast down by her failure to produce even one step of shoulder-in at the trot.

"How do you like my pony?" he asked. "I think he's going rather well with a strange rider in a strange place."

"He's lovely," answered Tina, patting the blue-roan neck, "but I'm not used to such a big pony, he feels a bit strange."

Vulcan reined back in a slow and stately manner, and then red-roan Berry took his place.

"She should know all about it, having been in harness," observed David. Berry backed briskly, rather too briskly. "Not quite controlled enough for a dressage test," said David, "but great for gates. Now you, Paul." Paul was inclined to pull on the reins, but as soon as David persuaded him that this was counter-productive, Banjo backed neatly.

"Right." David heaved himself off his shooting stick. "Form up the ride, walk round the school, and when we halt I want everyone but Sarah to rein back four steps and walk on. We'll let Rosie off with one or two steps," he added, turning towards Rupert.

"You'll be lucky. Without her hedge she'll never remember the aids," Rupert answered despondently.

There was a distinct improvement in almost everyone's rein-back. Saffron stayed on the bit; Jupiter still rushed back, but he was very nearly straight and didn't twirl at all; while Rosie, to Rupert's delight, produced two small, grudging steps.

"Good, that's very encouraging," said David. "Now, cross country stirrups and we'll do a little cantering before we go out on the course."

"About time too," said Paul in a dissatisfied voice. "He's not left much time for jumping."

"Shush," Lizzie told him, a shocked expression crossing her face, "David'll hear."

"Who cares."

Soon they were cantering round, circling, going faster and slower, changing the rein with a couple of trot strides at X to change the leg.

"Right," said David when he had called the blowing and steaming ponies to a halt. "Now we're going to have a couple of warm-up jumps, then we'll add a slip rail and a gate to the course, and we'll finish up with a new fence."

"A new fence?" asked the pony club members, standing in their stirrups and looking across the two valley fields. "Where, David? Where?"

"You'll see when we get to it, meanwhile could some of you go and build a fence in front of the bank? Mr Roberts and I left some poles and drums there, but we didn't have time to build it."

Half the ride volunteered and cantered on ahead, sailing confidently over the slip rails. Tina took them down for the Land Rover and by the time she'd climbed back on Vulcan, thanked Seb who had waited for her, and cantered over to the bank, the first jump was ready.

"Can everyone remember how to jump banks?" asked David.

"Yes."

"Yes, of course we can."

"The point is, do the ponies remember how to do it?" observed Rupert, ramming his crash cap on hard.

"Take a lead," David told him, "and you Sarah. Lynne, if you let Berry run out I may not be responsible for my actions."

"He means he'll turn purple with rage and probably kill you on the spot," Rupert threatened Lynne.

"If he does, he'll have Dad after him," she answered coldly. "And it isn't my fault that Berry's not much of a jumper."

"Right, James, over the poles and drums, over the bank, large circle round and, when the course is clear, come again. Anyone who refuses, get out of the way and wait."

James set off with Ferdie looking full of impulsion and confidence. They sailed over the drum jump and negotiated the bank neatly. Seb followed, looking much less confident, and he patted Jigsaw gratefully when they

269

had landed safely down from the bank. Jupiter started fast, but then seemed to remember that banks needed care and steadied himself, jumping prudently and with pricked ears. Saffron and Alice both looked as though they were enjoying themselves. Rajah was slow and careful, Stardust not completely confident. Bowie refused.

"Clear the course!" shouted David, as Sarah kicked and shouted at the agitated pony. Tristram whirled past Bowie and took the bank fast but neatly. Rosie pricked her ears, flung herself on and off and then gave a series of truimphant bucks as she raced after Tristram. Banjo made his usual stag-like leaps, Berry ran out. David was shouting insults at Lynne as the ride came round again. This time even the less confident ponies looked happy, and Lynne, who had joined on behind, rode with much more dertermination and went over with a shriek and a scramble.

"Well done," David shouted. "Make a fuss of the ponies." Then he limped over to Sarah. "What's the trouble, Sarah?" he asked.

"It's no good, he just *won't*." Sarah sounded tearful. "He's got a phobia."

"No, I don't think so, after all he jumped it with Alice," David reminded her quietly. "Are you going to try again, or shall I put someone else up?"

"I don't care what you do, he's a beastly pony and I hate him. I don't care what my mother says," Sarah flung herself off Bowie. "If she won't change him I'll have to go back to Chess."

"Supposing you swop with Tina." David seemed to be taking Sarah's tantrum calmly. "Tina," he called, "let Sarah try my pony will you? And I'd like to see you on Bowie. You can both have a ride round while the rest of us practise the slip rail. Now," he went on as the other pony club members gathered round, "try and see this slip rail business from the pony's point of view. If you gallop up to those rails he'll assume you want to jump them and,

270

if you do, you'll clock up sixty penalty points. So, explain that you're going to dismount. Instead of half-halting in preparation for the approach, take your feet out of the stirrups, dangle your legs down in an obvious manner and say 'Whoa'. If you have a nut like Jupiter, don't approach the rails head on, but from a slant. Three signals that you don't want to jump. O.K.? For the gate, you won't want to abandon your stirrups, so say 'Whoa' and use the slant approach, coming up to the hinge end of the gate and then riding alongside it."

"What happens if the pony won't jump the lower rail?" asked Rupert. "Can you take it down too?"

"I suppose so, but you'd waste a lot of time," answered David.

"Jupe will jump it, but I'll never get on again," moaned Hanif.

"Off you go, James, and remember to say 'Whoa' in the right sort of voice. Shouted briskly it sounds exactly like 'Go' to ponies. And when you're through the slip rails you can go on and jump the stick heap and the uphill log," he shouted after James.

The first three riders, James, Seb and Alice, had no problems, but Raj¬h was slow to understand what was expected of him and insisted on inspecting the rail carefully before making a large, cautious leap.

"Give him some practise at home," David, who'd driven over to the rails, told Lizzie. Rosie was even slower, she seemed to think it impossible that she should jump from a standstill and without a rider. Eventually, after a lot of dithering and some shooing from David, she crawled over, one leg at a time, knocking down the pole.

"Give her a lot of practise at home. Tie poles across all your gateways and lead her over them as you bring her in and out of the field," advised David as he tried to help Rupert to put up the rails.

Netti swept briskly through the slip rails and was followed by Hanif, approaching at a cautious trot, feet out of his stirrups and whoaing loudly. Jupiter made an enormous leap over the tiny rail, almost landing on Hanif, but then he refused to stand to be remounted.

"Stand, stand," intoned Hanif, hopping desperately in pursuit of his twirling pony.

"Clear the course," said David. "Over this way and I'll tell you what to do." He waved his good arm at Paul, awaiting his turn with growing impatience. Banjo was expert at slip rails. He nipped over neatly, turning as he landed so that his rider could stay beside the fence. Paul replaced the pole and vaulted on almost in one movement, then they raced away.

"That's the best so far," called David and, turning to Hanif, he went on, "Look, I know it's correct to face the tail when mounting, but sometimes, with a difficult pony, you do better to face the head. Give it a try, only don't stick your toe into him. You're not tall enough to get your toe right under the girth so turn it out, the whole foot along his shoulder. That's right. Now at least you're looking where you're going. Shorten the inside rein and let him turn round and round you for a bit. With luck he'll get bored, and at least you don't have to hop so far now that you're the centre of a very small circle. Well done!" he broke off to shout at Lynne, and then turned back to Hanif. "Keep the inside rein short, keep on saying 'Stand', and as soon as he does stand make a big fuss of him. This is one of those battles you've *got* to win."

"Supposing I don't?" asked Hanif, hopping desperately.

"You will." David turned his attention to Sarah and Tina. "How are you two getting on? Let's see you both over the poles a couple of times."

Sarah led the way. She had woken Vulcan up, shaken him out of some of his rather ponderous stateliness. Tina followed on a happy-looking Bowie, who was going smoothly, ears pricked.

"Good, now over the bank and through the slip rails," shouted David.

"He gave in, he stood," announced Hanif, with relief rather than triumph, and David, watching the two girls over the bank, also seemed relieved when the second pony landed safely.

"Great, we're all beginning to get somewhere then," he said. "Will you hang on and let me through the slip rails when those two have done with them?"

That was quite a test, thought Hanif, when Jupiter gave in and stood, much sooner this time. He knew he couldn't have done it last holidays. Mounting, he patted the sweaty liver chestnut neck and cantered after the Land Rover and the other ponies towards the stickheap jump.

"I like him far better than beastly Bowie," Sarah was telling David, "He's like a bigger Chess."

"I think Bowie's lovely," argued Tina, saddened by Sarah's rejection. "He's so slim and light and when he jumps you don't notice take-offs and landings, it's like sailing about on a feather."

"Different ponies suit different people," said David. "It's a great mistake to hang on to one you don't really like, because he'd probably be much happier with someone else, too. There's our hunting gate." He pointed along the edge of the wood. "And Mr Roberts has taken a stretch of the fence down here. You ride into the wood, come out through the gate and then jump our new fence into the quarry."

"Quarry?"

"Where?"

The pony club members looked round suspiciously.

"Hidden in that clump of trees." David pointed further along the field. "It's only a small one. But, first of all, do you know how to open gates correctly?"

"Depends whether they open towards you or away from you," observed Paul.

"Not entirely. Eitherway, you need whip and reins in the hand that's not doing the opening and you approach from the hinge end—if possible, keeping up your impulsion. If you overshoot the latch and have to start reining back you're bound to lose time. Try to hold on to the gate as you go through, turn the pony with your legs, ride foward again and shut it."

"But quite often in hunter trials if you slam them hard enough they shut by themselves," objected Seb.

"If you find you've got an easy gate in the competition, fine," agreed David, "but it's no good *schooling* the pony on the assumption that the gate will be easy. If he gets in the habit of racing on, he's not going to like it when you meet an awkward one that swings open rather than shut; he won't want to wait while you fiddle about, and you'll find yourself in trouble. Anyway, you must check that it's shut and stays shut, or you risk elimination from the whole competition."

Rupert shuddered. "Think of doing all that shooting, running and swimming, half killing yourself, and then getting eliminated at the gate."

David drove on towards the quarry, and the pony club members, all anxious to see the new fence, were soon cantering ahead.

"It's a bit steep," complained James, halting on the edge of the quarry and looking doubtfully at the fence which had been built halfway down the slope. "It's as steep as the hillside, and the jump's much higher than the one we practised over last holidays."

"Ugh! And it's solid," added Alice.

"*Very* solid," agreed Rupert, looking gloomily at the pole, so stout it was almost a log, which was lashed along the tops of three dwarf posts by a thick cord attached to large staples. "That's not going to fall down or bust when Rosie gets right under it and forgets how to take off."

"And there are two more of them," Lizzie pointed out.

"Oh, they're no problem," Seb told her. "This one's the killer."

The other riders kept their thoughts to themselves as they viewed the fence in apprehensive silence.

"I suppose you take it very slowly," said Lesley, as David limped over from the Land Rover.

"Not too slowly or you'll run out of steam and refuse number three," he answered. "You must maintain impulsion."

"Can you lean back?" asked Seb.

"You can, but I wouldn't advise it. In a steeplechase, with plenty of room between the fences, you can afford to lean back and let the reins slip—there's time to pick them up and balance the horse for the next jump. But if you lean back here, you'll almost certainly run out. These little fences are designed to need a bit more riding than anything we jumped last holidays," he went on, looking round at the gloomy faces. "But the ponies are going a lot better and you're all far more in charge. We've passed the creeping and popping stage of the very green horse, and now we're asking for impulsion, balance and obedience."

"But shall we get it?" asked Rupert, shaking his head gravely. "And supposing Rosie forgets to take off?"

"I was coming to that," said David, settling himself on his shooting stick. "Have we discussed how you indicate to a cross-country horse that he's to stand back, or take off close to, a fence?"

"No."

"I don't think so."

"Not these holidays, anyway."

"Well, imagine that you are going to jump a gate or other straight fence. You all know that you want to take off at least the height of the jump away, and up to the height-and-a-half away if your pony has a lot of scope. You want him to 'stand back', and to indicate this to him you approach with a 'holding' rein. You come to the fence at a steady pace, using your legs and keeping a constant contact with the pony's mouth. Now, supposing that you're approaching a triple, or a hedge with a large ditch on the *landing* side, you want to take off nearer the jump—with a triple only the height of the *nearest* pole away. You tell the pony this by riding with a 'giving rein'. This doesn't mean that you drop your hands suddenly or throw the reins away, but that during the approach your hands follow rather than hold. If you check or half-halt it must be a long way back and not during the approach."

David looked round at the members' faces and knew that his explanation had been too long, most of them had stopped listening. "Now apply all that to these three little fences," he said briskly. "You want to stand back for the downhill one. So sit up, look up and ride with a holding rein. The middle one is easy; just look at it, keep the pony straight, use your legs. For the uphill one you need impulsion and you mustn't stand back, so ride with a giving rein."

"People do lean back, really good riders do; I've watched them at horse trials," observed Sarah in an argumentative voice.

"Yes, they do," David agreed. "Sometimes they get away with it and sometimes they don't, but there's no point in copying even good riders' mistakes."

"Do you really think Rosie will survive the first one?" asked Rupert gloomily.

"Yes, if you sit up and help her. The riders have got to work, those who leave everything to the pony, look down, or rest their hands and weight on the pony's neck will come to grief," David answered. "All right, James? Start from here, into the wood, back through the gate and then the quarry. Harry, you go second, then Alice. Seb, Netti and Lizzie, you'll be the next three."

The waiting riders stationed themselves at the edge of the trees from where they could see the gate and down into the quarry.

Alice, rather ashamed at her own feeling of apprehension, wondered if James minded being the trail-blazer, the brave one, *always* going first. "Have you jumped one before?" she asked Seb.

He shook his head.

"It's much worse than the quarry at the Area Cup competition," complained Lizzie. "There the jump was at the very top of the slope, so you just had to pop over slowly."

"Yes, the take-off of this one is very scary," agreed Tina. "I can see Bowie missing the right moment and skidding down into the pole."

"Precisely. And then Rosie will muddle up her legs and collapse on her nose," observed Rupert gloomily.

"I'm not worried," giggled Lynne. "I know that Berry's not going to do it, whatever David says; she'll just run out."

"He's through the gate, the next one can start," called David, as James appeared looking calm and business-like. He steadied Ferdie and they started down the slope at a collected canter. Brown ears pricked, the pony gathered himself carefully and jumped neatly, then they were both looking at the next fence, and in a moment they were over that and pushing on for the uphill fence on the far side. As they cleared it the watchers cheered.

"A copy-book performance," shouted David, looking pleased.

"That was very cool," remarked Seb admiringly.

Alice started for the gate feeling much more confident. She was almost sure now that Saffy would also be capable of jumping the quarry.

"Steady, Jupe, steady." Hanif, sounding slightly apprehensive, appeared at a brisk canter. He half-halted on the brink, Jupiter looked down and, sizing up the new fence in a split second, swept confidently on, clearing it and then the other two with obvious zest.

David laughed. "Old Lionheart really enjoys his cross-country," he said and turned to watch Alice.

Alice was trying to warn Saffron that care was needed. "Sit down, a holding rein," she reminded herself. The dun pony stood back, jumped willingly and then cantered on to take the other two in a very matter-of-fact manner.

The watchers' spirits rose. They had all thought James might get over, but seeing Harry and Alice jump the horror fence so effortlessly had taken away most of its terror.

Jigsaw approached the fence cautiously, but Seb, on his mettle now that no one else had refused, gave an encouraging shout of, "Come on, boy," and used his legs,

277

and the skewbald jumped and then cantered on more confidently towards the next two. Tristram, who followed, flew over all three jumps as lightly and easily as any of the larger ponies. Then Rajah appeared, peering suspiciously and slowing down despite Lizzie's determined riding.

"Oh, go on, Ra," she shouted desperately as he began to slide to a halt, and, taking her whip in one hand, she whacked him. Surprised, Rajah took off, and Lizzie, grabbing back her rein, straightened him for the next fence.

"Well done, good timing," called David. He turned to the watching riders. "Whacking a pony like that on the approach can be a complete disaster, it's not to be recommended normally, but with a sticky old pony like Rajah, who knows all about jumping but prefers to take a good look, it can work marvels. Provided you get the timing right, of course, and Lizzie did."

Rupert, who had followed his sisters, was still struggling with the gate. Rosie, wearing her stupidest expression, was either moving in the wrong direction or simply standing stockstill and pretending not to notice that, despite Rupert's long arms, the gate was just out of his reach.

"Circle her," shouted David, "Small circle, but get her moving forward again; do a bit of shoulder-in."

Rupert, re-approaching in the shoulder-in position, managed to reach the latch, but having got through the gate, he had another battle before Rosie would agree to shut it. Then he set off at a rather sprawling canter for the quarry. As soon as Rosie saw the jump she began to brake, then to skid and, with terror in her bulging eyes, she slithered into the fence and almost overbalanced. Rupert sat tight, but several of the waiting riders turned pale.

"Perhaps we could have a groundline," he suggested cheerfully.

"If you clear the course you may get a lead," David told him, "Lesley's on her way."

But Lesley and Stardust, approaching the fence with a mutual lack of enthusiasm, came to a restrained halt.

"Oh, come on, you jumped downhill last holidays," protested David. "You've got to encourage that little mare, set her alight, throw your heart over. She isn't a brave pony, so you have to be the courageous one, Lesley."

They tried again and this time Stardust jumped. To everyone's amazement Rosie followed, flinging herself over with an enormous untidy leap and then pursuing the chestnut pony over the next two fences while Rupert cheered and waved one arm in triumph.

It was Banjo's turn next and he made one of his usual, unnecessarily high, stag-like leaps and then, surprised by the long way down, pecked on landing. Paul, who was sitting too far forward and resting his hands, went over the pony's head. He jumped up quickly and dragged Banjo out of the way as Tina and Bowie approached. The bay pony gave the fence a look of astonishment and stopped dead. Then he began to fuss, sweating and champing, ears back, eyes rolling.

"It's all right, Bowie." Tina tried to sound calm as she stroked his neck. "It's O.K., you'll do it next time."

"Clear the course!" shouted David, as Sarah and Vulcan arrived. "Tina, wait. Paul, follow my pony."

Vulcan cantered steadily down the slope, stood back and jumped the small fence easily, though Sarah was resting her hands and practically lying along his neck.

"Good, but he did it all, Sarah, you didn't help. Well done, Paul, he added as the little black followed, taking a small, cautious leap this time.

Then Lynne appeared and Berry cantered in pursuit of Banjo. Racing down the slope passing the first fence, her rider didn't seem to be making much effort to keep her straight and jumping the second. Despite David's roars of "Come back!" she chased Banjo over the third.

"Bowie refused then," said Sarah in a triumphant voice as she rejoined the group of riders at the top of the quarry.

279

"Yes, and I'm coming to that, it was quite an interesting one." David was looking round to see if he had their attention. "Have you heard of the 'refusal of the trained horse'?"

"No." They shook their heads, the braver riders wishing that he would hurry up as they wanted second turns.

"Well, I'm sure you've all seen top-class horses coming into a big fence, getting their stride wrong, and, realizing that they can't do it, that there's going to be an almighty crash if they try, refusing. It's a last-minute refusal and there's nothing mulish or obstinate about it—the horses are only too keen to turn round and try again. Full of confidence that they've got it right, they fly over at the second attempt. I'm pretty sure our fence took Bowie by surprise and by the time he saw it he knew he would be taking off too late, so he sensibly refused. You were quite right, Tina, to calm him down. Obviously one should never punish a horse for that sort of refusal as, if one forces them to jump at all costs, one could get a very nasty fall. O.K., let's go. Tina, Lynne and then everyone else; we won't bother about the gate this time, you can practise them at home."

Bowie pricked his ears and jumped the fence carefully and competently. Lynne cantered past again, but this time David pretended not to see. Everyone else went clear and even Rosie seemed quite confident.

"Remember, there's shooting on Tuesday and the rally on Friday," said David, as they parted in the sunken lane. "If I do have time for an extra cross-country practice next week I'll tell you on Tuesday. And *please* train. It's essential that you all do plenty of running and swimming."

"And shooting," added Seb as David drove away. "I mean to be a crack shot by Tuesday."

"Can't we all come and practise?" pleaded Netti. "We could borrow the pony club pistols and give David and Mrs Blazeaway a terrific surprise as we score bull after bull on Tuesday."

"There has to be an adult there," Lesley reminded

them, "and I'm sure my mother won't want to come. She's already complaining about the time she has to give to the pony club."

"But Seb's parents will be there, so that's O.K.," said Rupert.

"No they won't," Seb sounded savage. "I told you they had split up!"

"Sorry, sorry." Rupert looked suitably remorseful, everyone else was silent and embarrassed.

"Well, I suppose my father'll be around," Seb admitted after a pause.

CHAPTER SIX

We're In Real Trouble

"Seb's got his pistol and the Robertses are going to bring the pony club ones," Hanif told Alice, telephoning her on Saturday evening. "We're all to go to Kiddleworth tomorrow morning, but not before eleven; the Wheelers have just been on the phone to me."

"Terrific," said Alice. "What time do we start?"

"A quarter to ten?" suggested Hanif. "We're to take our lunches, and the Wheelers say they'll take us for a ride, either over the downs or round Beacon Hill, after the shooting."

"That sounds really great," said Alice. "It'll get the ponies fit, but what about swimming?"

"We could give the ponies a rest on Monday and spend most of the day at the pool. Let's try to persuade all the others to come too," suggested Hanif.

The ponies were very surprised on Sunday morning when they were not allowed to turn down Garland Farm lane, but were ridden on along the narrow, winding uphill road and through the village of Kidlake. Alice and Hanif looked into the Old Rectory's stableyard, but, though the weed-ridden cobbles were scattered with abandoned grooming tools, cans of hoof oil and plastic buckets, the blue stable doors stood open and there was no sign of people or ponies.

"They've gone on then," said Hanif with a worried look at his watch. "I hope we've allowed enough time."

"It won't matter if we're late," Alice told him. "There are no official characters like David or Mrs Blazeaway to make speeches and, if everyone's coming, the turns will take ages, even with three pistols."

But Hanif still fussed, so they trotted briskly along the grass verge, climbing all the time towards the muted green, and billowing bulk of the downs.

Kiddleworth was a hamlet, a small cluster of cottages, with an inn and a shop but no church, built round a crossroads in a sheltered hollow on the height of a windswept down. They found the Old Forge on the edge of the hamlet opposite the inn, which was called The Packhorse and had a very over-burdened and dispirited pony struggling across it's weather-beaten sign. The Old Forge was a white-painted cottage, thatched, with dormer windows and a small front garden. It was the last cottage in the row and from the paddock on the far side of it came a series of welcoming neighs. Lizzie appeared at the open five-barred gate.

"Seb's still getting the shooting range ready," she explained. "Jigsaw and Ferdie are in the shelter, but we've tied our ponies to the paddock fence. So have the Robertses. The Rookes and Tina haven't arrived yet."

When the two new arrivals had been unbridled and tied up in their headcollars, Hanif and Alice followed Lizzie through a small wrought-iron gate into the garden.

"What a lovely cottage; it's a real picture-postcard one," said Alice, looking from the hollyhocks along the wall to the roses round the porch.

"It's too small and upstairs the windows are only knee high, you can't look out properly," grumbled Seb, "The only decent room is the one which used to be the forge. I liked our old house *much* better. And it's boring here, I've no friends."

"Living on the downs must be terrific in some ways though," objected Hanif. "It's lovely riding country."

"Except in the winter. You try riding up here in a hailstorm, or in an icy east wind; it's bitter," Rupert told him.

"I won't be here in the winter. My father's only rented the cottage until we've sorted ourselves out and found somewhere else to live," Seb explained. "I want to go back to the Frogmorton country, that's where all my friends are, but my father's not so keen, he seems to have a girlfriend who lives somewhere round here."

James was setting up the targets, pinning them to three large cardboard boxes which stood on three tables ranged along the hollyhock wall.

"We'll have to mind out for the shiny table on the end," said Seb. "The other two don't matter, but I took that one out of the sitting room and it looks a bit posh. I don't want it embedded with pellets and the owner after us."

"You'd better put the best shots at that end then," Netti told him.

"Not me," giggled Lynne. "I even managed to put shot on the next-door target, or so Mrs Halford said."

"Have you any straw bales handy, Seb?" asked James. "We ought to put one behind each target to stop the pellets ricocheting off the brick wall."

"Yes, in the shelter. Everyone come and help carry straw bales," commanded Seb.

At the same moment as the range was ready, the straw bales arranged, and the pistols and round tins of pellets placed on a long bench the correct distance from the targets, a clatter of hoofs was heard in the road and the heads of Lesley, Sarah and Tina appeared above the wall.

"We don't want to waste time," said Seb in a businesslike manner, "so let's start the first detail; that's James, Rupert and Harry. I thought I'd do the commanding. Can the rest of you show the Rookes where to tie their ponies?"

"Hallo, have you gone back to Chess then?" Oliver asked Sarah as he opened the five-barred gate to let the riders into the paddock.

"I suppose I can let Tina ride Bowie if I want to. I don't have to ask *your* permission," snapped Sarah.

"Poor old Sarah's afraid he'll shy at traffic," Lesley taunted her sister. "She gets worked up whenever anything bigger than a car appears; she's *making* him nervous."

"I *hate* stupid, boring, nervous ponies," said Sarah, dismounting. "I can't be bothered with calming and soothing them, but I'm good at getting the best out of sensible ones like Chess and Vulcan."

The shooting went well, though, to everyone's surprise, Hanif still beat James who was using Seb's impressive-looking, brand-new pistol. Seb loaned it to Alice in the second detail, but her score was still much lower than Lesley's, and Lizzie, conscientiously taking deep breaths and remembering to squeeze the trigger, was worse still. Netti, with Seb's pistol, was better than Sarah and Lynne, and then Seb himself shot against Paul and Tina and was the best, though he was still very dissatisfied with his score.

"I'm afraid it *is* people, not pistols, who clock up the scores," observed Rupert sadly.

"Can I just have a couple of shots with it, Seb?" asked Hanif.

"O.K., and Oliver wants a go," agreed Seb amiably. "He can have one of the pony club ones."

"Can I have a second turn?" asked Tina. "I'm not being greedy, it's just that Lynne and I have much the lowest scores so we must need the most practise."

Seb let James command while he loaded for Oliver, and everyone else collapsed on the daisy-dotted lawn and began to argue about the best time for a swimming session on Monday. The shooters had fired their first five shots and were changing their targets when a sudden commotion broke out in the paddock: angry squeals, anxious neighs, the nerve-racking thud of kicks landing on another pony and then the crack of splintering, breaking wood.

They ran, propelling each other through the narrow gateway, all fearing that they would find their pony injured. Berry was loose—she was trotting up to Jupiter, squealing loudly, spoiling for trouble.

"Stop that!" shouted Hanif, racing to drive her away. Lynne ran too as the others looked round, checking their own ponies.

"Bowie's loose, he's broken the fence!" The panic-stricken note in Sarah's voice made them all turn. The bay pony was retreating across the paddock, snorting in terror at the fencing rail tied to his headcollar rope which pursued him as he fled.

"You fool, Tina! Why did you tie him to that rail? It must have been loose!" Sarah screamed. "He'll be killed and it's all your fault."

"Whoa, boy. Whoa."

"Stand Bowie, stand." Alice and Lizzie, talking soothingly, were trying to approach the terrified pony. "If we could both grab the rail at once we might be able to hold him," suggested Lizzie.

Alice was proffering the few pony nuts she had scraped from her pockets. Sarah was still screaming at Tina, who stood pale and horror-struck.

"Shut up, Sarah!" Netti turned upon her. "You're frightening Bowie, making things worse."

"Have you got a bucket of feed handy?" James asked Seb.

"I'll get one." Seb ran back towards the shelter.

"Make a half circle and trap him in the corner," suggested Rupert, as Bowie's snorting retreat took him to the far end of the paddock.

"Mummy'll kill me if he gets hurt," moaned Sarah. "She won't be able to get her money back and it *wasn't* my fault."

Alice and Lizzie were still whoaing soothingly when Berry, whom Lynne, Paul and Hanif were trying to catch, evaded her pursuers and galloped down to Bowie's corner of the field. The bay pony tried to dodge his tormentor and, as he swung away, the rail swung too, one end of it cracking against his forelegs. With a look of wild fear he fled, full gallop, across the paddock, the trailing rail beside him whacking and cracking against his legs, increasing his terror with every stride.

Rupert swore.

"Shut the gate!" shouted Alice, suddenly noticing that the five-barred gate into the road stood wide open. Lizzie took up the cry, "Ollie, shut the gate."

Oliver heard her, turned and ran, but he was too late. Bowie, galloping faster and faster in an attempt to leave the rail behind, had seen the open gate too and decided to escape. As he raced through, the rail caught between the spars and the sudden check caused him to skid and fall. As he lay struggling in the road the pony club members ran forward, but he scrambled to his feet and there was a sharp crack as the rail snapped in two. Then the terror-crazed pony was off along the road, the half rail still firmly tied to his headcollar rope, still cracking against his legs.

"Oh *no!*" said Rupert, watching helplessly. A sobbing Sarah and a white-faced Tina ran in pursuit.

"We'd better take the ponies," Hanif called to them.

"Would your father take some of us in the car?" Lesley asked Seb.

"No, sorry, he's gone to see someone."

Hanif and Alice were saddling and bridling hastily. "We'd better stay in groups," suggested Hanif. "We don't want the ponies going mad."

"Come on, Ollie, tack up quickly," called Lizzie as she grabbed Rajah's bridle. "Where's your crash cap?"

"Wait for me," Lynne was shouting. She'd caught Berry at last.

"I'd better lead Chess," decided Lesley, "or he'll break loose too."

"Could you hold Jupe?" asked Hanif, breathlessly. "He's determined to twirl." Alice, already mounted, held Jupiter.

"You two go on," Lizzie told them, "I'll wait for the others."

They galloped across the paddock, Paul on their heels. James was waiting for Seb who had had to fetch his tack. They trotted into the road, down which Bowie had turned towards Coombe Lentworth. A crowd of people in the

Packhorse garden were waving and pointing. Taking the ponies on to the grass verge, they cantered and soon overtook Sarah and Tina who had slowed to a painful, breathless jog.

"Can't you catch him? If he isn't killed by a car he'll break his knees!" Sarah screamed at them hysterically, "and it's not my fault."

They cantered on without answering, there was no point in wasting breath. The driver of the first car they met shouted rudely at them; something about not being fit to be in charge of animals. At least Bowie had survived *one* car, thought Alice.

They rode on, frightening themselves with images of the mangled body which could await them round each twist or turn in the road. They all knew that Bowie's flimsy form, fine-coated and spindly-legged, would stand no chance at all in collision with a lorry. The next car came slowly, the driver, expecting more loose ponies, looked relieved and waved them on, shouting that "he" wasn't far ahead.

Then, above the clatter and thud of their hoofs, they heard the roar of an engine; the road straightened and a large, red tractor towing a dray piled high with straw bales came into view. There was no sign of Bowie. They looked beyond the tractor, up the long straight road between hedges powdered with white chalk dust, but it was empty. The driver switched off his engine.

"You lost a pony?" he asked, shouting though the roar had stopped, and went on without waiting for an answer. "He didn't like the look of my tractor, it slowed him up a bit, so I turned him off the road, up the drive to the stud. I thought he'd come to less harm up there."

"Oh, *thank you!*" said Alice gratefully. "That's terrific, we ought to be able to catch him now."

"Yes, thank you very much *indeed*," added Hanif.

"He was in a fair old state, blood all over his legs," called the tractor driver as they cantered on. Ahead, a white-painted sign pointed to the right. "Coombe Manor Stud," read Alice. "That's it."

They turned up the weedless gravel drive, between white-painted posts and rails which fenced the well-kept paddocks on either side. Flat, symmetrical and evenly grazed they held large numbers of well-bred-looking horses, which, standing under trees or in shelters, dozed peacefully, shaded from the midday sun.

Alice pulled up. "One of us ought to wait on the road and tell the others where he's gone," she said. "We don't want them going on to Coombe Lentworth."

"I'll stop," offered Paul quickly.

"O.K.," they agreed and trotted on.

"I hope he's gone into the stableyard and not in there," shouted Hanif nervously as a long, low, old, but perfectly kept house, surrounded by a beautiful garden, came in sight.

But the stableyard looked perfect too, thought Alice, with its clock tower and centrepiece of mown turf; it was far too orderly to welcome runaway ponies.

"Oh, he has, that does it," groaned Hanif. "Prepare for fireworks," he added, slowing Jupiter to a collected trot.

They passed through the open white gate and saw Bowie standing in the middle of a velvet-smooth lawn, head down, sides heaving, his coat was dark with sweat and flecked with blood. A group of very smartly dressed and rather elderly people had gathered round him and they watched a tall silver-haired man, who, having unclipped the rope from the headcollar, was trying to loosen the knot which held the remains of the rail.

"Poor little wretch," said one woman loudly. "How *could* his owner have been so *utterly* stupid?"

"Criminal."

"Some people shouldn't be allowed *near* animals," the group agreed. Then, hearing the crunch of hoofs on gravel, they all turned accusingly on Alice and Hanif.

"Is this your pony?" shouted the silver-haired man aggressively. "Are you crazy? You look old enough to know how to tie a pony up or haven't your tiny minds grasped the fact that ponies can jump back? Hasn't anyone told you that if you don't have a ring in a wall you tie them to a loop of string, which breaks before the fence does? No one ties a pony to a fencing rail unless he's plain stupid."

Alice and Hanif looked at his angry red face in silence, not sure whether he expected an answer or a defence. "Thank you for catching him," said Alice politely.

"He belongs to a friend of ours," added Hanif.

"Well, give your friend my compliments and tell him or her that such a stupid clot doesn't deserve a pony. This nice little animal could well have been killed."

"We'll do that," agreed Hanif, who was desperately trying to prevent the impatient Jupiter from twirling on the velvet lawn. Alice had dismounted and was inspecting Bowie's legs. They looked awful, scraped and battered, scratched and bloody, but there didn't seem to be any deep gash or serious injury.

"Thank you very much," she said, taking the headcollar rope. "I'll walk him back. Can you lead Saffy, Harry?"

"Rotten, stupid children, not fit to have ponies," the silver-haired man stormed at their departing backs. He turned towards his guests. "Come on, everyone; back to lunch."

Hanif and Alice were halfway down the drive when Tina and Sarah came running to meet them.

"Is he hurt?"

"Is he lame?" they called breathlessly.

"He's a bit hurt and a bit lame, but he'll survive," answered Hanif who was in the lead.

Sarah set up a terrible wail.

"Look at those legs, Mummy'll kill me. He's all smashed up and he's limping—we're never going to be able to send him back like that."

"I don't think he's done any permanent damage," Alice tried to be comforting.

"You only say that because he's not your pony," Sarah shrieked at her angrily. "Anyone can see he's ruined his legs; it'll be months and months before they're properly better."

Tina seemed to want to lead Bowie, and Alice, glad to escape from Sarah's hysterical moanings, handed him over and mounted Saffron. The other riders were all waiting by the gate into the road.

"Seb went up some of the way and saw you'd caught him, but seeing what Mr Collingwood's temper is like I thought the rest of us had best wait down here," explained Paul.

"You mean you knew what we were letting ourselves in for," asked Hanif indignantly, "and you didn't warn us?"

"He's cunning, *that's* why he offered to wait for the others," observed Alice.

Paul smiled sheepishly. "Did he bawl you out? He's got a name for it round here. He's really hot-tempered; lots of the local people won't work for him."

"Dad says he can be really nasty," added Lynne.

"He was very rude to us and sent even ruder messages to Bowie's owner," Hanif told them. "We didn't answer back."

"He didn't complain about having his lawn trampled on, he gave us a lecture on how to tie ponies up and called us stupid clots. I think he was upset about the mess Bowie was in," added Alice, trying to be fair. "He said if you tie ponies to fences you must use loops of string which will break."

"He's got something there," said James.

"Yes, I suppose he has," agreed Hanif. "But he could have put it more politely."

"Never mind, it's marvellous that nothing *really* awful happened," Lizzie told them. "It could have been a real disaster."

Everyone was begining to feel better, and Sarah, muttering that there was no point in them both walking, had mounted Chess, when suddenly James shouted out, "The pistols! What did we do with the pistols?"

"We left them on the bench." Seb put a hand to his forehead. "Oh hell . . . I was loading for Oliver. I just put the blessed thing down and ran."

"So did I," admitted Hanif guiltily, "and so did Tina. But won't your father have heard the commotion, realized that something was wrong, and collected the pistols?"

"Not a chance. He went out before we started. He took the car. Oh *hell*," said Seb again, his face conscience-stricken.

"But Seb, you did say . . ." began James and then stopped. "Will you be O.K. if some of us trot on?" he asked Lesley.

"Yes, we'll just walk him home," she answered drearily.

"We could go on to Garland Farm and see if Dad's busy. He might be able to take you home in the cattle truck," suggested Lynne.

"We'd better make sure the pistols are all right first," Paul told her. "It'll be the last straw if something's happened to them."

"Yes, if they've gone we'll be in real trouble," agreed Rupert, urging Rosie into her fastest trot.

They were all worried, all reproaching themselves for their carelessness as they clattered back down the road to Kiddleworth, but they were still hoping to find the pistols lying where they had left them and promised themselves that, if they did, they would be much more careful in future. Then, as they came round the last bend they could see three motorbikes waiting in the road between The Packhorse and the Old Forge. Hearing the hoofs, the three helmeted riders looked round and then began to shout to invisible companions. A moment later three more helmeted figures came rushing out of the cottage gate and flung themselves on to the motorbike pillions. The engines roared and, as the bikes raced away, each of the pillion riders brandished something triumphantly, something which looked horribly like a pistol.

"Oh *no*!" cried Seb desperately as he jumped off Jigsaw, threw his reins to James, and ran into the garden. A quick look told him that the pistols had gone. The other riders had pursued the motorbikes as far as the crossroads.

"This way!" they shouted to James and Seb, pointing straight ahead to the road that led on over the downs. The grass verge was wide and they galloped recklessly along it, trying not to think of anything but overtaking the motorbikes. Hanif, in the lead, came to where a chalk track led up into the very heart of the downs. He pulled up and called to the middle-aged couple who were walking down it towards the road.

"Excuse me, did you see some men on motorbikes?" he asked, polite but breathless.

"Yes, we did. Young hooligans," answered the man angrily. "We're going straight home to phone the police, *and* I'll write to the Council tonight."

"They were waving guns," added the woman. "Pistol things. They looked real to me. You're not safe anywhere nowadays."

"Thank you," said Hanif, looking round to see if the other riders were following. As soon as they were all past the couple he gave Jupiter his head and led the long line of ponies up the grassy centre of the rutted chalk track at a brisk canter. When the track widened out they found themselves on top of the downs, which billowed wide and windswept in every direction, and with only a wire fence dividing their track from the carefully tended gallops where the local racing stables trained.

Hanif let Jupiter slide into a gallop, James and Seb passed Alice, Rupert hurtled after them, Netti followed him. Alice, determined not to ask too much of her unfit pony, found herself riding stride for stride with Rajah.

"I can't see any sign of them, can you?" she shouted to Lizzie.

"No, they seem to have vanished." Lizzie looked very depressed.

"It's no use galloping about without a purpose," shouted Alice, suddenly feeling angry with the leaders.

They came to one of the downland crossroads and pulled up the sweating, puffing ponies. Four tracks wheeled away, north, south, east and west. Shading their eyes with their hands the riders gazed into the glaring distance. They could see walkers, horsemen, but no motorbikes. They felt hot and tired and desperately worried; it was long past lunchtime and hunger was adding to their depression.

"There's no sign of them," Hanif admitted reluctantly.

"Perhaps they're down in some hollow," suggested James.

"Or they've dumped the bikes and are lying in the grass blazing away with our pistols." Rupert sounded aggrieved.

"If only we had some binoculars," sighed Seb.

"What *are* we going to do?" asked Lizzie.

"We'll have to tell David," said Alice sadly. "We really have messed things up."

Paul and Lynne, who had been very quiet since the theft of the pistols, were looking at each other with despairing expressions.

"We'd better own up," said Paul.

Lynne looked at James. "David wasn't about when we went to borrow the pistols, so we took them without asking. They were only locked in his tack room and we know where he keeps the key."

"Oh *no,* not on top of everything else."

"Hell, we are in trouble." The pony club members looked at Lynne and then at each other. "This makes it a thousand times worse."

"I can't see that it makes *all* that difference," argued Paul. "What really matters is losing the pistols, and Mr Fuller not being there."

"No it's not," Alice disagreed. "O.K., we all forgot to check that Mr Fuller was around, and though we were total idiots to leave the pistols lying on the bench in full view of the road, it was an emergency. But if the whole thing was taking place without David knowing, if the pistols were borrowed without his permission, then he's going to be really angry."

"Yes, there is going to be the most fearful row," agreed Rupert.

"And on top of that my father's going to go raving mad." said Seb gloomily. "I promised that I'd be responsible if he bought me a pistol and now I've lost it— on the very first day."

"It's no use standing here, we'd better go to Garland Farm and get it over," said Hanif wearily.

"Oh, let's wait a bit," protested Lynne. "Those boys probably took the pistols for fun, they may bring them back when they've finished larking about."

"Do you really believe that?" asked Netti.

"They could do." Paul supported his sister. "It's worth hanging on a bit to see."

"We'd better go back to my place and eat our lunches then," Seb decided dismally. "And hope for a miracle."

"I don't think you'll get one," James told him. "I think they've nicked them. You should have asked David," he told the Robertses, "I thought you had."

"That's right, blame us." Lynne's usually laughing face looked frightened and puffy, as though she was near to tears.

"There's no point in blaming anyone," said Alice. "It's just a terrible disaster."

"A real Woodbury-shaker," agreed Rupert gloomily, "and we're all in it, right up to our necks."

They rode slowly and sadly back to the Old Forge. They decided not to tie the ponies up, but to hold them as they ate their lunches. Seb hurried hopefully to the garden to see if the pistols had been returned to their bench, but he returned shaking his head dolefully.

"You start eating," he told the others. "I'm going across to the pub to ask if they know those blokes." He soon came back. "No luck, they don't belong round here," he told the other pony club members. "The guy at the pub says they're complete strangers and too noisy for Kiddleworth; he hopes he won't see them again."

"Now what?" asked Hanif, breaking a gloomy silence.

"We'd better ride to Garland Farm in a body and confess," said Alice. "I can't think of any other way out."

"What about the Rookes and Tina?" asked Oliver. "It's their fault too."

"Well they *had* to take Bowie home *and* they've got to face the old Rooke," Netti told him.

"Can we talk to Mum and Dad first?" asked Lynne. "They know how to handle David."

"Yes, if they break it to him we mightn't get quite such a rollicking," agreed Paul. "And there's still a chance those blokes will bring the pistols back."

"I think David would much rather we told him ourselves," argued Alice. "And shouldn't we tell the police too?"

"The trouble is that time is running out," said Hanif. "I've promised to be home for tea as we're going to visit relations this evening. So if it's not now, it'll have to be tomorrow morning as far as I'm concerned. And we ought to tell David *before* the police."

"I'm for putting the confession scene off, in case there *is* a miracle and the pistols reappear. We could put it to the vote," suggested Rupert.

"I agree," said Netti. "Those guys looked silly, but not mean. We don't want to get them into trouble if it *is* just a joke."

"And I agree with Alice," announced Lizzie. "Tell David now."

"Yes, let's get it over and let him tell the police," decided Hanif.

"Four against, three for telling him," said Rupert. "James, Seb?"

"Put it off," answered Seb. "I don't think I'd survive facing David *and* my father on the same day; let's spread it."

"Five for putting it off, three for immediate execution. Your vote doesn't matter, James, you can stop trying to make up your mind."

Hanif mounted. "O.K., so we telephone each other about developments?" he asked.

"Yes, if Seb can ring me and the Wheelers, I'll ring you,

296

Hanif, and you can pass the news on to Alice.. And the Wheelers can tell the Robertses and the Rookes," said James, glad to have something practical to settle. "I hope this doesn't ruin the whole holidays," he added gloomily.

"I'm afraid it's bound to," answered Alice sadly.

"Well, you can't shoot without pistols," said Netti, "so it looks like the end of the Tetrathlon. It's a shame, I was looking forward to it."

"You told me you were going up to see the Fullers' cottage and ride on the downs." Mrs Rooke glared at her daughters with angry, magnified eyes. "You said nothing about shooting, or tying the ponies to a fence for hours—of course I wouldn't have allowed that. What were you thinking of, Lesley? Surely you're old enough to know better?"

They stood at the open door of the loosebox looking at Bowie, who felt worse now that his battered legs were stiffening, and trembled pitifully at the pain as, with hanging head and dull eye, he tried to rest them in turn. Lesley shrugged her shoulders. "You can't blame me, you know Sarah doesn't listen to anything I say. She's supposed to be the clever one."

"Well, you tied Stardust to the fence too. It's not my fault if that beastly Berry picked on Bowie to kick," Sarah screamed at her sister. "It was Lynne's fault for not tying Berry up properly or David's, he allowed it, he let us have the pistols."

"You mean *David* gave permission for this shooting practice, knowing that there was no adult there to supervise?" demanded Mrs Rooke incredulously.

"We all thought Mr Fuller was going to be in charge," Lesley explained, "but he'd gone off somewhere. But the Robertses asked David for the pony club pistols so he *must* have known."

"It's disgraceful. I've never heard of such a thing. A pony club fixture without a single official present. In those circumstances our insurance would be invalid, and there could easily have been an accident to a child as well as a pony. I shall telephone David and have it out with him the moment we get home. Now the immediate question is—do we send for the vet? You've ruined an expensive pony—I can't see any hope of sending him back now, he's probably permanently blemished—and on top of that there'll be vet's bills to pay."

"He'll be all right, he's not very lame," Lesley told her mother. "Sarah had better hose his legs, that's what the vet told us to do when Stardust was caught up in the wire netting."

Paul and Lynne put off telling their parents what had happened until after tea, and then, when tea was over, they postponed it again until after supper. So when David came limping over to the farm cottage his face white and taut, his blue eyes hard and cold with suppressed anger, Mr and Mrs Roberts were taken completely by surprise.

"Lynne, Paul, Mrs Rooke tells me that you had a shooting practice up at Kiddleworth this morning, is that true?" he asked in a frigid voice.

"Yes," they answered, hastily averting their eyes from his furious face.

"She also tells me that the pony club pistols were used. I didn't believe her, but when I went to the tack room just now to check, I found they had gone. Did you take them?"

"Yes." Lynne and Paul nodded miserably.

"Without my permission and when you had been told that people of your age were only allowed to shoot with an adult present?"

"We thought Mr Fuller would be there, Seb said he would be."

"I see, but you thought it was all right to take the pistols? To unlock the tack room door and take the pistols without asking? I trusted you," he went on, when Lynne and Paul stayed silent. "It never occurred to me to hide the key in a place *you* didn't know about. I suppose I should have had more sense," he added bitterly.

"Here, David, hang on. It can't just have been these two, there must have been other kids involved," Mr Roberts protested.

"The others didn't know where I kept the tack room key." David's voice was sharp and unforgiving.

"Did they ask you to take the pistols up to Kiddleworth, Lynne?" enquired Mr Roberts.

"Yes." Lynne's voice came out as a whisper. "They all wanted to shoot so Seb's pistol wasn't much good on its own. We did *mean* to ask David."

"We did look for him." Paul, still staring at the floor, supported his sister. "But he'd taken the tractor somewhere and we didn't have much time."

David turned to the Roberts parents. "According to Mrs Rooke they tied the ponies to a fence while they shot. Berry broke loose and kicked Bowie who jumped back and then went off up the road with half the fence tied to him. They left the pistols on a bench in the garden while they chased and caught the pony. When they came back they saw six lads on three motorbikes making off with them. At that point the Rookes and Tina took Bowie home and the rest of you followed the motorbikes. Is that correct?" asked David, turning back to Lynne and Paul. Paul nodded.

"Yes, they went up on the downs and then we lost them," whispered Lynne.

"And you don't think you should have come straight back here and told me what you had done?" asked David.

"We thought the blokes might have taken the pistols for a laugh, that they might bring them back," explained Paul.

David gave an angry snort. "Well, that's the end of the Tetrathlon so far as I'm concerned," he said, in a voice that was still full of suppressed fury. "And now I suppose I had better ring the police," he added as he limped out of the cottage.

"Oh dear, oh dear," lamented Mrs Roberts. "Whatever on earth made you do such a thing, generally you're such sensible children."

Hanif didn't tell his mother and stepfather until late that night when they were driving home from Mr Franklin senior's seventieth birthday party.

"Your instincts were right, Harry," his stepfather said in the voice of certainty. "You all ought to have gone straight to David. Ten to one he'll now hear about it from someone else and, even if it's Mr Roberts speaking on your behalf, well, he'd have respected you more if you'd done your own owning up."

"It was difficult, Rupert was being democratic and my lot were outvoted," Hanif explained. "Now I don't know what to do."

"Sleep on it," advised Mr Franklin. "We'll talk about it in the morning. But I think someone must tell the police."

"I think you and Alice should ride over in the morning and tell David how very sorry you are. And how you did not know that the guns had been taken without permission," said Mrs Franklin. "You must never be too proud to say you are sorry when you know that you are in the wrong."

"Yes, I know that, Mum, but it's awkward; we oughtn't to put all the blame on Paul and Lynne."

"Sleep on it," advised Mr Franklin again.

Alice didn't tell her uncle and aunt what had happened but she went to bed that night feeling very sad. She had been enjoying the pony club so much and now it all seemed to be collapsing about her. Not only would all the Tetrathlon training be cancelled, but she had a feeling that David would never forgive them, never trust them again.

James told his mother and his older sister Nina the whole story. His father, a workaholic, was still out in the packing shed weighing plums, so he didn't hear.

"I'm the eldest," said James when he'd finished his story, "so I ought to give the others good advice, but I honestly don't know what we'd better do now." He looked hopefully at his mother, an anxious expression on his solemn face.

"A deputation to apologize to David and a collection to buy a new pistol for the pony club," suggested Mrs Morgan promptly. "I'm sure that Dad will pay *you* for some fruit-picking and he might take on some of the others as well."

Tina's mother was working. Fanny's Food and Wine Bar was shut in the day on Sundays and then opened at night, so Tina was alone in the flat. She felt very lonely shut up with her worries and the horrible thought that it was all her fault. If only she had tied Bowie somewhere else, none of the other disasters would have happened. She had been having such a good time, and now she had ruined every thing by one silly little mistake.

The Wheelers didn't tell their parents, who both seemed very busy and preoccupied with their work, but they discussed the whole disaster endlessly among themselves. Going over and over the same ground didn't make them feel any better and, by bedtime, Rupert and Netti, their hopes of the pistols returning miraculously, dashed, both wished that they had voted with Lizzie for telling David at once and getting it over.

CHAPTER SEVEN

Wider Repercussions

"The shooting practice is cancelled," announced Sarah Rooke in a dreary voice when she telephoned Alice on Monday morning. "David's dreadfully angry and, anyway, there are no pistols."

"Oh dear, did he give the Robertses a very rough time when they told him?" asked Alice.

· "They didn't tell him. And the worst of it was that Lesley and I thought they *had* permission to borrow the pistols. So, when my mother rang him, hopping mad that he'd given permission, he blew up completely. They're still hardly on speaking terms, but it wasn't our fault, we couldn't know."

"What a mess," said Alice sadly.

"Yes, it's not going to do the pony club much good. David's still in a really nasty mood. He's told the police, but it's awkward because we were breaking the law too. Though it wasn't our fault—I mean, we all understood Mr Fuller would be in charge."

"How's Bowie?" asked Alice.

"Making a fuss. We kept him in the stable last night and this morning all his legs were like bolsters; the vet says he's to stay out in the field. Stupid pony causing all this trouble."

Then Hanif rang Alice. "I expect you've heard the latest bad news from Sarah. My parents think we should ride over and apologize without any more delay. The Wheelers want us all to meet at their place at lunchtime and decide what we're going to say. James, Seb and Tina agree, so I suppose we had better go too."

"Yes, O.K.," Alice agreed. "What time do we start?"

"About twelve. We don't know if the Rookes are

coming, they say none of it's their fault. No one's dared to phone the Robertses."

They were all in very sombre mood when they met at the Old Rectory.

"We've left our ponies in the field so that you lot can have the looseboxes," Netti explained.

"James and I have spent half the morning trying to write a letter in case David's too angry to listen to what we want to say, but Lizzie and Rupert say it's no good," Seb complained, his wide mouth downturned, his brown eyes more mournful than ever.

"Was your father very angry about your pistol?" asked Alice.

"Not too bad. He came home in a good mood and was really quite restrained for him. He thinks we may be able to claim on the insurance. If we can't, it will be fifty quid gone down the drain. He said I was a prize fool and why hadn't I let the rest of you chase Bowie while I put the pistols away. But the thing that upset him most was that I'd let you all think he would be in charge. He said I hadn't made it plain why I wanted him to stay at home. He telephoned David to apologize last night, but it was after Mrs Rooke's fatal call, so he got a very frosty reception."

"Rubbing salt into the wound," remarked Rupert in a melancholy voice.

"Go on, Seb, you must tell them what David said," directed James.

"He said that 'unfortunately there had been wider repercussions, that the Woodbury Pony Club's reputation was mud with both the police and the public, and the pistols had been used to inflict cruelty and injure animals'—something like that."

Alice and Hanif looked at each other despairingly. "It gets worse and worse."

"Yes, they obviously rode round the villages shooting up old ladies' cats," said Rupert, "and we're getting the blame because we left the wretched pistols lying around."

"Oh blast . . ." said Seb despondently. "If only I had

303

thought and not rushed after Bowie. If only I'd told Dad he *had* to stay."

They all ate their lunches in the stableyard, sitting on upturned buckets. They had almost finished when the Rookes appeared.

"My mother wouldn't let us ride over, she says we're not fit to be in charge of valuable ponies," explained Lesley, "but Julia Cartwright offered us a lift. She dropped us at the lane and she's gone up to see David."

"She's mad. He's still in a *vile* mood and it won't do any good if he's made up his mind to resign," said Sarah.

"If he does resign it'll be the end of the Woodbury," Lesley told her. "Mummy says they'll never get anyone else."

"Well, the world won't end and perhaps we could get a sub-branch of the Cranford Vale going instead," said Sarah, trying to sound unconcerned.

"David's not really going to resign?" The other pony club members looked at the Rookes aghast.

"We don't know, my mother says he's in an impossible mood."

Lesley answered. "That's why Julia's coming here when she's seen him; she's going to advise us on what to do."

Tina was the next arrival, she looked hot and exhausted having ridden Oliver's elderly and neglected bicycle uphill all the way from Woodbury. While Lizzie fetched her a glass of orange the others told her the latest bad news.

"If only I hadn't tied Bowie to that rail, if only I tied him to something solid," Tina lamented. "I can't help feeling that it was all my fault."

"No, it was all our faults," Alice told her. "We're all saying, 'if *only* I'd thought of the pistols.'"

"Anyway, it was that beastly Berry who got loose first," Sarah reminded her. "If she hadn't kicked Bowie none of this would have happened."

"Don't go on about it," pleaded Hanif. "You might as well blame the Cranford Vale for challenging us to a tetrathlon. We were all idiots; we all forgot the pistols."

Julia's battered car stopped outside the gate long before they expected her. She got out slowly and, as they ran to meet her, they saw that her usually cheerful face was grimly serious.

"How did it go?" they asked, crowding round her.

"What did David say?"

"He's not going to resign, is he?"

"Not well," she answered. "I'm afraid there's more bad news. Those crazy wretches on the motorbikes took the track across the downs, the one parallel to the Coombe Lentworth road. They upset a lot of people by firing at dogs and birds, but they weren't very likely to hit anything while bumping along on the bikes. Then, when they reached the stud farm, they stopped and amused themselves by shooting at the foals. Of course, when the owner heard what was going on he was terribly upset, especially as the foals are all by famous sires, Derby winners and so on, and incredibly valuable. He sent for the police, but by the time they got there the horrible yobs had gone. Then, later on, the police told him where the pistols had come from, and you can imagine how livid that made him."

"Oh no," moaned Seb, holding his head.

"Unfortunately, Frank Collingwood knows David quite well," Julia went on, "so he got on the phone and tore him into strips. He's not a polite man at the best of times so I can imagine what sort of language he used. As far as I can make out, he told David that if he couldn't control his pony club he wasn't fit to be a district commissioner, and he was going to report him to headquarters forthwith. You know how people go on when they're angry and upset; they don't pull their punches, and the result is that David's very sore, very sore indeed. Then, this morning, he had a visit from the police and took a lot more stick from *them*."

"Oh dear, and it's all our fault," said Lizzie sadly.

"Yes," agreed Julia. "Anyone can make mistakes, but surely you *realized* that you were breaking the law? If the police do find the motorbike riders, they'll charge them and the whole mess will have to come out in court."

Seb groaned. "It was my fault. I was fed up with my father for going off like that when I needed him. It's impossible only having one parent. When James asked me, I said he was around somewhere, that he'd show up soon."

"It was all of our faults," said Lizzie. "We ought to have refused to shoot when we found he wasn't there."

"Yes, but at the time I forgot about needing a grown-up," explained Hanif, "Seb had everything so well arranged."

"So did I," admitted Alice guiltily. "It went clean out of my head." The others made agreeing noises.

"Were any of the foals badly hurt?" asked Tina.

"I don't think so, but of course being full of pellets is painful and they could cause trouble later."

"It was Mr Collingwood who caught Bowie," said Hanif. "He was very disagreeable to us, and Paul said he had a reputation for bawling people out."

"Yes, he has," agreed Julia. "And of course he's quite a figure in the racing world, which is making David extra sensitive."

"What are we going to do then?" asked Lizzie despondently.

"I honestly don't know, it's a real problem," sighed Julia. "You *can't* put things right—I mean it's all happened and that's it."

"My parents think we should all go and apologize," Hanif told her.

"I don't think that would do any good at the moment," said Julia thoughtfully. "I think he's still too sore to forget and forgive. He seems to be seeing the pony club as one more disaster on top of all his other disasters."

"My mother thinks we should apologize *and* start a fund to replace at least one of the pistols," James told her. "And my father's willing to take some of us on as fruitpickers, so that we can earn the money ourselves."

"Yes, that might help," Julia agreed. "I think David's one of those people who think actions speak louder than words. I think you've got to *convince* him that you're really sorry, rather than just say it. You've also got to convince him that you really want to do the Tetrathlon. I got the impression that, even before this pistol business, he felt that some of you were decidedly half-hearted about training, and that hurt."

"So we start a pistol fund," said James, glad to have something concrete settled.

"And you think we ought to go on training, in spite of everything?" asked Alice doubtfully.

"Yes, I think you've got to prove to him that you're keen enough to slog away at running and swimming. If you do that, keep the ponies fit and work really hard at collecting the money for a new pistol, he might change his mind about you. I can't think of any other way, but I will go and see him in a couple of days and tell him what you're doing."

"Thanks, you're a real friend," Netti told her.

"Yes," the others agreed gratefully.

"I'll come and pick fruit at your place, James," offered Rupert.

"Yes, so will I. I can come down on my bike. When do you want us, James?" asked Seb.

"I'll ask my father and phone you," answered James.

"We'd better try and find something nearer home," Hanif told Alice. "I could offer to wash my stepfather's car."

"Are you any good at painting?" asked Alice. "I mean the decorating sort of painting, not pictures. "Aunt Margaret is trying to find someone to paint the insides of her dog kennels and all the estimates have been very expensive. I could suggest that we do it."

"I've painted jumps," said Hanif, "and helped my stepfather to creosote a fence. He's the biggest perfectionist on earth so I'm probably quite good."

"Can I help too?" asked Tina. "I'm experienced, I painted all the doors in our flat."

"Yes, great, if Aunt Margaret agrees. I'll let you both know," said Alice.

"What about swimming, couldn't we all meet at Woodbury pool?" asked Tina.

"We could run through Alice's woods first, they're quite shady," suggested Hanif.

"Run from Alice's, all the way into the town, and jump straight in," said Rupert.

"In your clothes, I suppose," sneered Lesley.

"We have to exercise the ponies too," Hanif reminded them. "If anyone would like to come and have a school over my jumps they're welcome. They're only show jumps," he explained to Seb, "but better than nothing."

"Hang on, when are we going to fit in the fruit-picking?" asked Seb.

"What about now?" asked Julia. "I could spare an hour. What do you think, James? Would your father be willing to take on a whole gang of plum-pickers this afternoon?"

"He might be, I'll go on ahead and find out," offered James, running for his bike.

Twelve people picking with almost non-stop industry for an hour, earned twelve pounds. Julia and James picked more than their share, which made up for Rupert and Oliver picking less. Everyone felt much more cheerful at the sight of the pound notes, which Mr Morgan handed over when the plums were weighed and packed into boxes, for the replacement of one of the second-hand pistols was now in sight.

"You'd better look after it, Julia," said James, passing on the notes. "If any of us have it it's bound to get lost."

"I don't know that I'm all that reliable," answered Julia, but I'll give it to Mrs Rooke. I'm going to drop the Rookes and Tina at their doors, so I'll deliver it in person."

They parted outside Four Cross Fruit Farm. Hanif had invited everyone for a school in his field at ten next morning, and Netti had volunteered to telephone the Robertses and tell them about the schooling session, as well as the pistol plan and the running and swimming practice proposed for the afternoon.

"Did the police come to see you last night?" an anxious-looking Lizzie asked the group of riders gathered in the Franklins' small gravelled yard, a rectangle between the wooden loosebox and tack room and Mr Franklin's combined garage and workshop.

"Yes," answered Alice. "Aunt Margaret was horrified, but the policeman was quite nice, he calmed her down a bit."

"They went to our house to ask for everyone's addresses while we were at the Old Rectory," explained Sarah.

"The one who came to see me was very scathing about our lack of observation; he said surely taking the bikes' registration numbers would have been the first thing that came to mind," said Hanif.

"The landlord of The Packhorse was the only person who saw them without their helmets," observed Seb. "But no one got the registration numbers, not even those people walking on the downs."

"I've telephoned the Robertses," Netti announced, "but I only spoke to Mrs Roberts, who said that Lynne and Paul were outside somewhere. She sounded funny, a bit cagey. I explained about everything and she *said* she'd put them in the picture, but it didn't sound as though they'd be coming today."

"I do hope David's not being *especially* horrible to them," sighed Lizzie.

"It must be tough living right on his doorstep now we're in disgrace," agreed Alice.

"Worse than tough," said Tina with a shudder.

"Could some of you go into the field, please?" asked Hanif. "The yard's too small to hold all of you and we don't want anyone kicked."

"Aunt Margaret said yes to the kennel painting," Alice told Tina as they led the way into the paddock. "She's going to buy sandpaper, paint and brushes in Woodbury this morning, but she won't discuss payment until she sees how expert we are."

"I've put all the jumps at two-feet-six for the small ponies," said Hanif, who was wearing the harassed look of a hard-pressed organizer. "For the small ponies and inexperienced showjumpers. Then I thought we could raise them to three feet for anyone who wants them at that height, and the first lot could go again. Then three-feet-three and finally three-feet-six, or higher if you like, but no one to jump more than two rounds."

"Sounds great, I'd like to go at three-feet-six and three-feet-nine, if that's O.K.," decided James. "I don't often get the chance of a school round a set of show jumps."

"They're really classy," agreed Seb in an admiring voice. "How did you get them, Harry?"

"My stepfather made them. He had ambitions to turn me into a top-class showjumping rider, but I was a great disappointment," Hanif explained with a hint of bitterness.

"But he got over that last holidays," protested Alice. "He was terribly pleased when you and Jupe turned out to be good at cross-country."

"Can I go first, I'm ready," called Sarah, cantering at the first fence.

"And me second, Harry," shouted Oliver. "I want a go before Rosie smashes up the jumps."

"She'd better not," said Seb in threatening tones.

"I'll start at the lowest height too," decided Lesley. "David's always telling me to make it fun for Stardust."

Even Rosie managed a clear round at the two-feet-six height, though she jumped the wall from a standstill and made some very wild lurches to get herself in and out of the combination. Lizzie was the only rider who wanted to begin at three feet and, while she was trying to persuade Rajah to fly round fluently instead of slowing up and peering suspiciously at each new fence, Seb asked Tina, "Would you like to take Jigsaw round at this height? He's quite fit, he can go three times."

"Oh, I couldn't. He's lovely, but too good for me; I might spoil him," Tina answered, her freckled face flushing scarlet.

"Don't be wet. He's dead easy. And you've jumped Vulcan and Bowie," Seb told her impatiently as he dismounted. "Come on, don't hold things up. He's dead easy," he repeated as he helped her pull up the stirrups. "He's like Tristram, no peculiarities, just point him at the right jump and he'll do the rest."

Hobbit ran out when confronted by the heightened combination, but the three other ponies went clear. Rupert was delighted.

"I never thought I'd sail over real show jumps on Rosie," he told everyone as he patted her enthusiastically. "Did you see her go round the second time? She really whizzed. I think she was enjoying herself *and* she got her take-off right every time."

"Stardust went very well too," Lesley pointed out, "but I don't suppose you noticed *her*."

"A bit faster," Seb was shouting at Tina, as Jigsaw, surprised by his light and uncertain rider, drifted round the course. "Push him on."

"When everyone's jumped we could have a pair relay competition," Sarah told Hanif, who had fetched Jupiter and was trotting round and round in a large circle trying to settle his over-excited mount.

"No, we couldn't," answered Hanif firmly. "This is a school not a competition, and afterwards we're going down to the river; Alice and I have hidden some poles and drums by the ford."

The larger and more experienced ponies all jumped well. Rajah had a brick off the wall at his second height, but all the others jumped confident clear rounds. Alice was amazed at Saffron.

"I haven't practised over show jumps at all," she told Lizzie, "but now, suddenly, he can do them. At the beginning of last holidays I couldn't possibly have jumped a course like this ."

"David's always said that showjumping needs a better schooled pony than basic cross-country," Lizzie reminded

311

her, "so now the ponies are all better schooled I suppose it's almost automatic."

"It's a shame to think that we've all got this far, but now, if David chucks the pony club, we're stuck. We won't get much further on our own," said Alice, her elation over Saffron's jumping vanishing as she thought of the future.

"If *only* we could think of some way of putting things right," Lizzie sighed sadly.

Saffron and Jupiter, who crossed the river every time they went to Garland Farm or Kidlake, accepted wading through water as a very normal activity, and most of the other ponies remembered the day they had jumped in and out before the Area Cup at Easter. Jigsaw began by being suspicious, but when he saw the others splashing over the poles and drums, he followed them cheerfully.

"It's been great, really good fun," said Seb, when they decided that, if they were going to have time for running and swimming, they must take their ponies home at once. "Does anyone else have jumps we could practise over?"

"No, we've only a few cavalettis; my mother always schools over the riding school's jumps, but you have to pay," explained James.

"Ours are such a mess," Lizzie answered apologetically.

"Yes, they're disgustingly grotty: awful propped-up jobs and much too low for people with good ponies," agreed Netti.

"I've an idea for tomorrow. Well, it was my aunt's idea, actually," said Alice. "When I told her about the pistol thieves she said that when they got tired of shooting at the foals, they probably threw the pistols into the nearest hedge, so's not to be caught with them. I know the police have looked a bit, but they haven't had hundreds of policemen searching in rows like they do when someone's been murdered. I think we ought to ride over and take a look."

"That's not a bad idea," said Hanif.

"It couldn't do any harm," James admitted cautiously.

"Unless we meet the ferocious Mr Collingwood and he starts bawling at us," observed Rupert.

"If we stay on the bridle path he can't object," argued Alice, "and if we did find the pistols it might do us some good with David."

"And with my mother, she never stops going on about the money we've wasted," said Lesley.

"I'm for it." Seb sounded enthusiastic. "I'd give a lot to get my pistol back."

"I'm for it too," agreed Netti. "Why don't we meet at Kiddleworth tomorrow morning?"

"Yes, it's worth a try, but no tying up of ponies," stipulated Lizzie.

"I don't suppose we'll be allowed to come," Lesley's voice was gloomy. "The very mention of Kiddleworth makes my mother explode."

"Oh yes we will, I'll talk her round somehow," said Sarah.

That afternoon all the tetrathlonites, except the Robertses, met again at Hanif's house, and Alice took them for a run down Darkwood Lane and through the beechwoods. Despite the luxury of deep shade and a soft carpet of beech leaves, there was a good deal of moaning about the immense distance, the intense heat and terrible stitches. Most of it came from Rupert, Sarah and Oliver; Tina, who looked equally miserable, suffered in silence.

Then, when they had limped and puffed their way back to Barn Cottage, Mrs Franklin drove them, in two very squashed car loads, to Woodbury pool. They swam in three groups, slow, medium and fast, all ploughing up and down with grim concentration as they tried to add a few more metres to their scores.

Everyone improved, and Hanif, who in his second swim added half a length to his previous best, was delighted.

"It works," he said, "practising really does work. I'm coming every day from now on. Look, why don't we swim tomorrow morning and ride over the downs in the cool of the evening?"

"I don't think we can get here." Lizzie looked worried. "Mummy's got a deadline for this book she's illustrating so she's too busy, and Mrs Morgan, who brought us over today, is out all day tomorrow, isn't she, James?"

"Come on your bikes," Seb told her.

"They're a very geriatric lot, our bikes. Ollie's is about the best and Tina still hasn't recovered from borrowing it," Rupert told him.

"Why don't you mend them?" asked James briskly.

"Lizzie and I don't know how, Rupert and Ollie think they know but always make them worse," explained Netti.

"James and I had better look at them on our way home," decided Seb.

The pony club members met again at the Old Forge on Wednesday afternoon. The Woodbury people were all boasting about the number of lengths they had swum that morning while the Kidlake lot, which included James and Seb, competed with stories of bicycles restored, until suddenly they realized that Tina was riding Bowie.

"He's better then!" exclaimed Alice.

"How *did* you square your mother?" Rupert asked Lesley.

"I'm not sure. She seemed impressed with all the money we were collecting; Alice gave her their kennel-painting cash—six pounds—this morning. And she approves of us looking for the pistols."

"She was just in a better mood," said Sarah. "But she says David's still fuming, and he won't discuss what's going to happen at the rally on Friday at all."

"I'm not looking forward to that rally one bit," said Lizzie sadly.

"I don't want to go, but my mother says we've got to,"

Lesley told her. "She says it serves us right if David does bite our heads off."

"I think we'd be mad to go anywhere near him if he's still in such a raging passion," observed Rupert. "Especially when we don't know what's happened to the Robertses; they've never reappeared."

"Perhaps we'll find the pistols," suggested Alice optimistically, as they took the left-hand road from which the track led up to the downs.

"If we don't, my stepfather's offered to lend us enough money to buy one before the rally," said Hanif. "I think it would be better if we earned all the money ourselves, but I've agreed to him trying the sports shop in Brunstock and anywhere else he can think of for second-hand ones. I hope that's O.K. with all of you?"

"Yes, great."

"It would be a good idea to have a peace offering for David," said Rupert. "We'll send James in first, holding it out."

"We'd better concentrate on finding the old ones now and decide where we're going to search." James spoke in a rather reproving voice.

"Yes, do be sensible, Rupert; this is serious," pleaded Lizzie.

"I've borrowed my father's map of the downs," Seb told them, "and I took a good look at it before we started. When we chased the bikers do you remember coming to a meeting of four tracks?"

"Yes, that's where we turned back," said Alice.

"Well they must have turned left there," Seb went on, "because that track runs parallel to the Coombe Lentworth road and along the back of the Stud Farm."

"We couldn't see them," said Hanif.

"No, but they could have been in one of the stud farm fields, or there's a turn that takes you down to the Coombe Lentworth road, or there's a wood," Seb told him.

"And we know they went to the stud farm, so it's

315

obviously the one they took," snapped Lesley. "Let's stop talking, get over there and start looking."

"Can we gallop?" asked Oliver.

"Yes, come on." Sarah's legs flapped feverishly as she kicked Chess into a canter. Oliver followed.

"Steady," shouted James as the more excitable ponies took off.

"Ollie, do be sensible, let Bowie go first; we don't want any more accidents," called Lizzie.

With miles of open country ahead the ponies soon thought better of racing and settled down to a steady hand gallop. Jupiter had taken the lead with the other large ponies grouped just behind him. Behind them Tristram and Bowie galloped stride for stride, and further back Chess and Hobbit scurried along, their manes and tails flying.

At the downland cross roads Hanif pulled up and waited for the little ponies.

"Aren't they all being *good*," said Alice, patting Saffron.

"Yes, Jupe is a marvel of good behaviour," agreed Hanif. "And galloping really fast is bliss if you know that you can stop."

Tina had turned back to ride alongside Sarah. "Bowie's terribly fast and wonderfully smooth. Are you sure you don't want a turn on him, Sarah?" she asked. "There's no traffic up here."

"No, I'm not going to bother with him any more. I hate stupid, sensitive ponies, and now my mother's agreed to sell him and buy me a pony more like David's Vulcan there's no point."

"I think he's lovely," said Tina sadly as she stroked the slender bay neck. "I hope he gets a good home."

"I hope his legs hurry up and heal and that he isn't scarred for life," said Sarah. "I'm never going to hear the last of it from Mummy if he has to be sold cheap because he's blemished."

"Shall we have another gallop?" asked Seb, who was

316

leading them along the eastwood track. "Because once we reach the stud farm fence we'll have to ride slowly and look for the pistols."

They galloped until the dipping cornfields on the left side of the track levelled, became pastureland, and they recognized the high, well-made post and rails of the stud farm fencing.

"There's no horses in here," shouted Oliver in a disappointed voice.

"Look, there's Beacon Hill. Usually it looks so huge, but now it's suddenly tiny," called Netti, pointing away to their left.

"Shush everyone, we don't want to be heard by that horrible Collingwood man or he'll come out and give us hell," warned Hanif.

They rode in silence then, their eyes scanning the rough grass on either side of the beaten track for discarded pistols.

"It's a bit soon to start looking really," James pointed out, "because we haven't found the field with the foals yet and we know that the pistols weren't thrown away *before* the foals were shot up."

"No, but we don't know which field the foals *were* in," Rupert told him. "It *could* have been this one."

"Yes, he's probably moved them nearer to the house since the shooting," agreed Alice.

"And for all we know, they could have come back this way afterwards," added Seb, "though I think it's more likely they took the track down to the road."

They rode their ponies on loose reins while they stared fixedly at the turf, hoping to see the dull metal grey of a pistol butt among the fading green of the coarse summer grass.

"I can see horses in the distance," announced Oliver, bored with pistol hunting. "Lots of them." He stood in his stirrups. "They look like racehorses, but fatter."

"And that looks like the end of the stud's fields," said Seb. "There's the wood that's marked on the map. Now, there should be some sort of track going down between the field and the wood."

There was—a steeply descending chalk track, scattered with loose flints and shaded by the edge of a great dark wood which spilled down the slope towards the Coombe Lentworth road.

"If the mares and foals were in the corner field, the bike blokes could easily have thrown the pistols away here when they'd finished up their ammunition," decided Seb, dismounting and scuffling his feet through leaves and grass.

"They had a tinful of pellets each. I should think the pistols would have been red hot if they fired all that lot off without stopping," protested Oliver. But no one was listening to him, they had all dismounted and were busily searching on one or other side of the track.

"It's a yew wood," called Lizzie suddenly. "We must be careful. Ollie, do keep Hobbit away from those overhanging branches."

"Yew!" repeated Tina in horrified tones. "Bowie's not going near it." And she hurried him across to the field side of the track.

"Here, Ollie. If you'll lead Jigsaw for me, I'll search the wood side," called Seb.

"Good idea," said Netti. "If you'll take Tristram, Lizzie, I'll give Seb a hand." Sarah also decided to help the wood party and she handed Chess's reins to Alice.

"Horses at last!" called Hanif, who was being towed along in the lead by Jupiter. "A whole field full of really beautiful thoroughbreds."

"They look like youngsters," said Alice, joining him. "Yearlings do you think, or two-year-olds?"

"One-and-a-half-year-olds," answered Hanif, "because thoroughbreds are foaled very early in the spring, or so my book says." The young horses threw up their heads and began to pace about excitedly, snorting through wide nostrils at the sight of strange ponies.

"I hope old Collingwood doesn't come to see what

they're excited about," said Hanif, looking round nervously. The next field seemed to be empty. It was the last one; they could see that it ran right down to the road.

"The pistols will be here if they're anywhere," said Alice.

"I think the corner of the wood by the road is the most likely place of all," Seb called from the other side of the track. "They'd chuck them away when the fun was over and they were about to start for home."

"Fun?" queried Hanif in a disapproving voice.

"Well, they were obviously too thick to realize that foals had feelings, so I'm sure *they* thought it was just fun," explained Seb.

"The gate's open." Alice pointed. "Look, the field gate, it's been taken off its hinges."

They led their ponies over to investigate.

"This end's chained and padlocked," said Hanif.

"That's why it was lifted off its hinges. But whoever did it must have been a fairly hefty bloke," remarked James, testing his strength. "I can't move it on my own."

"Perhaps the thieves did this as well," suggested Rupert, "and the Stud Farm haven't sent anyone round to put it back yet."

"Except that it looks more as though a car had been driven through," Alice pointed out as she inspected the two parallel tyre tracks imprinted on the crushed grass.

"Someone's had a picnic," called Tina who had ridden Bowie a short way into the field.

"Here, come out!" Hanif shouted at her as he looked round apprehensively. "If Mr Collingwood catches you in there he'll blame us for the gate."

"There are lots of Coke cans and takeaway food boxes lying about as well as chicken bones," Tina told them as she rode back. "And the grass is all squashed down; it can't be long since people picnicked there."

"Well, it's nothing to do with us and luckily there were no horses in the field," said Lesley briskly. "Let's get on. Where have the others vanished to?"

"Sarah," called Alice, "Sarah, come and take Chess."

"I can't," came an answering shout from deep in the wood. "We've found a loose horse and we're trying to catch it."

"A loose horse?" The pony club members on the track looked at each other in consternation.

"Perhaps there *were* horses in the field then," said James.

"What sort of horse is it?" Hanif shouted into the wood.

"There are some more over here," Netti's voice came from higher up the wood. "Seb, can you come and help?"

"There's a gate down here and it's open," called Tina, who had ridden Bowie almost to the road and found a hunting gate into the wood standing open. The people who weren't hampered by having two ponies, mounted and rode to investigate. Oliver gave Lizzie Jigsaw to hold as well as Tristram and scrambled up on Hobbit.

"Can you drive them out?" James was shouting. "The gate's in this corner, we'll stop them getting on the road."

Rupert and Oliver had ridden into the wood to help and it rang with confused shouts as they tried to round up the horses.

"Someone ought to go to the stud and warn them," said Alice.

"Yes, and supposing they've eaten yew," added Lizzie anxiously, as a beautiful bay thoroughbred mare appeared in the lane being chivied along by Oliver and Sarah.

"Ollie," called Lizzie. "They mustn't drink, whatever happens, because if they've eaten yew it'll kill them. Go and stand by the water trough and drive them off."

The bay mare was reluctant to go back to the field without her companions, but with the track blocked by riders on either side of the two gates, and with Sarah and Oliver waving their arms threateningly behind her, she had no alternative. The moment she was through the gate, Oliver set off across the corner of the field at full speed for the water trough. Alice threw Chess's reins at Sarah and called to Hanif as she mounted.

320

"We must tell the stud what's happened. Will you come with me, Harry? We know the way."

"Make sure they realize the horses have been in the yew wood," said Lizzie. "They ought to send for the vet."

"We'll tell them," agreed Hanif. "I only hope they don't blame *us* for the whole thing." He followed Alice, who was urging Saffron into a gallop as she gazed across the field, searching for a gate in the fence on the far side.

The bay mare was neighing, calling to her companions to rejoin her, and suddenly six of them jostled their way through the hunting gate and trotted up the track, to be turned into the field by Lizzie and Sarah who guarded the gateway. Rupert and Netti went back into the wood to help Seb.

"Can you bring me a stirrup leather?" he was shouting. "There's one here who was actually eating yew. I've pulled most of it out of her mouth, but I know she swallowed some. I need something to lead her with."

A wild gallop across the huge field brought Alice and Hanif to a double fence, a spinney planted between the two sets of post and rail to act as a windbreak. Alice opened the first gate. While she was shutting it Hanif opened the second. They galloped on, skirting the groups of mares and foals, who stood, ears pricked, heads flung high, amazed at these sudden visitors.

"Make for the stables!" Hanif shouted. "See if we can find the stud groom; we don't want Mr C. bawling at us again."

The next gate led them into an all-weather training track. Fenced by walls of wood, it circled away in both directions. They found another gate and let themselves into a yard, where one huge barn housed horseboxes, and another, hay and straw. White-painted double gates stood open, and passing through they found themselves in a large, square stableyard, surrounded by looseboxes. Over the white painted doors appeared well-bred heads, neighing excitedly to the intruders.

A small, bow-legged, angry-faced man shot out of a loosebox.

"We've come to tell you that some of your horses are out," shouted Hanif quickly, forestalling a verbal attack.

"It's the field on the corner where the track from the downs meets the road," added Alice. "There seemed to be a lot of mares in the yew wood."

"It looks as though the gate was taken off its hinges, a car was driven through and the people in it had a picnic," Hanif went on explaining, but the bow-legged man had ceased to listen. He was calling names, shouting instructions.

The yard was suddenly alive with grooms, mostly girls, who ran about collecting headcollars and half-filling buckets with feed. The stud groom had rushed into a small office, the walls of which were lined with glass-fronted cabinets displaying very superior-looking rosettes. He grabbed a telephone, said a few words and rushed out, as a man drove a Land Rover into the yard. The grooms grabbed the buckets and piled into the back, the stud groom climbed in beside the driver, and in a matter of moments they were out of the yard, racing down the drive towards the road.

"Shall we go back the way we came?" asked Hanif.

They cantered sedately across the field with the mares and foals and, as they rode through the spinney, they could see the Land Rover swinging round the corner and through the open gateway at the far end of their field. The grooms jumped out, rattling buckets enticingly as the mares went to meet them.

"That was quick work," James called to Hanif and Alice as they rode past the Land Rover and into the lane.

"Did you explain about the yew?" asked Lizzie in an anxious voice.

"We explained, but I'm not absolutely certain we were listened to; everything happened so fast," answered Alice.

"We'd better tell them again when they've caught all the mares," decided James, as a continuous horn-blast drew their attention to the road and a large grey Mercedes speeding down it. The car stopped at the foot of the track with a squeal of brakes, and a tall, silver-haired man jumped out and came running up the track.

Hanif groaned, "It's Mr C. Now we're in for it."

But Netti and Sarah were emerging from the wood, where they had gone for a final look. "We've brought out nine mares," announced Netti briskly. "Does anyone know if that's the lot?"

"Nine is the full complement," answered Mr Collingwood, watching the scene in the field.

"The bay with the blaze and three white socks has definitely eaten yew," Seb told him. "The others were in the wood but we don't know whether they ate any or not."

"As you can see, the gate's been taken off its hinges," James pointed. "And it looks as though a car has been driven into the field—there's been a picnic."

As the last mare was caught, Oliver galloped over to the gate.

"We didn't let any of them drink," he told Mr Collingwood triumphantly. "My sister, Lizzie, says it makes the poison go round faster or something."

Mr Collingwood was hurrying into the field. "Is that the lot, Mason?" he shouted. "Right, run them up the road. Quick as you can, everyone. We haven't a moment to lose; I've three vets on their way with stomach pumps." He watched the mares trotting through the gateway beside their running grooms, then, muttering some very uncomplimentary remarks about townie picnickers, he followed them down the lane. Soon the Mercedes and the Land Rover were racing back along the road.

"Has anyone seen my stirrup iron?" asked Rupert, looking round vaguely. "Seb's given me back the leather, but I can't find the iron anywhere."

"It's hooked on the latch of the hunting gate," Lizzie told him.

"Was that Mr Collingwood then?" asked Lesley. "He didn't shout at us."

"That was him," agreed Hanif. "He didn't say thank you either."

"I expect he was much too worried to think about politeness," said Lizzie. "I do hope that all those lovely mares don't die."

"Don't mention dying," Sarah shrieked at her.

"*Three* vets ought to be able to save them," said Alice.

"Yes, you've got to give it to him—the whole set-up worked very efficiently," observed James.

"Could someone hold Jigsaw a sec?" asked Seb. "I want to make a quick search of the last bit of the wood for the pistols."

Back In Business

On Thursday the pony club members decided to give their ponies a rest and devote the day to running, swimming and tack cleaning.

"Still no Robertses," remarked Rupert, looking round the runners who had gathered in Hanif's yard. They were being offered orange juice and Samoosas by Mrs Franklin, elegant in a green morning sari.

"Do you think that David's cast them into some dark dungeon at Garland Farm, or given them some terrible punishment, like picking stones off fields, at which they labour night and day?"

"Of course he hasn't, don't be ridiculous," snapped Lesley. "My mother met Mrs Roberts in the supermarket yesterday and she said it was Mr Roberts who had forbidden them to ride for a week. She said it was very difficult for them, living right on top of David and having free run of the farm, to know what was theirs and what was his. But, after all this rumpus, she didn't think they'd ever take anything without asking again."

"They *could* have let them come to the running practices then," suggested Rupert. "I mean, running's a punishment in itself, especially if like me you've lost your track shoes and have to run in jodh boots."

"You look really weird wearing those boots with shorts." Lesley glared at him disapprovingly. "I hope you're not proposing to go to the pool dressed like that."

"Looks do not matter, but you will have blisters if you run in those boots," Mrs Franklin told Rupert. And then, if David should relent and take you to this Tetrathlon after all, you will be in very poor shape. I will find you a pair of my husband's tennis shoes."

"Do you think David *will* relent?" asked Alice. "I've lost hope, there are so few days left and he's probably cancelled our entry."

"No, my mother sees to the entries," explained Lesley, "and she keeps on and on about the waste of pony club money so I know they haven't got the fee back."

"Well, my stepfather's found a pistol—twenty-eight pounds. He say's it's a very good buy, and with our dog kennel painting tonight we'll have more than enough money."

"We've got to buy some ammunition," Alice reminded him.

"Yes, and with any extra we can start a fund for a second pistol. Seb and I are fruit picking again this evening," added James.

"If we *do* have another shooting practice with Blazeaway it'll take all day with one pistol," grumbled Seb. "It was bad enough with two. James is right, we'll have to go on earning."

"I don't think we can pick fruit tonight," said Lizzie, looking worried. "Our tack's *so* filthy and we can't risk upsetting David by looking grotty at the rally."

"I'm still trying to persuade Mummy that it's pointless for me to go as I haven't got a new pony," Sarah told them.

"We can't all chicken out," Rupert told her as he laced on Mr Franklin's tennis shoes. "Some of us have got to put our heads into the lion's den or normal relations will never be restored. Thanks, Mrs Franklin, they're terrific, and now Lesley will be proud to run through the streets of Woodbury with me."

"No I won't," snapped Lesley. "You're far too mad."

On Friday morning Hanif rode over to Garland Farm with a heavy rucksack. As well as his lunch and Jupiter's feed he carried the new pistol, a tin of pellets and Rupert's jodh boots which he had left at Barn Cottage.

"Who's going to give it to David?" enquired the pony

club members in anxious whispers as they crowded round to inspect the pistol.

"James," answered Hanif. "He's the eldest *and* he's collected the most money."

James looked horrified. "I won't know what to say. Besides, your father bought it and everything, Harry."

"Oh go on, James," pleaded Netti. "We'll tell you what to say, and you look so clean and shiny you're a credit to any pony club."

"Yes, go on, James," the others repeated.

"All you have to say is, 'Here is this pistol, David. We bought it to replace the others, with our own money,'" suggested Lesley.

"He ought to say *something* about being sorry that we lost the others," protested Lizzie.

"Yes, something," agreed Seb, "but we don't want to crawl."

"'I'd like to present you with this pistol,'" began Rupert.

"It's not for him, you twit, it's for us," objected Sarah.

"If I've got to do it, I'll just say that I'm sorry we lost the pistols and here's a new one," said James. "We don't want to go on and on about it."

"Here are Lynne and Paul," shouted Netti as the Robertses, dressed for riding and leading their ponies, emerged from the cattleyard. The pony club members cheered as they rode to meet them.

"You've been released from your dungeon then?" said Rupert.

"We heard you weren't allowed to ride for a *week*," objected Lesley.

The Robertses smiled sheepishly. "Dad said we weren't to ride for a week, but last night David came round and begged us off," explained Lynne.

"According to Dad, he said it had all gone on long enough," added Paul.

"Did he really? Oh, huge sigh of relief all round," said Alice delightedly.

"Do you mean he's stopped being angry?" asked Oliver.

"I wouldn't count on that," answered Paul.

All talking at once, they told the Robertses about the new pistol, and then, as the yard was becoming full of D ride people and their anxious mothers, James suggested to Julia that they should wait for David in Long Meadow.

"Good idea," agreed Julia. "Ollie, you go with them for the presentation, but you're to come back to my ride the moment it's over. I'll need you more than ever as I haven't got Tina."

"Yes, what are you doing on that Rooke horse?" Rupert asked Tina.

"Mrs Rooke didn't want him left at home on his own," explained Tina. "She thought he might jump out or something. Lovely for me."

As they waited in Long Meadow they all began to feel very nervous.

"Shall we get into a straight line?" suggested Alice, whose stomach was churning violently.

"Are you going to hand over the pistol mounted, James?" asked Seb, "or do you want me to hold Ferdie?"

"Dismounted," decided James after a few moments thought. "It's politer if the other person's dismounted, and I don't want Ferdie swinging his quarters into David and knocking him for six."

"The Land Rover's in the yard," announced Paul in a warning voice. They hastily organized themselves into an official-looking line across the school.

"I do hope he's in a good mood and doesn't notice Hob's green bit," said Oliver apprehensively.

"It's all right for you, trotting off to Julia's ride," Sarah told him. "We've got to put up with him for the whole morning."

"Sarah, he's a super instructor. We're terribly lucky to have him," protested Lizzie in a shocked voice.

"It's all right for you and Lesley too," Sarah went on, "and for Tina, Alice and Netti. He likes all of you. It's Lynne and me he picks on."

"Oh, do shut up, Sarah. He'll hear, and we don't want any more trouble," objected Netti.

Everyone looked anxiously at David's face as he stopped the Land Rover near the centre of the line.

"Good morning, all. This looks very formal," he said, opening the door and swivelling round to look at them.

James marched forward and cleared his throat. Everyone else stayed silent.

"We're very sorry about the pistols, David, and about the foals and all the other trouble we caused. We've managed to earn enough money to replace one pistol and here it is." He held out the box.

David lifted the lid. "It looks a good one, better than we had before; must have cost a packet. How did you manage that?"

"Honest toil," said Rupert, assuming a virtuous expression.

"Fruit picking mostly and dog-kennel painting," answered James.

"Could you hide it under the passenger seat for me?" asked David, looking at the box and evidently deciding that it was too big for one hand. "We don't want to lose this one."

"Now," he went on when the pistol was safely stowed away, "I've got something to say to you. I think you all know that when those stupid yobs took the pistols, they used them to take pot shots at the mares and foals at Coombe Manor Stud and, not unnaturally, Mr Collingwood, the owner of the stud, had some very hard things to say about the Woodbury Pony Club and its District Commissioner. Well, now, I'm pleased to tell you, he telephoned me yesterday and told me that he took back every word he'd said. That my pony club had spotted his visiting mares, let out into the yew wood by some diabolical picnickers. He was particularly impressed by your organization: two of you alerting the stud while the others caught the horses, keeping them away from the water trough, being able to tell him at once which mare

329

had actually been *seen* eating yew. He said your prompt action had saved the lives of all those beautiful and valuable mares and the lives of their unborn foals."

Lynne and Paul were looking very surprised, "What were you all doing up on the downs?" asked Lynne.

"We were looking for the pistols. We thought the motorbike blokes might have chucked them away," explained Rupert. "We found the mares instead."

"Mr Collingwood asked me to tell you that he would be eternally grateful," said David, climbing down from the Land Rover. "And, though I won't take back *every* word I said about you, I will take back *some* of them. Although, so far, the police have been unable to trace the thieves or recover the pistols, I suppose, now you've bought this new one, we're back in business."

"Great! Cheerio, David!" Oliver waved and set off. "Julia said I had to go back to her ride as soon as we had things sorted out."

David waved his good hand at Oliver as he went on talking to the others. "I'm presuming that you do want to go ahead with the Tetrathlon? I've heard that running and swimming training has been going on."

"Yes, everyone's keen and we've all improved a bit," answered James.

"Just as well, since we haven't much time left," David remarked dryly. "Right, lead on James." As they followed on round the school, David looked at Tina and Sarah. "Is that a permanent arrangement?" he asked.

"You mean Tina riding Bowie?" asked Sarah. "Well, only until his legs recover, then we're going to sell him and buy a sensible pony."

David settled himself on his shooting stick and looked at Lynne. "Would you like to try Vulcan today?" he asked her. "He's not brilliant but I think you might find him a bit more accomplished than Berry."

"Oh yes, I'd love to." Lynne's face suddenly recovered its usual smiling state. "Oh, thank you, David. Shall I go and fetch him now?"

"It *is* a phobia," Sarah shrieked angrily at David. "He *won't* do it."

"He jumped the water jump last holidays," David pointed out calmly. "But I haven't a lunge rein and Julia to pull him over today. Let's put Paul up and see what he can do."

"All right, I don't care." Sarah flung herself off Chess as David called Paul. "Ride him round, get him going and try him over a couple of small jumps first," he told Paul, then he limped across to the timber wagon builders. "Does that look frightening enough for you?"

"It's not bad, fairly realistic," admitted James.

"It's terrifyingly solid and has no groundline at all," observed Rupert gloomily.

"They all look terrifying when you're on your feet," Alice told him, "but they shrink as soon as you mount."

"Chicken coops, you said, James," David went on. "There are some old ones in the tractor shed, but I'll need a couple of you to load them in to the Land Rover. Lynne, would you run up to my tackroom and fetch one of those navy-blue day-rugs out of the chest. Now, can anyone else think of a scary object which we can incorporate in the course?"

"Yellow plastic sacks stuffed with hay," suggested Sarah. "Stardust won't go near them," she added with relish.

"Well, there are plenty of brightly coloured sacks in the tractor shed and plenty of loose hay in the barn. You go and fill a few of them up," David told her.

"Can I scout round?" asked Rupert. "I might find something . . ."

Alice and Hanif went with David to load the coops, Lynne told Sarah that she would help her with the sack-stuffing as soon as she had fetched the rug. Paul was schooling Chess over the small jumps. Everyone else was pony-holding and gossiping.

The four chicken coops, with a pole above, were positioned so that they could be jumped before the timber wagon, while the navy-blue, red-bound rug was draped over a pole and the plastic sacks were propped against another at the lower end of the field. The jumps were ready and everyone was mounting when Rupert appeared, carrying the top half of a trestle table and followed by Mrs Roberts with the trestles.

"What's that for? We can't jump tables."

"Oh Rupert, why are you such a nut?" the pony club members protested. Rupert looked at David.

"I don't see why not," David answered his silent question. "They sometimes have solid, flat-topped jumps they call tables, in horse trials. Put it down with the other scary jumps and give it a pole for a groundline."

"I'll just fetch the chairs," said Rupert, handing the table top to Lizzie and Netti who had gone to help him, and running back to the yard. He reappeared with two broken-down, canvas-seated chairs, which he arranged at either end of the table. "That's it," he said, mounting Rosie.

"Right," said David. "Now, let's be clear in our minds what we're doing. The rug, plastic sacks and table are to accustom the *ponies* to jumping unusual or scary jumps without a preliminary look. Therefore, we keep the fences low and simple and try to make them jump first time, from a standstill if necessary. The chicken coops and timber wagon are for the benefit of the *riders*. You think they are frightening, but horses, if they can do the height, generally jump much better over solid-looking obstacles. We'll try the scary jumps first. Start slowly, you've only got to pop over with the ponies full of impulsion and in an obedient frame of mind. Sit up, look up, and use your legs. Who wants to go first?"

"I will," offered Hanif who was already practising a little shoulder-in. He begun slowly. Jupiter didn't seem bothered by the rug, but he eyed the plastic sacks suspiciously and made a large, careful leap, then flew over the table.

"Good," said David. "Now for the water." He drove the Land Rover down the field to the four-feet-wide ditch, lined with black plastic and brimming with water, which the Robertses had dug at right-angles to the hedge. "James, you go first. Seb, take a lead from Harry; Tina, from Alice. Lesley, follow Tristram, and Chess, Banjo." He went on. "No, don't show it to them; they've now got to trust you to ride them correctly at unknown fences. As this is a wide jump with no height to it, you aim to take off fairly near, so come in briskly with a short stride and a giving rein. O.K."

Remembering his wetting at Easter, James sat down and rode hard. Ferdinand, feeling his rider's determination, didn't attempt to refuse and jumped easily. Jupiter followed, making the ditch seem nothing. Behind him, Jigsaw approached with goggling eyes and tried to run out, but Seb was ready and his long legs drove the skewbald pony on. Saffron followed eagerly. Bowie, to Tina's amazement, took the ditch in his stride. Rosie swept over fast, with pricked ears and shining eyes. The waiting ponies were twirling about impatiently, longing for their turns to come. Even Rajah forgot to be cautious, caught up in the rising tide of confidence. David roared at Lynne to ride on and not to hold Vulcan back. Banjo flung himself upwards and over. Only Sarah, waving her legs and shouting at Chess, refused.

"Seb and Lynne had better go again—and you, Sarah." decided David. "Could the rest of you build a timber wagon? You'll need three of the thickest rustic poles, two of the largest drums and four tyres. If you lean the tyres against the drums they'll look enough like wheels to fool the ponies."

"Where do you want it?" asked James.

"In line with the hedge," answered David as he watched Jigsaw fly over the ditch, "so that we can jump it and then the hedge from this side. Go on, Lynne." He waved his good arm at her. "Don't kick, use your whip if he's idle."

Vulcan jumped easily, but Chess, unmoved by Sarah's kicking heels and scolding voice, refused again.

"None of you should have any trouble over the hurdles or the hedge," said David firmly, "but do use your heads, *think* about what you're doing, especially when jumping into the pen. Warn your ponies when there are complications ahead. Collect them, *make* them attend. You're not beginners, so don't flap your legs or leave everything to the ponies. I want twelve clear rounds."

Ferdie jumped round neatly. Jupiter hurtled round and, despite Hanif's efforts, took the pen far too fast before sailing, with at least a foot to spare, over the hedge.

"These fences are much too small for that pony," announced David. "The sooner we get Harry riding in senior tetrathlons the better."

Saffron and Jigsaw both jumped calmly and competently. Rupert started when Jigsaw was only one jump ahead and, racing after him, Rosie took far too large a leap into the pen and then fell on her nose as she braked violently. However, Rupert sat tight while she found a fifth leg and scrambled out somehow. Then they galloped on, apparently unconcerned, and made a magnificent jump over the hedge.

Rajah began by peering distrustfully at the hurdles, but Lizzie, reins in one hand, gave him an indignant whack, and after that he behaved, jumping both the pen and the hedge in fine hunting style. Tristram whizzed round in his usual confident manner, and Lesley chased him, determined that Stardust should be inspired by his example. Bowie jumped the pen neatly and then carried a very faint-hearted Tina over the hedge. Lynne rode Vulcan slowly and carefully and was very pleased with her clear round. Chess jumped the hurdles and pen neatly, but then made an enormous and slow-motion leap over the hedge which left Sarah clinging round his neck.

"Stay on, Sarah, stay on!" the others shouted to her. "Or David won't get his twelve clear rounds." Sarah struggled back into the saddle as Paul and Banjo cleared the pen and then the hedge with their usual stag-like leaps.

"Bowie wasn't here at Easter, I don't know what he'll think of it," said Tina, turning pale.

"Jigsaw and I weren't here either," observed Seb, shortening his stirrups.

"Perhaps he'll drop you in it," suggested Hanif cheerfully. "That's what Ferdie did to James. Luckily I'd brought some spare clothes."

"There was a girl from the Cranford Vale at my sister's birthday party last night and she said they've built a new cross-country course. A really stiff one: not high, but it's all ditches and terrifically solid jumps. There are chicken coops and a *timber wagon*," announced James, looking at David with a worried face. "She said it wasn't really a novice course and she doubted if many people would get round."

"A timber wagon?" asked Lynne in horror.

"Oh dear, if there are going to be unusual jumps Ra's bound to stop for a look," said Lizzie despondently.

"And Stardust's not up to a *stiff* course," added Lesley.

"It'll be ghastly if we're *all* eliminated," observed Rupert in gloomy tones.

David laughed. "There'll be nothing over three feet," he told them, "and after all the time we've spent training the ponies to be brave and bold, I don't think we need be too downhearted. Come on, cantering, and then we'll see what we can do about a few strange jumps."

They warmed up over three of the Robertses' new jumps. A pair of hurdles across the gateway into the stubble field, a pen, built of straw bales and poles out in the middle of the field, and a section of the hedge back into Long Meadow, which they had layered and clipped until it was the regulation three feet.

"Ugh, I hate hedges, they look so scratchy," complained Tina, as they watched James start on his round.

"I like them, you can take off all wrong, plough through them and they never fall down," argued Rupert.

"Yes, you can leave Berry in his box and I have brushed him over."

They trotted, serpentining and circling as usual. Then they tried shoulder-in and Lynne, who was working very hard, persuaded Vulcan to take a few steps at the trot. Tina was also doing well, the smaller, slimmer Bowie suiting her better than Vulcan. Only Banjo and Chess were failing to carry out the movement properly. David, looking at the rest of the ride, seemed pleased.

"Good," he shouted, "those ponies are beginning to look like something. They're beginning to use themselves, to move with impulsion. Can you feel it?"

"Yes," the pony club members answered.

"Yes, it feels gorgeous, very powerful."

"It's quite different."

"And the extraordinary thing is that the ponies' necks seem to be *growing*," observed Rupert, who had been taking quick glances at the rest of the ride.

"They don't seem to be, they are," answered David and then called the ride to a walk. "Do you remember that last holidays I told you it was important to feel that two-thirds of your pony was in front of you and only one-third behind? Well, now that our schooling is beginning to take effect, most of you should have that feeling. If the horse's ears come nearer when you put him on the bit, you're pulling his nose in and that's wrong. If they go away from you, you're driving his hindlegs under, and that's right. Now," he got up from his shooting stick, "we'll do some cantering and then we'll try the Roberts's new jumps."

"New jumps, where?" asked the pony club members, looking round.

"They're not much," answered Paul. "The water is the best. It's not as wide as the one we had on the cross-country at Easter, but it's deeper; more of a ditch really. Gary helped us dig it, and Dad fixed up a hose from the water trough so we don't have to mess about with buckets."

"It's not black plastic?" wailed Sarah. "Oh, you are *mean*. You know Chess has a phobia. He *hates* it."

The pony club members cheered. Mrs Roberts and some of Julia's ride, who were looking over the fence between the fields, clapped.

"It's good for an over-confident pony like Jupiter to meet a few horrors," said David. "You could see him steady himself and *think,* instead of just charging at them."

Saffron wasn't worried by the strangeness of the jumps either, he looked at them attentively and jumped them extra carefully. Ferdinand tried to run out of the plastic sacks, but James, sitting tight, held him into the fence and he jumped reluctantly with goggling eyes.

"Good," shouted David. "That's how it should be done." And Ferdinand, suddenly accepting the domination of his rider, went on to jump the table with hardly a second look.

Jigsaw had run out of the plastic sacks. "Sit up, feel both sides of his mouth, ride every stride then he *can't* take you by surprise," David was shouting.

"Ra's put his spectacles on already," Lizzie called despondently, as Jigsaw jumped at his second attempt and she tried to shake Rajah into action.

"Try shoulder-in, you must get him going in front of the leg," instructed David, watching Seb push a disapproving Jigsaw over the table.

Rajah jumped the rug cautiously and then approached the sacks at a peering, snorting trot. He stopped, despite Lizzie's efforts, and stretched out his neck to sniff the sacks from a safe distance.

"Oh Ra, stop being so ridiculous: they're sacks," Lizzie scolded and then, since her legs could do no more, gave him a sharp whack. Ra took off at once, jumping from a standstill. Looking quite pleased with himself, and seeming to realize that he wasn't being asked to do anything really dangerous, he jumped the table without any fuss.

"Well done, that wasn't bad for old Safety First," shouted David, as he turned to watch Tristram who

337

popped over all three jumps with pricked ears and a smug expression. Rosie followed him, her toad eyes bulging with horror as she refused to approach the rug.

"She thinks there must be a poor, thin, half-starved pony inside that rug," announced Rupert, giving up a frontal approach and trying to edge her nearer from the side.

"We can't waste time on prima donna acts. Netti, ride Tristram over and let him sniff the rug," ordered David. Seeing Tristram sniffing, Rosie hurried forward to join him. Suddenly all her terror vanished and she turned away quite prepared to accept that this was a jump. But then, the moment she was over it, she began to gaze at the plastic sacks with equal horror.

The watching pony club members groaned. "Oh, do get on with it, Rupert. We want our turns," they complained, as Netti trotted back to go through the sniffing procedure again.

"She thinks they're crouching yellow cats, waiting to scratch out a pony's eyes," announced Rupert as she sniffed each sack gingerly. Satisfied at last that they were harmless, she allowed Rupert to take her back and then jumped eagerly. They cantered on towards the table. Rosie seemed to be attending, but then she saw the chairs, lost her concentration, missed her take-off stride and, with a tremendous crash, scattered the table top and trestles, landing on her nose and knees in their midst. Rupert was still sitting in the saddle as she heaved herself back on her feet.

"Sorry, David," he said, pushing his crash cap off his eyes, "I hope the table wasn't valuable."

"You must use your half-halt and *pop* over tricky jumps," David told him. "You're inclined to ride at a sheep pen and a steeplechase fence in exactly the same way. But the real trouble is that neither you nor the pony concentrate on the job in hand. Still, well stuck on. Go and give her a confidence restoring popover one of the little jumps and she can have another go at the table in a minute."

As soon as Mrs Roberts, Harry and Alice had restored the table, Paul, looking unfamiliar on Chess, started and went round neatly with no trouble at all. Sarah followed on Banjo, giving surprised shrieks at the powerful spring of his stag-like leaps. Then Vulcan cantered round soberly, the superior expression of an "old hand" on his blue-roan face. Tina started slowly, stroking and talking calmingly to an apprehensive-looking Bowie. She used her legs and seat to urge the pony on, but very quietly and in rhythm with his stride. They jumped the rug and then Tina began to persuade the nervous pony to approach the sacks.

"Stupid animal," said Sarah, and then, looking round, "Where's Lesley vanished to? It's going to take another half-hour to get Stardust over; she's got a phobia about them too."

"It wasn't very sisterly of you to suggest we jumped them then," observed Seb.

"Oh, I hate my sister, but she doesn't seem to be around. Do you think she's gone off and hidden herself?"

"No, she's been having a little school on the quiet," said Mrs Roberts. "She gave me the pony to hold while she filled a couple of yellow sacks for her own use. She deserves to go straight over the jump after all that patience."

When David looked round for her, Lesley was ready. She started at a very brisk trot, pushing Stardust into a canter as they came up to the rug and jumping it neatly. Then, as the chestnut pony's eyes began to pop with horror at the sight of more plastic sacks, Lesley brought her back to a powerful collected trot. The moment she was in complete control she drove the pony forward and, obedience triumphing, Stardust jumped the small fence with only a moment's hesitation. Lesley collected her again for the table and they hopped over easily.

"Well *ridden*!" said David. "You really made use of your schooling then. Now you can give Chess and Paul a lead over the ditch. Everyone else prepare to jump the chicken coops, timber wagon, hedge, pen, hurdles and finally the ditch in that order. At a fair hunting pace, I want clear rounds and no time faults."

Chess, who was now going forward freely, forgot about the black plastic until the very last moment. Then he tried to stop, but Paul had his whip ready in the hand on the non-hedge side and hit him on the take-off stride, whereupon the startled Chess flew over.

"Good, do it again from the other side," shouted David, turning to watch James sail over the timber wagon in fine style, and then back to Chess, who, intimidated by Paul and well aware that he had changed his whip into the other hand and was ready for any attempt to run out, followed Stardust over the ditch meekly. "Good, give him back to Sarah," called David, one eye on Seb who was approaching the hedge, the other on James who was sailing over the ditch.

Then Saffron and Rajah were on the course, both galloping round at a purposeful pace. Hanif waited until they were nearly home before he started as he didn't want Jupiter excited by the sight of a pony ahead. Rupert followed him, then Lesley and Netti. All the ponies were jumping well, full of confidence and apparently enjoying themselves. David held up the last four. "I'd like the poles over the coops and the timber wagon down a bit for you," he said. "I know you can do the height, but we want this to be fun for the ponies and not too much of an effort."

When the last puffing pony had returned, David called the riders together. "Have I convinced you that our *fairly* well-schooled ponies can now be trusted to jump new and unusual fences without a preliminary look?" he asked. "Or are you still quaking at the thought of the Cranford Vale's course designer's horrors?"

"You've almost convinced me," admitted James. "So long as he doesn't think up something we haven't practised at all."

"Or something very tricky," added Hanif.

"I'll be all right if they're not too high or too wide," decided Paul.

340

"Well, are the rest of you happy about the way your ponies are going?" asked David, looking at the faces of the people who hadn't answered.

"Yes, I'm terribly pleased with Saffy, but I don't want to tempt fate by saying so," explained Alice.

"I'm happy too," said Netti, "though I expect something ghastly will happen on the day."

"Yes, we'll all take the wrong course or something," suggested Rupert gloomily.

"Stardust's never got round a cross-country yet," Lesley admitted suddenly, "but if it's not too stiff I think she might this time." Tina and Lynne stayed silent, both wondering which pony they were going to ride.

"I discussed teams with the Cranford Vale secretary last night," David went on, "and she said that as it was a junior competition and boys and girls swim and run the same distances, they'd decided to let clubs which couldn't produce a single-sex team have a mixed one, so our third team will be mixed." He produced a rather crumpled sheet of paper and tried to flatten it one-handed. "Here we are. Girls: Lesley, Lizzie, Alice, Netti. Boys: James, Rupert, Sebastian, Harry. Mixed: Lynne, Sarah, Tina, Paul. Mrs Rooke has very kindly offered to lend Bowie to Tina." David ignored the disbelieving gasps which greeted this announcement, and went on, "I'd like Lynne to ride Vulcan. If that's all right with you, Lynne?"

"Oh yes. Thank you, David, I'd love to."

"Good, well I suggest that we look upon the competition as a trial run, an experience. We'll find out what sort of standards the other pony clubs have reached and where our weaknesses lie, then next year those who are still interested can start training much earlier."

"It's going to be a bit difficult with just the one pistol, isn't it?" asked James diffidently. "I know it's our own fault, but Nina's friend said that all the clubs shoot with their own pistols and that twelve of us sharing one would wreck the organization. We'd still be shooting when everyone else was swimming."

"We've sorted that out," David answered briskly. "Mrs Halford has managed to borrow two from rifle club friends. She'll be here tomorrow at nine-thirty for a final practice and we'll settle then who is to shoot with which pistol on the day. The organizers would like to know approximately how many lengths you all propose to swim in the time allowed, as then they can put you in heats with swimmers of more or less the same standard, but I'll get you all to write that down tomorrow. Finally, there is the problem of getting the ponies to Crocker's Farm, Ramsden—that's on the otherside of Brunstock, where the cross-country and running take place. The shooting, which is first, of course, will be laid on at Ramsden village hall, then the swimming in Brunstock pool and then, after lunch, the riding. This means that, ideally, the ponies should come on later. As it's Sunday, parents may be able to help, but can they load the ponies without you?"

Lesley put up her hand. "Yes, my mother says she and the horsebox driver and Julian can manage our three."

"No problem, my mother will cope with Ferdie," answered James.

"Mr Roberts has offered to load Wheeler ponies with Oliver's help," David went on. "Would it be possible for Jigsaw to borrow a loosebox?" he looked at Lizzie.

"Yes, he could have Hobbit's box."

"What about you, Harry?"

"My stepfather is O.K. with Jupiter and he'll take Saffron, but I'm not sure if Saffy will box for him," answered Hanif.

"I think he will, he's used to Mr Crankshaw," said Alice, "but it's putting your parents to a lot of trouble."

"We'll fix something. Julia might like to go with Harry's parents. Anyway, Mrs Roberts, Mr Fuller and Mrs Halford have already agreed to drive the teams over and we can settle the other details tomorrow, meanwhile I've a copy of the rules for each of you," finished David, handing the yellow booklets to Alice to distribute.

"It's terribly kind of your mother to lend me Bowie," Tina told Sarah as they mounted. "I never imagined such a wonderful thing happening. I do hope I don't let him down, but I'm afraid I will."

"I don't suppose you'll get round," said Sarah brutally, "but it won't matter because ours is a rotten team: you and Lynne hardly know your ponies, and you and Paul are both useless at swimming."

"Here, our other teams aren't all that much better," protested Lynne. "Lesley and Lizzie aren't *so* super at cross-country, and Lizzie's a terrible shot. And though James and Seb are good, Harry's hopeless at swimming, and Rupert, well, he's just Rupert, and goodness knows what he'll get up to."

"David said it was for experience, he doesn't expect us to win," Tina reminded her team mates.

"No, he doesn't expect much of us in the shooting, running and swimming," agreed Paul, "but I don't think he'll be too happy if we all mess up the cross-country.

CHAPTER NINE

Mixed Fortunes

"The Cranford Vale are tremendously good," said Alice, pushing her way through the crowded village hall where the shooting range had been set up, to meet the newly arrived Woodbury members.

"Yes, masses of bulls," agreed Hanif. "*We've* been here for hours, Blazeaway made us start at dawn. She said she wasn't going to miss a single shot."

"And the Cranford Vale teams are all dressed alike, they're the ones in white shirts, jeans and blue waistcoats," added Tina, a note of envy in her voice.

"Do you know their scores?" demanded Lesley.

"No, they're not being given out, and we're not allowed near enough to see exactly what's going on."

As David limped into the hall with Mrs Roberts walking slowly beside him, Mrs Halford left the firing range and came bustling over. She looked very official with binoculars dangling from her neck and a holdall, heavy with pistols, slung from her shoulder.

"The fifth detail are shooting now and our first competitors are in the eighth," she told David briskly. "The standard's fairly high so far, but we shouldn't have any trouble attaining it with regular practice."

Mr Fuller appeared with an armful of numbers. "The scoreboard's up in the farmyard, beside the Secretary's caravan," he told them, "but there's nothing on it yet. I've collected our swimming times and three maps so we won't lose anyone on the way to the pool."

"I've got the most terrible needle," said Alice, "I wish we could have a practice jump or something."

"You will be allowed your five sighting shots, dear, so just try to relax. Take a few deep breaths," advised Mrs

Halford. "Now, if the new arrivals have all had a look at the firing point, we'll take you outside. Standing in this crowd and breathing stale air won't do your shooting any good."

The Woodbury teams sat on the grass outside, all huddled miserably, grasping their knees, as they nursed the sick feelings in the pits of their stomachs. Mrs Roberts handed round barley-sugar sweets, Lizzie rolled her shoulders and looked more and more worried, Rupert tried to cheer things up by removing his sweet at regular intervals and taking exaggeratedly deep and noisy breaths. He succeeded in making Lynne giggle and Lesley glare, but the rest of them were too locked in their own variations of stage fright to pay any attention. Then Mrs Halford came bustling back.

"Right, we're ready for the first detail, that's James, Lizzie and Sarah. Don't panic," she went on as they grabbed their pistols and prepared for action. "You're not on yet, we've allowed a good five minutes for your eyes to get accustomed to the light."

"Are you sure this is Hollingsworth?" asked Sarah, looking at her pistol suspiciously, "because I hardly got a shot on the target with the stupid Woodbury pistol on Friday."

"Yes dear, all the junior team are having the Hollingsworth pistol, it's the best for small hands," answered Mrs Halford. "Now, the rest of you stay here and Mr Fuller will come for the next detail in about twelve minutes."

"Good luck," called Seb in a lugubrious voice.

"Yes, good luck," added Hanif and Alice with more enthusiasm.

"Think big, Lizzie, think BULLS," Netti instructed her sister.

"I have an awful feeling that Browne is in a missing mood," answered Lizzie, looking at her pistol apprehensively as she was led away.

The next three, Rupert, Alice and Lynne, were ushered

into the hall by Mr Fuller in time to watch the first three shoot, but found this very frustrating as the spectators were kept well back from the firing point and had no idea how their teams were shooting. Only the coaches, watching avidly through their binoculars and making notes on their clipboards, had any idea of the scores, and they were far too busy to be questioned.

"Nearly time for us," said Lynne with a bored sigh, as the others came to the end of their second targets. "I'll be glad to get it over."

"Yes, it's much worse waiting without a nice bouncy pony beneath you," agreed Alice. "Saffy always gives me courage."

"Rosie doesn't give me courage," objected Rupert. "In fact, I feel a lot braver without her. At least I know my trigger finger will take off."

Lesley, Seb and Tina all became very silent as their turn drew near, and Seb and Tina were white-faced and shaking as well. Mrs Roberts plied them with barley sugar and cheerful chat, and Mr Fuller found the first detail and dragged them over with instructions to talk bracingly. The last three, Hanif, Netti and Paul, were surprisingly calm. Then, suddenly, it was all over and they gathered in the dazzlingly bright sunshine outside the hall, talking excitedly and enquiring about each other's possible scores; except for Seb who sat on the grass, his head in his hands, and moaned, "Oh hell," at intervals.

"I wasn't spectacular, but I think I was quite reasonable," announced Rupert modestly. "At least I didn't shoot the chief steward."

"I mucked up my first target, but my second was quite good. I think I got somewhere around seven hundred," added James.

"I was spectacular for me," giggled Lynne. "Every shot on the target. What about you, Paul?"

"More or less what I usually get," answered Paul. "I wasn't expecting to do anything brilliant."

"I did better than I expected," Hanif told them. "If only we could add my shoot to Seb's swim."

"I was dreadful, I kept forgetting to squeeze," moaned Tina.

"It's that stupid pistol, it kept shooting to the left with me," Sarah told her, "I *know* there's something wrong with it."

"How did the all-girls team do?" asked James.

"Reasonably well for me," answered Alice.

"Yes, up to standard," agreed Netti.

"No worse than usual," said Lizzie cautiously.

They all looked at Lesley who was wearing her small, secretive smile. "I'd rather wait and see what the scorers say, but I think I managed a couple of bulls."

"Well done, all of you." Mrs Halford was looking quite pleased as she came out into the sunlight with David limping beside her. "It was really quite creditable for your first competition and with so little practise. Only three of you really tensed up and they'll do better next time."

"Yes, well done. First phase over and no one eliminated. Big sigh of relief all round," added David. "Now swimming. Can we have you in the same cars, please. We don't want anyone separated from their gear."

The first heat was already racing, and the pool was noisy with the echoes of splashes and voices, when the Woodbury people, shepherded by Mrs Roberts and Mr Fuller, appeared, ready changed for the fray. They looked doubtfully from the rows of spectators to the six-lane pool with the metres numbered down the sides.

"It's much smaller than ours," said Paul, his face brightening.

"Exactly half the size," observed Seb.

"Which means we have to swim twice as many lengths," added Hanif gloomily.

"Action, please. David's given me the lists, they've found him a seat and he's going to conserve his energy for the riding," said Mr Fuller, who, brown-eyed and wide-mouthed like his son, was paddling round in bare feet. "As you all know, they try to put you against people of the same standard, so: Tina, Paul and Harry are in heat three. Sarah, Lynne and Netti in four. Alice and Lesley in five. Lizzie, Rupert and James in six. We've no one in seven, but Seb's in the last one, eight. Now if you watch this heat you'll see the form, but remember that if there's a lot of frantic whistle-blowing just after you get going, it means there's been a false start and you have to stop and start again. You're each allowed a coach who can signal to you at half-time and again thirty seconds before the end. When you see this," he held up a card with a large figure thirty written on it, "go like mad. Anything else, Seb? You're our swimming expert."

"No, I don't think so, we went through the rules with David. As long as everyone remembers to touch the side of the bath before turning. Don't think a near miss will do, because there's a judge watching each swimmer and you won't get away with it."

After the cathedral quiet of the shooting range, all the pony club members were enjoying letting themselves go as they roared encouragement at their swimmers. The three-minute heats succeeded each other briskly, and soon the first of the Woodbury people were ploughing up and down the pool, swimming faster than they had ever swum before as they battled with competitors from the Northdown and South Barset. Alice was acting as Hanif's coach, Mr Fuller was Tina's and James, Paul's. They hurried from end to end, making encouraging faces, holding up the halfway cards and then the thirty seconds cards as, with waving arms, they spurred their swimmers to final bursts of speed amid the supporters' shouts and cheers.

Hanif struggled on painfully. He made his fourth length and then produced a final spurt which carried him halfway across the pool before the timekeeper blew his whistle. Tina and Paul, who were visibly tired, couldn't quite make four lengths. As they climbed out, Sarah, Lynne and Netti took up positions at the start.

"Four and a half, are you sure?" Hanif asked Alice. He was looking pleased. "That would be my best ever."

The next heat splashed in. This time the Woodbury were against the East Tulworth and the Brackenbury and at first the Woodbury three trailed, making it more of a procession than a race. Their dissatisfied supporters shouted disconsolately until, suddenly, the picture began to change. The leaders, who had set too fast a pace, slowed down and, when Netti produced a spurt, Lynne and Sarah followed her. Then Netti tired and it was Lynne who finished almost up with the East Tulworth girls.

Alice and Lesley were in another fast heat, and when the bobbing heads seemed too far ahead to catch, they raced each other. "Every metre counts," Alice kept telling herself as she fought, stroke by stroke, to keep level with Lesley. Thinking in metres, she lost count of lengths and was surprised when she climbed wearily out to be greeted as a heroine by the younger Woodbury people.

"Well *done*, Alice. You nearly made six lengths."

"You were as good as Lesley, though she's much older."

"Yes, you dead-heated," they told her jubilantly.

"I don't like the look of the opposition," James observed to Lizzie and Rupert as they lined up. "Those two Cranford Vales make us look very weedy."

"Yes, and they're the *worst* two in their team, the others are in the last heat with Seb," agreed Rupert gloomily.

"Still, none of the Woodbury were bad enough for the first two heats," Lizzie pointed out. "And all those really huge boys will be out of the juniors next year."

The Cranford Vale boys set off at a tremendous pace and the Woodbury people pursued them grimly; they had never put so much effort into swimming before. But there was no question of gaining on the Cranford Vale, it was all they could do to hold on, and the race was among themselves, for the sixth swimmer, who had been left at the start, never caught up. The Cranford Vale were into their sixth lengths and the Woodbury were roaring their team mates to greater efforts as the countdown began. They had all turned, getting their six lengths, before the final whistle blew.

"Now, if you want to watch Seb, can you do it from the corner by the changing rooms?" asked Mr Fuller. "We want to make a quick getaway and have lunch before we walk the riding course."

The heat before Seb's was mostly composed of Cranford Vale girls, and the competitors in the final heat were all much larger than Seb, who looked small and slim and very professional in his goggles. He dived straight into the lead, and then held it, to the delight of the Woodbury members.

"Look at that, he's going great guns," shouted James admiringly.

"And his tumble turns are a huge help; we *must* get him to teach the rest of us," added Alice, as Seb increased his lead with each turn.

"I hope he hasn't started *too* fast," worried Lizzie.

"Go on, Seb!"

"Keep it up!" they shouted, counting lengths excitedly.

When half-time was announced, Seb was still leading, though the other swimmers refused to be shaken off.

"Seven lengths. Terrific, he's going to get the best score of the day," shouted James. Mr Fuller was jumping up and down with excitement, the other pony clubs roared at their members to go faster, while the Woodbury shrieked at Seb to keep his lead. Then, suddenly, the sound of the whistle cut through the hubbub and it was all over.

"Well *done*, Seb," they called as, pulling off his goggles, he climbed out of the pool.

"See you in the car park," shouted Mr Fuller, as a flood of departing spectators cut him off from the swimmers who were making their way to the changing rooms, "Don't leave anything behind."

The Woodbury Tetrathonlites inspected their ponies, who had all arrived safely, and then sat down to eat their lunches without much appetite. They had almost finished when Oliver and Julian appeared from the direction of the cross-country course with long faces.

"There's a *staircase*," announced Oliver dramatically. "None of our ponies have ever seen anything like it before; I can't see any of you getting round."

"A staircase?" the others asked suspiciously.

"What *are* you on about?" asked Paul, swallowing his last mouthful of apple pie.

"They call it a staircase on the plan of the course," Julian explained, "but really it's four gigantic steps cut into a hillside."

"They're all sleeper-faced," added Oliver, "Rosie's going to fall over with fright at the sight of them."

"Oliver," called David from the Land Rover. "No subversion, please."

"Sub what?" Oliver rushed over, eager to tell his bad news.

"What's the rest of the course like?" Rupert asked Julian.

"Oh, it starts very normally, but when you get to that hill on the heath someone's gone a bit wild and made a whole lot of drops and slides and things."

"The timber wagon's enormous and there are two streams." Oliver, disappointed by David's lack of reaction, came rushing back.

David drove over. "Can you all fit in the Land Rover as far as the start? No, not you, Oliver; just the riders and Mr Roberts."

"The scores must be up, look at all those people round the board," shrieked Sarah. "Do stop, David. It won't take a minute."

"No, let's concentrate on the essentials," said David, driving past at a brisk pace. "Scores can wait. Very tempting," he added, stopping the Land Rover beside the first fence, a natural thorn hedge, clipped low and reinforced with a post and rails behind it. "But do make sure they know they've got to jump; collect them and then ride hard as it's a first fence."

They crossed the field, Mr Roberts walking with the members, David driving. The second fence was a straightforward one too, a hogsback of rustic poles set in a wire fence, but the wire had been made safe by two wings of brushwood.

"Keep them straight and keep riding," said David. "Remember that they're still going away from home and friends."

Hanif and Rupert tried to rock the top pole. "Great, it's solid. We don't have to worry about knocking that down," said Hanif.

"There are no faults for knockdowns," Lesley snapped at him.

"That looks like the opening and shutting gate," said Alice, pointing across the field, and they hurried on towards it. It was a free-swinging hunting gate, fastened by a square metal band which had to drop over the post.

"No use slamming that and hoping," said David with a sideways look at Seb. "Do make sure that the fastening drops *right* down before you gallop on. If it sticks halfway you'll almost certainly be eliminated; especially if the judge is a farmer." He left them opening and shutting it in turn and went to find a wider gate so that he could take the Land Rover on the heath.

"I just hope Jupe gives me *time* to shut it," fretted Hanif as they followed the uphill path through heather and pine and came to a stout tree trunk, flagged and numbered four.

"Nice, I like that," said Alice.

"It's *very* uphill," complained Rupert, "I hope Rosie doesn't run out of puff."

"She'll be all right, they'll all get their second winds at the gate," Mr Roberts told him and hurried them on to number five, which was over the crest of the hill. It was a sheer, sleeper-faced drop into a small hollow, followed immediately by a stout pole.

"Ugh! Chess isn't going to like that!" Sarah looked down in horror. Tina stood beside her, white-faced and quaking, while Lynne's expression was full of alarm.

"No problem," said David, rejoining them. "It's a test of the rider's seat. Wasn't it Seb who asked if you could lean back over drops? Well, if you lean back and let the reins slide here, you'll almost certainly have problems at the pole. Sit tight, keep contact and look at the pole. It's easy, the little ponies will just scramble and pop. It's easier than our bank."

"Rosie will probably collapse on her nose, but with any luck she'll get up again," decided Rupert in a resigned voice, and led the way on through the silver birch trees which had taken over from pine. A bend in the sandy track revealed the timber wagon, number seven.

"Oh, it's a real one," moaned Lynne.

"And it's *much* more frightening than the one we made at Garland Farm," added Sarah accusingly.

James measured it against his waist. "It's lower than the one the big ponies jumped."

"I like it," said Alice.

"Yes, it's a good solid jump, the bold ponies will love it," agreed David, "but it is slightly downhill and there's no groundline, so take it with a holding rein; you want to stand back."

The track continued downhill and brought them to a tiny stream, babbling and bubbling at the bottom of a deep ditch.

"If you just gallop on and hope to take it in your stride, you may get a last-minute refusal," David decided. "I'd collect them halfway down the hill, look up, sit down and ride."

"At least there's no black plastic around," said Sarah with relief.

"It's hardly a jump, but you can hear the sound of water; it's just the sort of silly thing Ferdie spooks at. I'd better have my whip ready," resolved James.

David had to cross the stream higher up, where there was a sleeper bridge, but the rest of them walked on unsuspectingly until they were suddenly confronted by fence nine, which seemed to tower above their heads.

Four giant steps, each about ten-feet wide and two-feet-six high, had been cut into the hillock in front of them and each wore a separate label; A B C and D. Halfway up, another group of pony club members surveyed the steps with hopeless faces. The Woodbury halted at the bottom and stood gasping with horror.

"Oh no! We're never going to get up there."

"Ra *might* do one or two, but not *four*."

"We'll all be eliminated."

"David, what do we do about this?"

"You jump up it," said David calmly. "It's a test of impulsion; you treat it like a grid. Get the pony going, ride dead straight and look at the last one. The lively ponies won't have any trouble, just keep them straight and look where you want to go. Stardust, Rosie, Rajah and Vulcan will need a bit of stirring up. Collect them after the ditch, build up some impulsion, and then, when you get here, some real cavalry charge stuff. The two little ponies will need to take a breather." He looked at Sarah and Paul. "Ease them up the moment you're over the timber wagon. And, if anyone does run out of steam, or nip out sideways, you can either retake the whole thing or a particular step, it's up to you."

"If we slow up too much we'll have time faults," objected Paul.

"And if you run out of steam you'll have penalties as *well* as time faults," answered David. "It's a junior competition so the time allowed's quite generous; the bigger ponies should have time to spare."

"It doesn't look much like a grid," said Tina as they climbed the steps. "I do hope Bowie will understand it."

"I suppose they see it as four banks in a row," decided Alice.

A left-hand turn brought them to the chicken coops, which looked comfortingly normal after the stairs, and they were followed by a pen of rustic poles with a sharp left turn for the out.

"Now, here we *do* have problems; a lot of good ponies

are going to sail straight through," said David. "If that happens to any of you, come back through the little gap and just take the out; they're numbered separately, so they count as two jumps. Now, to make it plain to the pony, take him as far to the right of the track as you can, get a bit of a left slant on the first fence, come slowly and, above all, look where you want to go."

James went back and walked along the extreme right-hand side of the track, planning his slant. Hanif was pacing out the pen.

"It's not as bad as the one we jumped at Easter," he announced, "but I think I'll trot if I can."

The course went on, steeply downhill and then over another tree trunk, followed almost immediately by another crossing of the stream, only here it had been dammed and widened into quite a respectable water jump with a pole over the centre.

"This is quite a test for a rider," said David. "You've got to keep the pony balanced on the bit when you jump down over the tree trunk or you'll be in no position to take the water. A half-halt as soon as you land—imagine you're on Coppice hill and halting beside the final flag—then push on with a giving rein; you don't want the ponies to stand back, for the pole is over the centre of the water."

The jump out of the heath was a narrow but stoutly built stile.

"Take it slowly, sit up, plenty of leg," said David. "You're homeward bound so it shouldn't cause trouble, but it is narrow."

Number sixteen was the slip rails. "I'm glad they're so late on the course," observed Hanif, "at least I shall have had some fun before I get here, and, with any luck, Jupe will be a bit tired."

"Feet out of the stirrups, plenty of whoas and approach on a slant," said David. "The ponies are now in the habit of jumping, their blood is up and there's nothing to tell *them* that this fence is any different from the others; you've got to make it crystal clear."

A yellow arrow, pointing sharply right-handed, brought them to the last fence. It was part of the same hedge as jump number one, but here it had been filled out with gorse.

"Look for the finish," David reminded them. "It's not dead opposite so it'll be easy to forget. Rupert, Tina, Lynne!" he roared suddenly. "Stop chattering and *look*. There's the finish. You'd better all walk through it. Then go and tack up. When you're ready, I'll be over there by the practice jump."

Most of the Woodbury members took a short cut across the next field to the horsebox park, but James, saying that his mother would tack up Ferdie and that it wouldn't take him a second to change, ran off towards the farmyard for a look at the scoreboard. Sarah and Paul, agreeing that they wouldn't be riding for ages and that they mustn't tire their poor little ponies by getting them out too soon, raced after him. They joined the crowd in front of an enormous blackboard, already teeming with numbers, and found themselves surrounded by Cranford Vale supporters all jubilantly noting down scores and telling each other:

"We seem to have it in the bag."

"Six hundred points, that's not a bad lead for Sandra after two phases."

"Our lot have certainly swept the board, it looks like an all Cranford Vale finish."

Sarah said, "I'm the best in our team. I've beaten Lynne by two points and you by more than a hundred, Paul. Poor old Tina's last."

Then Oliver appeared. "Your sister's done the best of the Woodbury, she's even beaten James," he told Sarah. "Rupert's third best Woodbury," he added proudly, "and Netti's beaten Lizzie."

"It doesn't matter who's beaten who in the Woodbury," James snapped at them. "Look at those Cranford Vale scores, all up in the seventeen and eighteen hundreds, and only two of us have made the fifteen hundreds."

"Yes, and the East Tulworth, the South Barset, the

Brackenhurst and the Frogmorton are all ahead of us too," agreed Oliver despondently. "I don't think we've much hope of coming anywhere now."

"At least we're not last," argued Sarah defensively.

"Your lot's third from last," Oliver pointed out.

In the horsebox park, the parents were holding the excited and restless ponies while their riders tugged on boots and polo-necked sweaters.

"I'm really surprised at you boys letting Lesley beat you in the shooting," Mrs Rooke reproached Rupert and Hanif. "And your swimming really let you down again, Harry. As for Sebastian's shooting, I think he must need glasses if he can't do better than that."

"Don't write them off yet," protested Mr Franklin. "By my reckoning the boys are in seventh place and the girls eighth, but there are still two phases to go and they might move up a couple of places: a lot can happen in the riding."

"The Frogmorton, that's my old pony club, say they're third at the moment, but they don't think anyone will catch the Cranford Vale now," observed Seb gloomily.

"Do you wish you still belonged to the Frogmorton?" asked Tina as she took Bowie from Mr Fuller.

"No, not really. Anyway, they wouldn't want me in their team with my pathetic shooting."

"Well, even if we're not much good, I'm enjoying myself," said Alice, "and I can't wait to get at the cross-country."

"Yes, it's really rather nice having no chance," agreed Lizzie. "We don't have to fuss about the riding."

"Look at Harry's crash helmet," exclaimed Netti as they all mounted. "I like the green silk and the matching sweater."

"Thanks, but I think it's too posh for someone who may get stuck at the slip rail," Harry muttered ruefully.

By the time the Woodbury teams arrived at the practice jump, the cross-country was well underway. Competitors were thundering confidently away from the start and urging their sweating, blowing ponies through the finish. When the Woodbury had jumped, David inspected their girths and reminded them that if their crash caps came off they *must* stop and retrieve them. Then they watched from the collecting ring, but it was only possible to see the first two and last two fences, the gate and the slip rails. All the fearsome fences on the heath were shrouded in trees, and so, as there was no public address, only a steward with a loudhailer, it was difficult to know how the early riders were faring.

David, with half an eye on his watch, said they all seemed to be taking their time about it. Then, just as the steward told James that he was next but one, Mrs Roberts and Oliver appeared, running red-faced and breathless across the field.

"Hardly anyone's getting over the staircase," announced Oliver, as Mrs Roberts stood speechless, a hand to her chest. "They're all getting stuck. The judge tells them to have three refusals altogether and then go on."

"It's true, David, they're having no end of trouble at those steps: some of them run out, and some of them just haven't the energy to get all the way to the top. And there's quite a lot of trouble at the other jumps too," Mrs Roberts added breathlessly.

"Well it proves that the Cranford Vale haven't practised over the course," said David calmly.

"We thought we ought to come back and warn you. I don't know if there's anything you could tell our children . . ."

"I've done my best," answered David. "I think they all understand how to ride it. Impulsion's the key, without that no pony could get to the top."

"Don't fuss, Mum. I'm going to slow right down after the timber wagon and give Banjo a breather. If the others are all refusing it won't matter if I clock up a few time faults," explained Paul.

"Lynne and I are going to give our lazy ones a couple of

waking-up whacks," added Lizzie, who was looking more cheerful and relaxed than usual.

"Well, I'm going back," said Oliver as James went to the start. "It's great over there, you can see the whole course from the top of staircase hill. Good luck, Rupe and Liz and Net; you're going to need it." He began to run.

"I think I'll go back too," said Mrs Roberts. "Good luck, all of you."

James had set off at a good pace. He jumped the first two fences easily, opened and shut the gate and vanished into the heath.

"I'm *willing* him to do well," said Netti, shutting her eyes and screwing up her face. "Go on, James, impulsion."

"Can you will Jupe to stand?" asked Hanif. "My stepfather's going to be over by the slip rails, but if I'm helped to remount it's eighty penalties."

"Turn Jupiter to the left and stand him up against the fence before you attempt to mount," said David, watching Seb jump the first fence. "Then he won't be able to swing his quarters away."

"I'd make him really belt round the whole course so he's longing for a breather by the time you get there," advised Paul. "Whew, did you see that? Seb was quick through the gate."

"Don't forget the finish," Netti told Rupert.

"Here's James, over the stile," shouted Lynne.

"He hasn't wasted much time," said David, checking his watch.

Rupert was started as James came through the slip rail. Rosie jumped the hedge well and then made a very large, cautious leap over the hogsback. No one watched Rupert through the gate, because the moment James was through the finish they all crowded round him asking questions at once.

"Did you have any refusals?"

"Was the staircase awful?"

"Did he mind the ditch?"

James patted Ferdinand and shook his head, then he jumped off and loosened the pony's girth. "It was great," he answered breathlessly and, leading Ferdinand over to David, he repeated, "It was great. He tried to stop and look at the ditch, but I gave him an almighty whack and he shot over. The staircase was fine—I think we ought to make one on Coppice Hill. Except for having to haul him round a bit in the pen, I didn't have any trouble. So I think I was clear."

"Good, well done," said David. "And here's Seb reappearing," he added, as the skewbald pony sailed over the stile.

Alice went to encourage the nervously circling Hanif.

"Seb's been so quick he can't have had any trouble at the staircase either," she told him.

"It's the non-jumps *I'm* worried about," said Hanif, obeying the starter's call. In a moment he was off, hurtling at the first fence. He let Jupiter have his head across the first two fields, hoping that he would then settle down.

Lesley was being called to the start as Seb came galloping in. "Terrific," he said, smiling broadly as he led Jigsaw over to the group by the Land Rover. "I really enjoyed myself. We almost ran out of steam on the staircase, we couldn't have jumped another step to save our lives, but everything else was easy; it really made up for the misery of the shooting." He patted Jigsaw lovingly. "How are the others doing?"

"James thinks he was clear, Rupert and Harry were both a bit slow at the gate," David answered.

Alice rode over to encourage Lesley who, reins lying loose on Stardust's neck, was polishing her spectacles. "I'm putting more anti-mist on," she explained.

"Here's Rupert," called Lizzie joyfully.

"It looks as though the boys' team are going to get three round," said Paul, a note of pride creeping into his voice.

"Lesley, wake that pony up," called David. "Get her on her toes."

"I'm willing Rupert to remember the finish," announced Netti, shutting her eyes.

Stardust jumped the first fence cautiously, but Lesley was able to galvanize her into life for the second. Rupert came home fast, flew the last hedge and remembered to alter course for the finish.

"I'm afraid I may have collected a few faults," he said, throwing himself off his blowing pony. "She did the staircase O.K. We took it at a hundred miles an hour, but she spooked at the ditch and nearly fell flat at the drop. The worst thing was the pen. I had a terrific job to turn her and we got entangled with the red flag—I heard the pole snap. Does it count? Are we eliminated?"

"Not if you were on the correct side of the flag," answered David. "Which bit of you or the pony did the damage?"

"My foot." Rupert rubbed his ankle gingerly. "I expect I can produce evidence."

"Your *right* ankle, that should be all right then," said David, looking at his watch as a shout of joy greeted Hanif's reappearance.

They watched Hanif's careful, slanting approach, saw him drop the rail and Jupiter follow him over willingly. Alice was praying that the pony would stand, Netti was willing Hanif to spring lightly into the saddle.

"Oh, stand still, can't you!" muttered James angrily as Jupiter twirled.

"Stupid unco-operative animal!" cursed Seb.

Hanif sprang, but was still only half on as Jupiter set off, full gallop, for the finish.

"Oh Hell!" said Seb as Hanif swayed precariously, hanging on to the pommel and vainly trying to swing his right leg over.

"He's going to take the wrong course and be eliminated," groaned James.

"He's going to fall off and be trampled to bits." Lizzie's face was desperately anxious.

Alice stood silent and aghast as they watched Hanif struggling. Then he stopped trying to mount and pulled really hard on the left rein, turning the pony away from home and making it appear that he had to go round the course again. Jupiter began to slow down and, keeping him on the circle, Hanif managed to scramble on. Then, pausing for a moment to get his right stirrup and gather up his reins, he rode at the last fence.

Lizzie started. There was no sign of Lesley yet. Hanif rode through the finish and then over to the Land Rover.

"Sorry, David. I had to circle, it was the only way I could stop him. It'll count as a refusal."

"No, I don't think so, you were still a long way from the next fence and you certainly hadn't 'put' Jupiter at it. But you nearly gave me a heart attack, you were supposed to be keeping him in a tight circle until you were on."

"Here's old slowcoach at last," announced Sarah as Lesley appeared.

"Good luck, Alice!" shouted Hanif, loosening Jupiter's girth.

"Did you have any other trouble?" James asked him.

"No, Jupe was brilliant; he loved it. He did a huge jump over the timber wagon, took the staircase as though he'd been jumping them all his life, and we went through the pen at a trot."

"It sounds as though we're all four round then," James looked pleased, "which means we can finish even if Rupert does something dotty in the running."

"She's taking her time about it," said Paul, watching Lesley at the slip rail.

"Oh, you can't hurry my sister." Sarah's voice was contemptuous.

"You won't have any problems, Tristram will just freewheel round there," Rupert told Netti who was waiting at the start.

"Don't. Touch wood!" shrieked Netti. "It's an awful responsibility having a good pony because if you don't go clear you know it's all your fault."

"Right, we'll have the last four over the practice jump again. Quickly." said David, noticing that Tina's face was greenish in colour and her teeth were chattering, while Vulcan, Chess and Banjo had all fallen asleep.

"I had one refusal," Lesley told David, "and I expect I got some time faults."

"Where did you stop?"

"The staircase—she didn't understand it and stopped to have a look. Then, when she realized it was just banks, she went up quite willingly. She cleared everything else. We did far better than I expected."

"Well done, she's learning." David patted the chestnut neck. "Have we lost Lizzie?"

"No, I can see her blue sweater coming through the trees," Hanif answered.

Alice was galloping, her blood was up and she was filled with elation, though, with her mind intent on remembering the course and taking the jumps correctly, she had no time for self-awareness. The first two fences had been easy, Saffron had co-operated over the gate, made nothing of the uphill tree trunk and taken the drop neatly. She asked him to stand back at the timber wagon and he soared over, making her conscious that he too was enjoying himself and being the perfect partner. He took a quick look at the ditch and jumped it carefully, then obeyed her call for acceleration. He summed up the staircase in a second and reached the top in four great bounds.

"*Good* boy!" shouted Alice, unable to spare a hand for a pat as she guided him round the sharp left turn to the chicken coops. Saffron jumped them with ease and then let her steer him to the right of the track and point him left-handed across the pen. Realizing the problem, he steadied himself and hopped swiftly in and out. They cantered down over the tree trunk, she sat tight, kept him balanced and then pushed on for the water. He flew over, ears pricked, already looking for the next fence. She collected him for the stile. They raced on across the flat grass field, and stopped at the slip rail. Saffron followed Alice over with a small, neat jump and waited for her to replace the rail and remount, with only a few small fidgets. Then they were galloping for the last hedge and remembering the finish.

"It was lovely, but I do wish it had gone on longer," Alice lamented as she led Saffron over to the group by the Land Rover. "It was all over so quickly."

"Any trouble?" asked David.

"No, Saffy thought it was great too." Alice patted him proudly. "How have the others done?"

"Lesley had one stop on the staircase and probably collected a few time faults," David answered. "And Lizzie thinks they may give her a refusal at the ditch. Rajah stopped for a look and jumped from a standstill. Netti's on her way; with luck she'll go clear. Cheer up, Lynne," he called, looking across at the junior team who were quaking miserably at the start. "My pony's an expert at this; just keep him informed about what lies ahead, he'll do the rest."

"We'd better take the ponies back and change," fussed James, who'd caught sight of a band of Cranford Vale people dressed for running. "We've still got to walk the running course."

Rupert groaned, "Do we have to?"

"*We* can't come until Netti's finished," objected Lizzie who was watching the stile anxiously. "Good luck, Lynne."

Lynne started slowly and Vulcan heaved himself ponderously over the first fence. But then she seemed to come to life and, stirring the pony into action, flew over the second.

Seb and Alice were trying to cheer up Tina who was looking green again.

"You'll enjoy it, it's really nice; I promise," Seb told her. "Every single jump was fun."

"And they won't look big now you're on Bowie," Alice reminded her. "It's the people on little ponies I'm sorry for; for Sarah and Paul and all that lot." She pointed at the two Northdown teams who had taken over the practice jump. None of them looked more than eleven and they were all riding twelve-two ponies.

"I'm going to take a look at the scoreboard," decided James. "They may have some riding scores up."

Sarah set off and Netti came galloping in. "He was really brilliant!" she told them as she patted Tristram enthusiastically. "He jumped them all perfectly, I didn't have to do a thing."

"Terrific," said Alice. "Now all our four are round too. You'd better start willing Bowie to go clear, Netti. Tina's got the most terrible needle."

"O.K., as soon as I've got my breath."

David had limped over to the start. "Cheer up, Tina, you've a good pony; just get going and throw your heart over. Paul, don't ride too hard. Save him for the fences, don't push him until you're coming back across these two fields."

Tina was still quaking as she started but once she was over the first fence she began to feel better, the awful coldness and the cramp in the pit of her stomach both disappeared. Bowie seemed a bit lacking in confidence. "Come on, the second one's easy," she told him, "and then it's the gate."

Paul waited, surrounded by Northdown members, for his sister to reappear. And then, as she landed sedately in the slip rail field, he set off; Banjo scuttling willingly towards the first fence, and Paul trying to curb his desire to ride at maximum speed.

"How did it go?" David welcomed Lynne home.

"I made a bit of a mess of it. Sorry, David," she answered. "We had a refusal on the staircase, we ran out of impulsion, just like you said. And we had to circle in the pen. I only just stopped him going straight on. But I did enjoy myself." Lynne jumped off and felt in her pocket for pony nuts. "It's quite different on a pony that likes jumping."

"Good, and two stops isn't bad for your first ride on him," David told her, as he watched a Northdown member refuse the first fence.

They waited impatiently for Sarah and at last she

appeared, cat-jumping the stile, whipping briskly through the slip rail, and then hustling a tired-looking Chess across the last field and over the hedge.

"Any trouble?" the Woodbury people asked her.

"A bit, the stupid pony had to have two goes at the staircase and then he stopped at the water, though it was on the way home. I made up as much time as I could."

"He's a game little pony," said David, patting the sweaty piebald neck. "Get off and give him a rest."

"Here's Tina, and she's going quite fast," Lynne called a few minutes later.

"Too fast. Here, take a pull, Tina," said David, watching anxiously as the bay pony raced across the field.

But Tina left it far too late. Bowie had seen the slip rails and was accelerating when Tina remembered that they were for taking down. He increased his stride and flew over triumphantly. Circling, Tina managed to pull up. The jump judge was calling to her and she rode back.

"Stupid pony!" stormed Sarah. "Spoiling our chances."

"Here, be reasonable, you can't blame the pony; it looked like any other jump," objected David.

"It's all right, they're letting her through," said Lynne.

"Oh, come on, stop talking to the judges, you're getting even more faults," muttered Sarah angrily. "At last," she added as Tina scrambled on and cantered for the hedge.

"I'm terribly sorry." Tina rode in looking very crestfallen, "I sort of forgot where I was on the course; we were whizzing along so beautifully the slip rails went right out of my head."

"Put it down to lack of experience," David told her. "Did you have any trouble on the heath?"

Tina thought back. "No, I don't think so, everything was so glorious I sort of went mad."

"You'll have sixty penalty points and masses of time faults," complained Sarah.

"She won't be any worse than us," said Lynne, staring at the stile as she waited for Paul to reappear.

"No riding scores yet," announced James, "but Mr

Franklin wants to drive us round the running course if you'll lend him the Land Rover, David. He says all the other pony clubs are doing it because everyone's so tired."

"Here's Paul!" shouted Lynne. They all turned to watch. He was through the slip rail in a few moments and vaulted on to Banjo. Urging the pony into a gallop he rode at the last hedge stirrupless and raced through the finish.

"How did you get on?" All the Woodbury people rode over to him.

"He went clear, I never thought he would, but he was really super," Paul told them with pride. "Drop, timber wagon, staircase, pen, stream; he did the lot."

Mr Franklin appeared. "Congratulations, David," he said, opening a garden chair. "Now, can we leave you to watch the scoreboard while I take them round the running course? You've done more than your share."

"Thanks." David sat down quite gratefully. "I'll accept your offer, particularly as it was your son who shortened my life by several weeks; I can't wait for him to grow into that pony."

"Yes there were a couple of hairy moments before he made the saddle," agreed Mr Franklin. "Harry's not firm enough with that pony, but I suppose it'll come. Get a move on," he shouted at the Woodbury members. "I'll fetch you from the car park in five minutes, so hurry up and change."

"Oh, David, they did do well."

"There were so many refusals and people were saying that the course was far too stiff, until our little lot came round and made it look easy."

"The way they tackled that enormous staircase."

"We really felt proud of them," said the Woodbury parents, flocking in from the cross-country course.

"We've heard so much about the Cranford Vale, but as far as the riding went our performance was a lot better. Those huge boys were having trouble all round the course."

All the Woodbury people, parents and competitors, met again at the start of the running. Mr Franklin had taken charge of the competitors, making them tie double knots in their shoelaces and lecturing Rupert on taking the right course, while Mrs Franklin handed round glucose tablets and sips of water.

The Cranford Vale boys, looking bigger than ever, went first, and were followed by their girls' team, which had done much better than the boys in the riding. Starting at one minute intervals, there was soon a long stream of competitors spread out all round the course.

"Even I can't possibly get lost with all that lot to follow," observed Rupert, as James started at his usual steady pace. Seb followed, equally steady but lighter on his feet, then Rupert, long and gangling.

"They all look rather like their ponies," observed Netti with a giggle. "Except that Rupert's eyes don't pop like Rosie's."

"No giggling," said Mr Franklin severely. "Keep your breath for running. It's a pity we don't know the scores, we can't tell you what you've got to do to get a place, but if you don't do your utmost you may be kicking yourselves afterwards. Chase Rupert with all you've got, Harry. Now Lesley, you're the first of our girls."

Rupert, running easily, gained on Seb, but Hanif, pushing himself to greater and greater efforts couldn't quite keep up with Rupert. Lesley was slower than Hanif and the gap between them grew, but Lizzie, running like the wind, drew closer to Lesley with every stride and left Alice behind. Netti almost kept up with Alice and, behind her, Lynne was doing well, but the last three, smaller and younger, were being left further and further behind.

They came home one by one, collapsing in stitch-tortured positions with agonized expressions, but quickly recovering and demanding to know their times.

Oliver appeared. "Still no riding scores," he complained. "The steward says that the riding always takes ages, but the running scores are very easy and that's why they're doing it last."

"Right," said David, when Paul had recovered from his collapse. "That's it then. You've all done very well, remarkably well as it was your first tetrathlon. It doesn't matter whether we've been placed or not, you all rode with intelligence and dash and you all finished in all four phases of the competition. Now, can we have tea and box the ponies while we wait for the results."

Everyone was very agreeable at tea. Mrs Rooke was heard telling Mr Fuller that she thought the Woodbury could have beaten the Cranford Vale if the unfortunate business with the pistols hadn't held up the practices. Seb was handing out envelopes. "It's an invitation," he explained. "Dad thought everyone would be too shattered for a party tonight, so he's set it up for tomorrow; I hope you can all come. We're having the barbecue in the paddock so that we don't set the cottage on fire."

Everyone was tearing his or her invitation open eagerly.

John and Sebastian Fuller request the pleasure of your company on Monday, 16th August at the Old Forge. 7.30 p.m. Barbecue. Cowboy clothes, but no ponies or pistols, please.

"Very posh," said Rupert, studying the Wheeler invitation. They were printed on orange-coloured cards.

"Dad's in printing, so he gets it done for free," Seb explained.

"You've asked all the parents too," observed Hanif.

"Yes, Dad thought they all ought to get together since David wants a pony club committee. We didn't ask your aunt and uncle, Alice, but it's O.K. if you want to bring them."

All the families were still consulting about the party when Oliver and Rupert came running. "The riding scores are on the board and we've nearly caught up," they shouted. "There are only about four people better than James now. The best person is in the South Barset, but two people in their team were eliminated in the cross-country," gabbled Oliver.

"The Cranford Vale girls are leading, but both our teams and the Cranford Vale boys are close," explained Julian more precisely. "But you can't work out which will be the three *best* scores in each team until they give us the running scores."

David limped over to inspect Julian's figures, while Mr Franklin and Mrs Rooke hurried to see the scoreboard for themselves.

"Yes, a couple of the high-scoring teams have been eliminated in the cross-country, so we may well move up a few places," agreed David. "I think you'd all better get dressed in some sort of matching gear."

"Track suits," suggested James.

"No, only about five people have them," objected Netti.

"Swimming trunks," proposed Rupert.

Seb thumped him in a friendly manner. "Don't be dead stupid."

"Riding clothes," said Alice. "After all, riding was our best thing." There was a general groan at the thought of getting back into jodhs and boots.

"Are you sure we need to bother?" asked Lesley. "I won't have done very well in the running."

"You're the best of the Woodbury girls," Julian told her.

"And Netti's beaten Lizzie," observed Oliver, looking over Julian's shoulder.

"I won't have after the running," Netti told him. "Lizzie was in terrific form."

"Has anyone seen my boots?" asked Rupert.

As soon as the last runner had finished, everyone, trainers, competitors, parents and supporters, gathered round the scoreboard to wait for the running scores and the final totals to be chalked up. A few teams were adding what they believed to be their running points and then comparing their best three against probable best threes from other clubs, but most people, either baffled by the sheer weight of figures or realizing that such suppositional calculations were a waste of time, merely waited impatiently for the official results.

"Well, we certainly haven't beaten the Cranford Vale," decided James, "because though we're about level after the cross-country, we know they all ran better than we did."

"And it looks as though some of the best people will have scores up in the four thousands." Seb sounded envious.

"It's terrific to see all those twelve hundreds for clear rounds though," said Alice. "You're the only team with four, and we didn't do so badly with three."

"Lizzie deserves a medal for going clear on Ra."

The official scorer was beginning to write up the totals when the organizer appeared and announced them through a loudhailer. "First Girls and overall winners: Cranford Vale Girls with 11,356," he boomed. "Second Girls: Woodbury with 11,026. Third Girls: East Tulworth with 11,012. First Boys: Cranford Vale again with 11,326. Second Boys: Woodbury with 11,290. Third Boys: Frogmorton with 10,890.

"Then we come to the individuals. First Boy: Charles Smith of the South Barset with a total of 4,424. Second: Stephen Sykes of the Cranford Vale with 3,910. Third: James Morgan of the Woodbury with 3,830, and Fourth, Woodbury again: Rupert Wheeler with 3,790. Individual Girls. First: Jane Ogden of the East Tulworth with 4,382. Second: Sandra Sykes of the Cranford Vale with 3,892. Third, Cranford Vale again: Mary Ann James with 3,782, and Fourth, Woodbury's Lesley Rooke with 3,734."

The Woodbury people were either jumping about with joy, gasping with amazement or merely looking dazed when the announcer went on, "The special prizes for under twelves go to Best Boy, Tom Scudamore of the South Barset, and Best Girl, Annette Wheeler of the Woodbury. Now, if you would all come up and collect your rosettes . . ."

371

CHAPTER TEN

No Pistols or Ponies

All the Woodbury Tetrathlonites slept late on Monday morning. Eventually they staggered out sleepily to inspect and offer delicious feeds to their ponies, though, as Rupert told a comfortably reclining Rosie, it was the humans who had done most of the work the day before and the ponies ought to be bringing *them* breakfast in bed.

After lunch they revived and began to search for cowboy-like clothes and by teatime they were all looking forward to the Barbecue and a chance to talk over the Tetrathlon. For, by the time the running was over, all three teams had been in an exhausted and bemused state. They had collected their rosettes in a daze and been packed into horseboxes and cars and taken home by bossily brisk parents without exchanging a word, except on the whereabouts of lost track shoes, towels and tail bandages.

Alice had decided not to take her aunt and uncle to the Old Forge. She couldn't see them enjoying a pony club party—they weren't very good at enjoying themselves at all. She would gladly have taken Clare, but her cousin was in Spain, so she arranged to go with the Franklins. Mr Franklin was always punctual so they were the first guests to arrive, except for Mrs Spencer and Tina, who seemed to be helping and were running round frantically with toasting forks and strings of sausages.

"What a perfect evening," said Mr Franklin politely, as Seb, resplendent in a full Western outfit from boots, leather waistcoat to hat—though the holsters on his belt were empty—greeted them at the gate.

"And what a perfect setting," added Mrs Franklin, admiring the thatched cottage and sniffing the scent of roses and honeysuckle.

"You won't be able to smell the flowers much longer," said Seb, "Dad's got two barbecues going. Come in and have a drink, there's wine for the adults and cider for us."

"There, you see, it was not essential that I came in jeans," Mrs Franklin, who was wearing a pink and gold sari, muttered at Hanif. "Mrs Spencer is wearing a beautiful skirt and blouse."

"She looks more like a gipsy than a cowgirl," said Alice. "Look at her huge earrings."

"She's a Spanish dancer, come to entertain the cowboys," explained Tina, hurrying by with an armful of plates. She *was* wearing jeans with a green shirt, her mother's short boots, a huge belt and a red, white-spotted handkerchief tied round her neck.

"Here are the Wheelers." Hanif sounded relieved and, leaving the four parents to talk, the pony club members hurried to the paddock. Except for Rupert, the entire Wheeler family was dressed in clean jeans and checked shirts. He had made a very old pair of jeans more ragged and wore them with a crumpled, faded shirt, and battered, shapeless hat and bare feet. He had rubbed charcoal on his pink and white Wheeler face, to give it an unshaven look.

"I *am* a cowboy, but a South American one, a gaucho," he told Hanif and Alice. "They didn't wear boots, because the leather shrank in the wet. They rode barefoot, with tiny stirrups for their big toes and they were poor and dirty. The North American cowboys were dirty too; Seb's far too posh, he looks like someone playing around at a dude ranch."

"It's really just a cover up, because he lost his clean jeans and couldn't be bothered to iron his shirt or wash his face," laughed Netti.

"I think Seb looks great," said Oliver enviously.

Then the Rookes and the Robertses and David all arrived at once and suddenly the party was in full swing. Mrs Spencer handed out sausages from one barbecue, Mr Fuller chicken joints from the other. Seb poured wine and cider with a lavish hand, Tina handed round plates and paper napkins.

They sat on straw bales and discussed the Tetrathlon. Lynne insisted on telling everyone exactly how Vulcan had jumped each fence, while Rupert's account of Rosie's mishaps grew more and more farfetched.

"Here's James, at last," announced Oliver.

"Where have you been, James? We missed you," Netti told him.

"We couldn't persuade my father to stop packing fruit. It got later and later, so in the end Mum and I came on. He may turn up—probably just when everyone's going home."

"Here, drown your sorrows." Alice passed him a mug of cider. "We've got to get you and Lizzie into a party mood."

"It's this field," explained Lizzie, "it keeps bringing back horrible memories."

They were all eating ice cream and Seb was explaining that he'd fixed up a disco in the shelter, which was well away from the other cottages, and that there would be dancing when everyone had finished supper, when Mr Fuller called for silence. Standing on a straw bale, he said, "As the father of the newest member I really have no right to speak, but I do want to propose the toast of the Woodbury Pony Club, coupled with the name of its boss—David. It may be a small pony club, but it's one of the friendliest, and I know that with the help of the committee of parents we've just been forming, it won't be long before it's one of the best."

"The Woodbury and David!" shouted everyone, holding up mugs and glasses and then drinking deep.

"Speech!" called the parents, who were becoming quite rowdy.

"Come on, David. Speech."

David climbed slowly to his feet. "I'm no good at speeches, so I'm not going to make one, but I do have a piece of good news for you. Frank Collingwood, the owner of the Coombe Manor Stud, just up the road here, was very grateful to those of you who rescued his visiting brood mares from the yew wood. When I met him the other day he was still talking about it and saying that, but for your prompt action, the British bloodstock industry would have suffered quite a severe blow; those nine mares are all classically bred and they can be expected to have six or seven more foals apiece. Anyway, he went on to say that he wanted to give the Woodbury a present. I suggested that he replaced the stolen pistols and got a very vehement and quite unrepeatable reply. I thought again and suggested jumps, which went down rather better. This morning he telephoned me to say that he had ordered a set of extra-stout show jumps, a complete set of twelve fences, to be delivered as soon as possible."

"Hurray!" shouted James. "That's really good news."

"Terrific. Decent jumps at last," agreed Paul. "I hope they come in time for the next rally."

"That's all," David went on when the parents stopped clapping. "Except to say that I was very pleased with the way things went yesterday. Though we only came second in both competitions we did have the best riding results and that's what really matters to a pony club."

"Here, here, here," Rupert shouted loudly as David sat down.

"You're drunk, Rupert Wheeler," snapped Lesley accusingly.

"There is one other bit of good news," said Seb to the other pony club members, as the parents began to talk among themselves again. He looked bashfully at Tina and then down at his boots. "Dad said it would be too embarrassing to announce it publicly, but that we could tell *you*. Tina's mother and my father have decided to get married.

"They've been seeing each other for quite a long time," he went on, when the others sat looking from him to Tina in speechless surprise, "but we didn't realize that it was serious, and they didn't want to involve us until they were sure it was going to work. Then they put off telling us because of the Tetrathlon—they didn't want us shooting with other things on our minds—so *we* only heard the news last night."

"Are you pleased?" asked Alice.

"Yes, I think so. Things have been so awful lately they *can* only get better," answered Seb sadly.

"I hope you're not going back to the Frogmorton country," snapped Lesley.

"Nothing's settled. We're going to start house-hunting tomorrow. We all like it round here, but it has to be a house with a field—a biggish field—because they're thinking of buying Bowie for Tina: she's obviously got to have a pony of her own."

"*You're* going to buy Bowie?" Sarah looked at Tina in amazement.

"It's not quite settled yet, but my mother's talked to yours."

"So that's why you were allowed to ride him yesterday," said Lesley in a knowing voice.

"I thought he was very expensive," observed Lynne.

"He is a bit," agreed Tina, "but Mum was saving all she could to buy us a flat or house one day, and now Seb's father's going to buy the house, she's going to spend some of the money on Bowie. I don't really believe it's all going to happen. It still seems like a dream."

"Do you *mind* having her for a sister?" Oliver asked, pointing rudely at Tina.

"No, I don't think so," Seb answered slowly. "I'd rather have a sister than a brother and I'm glad she's younger than me. I won't be like poor old James." He gave James a friendly thump. "His big sister's so superior she'll hardly speak to him."

"You *must* find a house near Woodbury, we can't afford to lose *two* super pony club members," Alice told them.

"She's right, you must forbid your joint parents to contemplate any house that isn't within easy hacking distance of Garland Farm," added Rupert firmly.

376

"Could you do some 'willing', Netti?" Hanif asked.

"Yes. If you stay, and Tina has Bowie, that'll mean two more good people for teams," decided James cheerfully. "By next year Paul and Sarah ought to have bigger ponies too and then we'll really show the Cranford Vale; it'll give them a real shock when they find that their days as the top pony club in Area Ten are over."

PONY CLUB TREK

CONTENTS

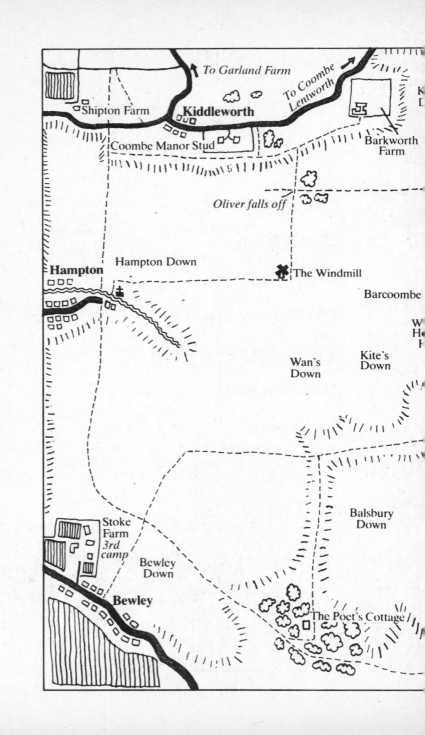

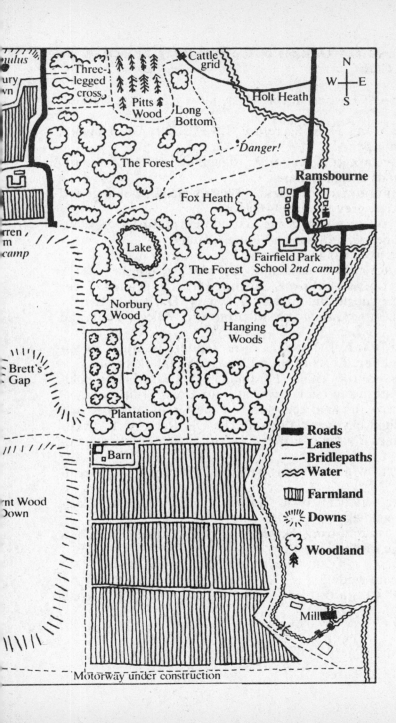

Three-legged cross

Cattle grid

Pitts Wood

Long Bottom

Holt Heath

Danger!

The Forest

Ramsbourne

Fox Heath

Lake

Fairfield Park School *2nd camp*

The Forest

Norbury Wood

Hanging Woods

Brett's Gap

Plantation

Barn

rnt Wood Down

Roads

Lanes

Bridlepaths

Water

||||| **Farmland**

Downs

Woodland

Mill

Motorway under construction

N
W E
S

rulus

ury wn

rren m camp

Members and Officials of the Woodbury Branch of the Pony Club

DAVID LUMLEY, ex steeple-chase jockey. Lives at Garland Farm.

MRS ROOKE, Hon. Secretary. Lives at 20, The Heights, Woodbury.

LESLEY ROOKE, her elder daughter. Owns Stardust, 14-hands chestnut mare.

SARAH ROOKE owns Chess, 13-hands piebald gelding, and Sparkler, grey gelding 14-hands.

MR AND MRS ROBERTS run Garland Farm for David Lumley. They live at Garland Farm Cottage.

LYNNE ROBERTS owns Berry, 13.1 red roan mare.

PAUL ROBERTS owns Banjo, 12.2 black gelding.

ALICE DRUMMOND owns Saffron, 14.1 dun gelding. Lives with her uncle and aunt at Shawbury, Darkwood Lane.

MARGARET AND PETER HUTCHINSON, Alice's aunt and uncle.

HANIF (HARRY) FRANKLIN owns Jupiter, 14.2 liver chestnut gelding. Lives at Barn Cottage, Great Coxwell.

JAMES MORGAN shares Ferdinand, 15.1 dark brown gelding, with his mother. Lives at Four Cross Fruit Farm.

RUPERT WHEELER, the eldest of the family, owns Rosie, 14.1 light bay mare. Lives at The Old Rectory, Kidlake.

ELIZABETH WHEELER owns Rajah, 14.1½ chestnut gelding.

ANNETTE WHEELER owns Tristram, 13.2 grey Welsh gelding.

OLIVER WHEELER owns Hobbit, 12.2 dark brown Dartmoor gelding.

TINA SPENCER owns Bowie, 13.3 bay gelding. Lives in a cottage on the Downs.

SEBASTIAN FULLER, Tina's stepbrother owns Jigsaw, 14.2 skewbald gelding.

JULIA CARTWRIGHT and JANET GREEN. Pony Club instructors.

CHAPTER ONE

"We're the Duds."

"Do come, Harry. I know we won't be chosen for the mounted games team, but it'll be fun and we'll see everyone," pleaded Alice Drummond, dismounting from her dun pony, Saffron, and leaning over the loosebox door. "The holidays are nearly over and I can't bear to waste a single moment of what's left."

Hanif Franklin dropped his body brush and curry comb into his grooming kit box and rumpled his curly blue-black hair. His brown face wore an obstinate look and his black eyes communicated nothing. Silent eyes, thought Alice.

"You're so sociable and the rest of the pony club is so competitive," he complained. "We spent the whole holidays training for the tetrathlon, and now it's over I want to relax. Why can't we go for a peaceful hack through the woods?"

"You'll be able to go for peaceful hacks every weekend when I'm back at school," Alice argued. "It's a lovely ride to Garland Farm. You can relax while you watch everyone else tearing up and down, trying to get into the Prince Philip team."

"Relax? With Jupe trampling on my toes, the Rookes quarrelling and people complaining that it's not fair and they ought to have been picked? Some hope." observed Hanif. He liked the Woodbury pony club members, but sometimes they all seemed terribly English while Alice with her tanned complexion, rich golden hair and dark blue eyes, could be Scandanavian. He liked her straight nose, wide mouth and determinedness, and the fact that she'd lived abroad and travelled a lot was another bond

383

between them. And she had no parents at all which was much worse than having to put up with a difficult stepfather.

Alice could feel him weakening. "You know you really love all the pony club scandals and dramas. Come on, tack up. We don't want to miss any of the excitement."

When Hanif had saddled and bridled the impatient Jupiter, a sturdy liver chestnut of fourteen-two, and collected his crash cap, they rode along Darkwood Lane and past Shawbury, the redbrick, gabled house among the trees, where, since the death of her parents in a plane crash, Alice spent the holidays with her uncle and aunt and a shifting population of grown-up cousins.

They took the path through the woods and forded the river Vole, low in its banks and flowing placidly after the long, sunny summer. The ponies jogged happily along the track which passed through the Waterford Farm meadows, where Saffron was turned out during the term. Then they crossed the main road and took the bridlepath, which led through stubble fields, towards Garland Farm, the home of David Lumley, who had been a well-known steeplechase jockey until a crashing fall had left him disabled, and was now District Commissioner and chief instructor of the Woodbury pony club. Soon they could see the farm, on the rising ground. It was sheltered by a half-circle of hills and, beyond the hills, in the distance, the smooth green humps of the Downs met the faded blue of the late summer sky.

The four Wheelers lived at the Old Rectory, Kidlake, a village just down the road from the lane which led to Garland Farm. Their house was old and large and rather tumbledown. Both their parents worked and no one ever had the time or energy to cut back the ivy which was gradually obscuring the upper windows, or to fix the dangling trellises, which were supposed to support the climbing roses on either side of the front door. Weeds had taken over the cobblestones of the stable yard and the sagging stable doors, clumsily re-painted bright blue by Rupert, were already peeling.

The Wheelers, who all had straw-coloured hair, blue eyes and pink and white complexions, were hard at work. Rupert, the eldest, was cursing as he pumped up the front tyre of an elderly and unloved-looking bicycle. His pink and white face was long and his blue eyes dreamy. Lizzie and Oliver were grooming chestnut Rajah and little brown Hobbit, while Netti had her grey, Tristram, tied up outside and was washing his tail.

"Why don't you hack over on Rosie?" Lizzie, the second oldest, who wore her straw-coloured hair in a single plait, called to Rupert. "You could tie her up in David's yard while you watch."

"Because I know what would happen," Rupert answered. "The old Rooke would soon bully me into joining in. She'd have me in some useless team, consisting of Harry on lunatic Jupiter and some horrid little children from the D. Ride, just to be slaughtered by Sarah Rooke and Netti and the other mounted games specialists."

"Don't talk to him, he's stopped pumping," Netti, whose straw hair was cut short and whose blue eyes were bright and challenging, told her sister. "And we're not going to slaughter anyone. We haven't a hope of making up a decent team. Except for Sarah, none of the good people have the right sort of ponies. Twelve-two is the best size, so even Tristram's too big and the fourteen-twos are useless."

"Hobbit's perfect then, and I'm bound to be picked," announced Oliver boastfully. He saw the Woodbury team winning at Wembley, cheering crowds and enormous rosettes.

"You are not." Netti looked at Oliver's round cheerful face, cheeky blue eyes and curly straw hair and decided that he needed crushing. "You're hopeless at vaulting on and you're too lazy to practise."

"Do tack up, everyone, we're going to be late," called Lizzie, interrupting Oliver's reply. "And Ollie, you *can't* go with your bit like that," she added in tones of horror. "It's *green*."

"Who cares. Boring old Janet Green only gives me a mingy three for inspection however hard I try. I can't think why David's made *her* the team trainer."

"Oh, come on, Lizzie, stop fussing," said Rupert as his sister ran to the tackroom for a wet rag. "I've got to start before this tyre goes down again, and surely everyone in the pony club *must* be used to Ollie's tack-cleaning by now."

James Morgan, large, solid and serious for his age, which was fourteen and a half, turned out of the gate of Four Cross Fruit Farm and bicycled slowly along the road in the direction of Garland Farm. Now that the tetrathlon was over the fun had gone out of the holidays, he thought gloomily. There wasn't much point in going to Garland Farm to watch other people practising mounted games, but he supposed that some of the older members might turn up, and, anyway, nothing could be more boring than staying at home. He hoped Sebastian Fuller, his best friend, would be there. He'd meant to ring up and find out, but Seb's father had just married the mother of another Woodbury member, which made it all a bit awkward. What if the new Mrs Fuller had answered the phone? James wouldn't have known what on earth to say to her.

Then James heard the sound of hoofs. He looked back and saw Alice and Hanif coming out of the bridle path at Four Cross. They waved, shouted and urged their ponies into a trot. Then there were more hoof sounds, ahead this time, and as he bicycled round another bend in the narrow road, he could see the Wheelers trotting towards him. They met at the Garland Farm lane and rode up together, all talking at once.

They were halfway to the farm when a car horn hooted imperiously behind them and turning in their saddles they saw Mrs Rooke, the pony club secretary, at the wheel, glaring at them through her thick-lensed spectacles.

"Car," shouted James as ponies and bicycles crushed themselves against the hedges and the car swept by towing a sparkling new trailer. Sarah Rooke sat beside her mother, Lesley, her older sister, in the back.

"They looked very tense, I think there's been another squabble in the Rookery," announced Rupert with relish.

"Yes, they were grim-faced. We didn't get a single wave," agreed Alice.

"Terrific new trailer, though. A much newer model than ours," said James enviously.

"But no Julian," observed Oliver. "I don't like him much, but he's the only boy in the pony club of my age even if he is a bit weird."

"His mother told ours that he was a mathematical genius," announced Netti. "He spends all day at his computer. Mum says she goes on and on about how marvellous he is, like she does about Sarah and her riding."

"So Lesley's the only one she doesn't like?" asked Alice.

"Yes, it's terribly unfair; I'm glad our mother doesn't favour Netti and Oliver," answered Lizzie.

"Life favours them though," said Rupert gloomily. "*They* get beautifully schooled ponies when you and I outgrow them, and we have to start all over again with dotty, new, green ones."

"I'd like a mother like James's," announced Oliver. "She cleans his tack."

The Robertses, Lynne and Paul, lived in the Garland Farm cottage. It was really two cottages knocked into one, built of red brick and covered in Virginia creeper. Mr

387

Roberts ran the farm for David Lumley and Mrs Roberts had done a great deal to help David through the difficult time after his accident. Paul, who was small for his age, with dark hair and grey eyes, was feeling quite hopeful of being chosen for the Prince Philip team. Banjo, his black pony was twelve-two, fast for his size, very handy, and good at most gymkhana events. But Lynne, who was a year older, much larger and looked quite different, with her wavy, light-brown hair, and wide, plump, usually cheerful face, felt very dejected. She was fond of Berry, her red roan pony, but she had to admit that her only talent was a fast trot and her habit of kicking other ponies had made her justifiably unpopular in the pony club. No one would want to be in a team with them.

It was a shame, thought Lynne. I'm better at games and races than most of the pony club members; I love them and I'd be willing to practise really hard, but without the right sort of pony, I've no hope at all of being picked.

Tina Spencer, small, reddish-haired and freckled, and Sebastian Fuller, who was tall with brown hair, brown eyes and a wide mouth, had ridden along the edge of the Downs and then through the woods to the rally. It was the same distance as going by the road, Seb had explained, but much more fun and, as it was only a boring mounted games rally, it didn't matter if they arrived on muddy ponies.

They didn't talk much. It's not going to be easy, thought Tina, as they rode side by side, Seb on skewbald Jigsaw, she on the smaller, bright bay Bowie. They were both embarrassed by their new relationship of stepbrother and sister. It was all very well for Mum and Mr Fuller, John, she corrected herself, to go on and on about how essential it was to communicate, about how they must talk everything through, and, if they were going to make a go of becoming a family group, each member must feel free to put a point of view or voice a complaint, but you had to find out what you *really* thought first. I keep changing my mind, thought Tina. Sometimes it's great: having Bowie and living on the Downs is like a dream come true, sometimes it's just O.K. and sometimes, when things are difficult or people are cross, I think we've made a terrible mistake. Better to keep quiet and see how things go, she decided as the ponies, sensing an occasion, pranced along the farm track and into the yard.

"Hullo."

"You've come too. Great."

"Here are Seb and Tina," The other pony club members gathered round, obviously pleased to see them.

"How are you two getting on?" Oliver asked the question that the rest were too tactful to put.

"We haven't had a stand-up fight yet," answered Seb, dismounting.

"And we've given the parents a week off—they've gone to Venice," Tina added. "We've Seb's grandparents staying with us; they're really nice and not a bit fussy."

"And when the parents come back we're going to do some serious house-hunting. My father only rented the cottage for the summer and it's much too small for four people," explained Seb.

"That's Janet calling us," said Netti, looking towards the paddock. "We'd better go. Come on, Ollie."

"We're only spectators," Rupert shouted to the waving figure at the paddock gate.

"Perhaps we'd better go and spectate," suggested James.

"A great mistake to appear too soon, she'll give us jobs," warned Rupert.

Sarah Rooke on piebald Chess and a stranger, a long-legged, long-haired girl who dwarfed her chestnut pony, were warming up. Paul, Netti and Oliver joined them.

Alice and Lizzie were dithering. "Does Janet want some impossibles to ride against the possibles?" Alice asked Lesley Rooke who was carrying a bundle of flapping flags on canes.

"I've no idea," snapped Lesley, glaring at them through her thick-lensed spectacles. "I didn't want to come. My mother made me; she said I had to help. I can't see why, there are plenty of other people standing about." She glared at the group of boys gossiping by the gate. "Why don't they help?"

"I'll help," Lizzie dismounted.

Alice looked from one Rooke to the other. It was unfair, she thought, that Lesley should be so much uglier than Sarah. It wasn't just the thick glasses. Her heavy face had a bovine look, her nose was too wide. Sarah had a heart-shaped face, pretty beneath a fringe, a small nose and a neat mouth, though that was slightly spoiled by thin lips.

"Who's the new girl?" Lizzie asked Lesley as she helped with the flags.

"Oh, you mean Lorna Mackintosh? She belongs to the Cranford Vale, but they always put her in their mounted games B team. Mother's more or less promised she can be in our A team if she switches clubs."

"Is that allowed?"

"I shouldn't think so. But my mother will go to any lengths to get her darling Sarah riding at Wembley."

"They have to beat the Cranford Vale A to get there, don't they?" asked Lizzie.

"Yes, in the area competition. And if you get through that there's the Zone round. They haven't a hope."

Janet Green was blowing a whistle. Then she shouted, but she had a high voice which didn't carry.

"I think we had better round people up," said Alice. "Janet looks a bit frustrated."

Alice rounded up Lynne and two small nervous-looking

children who said that their names were Jason and Melanie Clark and they were usually in the D ride.

Mrs Rooke was signalling to the gossiping boys by the gate. Hanif cantered over to explain that they weren't taking part

"You've no business to be here then," snapped Mrs Rooke. "Come along, Janet, do get them into teams. Sarah, Lorna, Netti and Paul are the A team. Who are you going to put in the B?"

"The minimum number for a Prince Philip team is five and the normal number is six." Janet's voice was peevish. "But not every member of the team competes in each race. Anyone who's chosen will have to be prepared to work really hard. We'll practise all through the term as well as the holidays. Winter *and* summer—because the Area competition is held at Easter, the Zone in the summer and, as Wembley's in October, your parents have to agree to you taking time off school."

"Great. Mine will agree," announced Oliver.

"Puts me out," said Alice. "I don't suppose Aunt Margaret would want me staying home from boarding school."

To his fury, Oliver found himself in the C Team with Melanie, Jason and Tina. The B Team, Lizzie, Alice and Lynne, were a person short, so Alice galloped over to the gate and persuaded Seb to join in.

"We're beginning with the Potato-picking Scramble," squeaked Janet Green. "Each team has a bucket. When I blow the whistle, two riders from each team ride to the pile of potatoes in the centre, dismount, pick up a potato, remount, gallop back and drop it in the bucket. Then they go back for another. When I blow the whistle, those two riders stop and the other two from each team begin. When I blow the whistle again that pair stops and we count the potatoes to see which team has won. Is that perfectly clear?"

"Yes." The pony club members, bored by the long explanation, surged towards the buckets. Mrs Rooke was lecturing Lynne on keeping Berry away from the A team as she didn't want their ponies kicked.

"Doesn't matter about the rest of us," grumbled Seb. "You look out, Tina. You know she hates Bowie."

The race started and it soon became apparent that those riders who could vault on were doing far better than those who had to use a stirrup to mount. Mrs Rooke, in her beige dress and sensible shoes, was encouraging the A team, clapping Sarah's better shots and admiring their vaulting ability. She ignored the problems of the Clarks, whose ponies took an instant dislike to the game. Tiger stopped dead and with a mean twist, tipped Jason over his shoulder. Grey Twilight stood midway between bucket and potato pile, ignoring Melanie's kicks, whacks and cries, and refused to move in any direction. Tina and Oliver went to the rescue of their team mates. Tina caught Tiger. A dun with black points, he was a miniature Saffron, except for his small, wicked, rolling eyes. Oliver administered a ferocious whack to Twilight's plump quarters and followed her, preparing to deliver another if she dared to stop again.

In the third team, Lizzie was proceeding at a stately pace, but Lynne's efforts to keep Berry away from the other ponies meant that she had to wait until there was a clear space at the potato pile, a handicap which soon left her trailing.

When the whistle blew for the third time Mrs Rooke hurried forward to count the A team's haul. Lesley, one eye on her mother, was surreptitiously adding extra potatoes to the other teams' buckets, before taking them to Janet for counting.

"Twenty-two," announced Mrs Rooke proudly.

"Eighteen and twelve," announced Janet, looking puzzled.

Alice and Seb, who had seen Lesley's action, began to giggle. Mrs Rooke gave them a glare and sent them to bag up the left-over potatoes. Lizzie was helping Lesley to arrange a row of dustbins opposite heaps of squeezy bottles with the tops cut off.

"This is the Litter Race," squeaked Janet, handing out long canes. "On the whistle, the first rider in each team gallops to the squeezy bottles, picks one up on the lance, rides on to the litter bin, drops it in, gallops back and gives the lance to the next rider."

Oliver decided to go first for the C team. "You'd better go next, I don't think they'll be able to do it," he told Tina, pointing at the quaking Clarks with his lance. The B team sent Lynne first, working out that this would give Berry least opportunity to kick their ponies. Netti went first for the As and this time the B team gave them a much better race. Alice and Seb rode fast and the bigger ponies had a slight advantage. But Oliver, to his chagrin, was left miles behind. He wasn't experienced enough to ride fast with one hand, nor was his seat strong enough for the sharp turns and rapid halts the others made. Then, when he handed over to Tina, Bowie fled from the lance in terror, shooting off across the paddock as though pursued by a demon.

"Drop it, Tina, drop it," shouted the other pony club members.

"Stupid pony," sneered Sarah. "Don't let *him* come again, Janet. He'll spoil the mounted games like he spoiled the tetrathlon, him and beastly Berry."

Tina dropped the lance and rode back on the still trembling pony. "Sorry," she said. "I'll practise at home. I think if I tried with a shorter one first I could get him used to it."

"Don't bother, we don't want *him* in the team," said Sarah spitefully.

"Don't you think you could weed out a few of the duds

now," Mrs Rooke suggested briskly. "Tina, Lynne and the two little ones are quite hopeless."

"Yes," agreed Janet weakly, "but I'll keep Oliver for the Grooms' Race; we need all the small ponies. Get into your teams," she squawked. "Numbers one and three stay here, two and four down the other end. No, that's wrong. Lesley, we want the bending poles."

Mrs Rooke made James and Rupert each stab a row of spiked poles into the ground, while Janet tried to explain to the baffled pony club members where they and their ponies were to go. "Number one starts here, leading number two's pony down through the bending poles. Number two is down there, holding number three's pony. She vaults on her own pony, bends back here leading number three's. Which means that number three stays here holding number four's pony. When number four gets her pony she gallops back here and that's it."

It took a long time to get organized. The pony club members wandered up and down with each other's ponies, arguing. Janet squeaked peevishly, Mrs Rooke glared. At last they were ready, and this time the people with small ponies had a huge advantage, vaulting on easily and racing away. It was becoming obvious that Hobbit was wasted on Oliver and that Netti would do even better on a smaller, quieter pony.

"Poor Ollie. Well, Hobbit *was* mine first," said Netti, trying not to feel guilty as she took over her brother's pony.

"Janet's finished with all of you. She's going to start training the *team*," said Mrs Rooke, gesturing the others away. "You can't expect her to waste her time on the bunglers and also-rans," she added, when Alice who'd been enjoying herself gave a sorrowful groan. "She has to concentrate on the good ones."

"We're the duds, the cast-offs," Alice told Hanif as they joined the group by the gate.

"You knew Saffy was too big," Hanif told her, "but you would come."

"Why don't some of you try those two little titchy ponies?" suggested Rupert. "If Netti's riding Hobbit, Tina could ride one of them."

"Oh yes, please do." Melanie and Jason brightened up. "It would do them good, they're getting worse and worse with us."

"I'll have a go," offered Oliver. "Come on, Tina, the others are all too heavy."

"O.K. Would you like a ride on Bowie, Lynne?" Tina suggested, worried by Lynne's despondent face.

"Thanks, but I'd better put Berry away first in case she kicks someone."

Tina and Oliver had appropriated a few poles and were teaching Tiger and Twilight to bend. Lynne was riding a dressage test in an imaginary arena on Bowie. Rupert was lying on the grass and Hanif was trying to persuade Alice that all the excitement was over and they could now go home, when David Lumley, in his specially adapted landrover with the disabled sticker, drove into the paddock.

"Good morning all," he said, pulling up beside the group of ponies and riders, "How have things been going?"

"Boringly," said Hanif.

"We're the cast-offs," added Alice.

"Janet needs six people, but she's only found four so far," explained Lizzie.

"Lynne would be good if she had a decent pony," said James.

"We'd all be all right if we had smallish nippy ponies," protested Seb.

"I've had a thought, something the rest of you might like to do," said David, looking round at the bored and disappointed faces. "What about a trek? A short one, say three days. You could ride over the Downs to the forest and back. I think I could fix up fields for the ponies and you could take tents."

"A trek?" Alice's face lit up. "What a lovely idea—but do you mean these holidays?"

"I don't see why not. September's a good month."

"It *sounds* great," said James in a practical voice, "but how would we carry the tents and food and cooking things? It's not much fun riding with a backpack."

"Pack ponies," suggested Rupert.

"I thought a rota of parents could deliver the tents, grub for humans and ponies and all the rest of it, to each campsite in turn. You're too young to be left entirely to your own devices, so we could look you over night and morning, but otherwise you'd be on your own.

"I think it's a terrific idea," said Alice enthusiastically. "Don't you, Harry?"

"I was wondering how Jupe would fit in," answered Hanif.

"Berry wouldn't. She'd spoil it for everyone," said Lynne sadly.

"No problem. If you want to go you can take my Vulcan," David told her. "He'd love it. We'd need two fields each night, one for mares, one for geldings, otherwise there'll be jealousy and kicking." He went on thoughtfully, "I think it could be done; I've some useful friends scattered about in that area."

Seb had called Tina over and was explaining about the trek. Rupert got up and brushed the grass from his clothes. "I'm willing," he said. "When do we start?"

"I'd like to go too," James told David, "but I'll have to ask my mother first. I'm not sure if she'll trust me with Ferdie. He's hers really, and she does all the stablework and grooming—I'm only allowed to look after him if she doesn't feel well."

"I'm putting my name down. What about you, Tina?" asked Seb.

"Three days beginning when? It would be awful if we went away the minute the parents came back," answered Tina.

"I want to go like anything, but if Netti's taking over Hob I haven't anything to ride," moaned Oliver.

"Yes, you have. You swop Hobbit for Tristram, you dope," Rupert told him briskly.

"Oh, we don't want him, he's too young," complained Lesley, who had been fetched by Lynne.

"You don't mean that *you're* coming?" asked Rupert, gazing at her with a shocked expression. "Do you really think you should? I mean, I know we all drive you mad with our horrible habits and general incompetence; you'll be worn out with scolding me all day long. I don't think I'd advise it, Lesley."

"Anything would be better than staying at home and hearing about potato scrambles and flag races from morning to night," snapped Lesley.

"And I'll look after Ollie, so he'll be all right," said Lizzie.

David had limped across the paddock to watch a final run through of the flag race.

"Those four aren't half bad," he said, joining Janet and Mrs Rooke as the race ended.

"But there are only *four* of them," Janet complained peevishly. "Where are we going to find the other two?"

"I'll talk to Derek Roberts again about getting a suitable pony for Lynne. She's good enough to train a pony on now and they could make a lot of money when she outgrows it. I'm told the richer pony clubs pay a fortune for their Prince Philip ponies. Ironic, since the whole idea when the Prince started the games was to give the poorer children on cheap ponies a chance."

"That's five, we still need six," snapped Mrs Rooke, looking round the pony club members with a dissatisfied expression.

"Bowie's too nervous and Tristram's going to hot up if we keep racing him; he hasn't the right temperament for mounted games," explained Janet.

"What about that little grey fatty?" asked David pointing his good hand at Twilight.

"Useless, it won't move," snapped Mrs Rooke.

"She was moving just now when Tina was riding her. I'm sure if she had a couple of weeks with an experienced kid like your Sarah she'd be a different pony," David told Mrs Rooke. "Give it a try, Janet, even if she doesn't make the team you'll have done the Clarks a good turn."

The group of pony club members by the gate came to a sudden conclusion and walked over to meet David.

"Yes please, David," said Alice

"We think it's a great idea," added Seb.

"There are ten of us who'd like to go, but Ollie and I have to ask our mothers," explained James.

"You *all* have to ask your parents' permission. You do that, and I'll find out about fields; then we'll discuss dates and equipment."

"It looks as though there'll only be two mares," said Lesley.

"But five boys and five girls, which is going to make it awkward over tents; most of them hold two," observed James.

"What is all this about tents?" asked Mrs Rooke, bustling up.

"We're going on a *trek*. We're going to camp on our own, without any grown-ups. Much more fun than boring old mounted games," exulted Oliver.

"It's only for people who aren't in the Prince Philip team," Lesley told her mother.

"Nothing's definite until you've asked your parents," said David. "If they say 'yes', give me a ring."

"Our parents are in Venice," Tina's freckled face looked worried. "Seb's grandparents are looking after us.

If they say yes, will that do?"

"Of course. Tell them that you will be inspected night and morning by a pony club official, but otherwise you'll be on your own." said David.

"Come on, let's go home and start working on Mum," shouted Oliver as he struggled to mount Tristram. "We don't need to wait for Netti."

All the would-be-trekkers were suddenly galvanized into action. There was a great packing up of half-eaten lunches and a general tightening of girths. Waving goodbye and shouting their thanks to David they clattered down the lane, talking excitedly. Only Hanif seemed silent and unenthusiastic.

"What's up?" asked Alice, when they had parted from the main body of riders. "Do you think your parents will be difficult? Will they object to us camping on our own?"

"No, quite the opposite. My stepfather will be all too keen, he'll be buying me the latest in camping equipment and teaching me how to cook a four-course meal in one billy can," complained Hanif. "I want to be left alone and allowed to make mistakes and do things badly like everyone else."

CHAPTER TWO

Getting Ready

Alice turned Saffron out in the paddock behind the dog kennels and went in search of Aunt Margaret. She found her grooming one of her prizewinning Springer spaniels. The large brown and white bitch seemed to be enjoying the attention.

Alice explained about the trek. "It's not quite definite yet," she finished, "We're all asking our families and then reporting back to David."

"Three days. I suppose that *would* fill in the time before you go back to school," said Aunt Margaret, her always pale and unsmiling face made to look paler by the harsh reddish-brown of her hennaed hair. "And it doesn't sound as though it would be an expensive trip."

"No, sleeping in a tent and eating baked beans; couldn't be cheaper," Alice agreed cheerfully. "And we're going to be checked night and morning by a pony club official."

"I hope the boys are a well-behaved lot. I don't really like these mixed parties, but I suppose there is safety in numbers," said Aunt Margaret doubtfully.

"James Morgan's *very* sensible," Alice spoke in reassuring tones. "And Harry and Seb are models of good behaviour. Rupert's the only dotty one, but Lizzie will keep him in order. I expect I'll share a tent with her or Lesley Rooke."

"Well, if Mrs Rooke is letting her daughter go it must be all right," decided Aunt Margaret. "And don't go wasting your money on camping equipment. Your cousin Andrew insisted on our buying him a complete set when he went to Spain and then never used it again. You'll find it all in the cupboard in the garage."

"Oh great. Thank you very much," said Alice gratefully. "I'll take a look at it and then telephone David."

"Wait till the cheap time, dear," Aunt Margaret called after her.

At Four Cross Fruit Farm James was arguing with his mother. "Of course I'll remember to water before feeding, I'm not a complete twit," shouted James, red-faced and indignant. "Just because you usually look after him doesn't mean I *can't*."

"No, I know, I didn't mean that" said his mother hastily. "It's just that I love him so much that I can't bear the thought of anything happening to him."

"I wish I had a horse of my own, it's such a responsibility riding someone else's," complained James. "And then I could go to rallies with dirty tack if I wanted to, instead of always getting ten for inspection and hearing everyone making snide remarks, because they know it's all done by you."

"It would be madness to have two horses, darling," said his mother. "We couldn't possibly aford it, and anyway neither of us has enough time for a horse of our own. I'd never get the farm accounts done if you didn't do all the exercising in the holidays, and you could never cope with a horse in the term. No, you take him on your trek. I don't suppose a little healthy neglect will hurt him, but you must ring me at once if you think he's starting colic or coughing or anything."

"I don't suppose it'll come off, probably half the parents will say no," James retreated into gloom. "But if it does, we're going to be inspected night and morning by a pony club official and now you're on the committee I suppose you count as one and could come and inspect Ferdie yourself."

"Why should I feed Chess for you this evening?" In the red-brick Victorian house on Woodbury Heights the Rooke sisters glared at each other. "You and Mother are only going to buy *you* another pony. I'm not going to be your groom. You can feed him yourself when you get back."

"I don't care," retorted Sarah. "It won't hurt him to go without his stupid feed for once. It's Mother who wants you to do it, not me."

"I'm not going to do all the work just so that Mother's little pet can be in the Prince Philip *and* the show-jumping teams," Lesley stormed. "Nor am I going to spend my time dragging sacks of potatoes and bending poles about. I'm going on the trek."

"If I get another pony I think I'll come too," said Sarah in a provocative voice.

"You can't, it's for people who *aren't* in the team, David said so," Lesley snapped back. "Paul's not coming and Netti's letting Oliver have Tristram."

"I don't care what the Wheelers do, and Mother will take care of David. If I can get another pony, I'm coming. You try and stop me," sneered Sarah.

"Do you think Ollie's really up to a three-day trek?" asked Mrs Wheeler, turning reluctantly from her easel to look at her children, who had burst into the bare attic room which she used as a studio. "Of course the rest of you can go, but Ollie riding Tristram? I don't think it's on."

"Oh really, Mum, I'm ten and a half now," Oliver told her in a pained voice. "I'm only a year younger than Paul and a year-and-a-bit younger than Tina. She's going, and Paul *would* be going if he wasn't in the team."

"I'll give him some lessons first, because *I* don't want him riding Tristram badly," said Netti in a reasonable voice. "He can't go unless he sits properly and is in control, don't you agree, Lizzie?"

"Yes, you can't slop about on Tristram, Ollie."

Oliver made a face. He hated riding properly, but this wasn't the moment to say so. "O.K.," he agreed. "If I take lessons and ride properly, can I go?"

"I'll look after him," offered Lizzie.

"We'll see, I'll talk it over with Tim," answered their mother, buying time.

"You'll have to remind Dad that time has passed and Ollie's nearly eleven," Rupert told her. "You used to let me do all sorts of daring deeds when we first had Tristram and he wasn't nearly as well-schooled as he is now. James used to come on Toffee and we played Cowboys and Indians for hours."

"I know, but we were younger then. You lose your nerve when you reach middle-age," Mrs Wheeler explained.

"Well, can we tell David that Ollie's *almost* certain to be coming?" asked Lizzie.

"Ninety-nine per cent certain," insisted Oliver. "I am quite sensible really, Mum. It's being the youngest. The others are always telling you what to do, so you have to go a bit mad and let off steam sometimes, but I promise not to on the trek."

Seb and Tina went home by the road. They parted from the Wheelers at their gate and then rode on slowly, the reins lying slack on the ponies' necks.

"Do you think that your grandparents *will* let us go on the trek?" Tina asked Seb.

"Oh yes, it's nothing to do with them really. I'm sure Dad would agree. He doesn't much care what I do as long as I do *something*. What he hates is my spending all morning in bed, that drives him raving mad. Anyway they said they'd phone, didn't they? To make sure we were O.K. With any luck they'll do it tonight and that'll settle everything.

"Yes, and I'll be able to ask Mum what she thinks," agreed Tina. In her mind's eye she could see her mother. She was so young-looking, with her shining eyes and wild hair, that people often thought they were sisters. Tina was missing her dreadfully. They'd never been separated before, and it would be awful if her mother came back and found they'd gone off on a trek. But she couldn't explain that to Seb.

Paul Roberts was delighted with Banjo's performance. They'd held their own with Sarah and Netti and even with the Cranford Vale girl, once they'd got the hang of things. They were good, good enough to be in the team, to compete in the area round. He couldn't see them getting to Wembley, not next year, anyway; but Janet had said they were a young team and time was on their side. He didn't say anything, just harboured the feeling of warm, quiet, pride that was swelling up in him, and mixed Banjo an extra special feed. It wouldn't be fair on Lynne to make a song and dance about it, he thought, as they headed for the cottage. Berry didn't seem to be much good at anything and Mrs Rooke wasn't going to let anyone forget that she'd kicked Bowie. It was mean, the way she'd kept picking on poor old Lynne all morning.

Lynne felt near to tears. She wasn't used to despair. She didn't know what to do with her face which kept sagging into unfamiliar and sorrowful lines. She'd never cared about being a good rider, about being in teams. She'd been content to hack about and have fun. She'd been proud that Berry was one of the best groomed ponies in the Woodbury, bettered only by Ferdinand, and every one knew that that wasn't James's work. But then, when David took over the club, things had changed, and they'd all begun to ride better. It was riding Vulcan in the tetrathlon that had changed her, she'd found she *could* win prizes. And now Paul and *both* her special pony club friends were in the Prince Philip team, and she'd been left out.

"What a face, Lynne," Mrs Roberts noticed at once. "Was it that bad?"

Lynne nodded, she couldn't trust herself to speak.

"Mrs Rooke keeps on about Berry being dangerous. They won't let her near the other ponies. Lynne ought to have a new pony," Paul spoke for his sister. "She's good, just as good as the rest of the team, Janet Green said so."

"Wouldn't David lend you Vulcan again?"

"He's no good, you need little nippy ponies," Paul explained.

"He said he'd lend me Vulcan for the trek," said Lynne, her face brightening. "The people who aren't in the team are going. It's for three days, over the Downs and through the forest. We're going to take tents and do our own cooking."

"You mean he's turning you loose on your own?" Mrs Roberts sounded shocked. "I'm not sure your Dad's going to like that."

"Not completely on our own. Someone from the pony club's going to check us night and morning and David said he'd ask friends of his to lend us fields."

"Oh go on, Mum. You must let her go," persuaded Paul. "It's a real shame she can't be in the team, but the trek will make up for it."

Hanif broke the news to his mother in the sitting room at Barn Cottage. He had turned Jupiter out in his paddock and then cut across the tamed and flawless lawn and entered by the french windows. Mrs Franklin was giving a lesson in English conversation to two Pakistani friends. In their bright summer saris they looked a bit like butterflies, thought Hanif as he shook hands politely, and quite unlike the pony club mothers; *their* uniform of drab trousers, green huskies and wellies, scarcely changed from summer to winter.

Mrs Franklin was pleased to hear about the trek. She worried a lot over Hanif and whether she had done him great harm by leaving her own country and giving him an English stepfather. She was always afraid that he was becoming a loner and making no English friends, but he'd joined in the tetrathlon and now this trek, her black eyes lit up with happiness.

"It will be very beautiful," she said, "to ride over the Downs and through the forest. And you say the tents will be put up on the farms of David's friends?"

"That's the idea. It's not completely settled yet. He's asking his friends and we're all asking our parents. About ten people want to go, five boys and five girls. No adults, but they'll come and check us out night and morning." Leaving his mother to calm the Pakistani ladies, who were so appalled that girls were to be allowed to trek with boys that their carefully acquired English conversation deserted them entirely. Hanif went off to drink orange juice and clean his tack. He would let his mother tell his stepfather, who was tall and fair and very English-looking, about the trek, he decided, dropping bit and stirrup irons into a bucket of water. He didn't expect any trouble. In fact, as he had told Alice, he anticipated being swamped by enthusiasm. For his stepfather, who had been good at all games—the house was full of silver cups and photographs of teams—thought his stepson too much of a swot and a bookworm and was trying to change him.

Hanif was right. Charles Franklin was as pleased with the idea of the trek as if he was going on it himself. All through supper he enthused about the stretching and character-building aspects of going off into the unknown and coping with the unexpected, until Mrs Franklin became quite nervous and said that surely David would tell them where they were to go.

"He'll give them maps and compasses, of course," her husband explained. "You and I had better have a couple of sessions with the map and put in a bit of compass work, Harry," he went on. "We don't want you getting lost and I don't suppose any of the pony club kids have a clue."

"But there are huge tracks across the Downs, made by the Ancient Britons or someone. If you follow them you arrive at the next place," objected Hanif. "It's easy."

"Well, it would be a bit tame if you stuck to the obvious tracks. We don't want you drifting around like a riding school out for a hack. I must think up something a bit more testing and put it to David."

Hanif groaned inwardly. He could see his stepfather ruining everything. He would bulldoze David into some horrible regimented scheme and all the fun would disappear. He began to hope that the other pony club parents would all refuse to let their children go.

"The trek's on." Alice recognised Lizzie Wheeler's voice on the telephone. "Lesley Rooke's just rung us. She said I was to tell you and you were to tell Harry."

"Great, when do we start?" asked Alice.

"Thursday. There are only three days to get *everything*. Oh, and the most important thing of all is to get the ponies shod. David says no one with risen clenches or grotty shoes will be allowed to start."

"That's not too bad," said Alice.

"It's going to be an awful rush for us. *All* the ponies have risen clenches," there was a rising note of desperation in Lizzie's voice, "and usually we share everything so, as Netti's not coming, it means buying an extra tin of saddle soap and a new hoof pick as well as organizing tents and frying pans and food."

"We don't *all* need frying pans, surely?" said Alice. "Some of us had better bring saucepans and kettles."

"Yes, I know. David says we're to meet at Garland Farm tomorrow morning to discuss who brings what.

Ten o'clock; mounted, because he says the ponies are to be kept in work."

Alice telephoned Hanif and gave him David's messages.

"Isn't it great?" she asked.

"No," Hanif answered, "My stepfather's gone mad. He's erected two tents on the lawn, produced three cooking stoves, a whole collection of lamps and billy cans and he goes on and on about grid references and the magnetic North."

"Oh, you are lucky," Alice told him. "Aunt Margaret only looks gloomy about the expense and Uncle Peter won't take any interest. They said I could have my cousin Andrew's camping gear, but it's all for one person. The sleeping bag's fine, but who wants a tent for one? All his cooking pots are tiny and so's the stove. Are your stepfather's bigger? Do you think he'd kit me out too?"

"Delighted, I should think. But you'll have to listen to never-ending lectures on prevailing winds, learn safety drills for the use of lamps in tents and how to use your watch as a compass if you lose the two he's just given you," answered Hanif in a voice bitter with indignation.

Lesley Rooke had given the information for trekkers to James and told him to pass it on to Tina and Seb.

"Are you definite about coming?" James asked when Seb's grandparents had called him down from his room.

"Yes, we're both coming. Our parents phoned from Venice last night. They said 'Fine' and that they'd stay on an extra couple of days. What about you?"

"My mother's reluctantly agreed to trust me with her precious Ferdie. Well, not trust exactly, she's agreed to risk it. Oh, and David says you're to check your ponies' shoes. No one will be allowed to go who has risen clenches or worn-out shoes. And we're all to be at Garland Farm tomorrow at ten, to settle the details."

The pony club members were all sitting on their ponies in the yard at Garland Farm and arguing about frying pans and tents and who would share with whom, when, punctually at ten, David appeared. Like most jockeys he was slightly built and not particularly tall. He wore jeans and a checked shirt.

His face looked healthy and suntanned now, thought Alice, much better than last Easter, and when you were looking at it you noticed that he had blue eyes and nice hair, brown, thick and vaguely curly, but not that he was disabled. It was only when he walked that you realised how lame he was and observed the useless arm dangling at his side.

"Good morning all," said David. "You're in very good time. Julia's about somewhere. I think she's nicking a bale of my hay. She's going to inspect the ponies' shoes, hoofs, etc, while I take a look at your tack. Then we'll get down to the paperwork." He looked round. "Where's my writer?"

"I'm here," Paul rushed up with biro and notebook ready.

"A *tack* inspection!" the pony club members muttered guiltily. Rupert and Oliver exchanged anguished glances. Then Oliver remembered that he was riding Tristram, whose tack had been regularly cleaned by Netti, and relaxed. Rupert dismounted hastily and, spitting on his handkerchief, tried to remove the ancient grass and grime from the rings of Rosie's snaffle bit.

"Serves you right. David should do more spot checks," Lesley glared at him reprovingly.

"Counter productive," Rupert told her. "More checks wouldn't make me clean my tack more, they'd simply depress David and the other pony club instructors. Look, Seb, I'll stand between you and Tina, you're not *too* brilliant. Lesley, you go next to James, his mother's achieved perfection as usual. Lynne, you go last. You're nearly as good as James and we want David to end on a good note, thinking that he has a clean and shining pony club."

They lined up across the yard and David began with James, while Julia Cartwright, who wore her brown hair in a pony tail and was much preferred to Janet Green by the members—she smiled and laughed a lot, as well as being a better instructor—began with Lynne.

David seemed more interested in nosebands, than in the actual cleanliness of the tack. He explained that he would like the ponies to wear their headcollars under their bridles, but that this was impossible if they also wore dropped nosebands or standing martingales. "It's a question of priorities," he told Hanif. "If you *need* your dropped noseband you'll have to carry your headcollar. Don't put it over your bridle. We don't want uncomfortable ponies with sore cheekbones." He was also checking the condition of reins and the stitching near buckles and billets, especially on girths and stirrup leathers.

"I'm not being fussy. We don't want the whole expedition spoiled because of broken tack," he explained. "We'll give each group a spare pair of reins and leathers for emergencies, but *starting* with rotten tack isn't an emergency, it's bad management. Paul, we need to make a note of all the saddles with two decent D's for carrying saddle bags."

Julia was rather shocked by the state of the ponies' shoes.

"I suppose you were all hoping that they'd last out the holidays," she said. "Well, they won't, and certainly not a trek. How many of you go to Mr Barret? Perhaps we could arrange a joint shoeing session."

James, Lynne, Lesley and Hanif were all smugly perfect, but the rest of them needed stitching or shoeing or both.

"Aunt Margaret isn't going to survive the shock of new shoes," observed Alice. "She's been counting the days and convinced herself they'd last the six weeks."

"Break it dramatically," advised Rupert. "Tell her that something really shocking has happened, that you're terribly sorry, but it'll cost a fortune, then, when she hears it's only shoes, she'll be so relieved she won't fuss at all."

"I wish you lived nearer," said Alice. "I'd send you to break the news."

"Now, groups," said David, when the inspection was over. "You won't enjoy a whole day's ride if you go in one great gang. Two groups of five is a much better idea. How would you like to split up, remembering that you'll all be together each night?"

"Boys and Girls," suggested James. The other pony club members looked at each other doubtfully.

"No, Ollie's only allowed to come if I look after him." objected Lizzie.

"Well, that's a start," said David. "Group I: Lizzie and Oliver," he told Paul. "Now is there anyone else who has to be with someone special?"

"I don't exactly *have* to be with Lizzie, but we share things so it's more convenient," Rupert explained.

"Seb and I want to be together," announced James.

"And we'll have Tina," added Seb, "because Jigsaw and Bowie are just getting used to each other."

"And I'll go in Tina's lot," Lynne told Paul.

"Shall we go with the Wheelers?" Alice asked Hanif.

"O.K." He seemed relieved to have his mind made up for him.

"That means Lesley goes with James's lot. All right?" asked David.

"I don't care which lot I go with," Lesley made it sound like an insult to both groups.

"I do," Rupert muttered at Alice. "She scolds me every time I draw breath."

411

"You like it, you provoke her on purpose."

"I should stay in the same groups for cooking," David was saying. "Most people's saucepans and frying pans cater for about five."

"Yes, and we'd never get ten people to agree about food, but it's just possible five might be able to," added James.

"Have we any vegetarians or people with allergies?" asked Julia.

The pony club members shook their heads.

"Does everyone like sausages, beans, eggs, bacon and beefburgers?" asked Seb, "because that's all I *can* cook."

"I can make curry, choice of chicken or prawn," offered Hanif.

"Ugh, I hate curry, I'm glad I'm not in your group," giggled Lynne.

"Fruit for pudding?" suggested Alice.

"*No*, ice cream," demanded Oliver.

"Don't be silly, we can't take a freezer camping."

"Yes, ice cream every night," agreed Lynne, "Whoever comes to check up on us can bring it in Mum's cool bag."

"They might as well bring the whole supper," suggested Oliver. "Lizzie and Rupert are useless cooks, they burn everything. We have disgusting meals when our mother is too busy to make them."

"Each group will settle its own food," said David firmly. "You'll need enough for three breakfasts, three teas and three suppers. I'll arrange for your morning visitor to deliver sandwiches for lunch. When you've made your lists you'd better consult a mother about quantities. Remember that you'll be extra hungry."

"Now, ponies," he went on, sitting down on the end of the water trough. "One bucket and a sack of feed per pony. Enough for two feeds per day. You'll all feed before breakfast and before turning them out at night—at the same time, to avoid kicking. A headcollar and rope with a

412

quick release fastening. *And* a length of baling string. This is important because we don't want a repeat of Bowie's accident. *No* pony is to be tied to anything by the headcollar rope. Tie the baling string to the fence, tree or whatever, make a loop, tie the headcollar rope to the loop, preferably with a quick release knot. Is everyone clear on that?"

"*Yes*," the pony members answered. None of them were likely to forget the day Bowie had bolted away with a fence attached to him.

"Grooming tools," David went on. "Well, the ponies will be living out and autumn's coming on, so really the less the better. No body brushes, just a dandy brush for knocking the mud off. A share in a hoof-pick and perhaps a share in a water brush for manes and tails. Tack-cleaning is really a matter of washing the bits each evening, but I won't stop you taking saddle soap and it might come in useful if it rains."

"I think I may have to take a complete grooming kit for Ferdie *and* clean my tack," said James apologetically. "My mother doesn't like him to rough it."

"Doesn't matter, you haven't got to carry it. Everything will be delivered by car or in the trailer, but please pack it sensibly.

"Now, what else?" he looked at his list. "Fly spray, not essential for the Downs, but very useful in the forest. Pocket knives, yes, but not sheath knives and nothing that could hurt you if you fall off and land on it. Money, especially telephoning money. Normal riding clothes except that anoraks are better than jackets, sensible shoes or boots and hard hats *must* be worn.

"Have I forgotten anything, Julia?"

"Lots, Mr Franklin's made a huge list with everything like knives and forks and spoons on it, but he's getting it photocopied so they'll each have one."

"Yes, the committee are being a great help," said

David. "Mr Franklin's providing the maps and compasses and he's going to give you a short talk on how to use them. He's also in charge of tents. Mrs Roberts is in charge of the first aid kits and she's arranging for someone from the Red Cross to come and tell you about the basics of First Aid. So now the only question is can you all meet here on Wednesday evening for the talks and final arrangements? Then on Thursday morning you'll all start from here, but the groups will be given different routes."

"I knew my stepfather would ruin everything," groaned Hanif, when, having thanked David and Julia, the pony club members set off for home. "I knew it would be fatal once the parents were allowed on the committee. My stepfather will take over, he always does."

"But poor David can't do everything, he's only one working hand," protested Alice, "He *needs* people to help."

"And we need to be taught to understand maps and compasses," said Lizzie. "We don't want to be lost for days in the forest."

"No we *don't*," agreed Oliver. "And we won't have Netti, she's the best at knowing the way. Rupert and Lizzie can get lost on Beacon Hill."

"I'm not bad at maps," announced Seb, "and I know some of the ways across the Downs."

"I think a couple of talks before we go is quite a good idea, but I'd rather learn to use a map and compass than do first aid. I hate blood," James admitted sheepishly.

"I've got to persuade Aunt Margaret to teach me to *cook*," said Alice, "and there's not much time left."

"We've *three* tents on the lawn now," Hanif told Alice when she and Saffron called in at Barn Cottage on the way home from their visit to the forge. "And you needn't bother to learn to cook, my mother's made enough food for ten people. She's made a selection of curries and

414

frozen them, she says she'll send them up daily, and then we'll only have to boil them in the bags and cook some rice."

"Oh great," said Alice. "Even *I* can cook rice and I love your mother's cooking."

"My stepfather's furious," added Hanif in a voice full of satisfaction." He wanted us to scrape carrots and peel potatoes as he had to at scout camp. He doesn't think eating boil-in-a-bag curry will develop my character at all."

"At least he cares about your character and he's right behind you if you *want* to do anything. Aunt Margaret only points out the difficulties. She's not a bit encouraging. If it wasn't for the pony club I don't think I'd have any fun at all in the holidays. Still, she is taking a bit of interest in the trek. She's arranged with the other mothers that she'll provide fresh fruit. She thinks we'll all be coming home with spots and scurvy after a diet of sausages, beans and chips."

"My mother's bought two enormous cans of fruit salad, the exotic kind with mangoes and passion fruit. We're going to have far too much to eat," fussed Hanif.

"Don't worry, I expect Rupert eats masses, he's so tall and thin," said Alice. "And I don't altogether trust the Wheelers. I know they've agreed to do all breakfasts, but we may find they've forgotten the bread or dropped the eggs. Anyway I've bought three malt loaves, three cakes, three packets of biscuits and a collection of mince pies and jam tarts, so our group's teas are organized."

"We're giving you a lift to this hideous meeting tomorrow, aren't we?" asked Hanif. "I'm afraid my stepfather wants you to bring your sleeping bag and as much of your other gear as you can then. He's found two canvas kit bags and they're all cleaned up and labelled, one for each of us. Honestly, you'd think we were going to the North Pole."

The First Aid lecture was first because Mr Franklin had to give his map reading talk after work. Lynne and Paul, lining up chairs and benches in David's large farmhouse kitchen, were feeling nervous.

"I hope Mum knows what she's doing. It's ages since she was a nurse. She stopped before I was born, didn't she?" worried Paul.

"But Mrs Gail's right up to date, and they're going to do a double act, Mum said, not a proper lecture. There," Lynne dragged the second basket chair into position. "That's fifteen places if they use the window seats. We can't need more than that."

"They're coming," Paul was looking out of the window. "All four of the Wheelers and Mrs Rooke and Sarah have arrived; I think they're coming in too."

"It's not meant for the Prince Philip people," Lynne's voice was full of indignation. "They'll have to sit at the back."

The kitchen was soon full of pony club members arguing over menus, and how much coke and orange juice ten people would drink in three days.

"Depends on the weather, surely that's obvious," said Seb.

"And it doesn't matter,"Rupert pointed out. "If the coke runs out, we drink water. No problem."

Mrs Rooke was clapping her hands at them.

"Shut up and sit down," Sarah bawled in a rude voice, as an official-looking lady in a dark blue uniform with red crosses on her shoulder and cap badges, was ushered in by Paul and Lynne's mother.

"This is Mrs Gail, a very prominent lady in the Woodbury Red Cross," announced Mrs Roberts briskly."She's a very busy person and an expert on first aid so we're very lucky that she's found the time to come and talk to us."

Everyone clapped loudly as Mrs Roberts sat down.

"Now this is a short practical talk," began Mrs Gail. "And the first thing I need is a volunteer, a guinea pig to demonstrate on."

"Me," Rupert's hand shot up at once. "I'm so tall that there's a nice lot of me to practise on and so thin that I don't use up too many bandages."

"Oh me, please," wailed Oliver.

"You're too young and you'll wriggle," Rupert told him firmly. "I'm brilliant at sitting still."

"You may *sit* still, but can you keep your tongue still?" asked Mrs Roberts as Rupert picked up his chair and joined the speakers.

"Now when you come upon an accident you have to keep calm and remember three things." Mrs Gail went on. "First, will the casualty come to more harm if you leave him where he is? Rupert has fallen off his horse and is lying in the middle of a busy road. The question is, do you stop the traffic or, if he's not too badly hurt, move him to the side?

"That question settled, the next is, does he need an expert, should you send for help? If the casualty is unconscious, in great pain, has obviously broken limbs, head injuries or is bleeding a lot, you should see that an ambulance is summoned right away. You all know to dial 999 of course, but as you hurry to the telephone prepare a brief statement of the facts and make sure you can explain where you are.

"When you've dealt with those two points you can think about attending to the patient. You've found Rupert lying at the side of the road, he's unconscious," she pointed at Alice. "You've sent your sister to telephone for help, what are you going to do next?"

"I can't imagine," said Alice, obeying Mrs Gail's beckoning finger and advancing on Rupert who lay groaning on the floor.

"You're going to move him into the coma recovery

417

position. Kneel down beside him and arrange his arms close to his sides. Watch everyone, because this is one way a first aider can save a life. Now, very gently, roll him on to his side; that's right. Draw the upper arm towards you," she instructed Alice, who arranged the giggling Rupert obediently.

"Now all his airways should be clear, but you must look in his mouth and check that it's clear of mucus, false teeth, or, if he fell in the river, weeds."

Alice said, "Open, please." Rupert made strange gargling noises and Oliver collapsed in giggles at the thought of false teeth. Mrs Roberts gave him a ferocious glance.

"Right, you can get up, Rupert, and we'll go on to fractures. But do remember that unconscious people should be put in that position, unless you suspect they have spinal injuries."

"What do you do then?" asked Seb.

"Wait until skilled help comes. Now you recognize a break or fracture, by pain, swelling and deformity, but if you suspect a broken leg, don't pull off boots and jodhpurs to make certain, you could make the break a great deal worse; send for an ambulance."

Mrs Gail went on to name the symptoms of shock: the patient would be pale, shivery, have a rapid pulse and might feel giddy, sick or faint, while Mrs Roberts supervized the splinting and slinging of both Rupert's arms.

Then they went on to wounds and everyone was bandaging someone else. Long experience with tail and leg bandages, had made them all expert, and Mrs Gail was quite impressed.

"Burns," she said, trying to shout the pony club members down as they re-rolled bandages. "This is probably the most likely injury to occur in your camp. What do you do when you burn or scald your hand?"

"Blow on it," answered Rupert.

"No. Put it in cold water until it stops hurting," said Tina, who, belonging to a one-parent family had learned to cook young.

"Correct, a burned finger can be held under a running tap. A badly burned person should be put in a bath of water until the ambulance arrives. In camp you could pour jugs of water over a burned arm or leg. You cool the burn down, then bad ones go to hospital to be dressed. Small ones merely need a plaster.

"Stings—well, you will have anti-histamine cream in your first aid kit. But some people are allergic to stings and anyone who swells up excessively should be sent straight to hospital. Then there are snake bites. In England the adder is the only poisonous snake, but there are a few in the forest so perhaps we ought to go into the first aid treatment. The idea is to stop the poisoned blood going back into the body so you bind something tightly round the limb, between the bite and the body. Got that? You can wash the wound, but you must keep the area as still as possible and keep the patient quiet until the ambulance arrives. On no account allow him to walk."

Mrs Gail summed up her talk and Mrs Roberts was in the middle of thanking her when David's head appeared round the door.

"Next speaker's arrived," he said when the applause had died down. "I'm sorry I chickened out of yours, Mrs Gail, but I feel I've had enough hospital talk to last me a lifetime."

When Mr Franklin, tall, fair and exuding authority, strode into the room all the giggling stopped abruptly and the pony club members retreated to their seats, leaving Mrs Roberts and Mrs Gail to finish clearing up the tangle of splints and bandages.

David said, "You all know Mr Franklin and he's volunteered to explain the mysteries of map reading and the management of compasses to you. I don't know anything about them myself—you don't need them on racecourses—so please listen carefully. We want you all home safe and well on Sunday. Now Mrs Rooke and I have some pony club business, so I'll leave you to it," he added and limped out of the kitchen.

"I'd like you to divide into the two groups you'll be riding in," began Mr Franklin. "Move the chairs, leave a space between you."

The pony club members got up and began to move reluctantly out of their happy huddle.

"What shall I do?" asked Netti. "I'm in the mounted games team, but I'd like to listen to your talk."

"Sarah and Paul shouldn't be here either; they're not trekkers," snapped Lesley.

"Oh, yes I am." Sarah gave her sister a triumphant glare, as she told the others, "we've just bought a new pony, grey, fourteen hands, perfect for trekking, so I can keep Chess for the Prince Philip."

"But you can't be in two places at once, Sarah," Lynne pointed out. "You'll miss the team practices."

"No, I won't. My mother will collect me from wherever we're camping at tea-time and drop me back after supper."

"That's not fair. The trek is for people who aren't in the team," objected Oliver.

"It does seem just a trifle greedy," observed Rupert.

"Can Paul and I do both? We could borrow the Clark ponies," suggested Netti.

"You can't come, Sarah. The tents are full and we've fixed the food; it's too late," Seb told her.

"My mother says I can and she's the secretary, not you," sneered Sarah.

"Look, this is all outside my province. Could the extra people attach themselves to a group temporarily and sort the matter out with David afterwards."

"I'm not going in the same group as my sister, thank you," snapped Lesley.

"Well, I'm going with Tina and Lynne, whatever you say, so if you don't like it, *you* change, and good riddance," sneered Sarah.

"You're making the numbers uneven; one group will have six in it. It's going to mess up all our calculations," complained James.

"No Lesley, you *can't* come with us," moaned Rupert. "You know my strange habits drive you mad. You'll be quite worn out with scolding me. You won't enjoy yourself one bit."

"Harry, will you hand out the maps and compasses," Mr Franklin shouted to be heard above the racket. "Two per group.

"Now, this is only a brief introduction to elementary map-reading and compass work," he began firmly. "Take a look at the maps, your three camping sites are circled in red. Warren Farm, Charlton, Fairfield Park School, Ramsbourne, and Stoke Farm, Bewley. Got them? It looks easy, as though you've only to ride round the four sides of a rectangle, but we've devised some interesting diversions and each diversion entails a small task. The leaders of the groups will be given the day's task in a sealed envelope each morning."

Hanif sighed despondently. Tina asked, "A sort of treasure hunt?"

"No, more technical. You'll be given a map reference and, when you've found your way to the right spot, using your compass and map, you'll know the answer to the question in the envelope."

"Map reference?" The pony club members looked at each other doubtfully.

"I expect most of you know how to read a map," Mr Franklin went on confidently. "You know that it's merely a bird's eye view of the ground with the different features indicated by colours and symbols. The key to the symbols is on the left side of our maps. Could group J identify the sign for a church with a spire and then find as many as they can on their map, while group A does the same, but for churches with *towers*."

The pony club members looked at him with baffled expressions. "We didn't know we had letters. Which group is which?" asked Seb.

"Sorry. David and I had to have some way of referring to the groups. We decided on an initial and picked the first name, alphabetically, in each group, so Alice and James. You'll find all information labelled A or J. Right?"

"Right, we're spires then," said James. "You lot do that half of the map, Seb and I will do this side. Look in the towns and villages."

The Js searched industriously, giving cries of excitement on the discovery of each spired church. The As took the search in a leisurely manner and Rupert insisted on looking for chapels instead.

"Now look at the colour key," said Mr Franklin. "As you can see there are different shades of green for woods and fields, different browns for heaths and downs. Take another look at the map and you'll begin to get a picture of the country you'll be riding through. Then look at the contour lines, they tell you whether the land is flat, hilly or mountainous. The numbers give you the height in metres. This enables you to make a choice, whether to take the path over the down or the easier track round the valley. I'm sure you're all beginning to realise that studying a map is very rewarding."

"Yes, I'm making a collection of windmills," announced Rupert.

"What a waste of time; it would be more useful if you learned the route we've got to take tomorrow," snapped Lesley.

"We don't know it yet," Alice reminded her.

"Now, imagine that you are up on the Downs and for some reason you've missed a turning and lost your way," instructed Mr Franklin. "You get out the map and then find it's not much use to you. You know where you're going, but you've no idea where you are. Then suddenly you see a land mark, a windmill or the famous White Horse. Now you're all right. There they are marked on the map; you turn it round until you've got them lined up in the right places, and you're off.

"But now suppose the same thing happens in a wood. All you can see is trees stretching away in every direction, the map on its own is useless. You get out the compass." He glanced round at the pony club members, "Will you all take a look at the compasses. First line up the magnetic needle with the orienting arrow, you've now found the magnetic north, turn the map until its North, that is always the top of the map, agrees with the compass North. You still don't know exactly where you are, but you can suddenly see the *direction* in which you have to go. Mr Franklin turned to James. "Have a try, you're lost in the forest and you're trying to find Ramsbourne."

"I'm glad you're in our lot, Harry. You're brilliant at it," said Alice admiringly, as he lined up the map and compass.

"Only because I've done it before."

"Got it," said James, looking pleased with himself, and gave the compass to Seb. Tina was awaiting her turn eagerly, but Lynne and Sarah had lost interest and were discussing Sarah's new pony.

"I love the names. Let's make a detour and visit Black Gutter Bottom," suggested Rupert, "Or Camel Green. Do you suppose there were once camels tethered all over the green?"

"A circus came and the owner fell ill so it stayed for months or even years," said Alice, passing the compass to Lesley.

"Much more likely that a Mr Camel lived there," snapped Lesley, taking off her spectacles and peering intently at the map.

Mr Franklin began to speak. "Right, everyone out of the forest? Good. Well, there are many more complicated ways of using a compass, too complicated for us to go into this evening, but I think you all see that it's a trusty friend and will get you out of trouble.

"Now we come to Map or Grid references," he went on. "As I said earlier, when we give you your tasks we shan't tell you where to go in words, but in numbers; we'll give you a map reference. Six numbers, four representing the grid square and two the point within it." He glanced round at the pony club members. They were looking baffled again. "You see these criss-crossed lines on the map? They are the grid lines, one lot are vertical and are called eastings, because they cross the map from left to right, that is from west to east. The horizontal lines are called northings and you read them from the bottom of the map, that is from south to north. Where the two lines intersect you have a grid point and this is identified by combining the numbers of the two lines. Can you see the numbers along the side and top of the map?"

"Yes," the pony club members answered warily, even. the interested ones were beginning to think that two lectures on one evening was excessive. Sarah and Lynne were whispering and Oliver was torturing a compass with disorientation techniques.

"Begin with the eastings," said Mr Franklin. "It's essential to get this right, tell yourself that E comes before N. Take easting 91 and northing 42. They meet at a grid point. But I actually want to send you to the Roman villa in the square made by the lines so I must give you a more exact reference and I do this by dividing the square into tenths. First the easting: the Villa is one tenth from the line and the number becomes 911, but it's three tenths from my northing line so that number becomes 423. And the complete MR or map reference 911423. Do you get it?"

"No," said Alice.

Hanif demonstrated to the As very patiently while his stepfather repeated his explanation to the Js. Then they all practised, giving each other numbers and demanding to know what lay at the spot.

"Well, I think quite a few of you have mastered the basics," said Mr Franklin, glancing anxiously at his watch, "and you'll find experience a great teacher. That's all we've time for, I'm afraid. Hang on, hang on," he added as the pony club members leapt to their feet.

"I think before you go, each group should elect a leader," he went on as they sat down reluctantly. "I'm proposing to introduce a slight element of competition to the trek." Hanif covered his face with his hands and groaned. "And to provide prizes for the group giving the best all-round performance: map reading, care of ponies, performance of tasks and camp duties will all be taken into account in the final assessment. Oh yes, and we're going to ask each group to keep a log in which they jot down the day's doings. Don't you think electing a leader *before* you start could save a lot of trouble later? He or she could carry the map and compass and be responsible for the route."

"No," said Hanif in a muffled voice. The other pony club members looked thoughtful.

"It might be an idea to appoint a navigator," admitted Seb, "but I don't see the point of electing a sort of tribal chief."

"And there are a lot of other jobs." Lynne pointed out. "Someone will have to carry the first aid kit and Mum says whoever does, ought to know what's inside, in case there *is* an emergency."

"Couldn't each member of the group be in charge of something?" suggested Alice.

"Not a bad idea, I'll be the Scribe and write the log," offered Rupert.

"Lynne better do our first aid," said James.

"And Lizzie ours. She's brilliant at repairing wounded horses," Rupert explained.

"You can be Navigator, you're good at it," Hanif told Alice.

"I'm nothing like as good as you," objected Alice.

"But your pony's sensible. I'll never be able to read a map on Jupe, and think what his twirling would do to a compass; it might never recover. No, I'll be chief cook, a position of great power."

"Can I be assistant cook?" asked Oliver.

"Well, I'll leave you to settle the duties among yourselves," said Mr Franklin. "One last word though. A new motorway is being built along the southeastern edge of the Downs. It's not marked on the map, but you'll see that I've plotted it in with two broken red lines. You've no reason to go near it, in fact you should give it a wide berth, but I think it's worth a mention because it's very disconcerting to stand on a hilltop and see something that doesn't appear on the map and so shouldn't be there."

He collected his lists. "Well, good luck. You have the compasses and maps, keep them in the map sleeves. David will give you the route cards and map references and if you've forgotten how to work them out ask Harry."

"What's the good of that? He's in the other group, he won't help *us*," complained Sarah.

"Oh, don't be so *boring*, of course I'll help your lot," said Hanif in a pained voice. "We're not going to take this idea of a competition seriously; we're not riding against a rival pony club."

CHAPTER THREE

Day I: The Downs

On Thursday morning the yard at Garland Farm was full of excited ponies, all tied to fences, rings in the walls, or the stanchions of the dutch barn, with lengths of baling string as decreed by David. The pony club members helped their parents to unload their cars. An extraordinary assortment of bedding rolls and cooking pots, cardboard boxes full of human food, heavy sacks of pony food, was dragged out and carried across to Mrs Rooke's new trailer.

To Hanif's relief his stepfather was at work, so his mother, dressed in a green morning sari, had brought his and Alice's gear.

"I hope I have forgotten nothing," said Mrs Franklin, gazing at their neat pile, which, with everything packed in kitbags and efficiently labelled by Mr Franklin, was in direct contrast to the Wheelers' chaotic heap of bulging bundles, overflowing boxes and bursting carrier bags; two of which had already spewed their contents over the concrete.

"We'd better re-pack it all in these plastic rubbish sacks," suggested Hanif gloomily. "My stepfather said they would come in useful."

"*And* he gave some extra labels and a biro," Alice grinned at Hanif.

"Bad luck, you won't get *any* marks for camp efficiency with the Wheelers in your group," Sarah taunted her sister. "We'll win easily. I wonder what the prizes are. Mother doesn't know, but she said she might find some rosettes for the winners."

"Efficiency is not our strong point," agreed Rupert equably, as he held open a plastic sack for Oliver to fill. "But don't underate us. Lizzie's brilliance at first aid, my lateral thinking and Ollie's willingness to journey into the unknown on a strange and fairly vicious steed will all count in our favour."

"Strange and vicious steed?" Alice looked up from her labelling. "Oh *no*, I wondered what the Clarks' horrible little Tiger was doing here. You don't mean Ollie's riding him. What's happened to Tristram?"

"We had a drama last night. He suddenly produced a warble fly lump, just where his saddle goes," Lizzie explained. "We brought him over here and David took one look and said he wasn't to be ridden until the warble maggot came out. So definitely no trek."

"Whereupon Oliver's cries of rage and anguish echoed along the Vole valley," Rupert took up the story, "until someone suggested a Clark pony. Netti had agreed to see if they could be taught normal equine behaviour, so she's schooling Twilight and Ollie's trekking Tiger."

Hanif, tying the top of a plastic sack, groaned. "What about his bucking? Oliver's never going to stay on."

"He only bucks when you try to make him go on his own," explained Lizzie. "We think he'll be all right following the others."

"My mother doesn't think he ought to come, but David gave way over Sarah so now she's had to give way over Oliver, serves her right." snapped Lesley contemptuously.

"You'll want to *un*load the buckets and feed sacks first," David was telling James and Seb. "Tents next, in case it's raining, food and bedding rolls last, so don't forget to load in reverse order."

"Can't we leave everything in the trailer until we need it?" asked Seb.

"No, Mrs Rooke will be taking it to the mounted games practice each evening, but when she brings Sarah back you can use it for the tack for the night."

"Supposing it pours with rain?" asked James indignantly.

"The practice will be cancelled," answered David. "But anyway you can put the tack in the tents."

"We've four tents?" asked Oliver, helping to load.

"Yes. Seb and I are sharing the small one, the rest of you are in three's," James told him.

"Where's Sarah's new pony?" Tina was asking Lynne.

"In the loosebox next to Vulcan. Mrs Rooke said he had to have a box," Lynne answered. "He's called Sparkler and he's a lovely dapple grey; Sarah says he's won masses in juvenile jumping classes," she went on, trying to keep an envious note out of her voice.

Only Mrs Roberts, Mrs Franklin and David saw the trekkers off.

"There is the first curry, four rices, three jars of chutney and three cans of fruit salad, I hope it will be enough," Mrs Franklin fussed as Hanif mounted.

"Plenty. Don't forget the others have brought food too."

"Have you remembered your pieces of string?" asked David.

"And your lunches?" added Mrs Roberts.

David was handing the route cards and sealed envelopes to James and Alice. "I wouldn't open them until you reach the Downs," he told them. "Give the ponies a chance to settle. Your ways don't divide until you reach the top of the Kiddleworth track. There's a list of emergency telephone numbers on the back of the route card."

"There's a second list in with each first aid kit," added Mrs Roberts, who'd been helping Lynne and Lizzie to stow the kits away in their saddlebags. "Good luck, all of you."

"Be sensible and stay in your groups," said David. "If there *is* an emergency, two go for help and the rest stay with the casualty, don't forget."

429

"Take care," called Mrs Franklin as they set off down the farm track. The ponies, sensing adventure, jogged with pricked ears and tossing heads, vying for the lead.

They crossed the sunken lane, jumping the slip rails into the Coppice Hill field. Sarah insisted on going second. She followed Jupiter, and Sparkler sailed over and landed lightly. The other large ponies followed, all eight of them, jumping eagerly. Then Rupert turned back to lower the top rail for Oliver. Tiger refused, dropping his head in his usual mean way, tipping Oliver over the rails, but the boy landed on his feet and holding on to the reins. He mounted and tried again, riding in his usual untidy style. Tiger refused again.

"Well, do you like my pony?" Sarah asked Hanif. "He's the best jumper in the pony club; he's cleared five feet."

"Great," answered Hanif, "but he looks a bit like Jupe used to. When I first had him I thought I had to ride in pelhams and martingales and several nosebands, but David persuaded me out of them gradually."

"He's not persuading me out of them," retorted Sarah. "I want to show jump, I hate boring dressage, and all the best showjumpers are ridden in running martingales and lots in pelhams."

Tiger over, they cantered on up the hill and Alice opened the hunting gate into the woods. The long climb quietened the ponies and by the time they had crossed the Kiddleworth road and taken the track to the Downs, they were all behaving soberly.

"Here?" James asked Alice as they came to the top of steep chalk track and could see the tops of the Downs billowing away on three sides of them, the irregular crests and troughs of a green sea.

"Yes, O.K.," agreed Alice, unbuckling her saddlebag. They opened the envelopes, their reins hanging loose on their ponies necks. Rupert and Oliver were standing in their stirrups, trying to see what was written on the As' single sheet of paper.

"Oh come on, Alice, read it out," demanded Lesley impatiently.

"At M.R. 096121 you will find a stone erected in memory of Emily Jakes. Write down the rest of the inscription and take it to Camp One." read Alice.

"A stone? What *is* he on about?" demanded Oliver.

Alice passed the paper to Rupert. "I'll have a look at the map," she said, dismounting. Saffron, fascinated by the unfolding map, insisted on snuffling over it and then jogging Alice's elbow as she tried to identify the grid numbers.

"Will someone please hold him?" she asked exasperated, "and someone else come and help me to find this horrible map reference."

"I told you my stepfather would spoil everything," said Hanif as he took Saffron's reins.

Alice spread the map on the grass and gazed at it stupidly. Her mind had gone blank. "Do you remember which number came first?" she asked Rupert and Lesley as they knelt beside her.

"No. Harry, which number came first?" bawled Rupert.

"Eastings. They're the vertical lines and you read them from west to east. From left to right," Hanif answered, in a bored mechanical voice.

"Thanks Harry, we'd forgotten too," called Seb.

"There," Alice captured the vertical line with a triumphant finger. "You work out the tenths, Rupert, while I do the northings. South to north," she told herself. "It's all coming back to me."

They followed the grid lines to their intersection and used the millimetre scale on the plastic base of the compass to work out the tenths.

"It's a church. A church with a tower," called Alice.

"Which means the stone is a tombstone," added Rupert.

"Are you sure it's not that farm?" asked Lesley, taking

off her glasses for a closer look. "No, you're right. It's a church in a village called Hampton."

"Which direction do we go?" asked Lizzie.

"Over there," Oliver who had dismounted and was looking over his brother's shoulder pointed eastward.

"No, hold on, we haven't set the map yet," Alice told him. "We don't need the compass, do we?" she asked Rupert, as she turned the map. "I mean, we know Kiddleworth's there, Woodbury's behind us and we're here."

"So Hampton's there. Due south," agreed Rupert as Alice turned the map. "Brilliant, we've got the idea."

"We follow this track for miles," said Alice. "Then we can either go right into the village or take this path on the left which goes to the church. It looks quite easy." She sounded surprised.

"There's a stream, we'll be able to water the ponies," Rupert pointed.

"We must let the others look. We all have to agree on the way," said Alice.

"Ours is a tombstone in a churchyard, about a hundred miles due south," Rupert shouted to the other group. "What's yours?"

"Something to do with a tumulus, we think," answered James.

"Don't tell them, they may have to find ours tomorrow," objected Sarah.

"Oh shut up," Seb sounded disgusted. "We go east, then? No, I mean west. You haven't oriented the map properly, you great twit," he told James in a friendly voice.

"Past the stud, straight on for about six miles," muttered James. "Then we veer north. Perhaps we'll be able to see the Down with the tumulus on it; it's quite a high one."

They stowed away the maps and compasses and mounted.

"See you later," they called to each other, waving cheerfully as they parted. Only Stardust and Sparkler objected to the separation. They looked back longingly and gave sorrowful whinnies.

"Oh come on, Stardust, you've only known him for a few hours. You can't be *that* fond of him," snapped Lesley.

"Perhaps it was love at first sight," suggested Alice as the pretty chestnut pony raised her head for another long, sad neigh. "It's all right, Stardust, you'll see him again this evening."

Sparkler neighed even louder and more persistently than Stardust, deafening all the J group as, with the boys in the lead, they set off at a brisk trot along the track which would pass Coombe Manor Stud.

"I know the way as far as Barkworth Farm," Seb called, shouting to be heard above the neighs and Sarah's yells of displeasure. "When we get there we'd better stop and take another look at the map."

"O.K.", James's solemn face looked worried. Conscious of being the eldest, he felt overwhelmed with responsibility.

Sparkler neighed again. "Stop it, you stupid pony," shrieked Sarah, yanking at his mouth.

"Don't," Tina protested, as the grey pony flung his head up. "You hurt him. You'd be feeling sad if you had a new home, a strange rider and the only pony friend you'd made was taken away."

"I'll do what I like," snapped Sarah. "They said he was a sensible pony," she turned to Lynne. "I can't stand silly hysterical ponies; I don't want another Bowie, *thank you.*"

Tina, patting Bowie's bright bay neck, below his fine black mane, tried to think of a crushing reply. She loved the slender, well-bred pony, whom Sarah had owned for a short time at the beginning of the holidays and sold to her after his accident. *She* didn't mind him being nervous.

"Different ponies suit different people," said Lynne hastily, hoping to avert a quarrel. "Bowie's perfect for Tina, everyone says so."

"Thanks," said Tina, but she held Bowie back and let the other two ride on side by side. She was beginning to wish that she hadn't come on the trek. She didn't know any of the pony club members really well, not even Seb, though he was her stepbrother. He was too new. She would rather have gone with the other group, she liked Alice and the Wheelers. But Seb had to go with James, who was his great friend. They went to the same school and had known each other before Seb's parents split up, long before his father met her mother. They'd been friends in the days when Seb belonged to the Frogmorton pony club and despised the Woodbury.

Still, even if things aren't perfect, they're not that bad, thought Tina, looking from the Downs to the sky. We're on top of the world, it's really beautiful and I've got Bowie.

When they reached Barkworth Farm, James stopped to consult the map again. He dismounted and studied it carefully. "I *think* it's up there," he pointed across a valley. "On top of that tall Down, the very green one."

"Don't you *know*?" snapped Sarah. "We don't want to climb all the way up there and then find it's the wrong hill."

"Let's have a look." Seb gave his reins to Tina and joined James in poring over the map. "We go up the valley until we've crossed Kites' Ditch, then it's the next sort of summit on our right," he decided.

The A group cantered along their track, a warm breeze blowing in their faces and the downland world unfolding before their eyes. Jupiter, in the lead, had settled and stopped fighting for his head. Tiger at the back had no

434

energy left for wicked deeds as his short legs worked overtime, struggling to keep up with the larger ponies. When he began to trail Lizzie took pity on him and called for a walk.

As they slowed down, Alice rode alongside Hanif. "Isn't it lovely now that we're on our way; now all the boring arrangements are over?" she asked.

"Not bad," Hanif answered cheerfully, "but you wait until all the hassle starts again tonight: getting those tents up, and finding what we've left behind."

When the ponies were rested and the track ahead looked temptingly soft and un-rutted, they decided on a gallop and rode full tilt until the puffing ponies were strung out across the hilltop. Jupiter was the last to tire and, when Hanif pulled up to wait for the others, he was in sight of Hampton, looking down on the cluster of houses, cottages and gardens, tucked away in a fold in the Downs.

"There's our church with a tower," he called triumphantly, pointing it out as the other riders came up.

They rode downhill, and on the outskirts of the village they came upon the stream. Suddenly widening it flowed across the track, shallow and gravelled bottomed.

"How very convenient," observed Rupert as the thirsty ponies rushed to drink. The riders sat talking as their mounts drank and paddled, cooling their legs, and sampled the various cresses which grew along the bank.

"Do we look for the stone or do we have lunch first?" asked Alice.

"Lunch," answered Oliver without hesitation. "I'm starving."

"Lunch," agreed the others.

"If we go back up the track a bit, there was a wider place with a gate and some trees we could tie the ponies to," suggested Lizzie.

After lunch they rode through the stream and on into

the village. The cottage gardens were still full of flowers and the warm air was sweet with the scent of roses. The church stood alone on a hillock at the edge of the village, the Downs rising behind it. They decided to send Lesley and Lizzie in to look for the stone, and the boys held their ponies while they climbed the steps to the lych-gate. Alice unfolded the map and began to work out the way to Warren Farm.

"We've found it," Lizzie shouted from the churchyard. "Lesley's written it down."

"What does it say, Lesley?" asked Rupert.

But Lesley had no intention of shouting the information. She descended the steps and crossed the road before she answered. "The inscription reads: 'In loving memory of Emily Jakes wife of Joseph Jakes she departed this life on January 6th 1843 aged fifty-nine years. R.I.P.' That's word perfect, we've both checked it," she added, glaring round at them.

"Great," said Oliver, as Lesley folded the sheet of paper, restored it to its envelope and handed it back to Alice. "*We've* found our objective, I wonder how many points we get for that, and whether the other lot have found theirs."

Hanif groaned. "Don't you start, Ollie. Trekking's a pleasure; you don't have to win."

"But your stepfather said . . ." Oliver began to object.

"Never mind his stepfather," interrupted Rupert. "We're not going to be lured into competition by the promise of a few rotten old rosettes. It'll only lead to polishing saucepans and keeping our tent pegs tidy. Agreed?"

"I know I'll never hear the last of it if we *lose*," answered Lesley, "but I'm used to Sarah's crowing; it won't worry me."

"The trouble about competing is that I'll feel sad for us if we lose and for them if we win," explained Lizzie. "It's all right if you don't *know* the other people."

"I'm against spoiling the trek by fussing," said Alice. "I mean, we're going to be sensible and try not to get lost. Obviously we'll look after the ponies properly and cook as well as we can and clear up our litter. If we're given a prize for that it's O.K. by me."

"Ollie?"

Oliver avoided his brother's eye by fiddling with Tiger's bridle. Secretly he longed to win, longed for another rosette to join his tiny collection on the tackroom wall, but he couldn't say so. He swallowed and persuaded his voice to sound indifferent. "Oh, let the other lot win if they can be bothered."

The narrow path led up from behind the church, climbing the Down in a steep zig-zag. The ponies, lively after their rest, took it fast, but they were all reduced to a walk before they reached the top. Alice led the way to a wider track.

"Now it's easy. We go along here until we come to a windmill where two tracks cross, then we turn left, that's north, and head for Warren Farm which is northwest, somewhere over there," she pointed.

"Why don't we cut across the middle?" suggested Rupert.

"Because there's no path marked on the map and we're bound to get lost," answered Alice.

"And look at all that up and down," protested Oliver.

"We'll do much better to follow the ancient Brits," said Hanif. "They made the tracks and they'd lived here for years."

The ponies, who had expected to turn for home, were very disgruntled. They argued with their riders, edging in a homeward direction and, when they were made to go on, they sulked, ears back, trotting without impulsion.

"It's what they call a post trek," Alice explained to Saffron. "You stop at a different place each night. It's great, Saffy, you don't have to go back to your boring field at Shawbury for three whole days."

"Let's cheer them up with another gallop," suggested Rupert.

"Are your girths tight, Ollie?" asked Lizzie, looking back anxiously.

The windmill was derelict, a sail-less shell. They rode right up to the fence and peered over.

"It's a bit of a mess," said Oliver.

"Yes, someone ought to restore it," complained Hanif.

"A waste of money," snorted Lesley. "There's no road to it so what's the point?"

"It's a lovely spot, I'd like it as a house. Look at the view," said Alice.

"Too windy," objected Rupert. "Now, where do we go next?"

"It gets a bit complicated," said Alice, unfolding the map. "I think everyone ought to look; don't leave it all to me. We follow *this* track north, but then we have to take *that* path and it wanders around a lot before it arrives at Warren Farm." She held the map out for Lizzie to see.

"Yes, that looks O.K.," agreed Lizzie weakly, and passed the map to Lesley.

Lesley had taken off her spectacles and was peering closely at the map when a gust of wind caught it, making a loud flapping noise, terrifying Stardust, who leapt in the air and fled, straight down the Hampton track, heading for home.

"Drop the map," they shouted at her. Lesley let go of it, and then with two hands for the reins, she managed to slow the frightened pony. Then she stopped; turned the pony and rode back rather uncertainly.

"Can you see my spectacles?" she called. "I dropped them with the map, or just afterwards. Now I'll never find them, I can't see a thing." Without the glasses her face looked naked and vulnerable; she no longer glared.

438

"Don't worry," Rupert told her soothingly. "We'll spread out and search."

"Not with the ponies," snapped Lesley, "they'll tread on them, and they won't be much good to me if they're smashed to bits, will they?"

"Absolutely not," agreed Rupert in reasonable tones. "I'll hold ponies. I'm not much good at looking, but Lizzie's brilliant. Get looking, Lizzie."

Hanif gave Jupiter to Lesley and joined the search. They walked cautiously over the short grass, peering into the clumps of clear blue Chicory and muddy blue Scabious, and along the rutted chalk track.

As they searched they became aware of voices. Voices calling repetitively and, in between the calls, the silence was filled with whistling.

"Sounds as though someone's lost a dog," said Rupert.

"Why bother to state the obvious?" scowled Lesley, furious with the humiliation of not being able to see.

As the voices came nearer, the trekkers could hear the dog's name. "Dirk, Dirk," they were calling. A man's voice and a woman's.

"It's a pity specs don't come when they're called," said Rupert. "But perhaps they do. Better give it a try. Specs, Specs," he began to call in a high voice, interposing his calls with whistles.

Oliver collapsed in giggles.

"There's no need to make yourself seem madder than you are, Rupert," scolded Lesley.

But Rupert was watching the two weary-looking people climbing up the dusty track to the windmill. They were grey-haired, drably dressed, hung about with binoculars. They stopped and the woman, getting her breath first, said "Good afternoon. Have you seen a Jack Russell terrier?"

"No," Rupert shook his head.

"A small terrier, mostly black and white but with a

couple of brown patches. He's called Dirk," appealed the woman as if by trying harder Rupert might remember the dog.

"No, sorry. I can't remember seeing a single dog since we left Hampton. Can you, Lesley?"

"No, just the fat spaniel by the church," said Lesley.

"Have you lost something too?" asked the grey-haired man, watching the searchers who were still wandering up and down, gazing fixedly at the ground.

"Only a pair of glasses," Rupert answered.

"You wouldn't say *only* if they were yours, and *you* couldn't see a thing," snapped Lesley.

"Where did you lose Dirk?" asked Rupert.

"Somewhere on the top here. We come from Hampton and we're making our usual circle. We were about halfway round when we realized he was missing," the man explained, "so we retraced our steps."

"We saw a bird we couldn't identify. We were halfway along that track," the woman pointed in the direction the trekkers were to take. "A few minutes' inattention and he vanished. They say thieves take them for vivisection nowadays," she added with a break in her voice.

"I don't think there are any bad characters lurking up here," Rupert told her comfortingly. "We haven't seen anyone except you."

"I expect he's gone home," said the man in matter-of-fact tones. "You'd better go back, Anne. I'll have a look down the Barcombe track and follow you in about twenty minutes. Then, if he hasn't turned up, we'll get on to the police. I hope you find the spectacles," he added politely as they took their opposite paths.

"Where do you live in Hampton? In case we find him." Rupert shouted after their departing figures.

"Hampton 231, the name's Mottram," the man shouted back.

A few moments later there was a cry of excitement from

440

Lizzie and she pounced on a tuffet of grass. "I've found them and they're O.K.," she called joyfully.

"Thank goodness for that," Lesley went to meet her. "I wouldn't have been able to see a thing till I got to Warren farm and found my other pair and my mother makes such a fuss when I lose them."

They mounted and rode on downhill. Everyone was feeling cheerful, even Lesley, now that she could see again.

"What about a canter?" asked Hanif when they reached the bottom of the dip and were faced with a long, gently rising slope.

"A gallop," demanded Oliver checking his girth.

"Remember we have to turn right somewhere along the top," called Alice as they set off.

They raced up the hill and then slowed to a steady canter, Hanif, in the lead, was watching for the turn. "There, by that clump of trees," he shouted over his shoulder, and steadied Jupiter. The riders following him collected their ponies too, sitting down, using their legs, steering them in the new direction, but not Oliver. Riding with flapping legs and a loose rein, he wasn't in control. He expected Tiger to follow the other ponies, but the little dun had other ideas. Too late, Oliver hauled on the reins, the pony swerved, then finding himself among the scrubby bushes at the foot of the clump of trees, stopped dead. Oliver shot over his head.

Lizzie, looking back, saw what happened. "Ollie's fallen off," she shouted. Cursing, the pony club members pulled up and turned back.

Oliver was emerging from a bush, cross, but unhurt, Tiger, reins and stirrups flying, black tail blowing in the breeze, was cantering away across the Downs in a very purposeful manner.

"Hell, he's going home," shouted Rupert, and urged Rosie in pursuit.

"You shouldn't chase loose ponies," began Lesley.

"I think we'll have to. We'll have to try to head him off," said Hanif. "We can't let him go all the way to Woodbury." And giving Jupiter his head he raced after Rupert.

"If they managed to turn him we'd better be ready to circle round him," said Alice watching anxiously. "If you go to the left, Lesley, I'll take the right. Will you go between us, Lizzie?"

"O.K. Have you any pony nuts, Ollie? You'd better be ready to catch him when he's tired. Here," Lizzie handed her brother a handful of nuts from her pocket.

Rosie was fast, much faster than Tiger, thought Alice, watching the bay, mealy-nosed and usually gangling mare racing across the Downs. She was one of those ponies which only look completely coordinated at the gallop. Rupert looked good too, like a real cross-country rider. He was using his head and had stayed on the high ground, when Tiger had gone down into the valley. Now the little dun was faced with an uphill climb and Rupert, galloping round the heights, would be waiting for him on the top.

Harry would be there too, she thought. He was following Rupert's route and lessening the distance between them, as Rosie slowed down. She decided to follow Tiger into the valley, she could catch him if he turned back.

Calm and balanced, Saffron cantered down the hill and along the valley. Ahead Alice could see Tiger losing heart as he struggled up the hill. When Rupert appeard over the brow, he gave in and let himself be caught.

"That was a nasty moment," said Rupert leading Tiger down to Alice. "I had horrid visions of David's face as Tiger trotted to Garland Farm. Is Ollie all right?" he asked Lizzie, who had followed Alice into the valley.

"He's O.K., but he seems to have stuck halfway up that hill."

"Come on, Ollie."

"Come on down," they shouted waving at him. Oliver waved back, shouted and pointed at the ground, but didn't budge.

"Oh, dear, what's happened now," worried Lizzie.

"Perhaps he's sprained his ankle," suggested Alice.

"We're not going to make a very brilliant impression arriving hours late at Warren Farm," sighed Rupert. "If he *is* sprained you'd better do some really dramatic bandaging and slinging, Lizzie."

Tiger jibbed at the hill, but Alice went behind him and waving her whip threateningly, got him going before he pulled Rupert off backwards. Lizzie had gone ahead and was hurrying the puffing Rajah up the steep climb.

"What's up, Ollie?" she called.

"It's the dog," Oliver shouted back, he was kneeling now with his ear to a rabbit hole. "*A* dog, anyway. I think it's stuck, it keeps barking."

Hanif and Lesley, realizing that something was wrong, were riding down the hill. The riders dismounted when they reached Oliver and, learning what was wrong, were soon all putting their ears to the many rabbit holes which honeycombed the hillside.

"It's certainly a dog," agreed Rupert lying on his stomach and thrusting an arm down the rabbit hole, "but he's a long way in; miles out of reach."

"I think he's between these two holes," Oliver pointed. "If only we had a really long stick."

They all looked round at the bare Downs, there was no help there.

"I doubt whether we could prod him out even with a stick," decided Rupert, getting to his feet. "The tunnel doesn't run straight. He'll have to be dug out."

"We'd better gallop after his owners then," suggested Alice.

"We *can't* go all the way back to Hampton," moaned Oliver.

"It sounds as though we'll have to," said Hanif.

"We could go on to Warren Farm and phone them from there," suggested Lesley. "I memorized the number."

"That would be an easy way out," agreed Hanif, "and we wouldn't be so late at the camp."

"But would they ever find the dog? There are the hell of a lot of holes here," said Rupert, looking at the slope.

"They'd hear him barking."

"He may lose his voice or get exhausted and stop."

"Some of us could go on to the farm and explain what's happened, while the others ride to Hampton and find the Mottrams."

"But we need to leave some people here too. Supposing he comes out?"

"David said we were to stick together."

"Two parties then. Who wants to go, who to stay?" asked Alice.

"I'll go," offered Hanif. "Jupe's still full of go."

"I'll come with you then," said Alice.

"The name's Mottram," Rupert reminded them. "What was the telephone number, Lesley?"

"231 and do be quick. We don't want to hang about here all evening," replied Lesley crossly.

The J group had found their tumulus, a round green hump on the top of Whitbury Down, noted the inscription on the board erected by the Ministry for Works, and eaten their picnic. They had had trouble finding water for their thirsty ponies and, in desperation, had ridden boldly into a field of cows and watered them at the trough, while watching nervously for an angry farmer.

Now, having found their way to the north-east corner of the Downs they stood on the edge of the escarpment and looked across the cultivated land below: squares of green checked with the straw-yellow of stubble, or the chalk-streaked brown of newly-turned plough, and, beyond the plain, stretching away to the south, the dark line of the forest.

"That *has* to be Warren Farm," Seb, who was consulting the map, pointed to the pygmy farm at their feet.

"Looks O.K., all arable," said James.

"A bit dull, huge fields and no animals," complained Tina.

"Isolated too," observed Lynne, "even further from the shops than Garland Farm. I hope we haven't forgotten anything."

"There's not a sign of the others," announced Sarah complacently. "Come on, let's hurry down and bag the best places for our tents and ponies." She hurried Sparkler forward, leading the way down the stony track that zig-zagged its slow journey down to the land below.

At last they reached the open white gate which led both to large, modern farm buildings and a much older farmhouse, built of mellowed red brick. The house, half-hidden and sheltered among the trees and shrubs of a long-established garden, made the vast expanse of corn-growing land, unfenced and unhedged, which surrounded it, look bleak and inhospitable.

"Now we have to tell Mrs Shambrook we're here," said James, straightening his crash cap and putting on an official expression. He dismounted on the waste of concrete and disappeared through a side gate into the garden. The others looked at the rows of shining machinery housed in huge barns. A combine harvester, several tractors and a miscellaneous collection of muck spreaders, disc harrows and ploughs, were lined up tidily.

"Not even a sheep," complained Tina.

"I like the house though," said Seb. "That's the sort of place I want, but my father says I'm out of my mind."

"I don't want to be *too* grand," Tina told him. "You have to think about the housework," she added as James appeared, opening the gate politely, for a tall, elegant woman with white hair.

"What nice ponies—but this is only half of you," exclaimed Mrs Shambrook, looking round for the missing riders.

"We're in two groups," James explained, "but if you'll show us where everything is, we'll show them."

"We might not," Sarah whispered to Lynne as they followed Mrs Shambrook round behind the house. "We could refuse to tell them where the water tap is so they have to waste hours looking for it."

"Don't be horrible," Lynne was shocked. "They're our friends."

"My sister isn't," snapped Sarah.

"There *are* only two small fields," said Mrs Shambrook, opening a gate. "When our children were at home they kept their ponies here. I suggest that the tents and whichever sex of ponies you have fewest of, share the orchard and the rest go in the paddock."

"We've mostly geldings, only two mares," James explained.

The two fields ran side-by-side with a post and rail fence between them and a thick hedge round the outside. The orchard had a few old, gnarled apple trees.

"The water trough serves both fields," Mrs Shambrook pointed, "and there's a tap by the old stable, over there where we've parked your trailer. Now I'll show you the washroom. It's next to the grain dryer and rather basic, but since you're camping . . ."

"It's lovely, thank you very much for having us," said Tina politely, as Lynne handed her Vulcan's reins and muttered that she couldn't wait to see the basic loo.

"Well, don't hesitate to come to the house and tell us if you need anything else," answered Mrs Shambrook. "David Lumley is coming over to dinner with us tonight so he can deal with any major problems."

446

"Shall we turn the ponies out and start on the tents?" suggested James, when Mrs Shambrook had gone.

"We're supposed to feed them," snapped Sarah.

"We can't till the others get here, or there'll be kicking when they feed theirs."

"That's their look-out."

"No it isn't," Seb supported James. "Let's turn the ponies out, have a drink and then start on the tents."

"But I *have* to feed Sparkler before I go to the Prince Philip practice," objected Sarah.

"They may arrive at any minute," Tina told her. "And if they don't come in time Lesley can feed him for you."

"Lesley feed *my* pony?" Sarah gave a scornful laugh.

As the freed ponies trotted away to explore their field, or lay down for long luxuriant rolls, Seb ran to the trailer and began to unload.

"David was quite wrong," he complained, dragging out sacks of feed and tents. "We should have put the drinks in last."

"If I could find a squarish cardboard box, there's a chocolate cake Mum made which we could have for tea," said Lynne, looking helplessly at the confusion in the trailer.

"We'd better get it all out, Mrs Rooke will be arriving soon," decided James, heaving boxes cheerfully. "Look, put all the sacks of feed in the stable. We don't want the mares getting at them."

"I don't see why we should unload the A group's beastly luggage. It's not fair," protested Sarah. "They ought to have got here on time and done it themselves."

"Oh, stop griping. It won't kill you to move a couple of sacks and they'll probably do the same for us tomorrow," Seb told her.

"Here's one of the cooking stoves, I'm going to put the kettle on," Tina announced happily.

"And I've found Mum's cake," Lynne told her. "Great, we can have tea."

They put all the ponies' feed and grooming tools and buckets in one loosebox and all their supplies and cooking pots in the other and then, feeling rather pleased with themselves, they sat on their bedding bundles and had tea.

I like this place, thought Tina, giving a contented sigh as she listened to the rhythmic coo of the woodpigeons and watched the apple trees casting longer and longer shadows across the grass, I'm glad I came now.

"Where are we going to put the tents?" asked Seb.

"Facing the stable," suggested James. "We could make a square."

"No, I want a view," protested Tina.

"I don't care as long as I'm miles away from my sister," said Sarah.

"Then you'll have to sleep in the trailer. We want to be right next door to Alice and Lizzie, don't we, Lynne," replied Tina, quite surprised by her own firmness.

"Why don't we move the trailer and put the tents on a line with the stable," proposed Seb.

"Yes, they'd be facing east, we'd get the morning sun," agreed James.

"Let's put ours next to the stable then," said Seb.

"And leave a space for the other boys next to us," added James.

"*If* they ever turn up," jeered Sarah.

"It is getting a bit late," James looked at his watch, his solemn face worried. "I hope nothing disastrous has happened. We don't want the whole trek called off on the first day."

"I expect it's Tiger," said Lynne, gathering up cake wrappings. "He's a real little menace according to Janet Green."

Seb and James had their own tent up, an elegant blue affair, and were battling with the larger old-fashioned green one, which had been allocated to the other boys, when a horn tooted and they saw Mrs Rooke's car at the orchard gate.

448

"She wants the gate opened. Go on, Sarah," called Seb, who was banging in pegs.

"Oh, she's brought David," said James, emerging from the sagging tent. They all abandoned work and went to meet the car.

"Hullo, this is all beginning to look very cosy," said David, glancing from the grazing ponies to the half erected tents, "but where are the others?"

"We don't know. They simply haven't turned up," answered James.

"Which means that J group has won the first day by miles," Sarah told her mother in triumphant tones.

David looked up at the Downs. "Oh it's all right, there they are." He pointed to the track zig-zagging down the escarpment. A long file of ponies was plodding soberly down. The anxious watchers looked up and counted six. Then Seb put two fingers in his mouth and emitted a piercing whistle and suddenly the distant riders were all waving frantically.

"Big sigh of relief all round." said David. "They look cheerful enough, so it's nothing serious."

"Come on, let's get these tents up," said James, "then we can feed the ponies as soon as the others arrive."

"I'll put the kettle on for *their* tea," decided Tina. "It takes ages to boil."

"I'll leave you to it." said David. "I'm having supper with the Shambrooks. So I'll be in the house if needed," he added as he limped away.

"Boys," called Mrs Rooke, "I want the trailer hitched on, please, before you start messing about with tents."

All four tents were up and Mrs Rooke and Sarah had departed, when the sound of hoofs announced the arrival of the As. Everyone hurried to meet them. David and Mrs Shambrook were at the front door as they rode into the yard.

"Sorry we're late," called Alice, waving cheerfully.

"Any problems?" asked David.

"Nothing serious."

"Nothing *we* couldn't cope with."

"Everything's under control," they shouted as they slid off their weary steeds.

"The water troughs are in the fields."

"The mares go in the orchard with the tents," explained the resident campers, hurrying the newcomers along.

"What did happen to you?" asked James, opening the gate into the field.

"I found a lost dog stuck down a rabbit hole," said Oliver. "We knew he was lost because we'd met his owners earlier. His name's Dirk and he'd probably have died if I hadn't heard him barking."

"Yes all right, Ollie, we know you're the greatest, but could you get out of the gateway?" asked Rupert running to slam the gate in Sparkler's face. The two Rooke ponies had seen each other and all human conversation was drowned in their noisy reunion.

The sun set, dropping suddenly behind the Downs, as the As drank mugs of tea and munched slices of malt loaf while being suitably grateful for the erecting of their tents.

"I was dreading it. I saw us hammering in tent pegs by torchlight," confessed Hanif, pulling on a sweater.

"How lovely to arrive and find you have a house," said Alice, crawling in with her bedding roll. "Has anyone worked out how it's best to sleep, three in a row, or one across and two down?"

"I wish *ours* was blue and really new, like James's" complained Oliver.

"Appearances don't matter, as long as they keep out the rain," Rupert told him. "This one *looks* good and solid and we've more headroom than they have."

The ponies fed, the campers embarked on cooking supper. They began tidily divided into their two groups, but when Oliver started to moan that he hated curry and

450

would much rather have the Js' fry-up, Seb, who liked curry, offered to swop. Then several people arranged partial swops, in order to sample the other group's cooking, and when it came to pudding everyone elected to have a mixture of the Js' half-melted icecream and the As' exotic fruit salad.

Then they sat on in the dusk, putting off the washing up and discussing the day's adventures.

"You seem to have had a much more exciting time than we did," Tina's voice was tinged with envy.

"Don't worry, it'll probably be our turn for trouble tomorrow," laughed Lynne.

"And it was all a bit boring really, there was a lot of hanging about," Oliver admitted. "Alice and Harry took ages finding the owners."

"We had to go right back to Hampton, and then we didn't know where they lived; so we rang the number they'd given us from the call box by the church," explained Alice.

"They told us to start back and said that as soon as they'd borrowed a land-rover and collected some tools, they'd catch us up," Hanif continued the story. "They did too and they brought some extra people to help with the digging, so we didn't have to stay."

"Mrs Mottram cried when she recognized Dirk's bark," added Oliver.

"It was rather embarrassing," said Lizzie. "They were so terribly grateful and kept thanking us."

"And quite right too, considering all the trouble they'd put us to," added Lesley.

It was dark and they were washing up by lamplight, when Mrs Rooke and Sarah returned.

"So the poor little As found their way here in the end, did they?" mocked Sarah. "Well you've lost hundreds of marks and we're leading by miles."

"That's right, we got our map upside down," agreed

Rupert as Hanif went to help James unhitch the trailer. "We rode miles in the wrong direction. We'd be somewhere in the Cranford Vale now if we hadn't met a friendly policeman."

"Then Oliver fell off, Lesley lost her specs, Bowie slipped his stifle and Ra swallowed his bit," added Seb.

"And *then*, to make matters worse, we found this half-suffocated doggie," Rupert finished.

Sarah shone her torch on their faces. "You're just being silly," she snapped. "What really happened?"

"Now, see that the trailer is loaded by nine tomorrow morning," commanded Mrs Rooke, "and don't leave anything behind. I'm not trailing back here for any of your odds and ends. Oh, thank goodness, here *is* David. I thought he was going to keep me hanging about half the night."

"Message for the As," said David, looking cheerful. "A Mrs Mottram has just telephoned. She said to tell you that they'd dug Dirk out, exhausted but unharmed, and no words can express her gratitude for the part you played in his rescue."

The older As looked at each other slightly embarrassed.

"We didn't do *that* much . . ." began Alice but Oliver was patting himself on the chest. "All due to me," he announced loudly.

"Don't show off, Ollie," pleaded Lizzie.

"I think it was all due to Tiger," said Alice. "You wouldn't have heard the barking if he hadn't chucked you off."

"And then there's Tristram's contribution," said Rupert in a serious voice. "But the person Mrs Mottram should really thank is the warble fly who laid her egg on Tristram's leg last summer. But for her, Dirk would still be down that hole."

Lynne collapsed in giggles and Sarah said, "Oh very funny. What is all this about a dog?"

"Are you ready, David?" asked Mrs Rooke, settling herself in the car.

"Yes, just collecting today's completed tasks," he answered, as Lesley and Seb produced them, crumpled, from pockets. "Two more tomorrow morning," he reminded them. "Have a good night all of you."

CHAPTER FOUR

Day II. The Forest

They woke to another fine day, brilliant with sunshine, noisy with birdsong. The ponies welcomed the sleepy voices from the tents with encouraging neighs; neighs that hinted at buckets and breakfasts.

"The geldings are all lined up along the fence, watching the tents, they look terribly sweet," reported Tina, un-zipping the tent flaps and peering out.

"When I woke up in the night Rosie and Stardust were standing just outside," Alice's head appeared from the next tent. "They were fast asleep and each resting a hindleg, it looked as though they were trying to be as near their owners as possible."

"Does Ra look O.K.?" asked Lizzie with a yawn.

"Fine, except for hunger. They're all willing us to get up."

The pony club members began to feel for their clothes and suddenly there were cries of rage from Oliver, whose socks had somehow escaped from the tent and were soaking wet with the heavy dew, followed by cries of anguish from Lesley, who couldn't find her spectacles.

The people who had pulled gumboots and anoraks over their pyjamas emerged first, and were greeted with an even louder chorus of neighs.

"If you'll do Saffy's feed for me, I'll start putting the kettles on," Alice told Hanif. "He has a good half-bucket and it's mixed. However high you turn the stoves, those kettles take ages."

"O.K., I'll get the feeds," agreed Hanif, trying to rub the sleep from his face.

The ponies caught, tied up and fed, the campers turned their attention to breakfast. They transferred the kettles to the smaller stoves and had two frying pans at work on the large one, which meant that, except for Lesley, who ate only muesli and fruit, people were to be fed in pairs and in alphabetical order, announced the cooks, Hanif and Tina. Those who found themselves with a long wait, went off to dress; some even washed.

Sarah refused an egg with a broken yoke and Oliver insisted that his sausage must be split, but everyone else was complimentary, though Rupert announced that he was still hungry and fried himself two slices of bread and a spare egg as a second helping.

Then they began the horrible task of washing up. They let the cooks off, but when Sarah tried to escape, saying that she had "done hers", Seb dragged her back, pointing out that all the really disgusting pans were communal.

The tents and bedding rolls were packed away in the trailer and the campers were all grooming, brushing off mud and sweat marks, picking out hoofs, when two cars drove into the yard. Mr Franklin parked his and jumping out briskly, opened the orchard gate for Mrs Rooke. Hanif groaned at the sight of his stepfather and became immersed in his grooming, but James threw down his water brush and went over to help hitch up the trailer.

"We've brought your lunches. Sandwiches, apple turnovers and a banana each," called Mrs Rooke. "Lesley, you can hand them round."

"What's in the sandwiches?" asked Oliver suspiciously.

"I don't want a banana with any black on it," began Sarah.

"One packet each and no picking and choosing," said Mr Franklin, taking over the distribution, and firmly placing a lunch packet in each crash cap.

"Sarah's met her match," Rupert grinned at Hanif.

Alice was asking Mr Franklin about the day's tasks.

"Could we have them *before* we untie the ponies. It's much easier to look at maps without them, even the sensible ones like Saffy keep pushing you and Stardust is terrified if they flap."

"Right, I'll hand them over now, if everyone's tacked up," agreed Mr Franklin, "but first I'd like to say that I'm very impressed by the state of the field. I've had a look round and found only one sweet paper. Well done. David says you all did very well yesterday, so keep your high standard and have a nice day," he finished, handing the sealed envelopes to Alice and James.

"What have you been given, James?" demanded Sarah impatiently.

"I bet *we've* got a mouldy old tumulus," grumbled Oliver.

"We've got *two* map references," announced Alice.

"So have we," said James as both groups squatted round the maps.

"There, that's it," Hanif pointed. "Three-legged cross. It's a cross roads."

"Cross tracks really," said Alice, "and deep in the forest."

Lesley read out Mr Franklin's instruction. "'Write down the warning given'. I suppose it's some sort of sign," she added doubtfully.

"Beware of the wild boars," suggested Rupert with relish.

"Circle it," Hanif told Alice, passing her a biro. "Now, where's the next one?"

"Somewhere in this direction," answered Alice. "Look, I've found Ramsbourne. That's where the school is."

"Oh, do hurry up, James. You're so *slow*," complained Sarah. "The others will be starting in a minute."

"If you're so brilliant why don't you help, instead of always moaning?" demanded Seb.

"I'll have my own map tomorrow. I've told my mother

to get me one, and a compass. I bet I'll find the way a lot faster than you do."

"We've got a lake," James sounded pleased. "At least we'll be able to water the ponies. And the second reference is quite near."

"It looks as though we have to ride right round the lake," said Seb.

"And through Fox Heath for miles," added Tina, "until we leave the forest and take the road to the school."

"Long Bottom, Pitts Wood, Holt Heath," muttered Alice.

"It looks as though we may meet up with you lot," James told the As. "There's only the one track leading out of the forest to the Ramsbourne road."

"Yes, but I don't suppose we'll get there at the same time," answered Hanif. "I don't think even my stepfather could work out two routes that were *exactly* the same length."

"Let's make sure we know what to do when we go out of the gate," said Lizzie to Alice. "We can always stop for another look at the map when we get to the forest."

"I wish *we* had a lake," grumbled Oliver.

"We ought to thank Mrs Shambrooke," Lizzie reminded the others as they mounted.

"Yes, one from each group," agreed Hanif. "It's the navigators' job."

"No, it's nothing to do with maps, it's a domestic matter. Definitely a job for the cooks," retorted Alice.

"I think the two eldest should do it," said Lynne.

"That's James and Lesley, good idea." Sarah gave her sister a spiteful look.

"I don't mind doing it on my own," said James hastily, handing his reins to Seb.

"I'll come with you," offered Alice, "but you can do the talking."

Mrs Shambrook thanked, they set off down the road.

457

The ponies jogged with pricked ears and expectant expressions, they seemed to have forgotten about home and to be eager for new climes and experiences.

When they reached the first crossroads, where the two groups had to part, Stardust and Sparkler put up a spirited resistance: jibbing, swinging round, ears back, eyes rolling, they fought their riders. The usually meek Stardust even attempted a threatening half-rear. The Rookes shouted, kicked and tugged and whacked irritably. The riders won and the ponies, forced apart, neighed desperately as they took their separate roads.

"Oh, shut up you stupid pony. What on earth do you want to make such a silly fuss about boring old Stardust for?" Sarah scolded Sparkler. "If you go on like this, I'll send you back, you're only on trial."

"You wouldn't? I think he's a lovely pony," objected Lynne.

"And I think Stardust's very pretty. A lovely chestnut with a beautiful arab head," added Tina.

"She's *never* behaved like this before," Lesley complained to the As. "And it's so ridiculous. I know he's grey, but otherwise he's just a cob with rather a large, coarse head."

"He's not that bad-looking," objected Alice.

"It's his dapples she's crazy about," decided Rupert. "She's besotted and dreams of him every moment they're apart. You realize that you're being cruel, Lesley. You ought to change groups for your pony's sake."

"It would take more than that to make me ride with my sister," snapped Lesley.

They came to the edge of the forest. Huge ancient oaks lined the roadside and grassy rides led temptingly into the interior. Across the entrance to each ride was a stout wooden barrier, leaving a gap on either side, so that pedestrians and riders could enter, but not cars.

"Let's have a jump," suggested Hanif. "They're nice and solid, so Jupe will look what he's doing."

"Yes, let's."

"Great idea, I'll go second," answered the older Wheelers, but Lesley said, "No thanks, they're too solid for Stardust."

"And much too high for Tiger," moaned Oliver.

"Have a look among the trees, you might find some tree trunks to jump," suggested Lizzie, tightening her girths.

The larger ponies, already in an adventurous mood, all flew over the barrier. Their riders stopped them someway down the track, turned back and jumped again, pulling up sharply on the edge of the road.

They jumped the next two barriers and then reached the fifth track, which Alice said was the one which would take them to Three-legged Cross. The track ran straight and shady, suddenly emerging into forest clearings, where the grazing deer, hinds and fawns, fled, startled, at the approach of the riders. They cantered and walked and cantered again until their track ended, merging with another, which, skirting a fir plantation, made up the three-legged cross.

"I think this is it," said Alice, looking round the clearing which lay alongside the plantation. She dismounted. "I'll check the map and work out the next reference."

"We'll look round for the warning. Can you see anything, Ollie?" asked Lizzie.

"I've found it," called Rupert. "It's a fire warning, just inside the plantation gate. Come and write it down, Lesley."

"Oh great, can we have lunch now?" asked Oliver, riding over to inspect the warning sign.

"There's no water for the poor ponies here," complained Lizzie.

"And Rosie is a terrific drinker, we'd better ride on a bit," agreed Rupert, holding Stardust while Lesley copied the warning notice. "Can you find a stream on the map, Alice," he called.

Alice had persuaded Hanif to study the map too. "You can see that the stretch across the heath is complicated," she pointed. "There are so many paths criss-crossing, it'll be all too easy to go wrong, and there don't seem to be any landmarks."

"We'll have to check with the compass," said Hanif, "as long as we head east we can't go far wrong, we'll hit the Ramsbourne road eventually. But first of all we've got to go round the plantation and find our second warning. Then along Long Bottom!"

"There is a stream, but it's rather a way off. We'll all starve to death before we get there."

"Unless we make a detour and meet it earlier. Look, it's not far from our track if we go down there."

The As' second map reference led them to the spot where a narrow road entered the forest over a cattle grid. Avoiding the grid, the As gathered round the sign beside it. "'Drive Slowly Animals on Road. Speed Limit 20 mph.,'" Rupert read out slowly for Lesley to write down.

"*Now* can we have lunch?" asked Oliver in a grumpy voice.

"By the stream," Alice told him. "It's not far."

The ponies were pleased with their stream and drank deeply, but Alice's plan to picnic on the bank proved a disaster. The grass was already grazed to the ground, there was nowhere to tie the ponies and clouds of flies appeared and seethed round their heads, maddening both ponies and riders.

They unpacked the cans of fly spray and Lizzie and Hanif raced round spraying each pony in turn. Then they ate their lunches standing, and were glad to mount and ride on slowly across the heath, first along shady, bracken-edged paths and then over a dry, stony stretch, supporting only heather and scrub.

They seemed to be miles from anywhere and quite alone in an empty landscape, until they saw the girl coming towards them. She was wearing jodhpurs, a blue and white checked shirt and a crash cap and seemed to be walking unsteadily. As she weaved her way towards them they noticed that she was supporting one arm across her chest.

"Excuse me, have you seen a roan pony? A red roan with black points and a star, about thirteen-two."

"No, sorry. No ponies at all," answered Hanif who was in the lead. "Have you fallen off?"

"Yes," she nodded. Her face was white and she swayed as she spoke.

"Have you hurt yourself?" asked Alice.

The girl nodded again. "Yes, my arm. I think it's broken, my hand won't work and my wrist is throbbing dreadfully . . .," her voice trailed away.

"Lizzie, your services are required." Rupert dismounted and took Rajah's reins.

"A broken arm?" said Lizzie, desperately trying to remember the treatment; her mind had gone blank.

Jupiter had begun to twirl impatiently. "Could you walk back to that clearing?" Hanif asked the girl.

"Wait a minute, let Lizzie help her," advised Alice as the girl swayed dangerously. Lizzie took the girl by her good arm and led her back along the path to where two paths crossed, making a stony clearing among prickly gorse bushes. There she sat her down on a convenient hillock.

While Lizzie rifled through her saddlebag, Alice knelt beside the girl.

"I'm Alice Drummond," she said. "What's your name?"

"Amanda Quale."

"And you live near here?"

Amanda nodded, as Lizzie approached with a coarse cotton sling.

461

"Do you think it needs a splint?" asked Lizzie looking anxiously at the deformed and swollen wrist.

"No, it's fairly O.K., if I hold it like this. It doesn't like being moved."

"Lay the free end over the unafflicted shoulder," said Lizzie, suddenly remembering what Mrs Gail had told them she began to place the sling in position. "You hold the wrist steady while I slide the sling between it and your body," she told Amanda. "There. Now you must tell me which is the most comfortable position," she went on, going round behind the girl and preparing to knot the two ends of the sling. Amanda who seemed terrified of moving the wrist at all, allowed it to be raised a few centimetres.

"Yes, that is better," she admitted in a faint voice.

"Would you like a drink of water?" asked Lesley, unscrewing her water bottle.

"Not much," objected Lizzie, "just a sip. Remember they can't give anaesthetics if you've been eating and drinking."

"Do you think they give anaesthetics for a broken wrist?" asked Alice.

"Depends if it's a clean break," said Rupert knowingly.

"And it's going to be ages before we get her to hospital," added Hanif. "I can't find one on the map."

"How far is it to your home?" asked Alice.

"I'm not sure exactly. We've only just moved here. It's a place called Ramsbourne."

"That's where we're going, to the school. Fairfield Park School," explained Alice.

"My father's going to teach there next term. Robin, that's my pony, may have gone back to our old home. I don't think he likes it much here. He misses the ponies he used to share a field with."

"If we put her on one of our ponies we could lead her to Ramsbourne," suggested Alice.

"Yes, we're not going to get an ambulance to come

462

here," agreed Hanif, looking helplessly across the rough and stony heath.

"Do you think you could ride one of our ponies, if we help you to mount and then lead you?" Lizzie asked Amanda.

"Yes, O.K., I'll try," Amanda agreed.

"She'd better ride Saffy or Stardust, they're the smoothest," said Alice, looking round at the ponies.

"Saffron," said Hanif. "Stardust might suddenly think of her lost love."

"Yes, she's not as trustworthy as usual," agreed Lesley, "but I'll do some of the leading."

Alice stood Saffron beside the hillock and let his near stirrup down several holes. Lizzie stationed herself behind Amanda ready to give a helpful push. Lesley went round to the other side prepared to give a pull.

Amanda winced at the jolt as she swung her leg over and landed rather heavily in the saddle. Saffron seemed to realize that his new passenger was hurt and walked quietly at the back of the cavalcade.

Oliver, riding near the front, sighed, "This is going to take hours," he said. "Why does our group have to have all the problems? I expect the others are just sailing along again."

"Our log will be the best though," Rupert told him, "plenty of juicy material. 'Crossing the bleak and deserted heath we suddenly heard a faint cry for help . . .'"

"Did you see which way your pony went?" Alice asked Amanda.

"Not really. You see I'd never ridden on this heath before. I went to the lake first and then I was coming back when Robin suddenly went mad. He bucked and bucked. He's never done that before, and when I came off he went off at full gallop. I was feeling awful, faint and sick, so I didn't get up very quickly, and when I did he'd vanished. All I know is that he didn't go towards home, our new house, that is. I'm afraid he may try to find his way home to Crofton."

"Where's that?" asked Alice.

"About twenty miles away, over the other side of the Downs," answered Amanda.

Group J had enjoyed their ride by the lake. They had found their warning sign without difficulty. Attached to a post which also held a lifebelt, it warned against the dangers of bathing in the deep waters of the lake.

"If it was really hot I wouldn't mind a swim in there," decided Seb, who was the Woodbury pony club's best swimmer.

"I would. The water looks so dark and gloomy with the trees all round. Ugh," Lynne shivered.

They found a less thickly wooded section of the lake for lunch, with a sunny, gently shelving beach running down to the water. They tied the ponies to trees and, though there was nothing to eat, they seemed content to rest in the shade. The riders flung themselves down on the pine-needle carpeted sand, and ate their lunches to the sound of lapping lakewater. The sandwiches tasted delicious. Seb devoured Sarah's discarded banana with relish, and everyone cheered greedily when Lynne produced a bag of her mother's fairy cakes.

"This is the life," said James, stretching out contentedly, when they had finished eating. "I wouldn't mind a couple of hours here."

"I would, it's boring," objected Sarah. "We ought to get going and do something really clever so that we win by miles." She turned to Seb. "You realize that our log is really boring compared with the As'?"

"Who cares, we're having a great time and seeing new places. Can't you get it into your thick head that it's the *journey* that counts, not prizes."

"You wait until you see the As getting them, you won't

like that," taunted Sarah, "and I shall go really wild if my sister wins."

James got up, brushing sand and pine needles from his clothes. "I suppose we had better get moving," he said, taking a farewell look at the placid waters of the lake. "Come on, Seb. Let's check the map."

"Haven't you worked out where we're going *yet*?" snapped Sarah. "I don't know why we picked you as a navigator. I can't wait to get a map of my own, then we won't have all this hanging about."

James went his way without a word, but Seb, getting up to follow him, said, "You're a poisonous little creep, aren't you? A real troublemaker."

"No, I'm not," Sarah shouted after him. "It's you great slobs of boys who are useless. If we lose it'll all be your fault."

"Oh, do shut up, Sarah. Why are you trying to spoil our lovely ride?" demanded Tina. "Because that's what you're doing, isn't it, Lynne?"

"Yes, you are. We were all really happy until you started," agreed Lynne.

They tacked up and rode on, away from the lake. Sarah, finding everyone against her, sulked. They found their second map reference without difficulty. The warning was another of the fire danger signs, and then they turned eastwards, and rode uphill to Fox Heath.

Sarah, still sulking, disassociated herself from the group by following separate paths through the heather and scrub, and gradually increasing the distance between them.

"You know what David said about no one going off on their own," called James.

"I'm not on my own. I've got good eyesight and I can see you perfectly," Sarah's defiant shout came back.

After that they ignored her. When they trotted she trotted and though it looked as though Sparkler was

465

objecting to the separation, Sarah seemed to be enjoying the battle, and was forcing him to obey.

They were riding downhill and the heath was losing some of its harshness, with grassy clearings and larger trees ahead, but not yet the telegraph poles that would tell them they were coming to the Ramsbourne road, when a piercing scream shattered the drowsy calm of the afternoon. They swung round in their saddles.

"It's Sarah," shouted Lynne, and they all saw the grey figure of Sparkler, bucking and kicking as he raced westward, while Sarah, unseated, clung round his neck.

"He's gone berserk," cried Lynne, as another shriek stabbed the air.

"Hang on," Seb shouted to Sarah. "We'd better try to cut him off," he added, turning Jigsaw, and cursing the runaway's long start.

Tina, who had been at the end of the line, was now the leader, but Bowie was fast for his size and they set a reckless pace. It was no use cutting across to Sarah's path until they had drawn ahead, thought Tina, urging Bowie faster. Sarah was clinging on, still shrieking, "Whoa" and "Stop!" in a hysterical voice which did nothing to calm the fleeing pony.

They galloped and Sparkler galloped. But the grey's path was twistier, thought Tina, and the pursuers were gradually gaining. Then ahead they could see the place where Sarah's path rejoined the main one. James shouted something and Tina drew to one side to let the larger and fitter Ferdinand pass. James was riding really hard, his whole being dedicated to reaching that junction first. Ferdinand was going flat out, ears back, eyes fixed, nostrils flared and Sparkler, sweat-covered and wild-eyed was travelling almost as fast. There was going to be a collision, thought Tina, taking a pull at Bowie. Sparkler was going to crash into Ferdie's side, it was unavoidable. As she watched them racing for the junction, she felt like shutting her eyes. But then, at the very last moment the grey pony swerved. Swerved and braked. Sarah lost her hold round his neck and fell. With a desperate neigh, Sparkler was among the other ponies. Pulling up hastily, Tina grabbed his rein.

With a feeling of enormous relief they all turned to Sarah, but she was already screaming at James, who stared at her, baffled.

"Where's the first aid kit? Why don't you *do* something. He'll die if you just stand there gaping."

"What's the matter, Sarah?" Tina gave Bowie to Seb and led Sparkler over to her. "He looks fairly O.K."

"Well, he isn't. A snake bit him, that's why he went off like that. He'll *die* if you don't do something."

"Where, Sarah?" they asked, crowding round the grey.

"I don't know, do I? On his foreleg, I suppose," sobbed Sarah hysterically. "I saw a snake on the path and then he went mad, so it must have been a snake bite. Look, there, his chest is swelling. That's the place," Sarah shrieked at them accusingly.

"It would have to be a fairly tall snake to get him there," said Seb. "Does anyone know how long adders are? Do they rear up before they strike?"

"You're supposed to bandage tightly between the bite and his heart, but that's impossible," wailed Lynne. "I mean it's right by his heart and there's nowhere to put the bandage."

"And we should have kept him still, not let him gallop a mile," added Tina.

"Are you absolutely sure that it was a snake that bit him? What colour was it?" James asked quietly.

"How should I know? I didn't sit there looking at it, did I?" shrieked Sarah indignantly.

"Surely you noticed whether it was black or green?"

"No, I didn't and if you don't get a vet quickly he'll die. Look, he's trembling all over and his chest's swelling."

The other trekkers looked at Sparkler gloomily. He was sweating and trembling and there was no doubt that his chest had a hot and swollen area to one side.

"There's nothing much we *can* do except keep him still, is there?" James asked Lynne. "I mean until we get the vet."

"I can't remember anything else, can you, Tina?"

"No. Come on, let's find a telephone."

"We've got the numbers of a couple of vets on the route card, but you're supposed to tell them what the snake was like, otherwise they bring the wrong serum," worried James as he mounted.

"They said there were adders here. Tina, are you coming with us or staying with Lynne?" asked Seb.

"Will you be O.K.?" Tina asked Lynne. It seemed mean to leave her with Sarah and a dying pony.

"I expect so," Lynne answered uncertainly.

"I know more or less where it happened. We'll go down Sarah's path and see if we can see the snake," decided James. "It's on the way to the telephone."

"They're so slow. He'll be dead hours before they get the vet," Sarah snapped despairingly. "It's no use my mother blaming me. I told them to go as soon as I could."

"We have to keep him still and calm," said Lynne. "Look, you hold Vulcan, Sarah. You're too upset to be a good nurse." She took the trembling Sparkler's reins and began to talk to him soothingly.

"We're nearly at the place," said James, slowing down. "We don't want to risk the ponies, so if you'll hold Ferdie, I'll go and have a look on foot."

"Do be careful," Tina told him anxiously.

"I've got boots on, so I'm O.K. Seb, lend me your whip. It's much heavier than mine." Armed with the whip, James set off down the path, poking and prodding the heather on either side and looking about him in a very alert manner.

"Do you think I ought to go with him?" asked Seb.

"No, you've only got jodh boots, but we'd better be ready to rush to his aid if he shouts," decided Tina.

"Yes, I'll do that, you hold the ponies," said Seb in his older brother voice, as they watched, tense, anxious and ready for action. They waited in silence, Tina was thinking, that in his quiet way, James was brave. Seb was wishing that he had gone with his friend; he felt feeble, just watching.

Then James stopped dead, gave a cry of pain and came running back.

"What's up, did you see the snake?" Seb ran to meet him.

"No, it's wasps! Come on, let's get away, they're still after me," shouted James, putting on a spurt. The boys grabbed their ponies, mounted and the three riders fled in an undignified manner.

"There was a nest of them. They seemed to be pouring out of a hillock at the side of the path. They were in a real fury," explained James as they slowed to a trot. "I'm not surprised poor old Sparkler went off like he did. They were really vicious. One got me on my hand and one on my cheek."

"Lynne's got a huge tube of anti-histamine cream," Tina told him as relief surged through her. "Let's keep going and put poor Sarah out of her misery."

"That girl deserves to suffer," said Seb.

They rode back at a brisk trot, feeling quite pleased with themselves, they had done the right thing as it turned out; they hadn't panicked.

"Wasps," they shouted, waving cheerfully, as soon as they could see Lynne and Sarah. "Don't worry, it was only a wasps' nest."

"Look, they got me too." James displayed his stings proudly. "I don't know why they were in such a fury, but they came pouring out, determined to sting me to death."

"I didn't see any wasps, only the snake," said Sarah, clinging to her story. "How can you be sure it's a sting?" she demanded as Lynne began to apply liberal dollops of cream to Sparkler's swollen chest.

"Give me a couple of blobs," asked James, holding out his hand. "I sympathize with you, Sparkler, mine hurt too."

"But you're not trembling," said Seb.

"Lynne, I think he's got some more round here on his quarters," Tina pointed.

When they looked for stings they found eleven hot swollen patches on the trembling pony. Lynne treated them all and even Sarah was prepared to admit that a snake could hardly have bitten a fleeing pony's quarters.

"He might have been *stung* to death," she said as they all mounted.

They set off across the heath, riding slowly, until they were satisfied that Sparkler was recovering.

"We're getting near the place where Robin went mad," said Amanda Quale as the path meandered downhill and they could see grassy clearings ahead. She hadn't spoken for some time and she was still very pale, thought Hanif, who was leading her. He'd taken over from Rupert, who had spent *his* turn trying to cheer her with absurd jokes. Hanif had decided to leave her in peace, and walked beside Saffron in silence. "Was it this path?" he asked.

"I'm not sure, but it was near here," answered Amanda.

Then Stardust raised her head and neighed. It was a long, loving neigh and she was looking across the heath.

"It's the others, look," Lizzie pointed as all the ponies raised their heads and answering neighs rang out.

"Great, I wonder if anything exciting has happened to them," said Oliver, waving.

"What's up with Seb?" asked Rupert, as Seb and Jigsaw

470

left the main party and began to cross the section of heath which separated the two paths. "Can anyone hear what he's shouting?"

"Perhaps they want to know why Harry's walking," suggested Alice. "You'd better tell them, Rupert. You've got the loudest voice."

"Can't we wait till he gets here?" snapped Lesley. "I don't want to be deafened for life."

"I think he's shouting 'stop'," said Lizzie. "And look, he's holding up one hand like a policeman."

"Yes, it is 'stop'," agreed Oliver, "but I can't see any reason for stopping. What *is* he on about."

"We'd better stop," said Lizzie. "Something may be wrong. Whoa, Rupert! Seb wants us to stop," she shouted to the front of the ride.

"Perhaps there's been a landslide," suggested Alice, as they all pulled up and concentrated on the approaching Seb.

"Hold it," he was calling, "you're riding into a wasps' nest. Can you come across to our path. They're swarming or something. They've half-murdered Sparkler and they got James when he went to investigate."

"A wasp nest, on this path?" asked Amanda.

"Who's she?" muttered Seb.

"Amanda Quale. We think she's broken her wrist. Her pony bucked her off and disappeared." Alice told him.

"Another victim of the wasps," said Seb. "Were you on this path," he asked Amanda. "Did your pony suddenly go mad?"

"Yes, poor Robin. He's never done anything like that before. Do you think they were stinging him all the way up the path?"

"Yes, that's what they did to Sparkler. Sarah came off eventually, but we were there to catch Sparkler. Where do you think your pony's disappeared to?"

"I'm afraid he's lost. We only moved here a couple of

days ago. He's either lost or trying to find his way back to our old house, poor Robin." There was a sob in Amanda's voice.

"Once we get you off to hospital we'll start telling people about Robin," Lizzie tried to comfort her.

"And tomorrow we'll be riding over the Downs," added Rupert.

"But he'll be spending all night in a saddle and bridle," sniffed Amanda.

"She's suffering from shock," said Lizzie.

"Yes, her wrist looks nasty and you can see it hurts like hell if it gets a jolt," added Rupert.

"Seb, do you think your lot could go on and get help?" asked Alice. "Perhaps her parents could come and collect her in a car."

"Where exactly do you live, Amanda?" asked Hanif.

"In the village, right by the church. It's called Kingcup Cottage and you get to it by a little bridge," she answered.

"Right, we'll go on then," Seb sounded business-like. "Amanda Quale, Kingcup Cottage. And if Sparkler isn't up to it we'll send him to join your group," he called over his shoulder as he cantered away.

"That's the last thing we want," snapped Lesley.

Seb explained matters to the Js in as few words as possible and tried to persuade Sarah to join the As. "We've got to ride fast," he told her.

"I'm not going with my sister and anyway Sparkler's better," she answered obstinately.

"Right, we're off then," said Seb, urging Jigsaw into a canter and waving encouragingly to the As.

The first grassy clearing was succeeded by another and the track led on, soft and peaty, through the trees, until they saw the road ahead. They hurried through the gate beside the cattle grid, turned right and clattered up the road into the village. The church, with its turreted tower, stood in one corner of the square. The picture postcard

472

cottages faced each other, and the stone wall and high wrought-iron gates of Fairfield Park faced the trekkers.

"Near the church, bridge over the stream," Seb muttered. "It must be over there."

They inspected the row of cottages, each one reached by its own tiny bridge over the narrow stream. Kingcup Cottage was one from the end. Seb hurried over the bridge and began to hammer on the door. No one came.

"I bet you've got the wrong cottage," sneered Sarah as he peered through the windows and then knocked again. But James and Tina had found a neighbour in the square and were asking for Mrs Quale.

"I don't think there *is* a Mrs Quale, dear," explained the neighbour. "They've only just moved in, but I think it's just Mr Quale and the little girl. We heard there had been a recent bereavement."

"Oh, then we need Mr Quale," said Tina. "Amanda's fallen off and broken her wrist, our friends are bringing her back from the forest, but she needs a hospital or a doctor.

"Oh dear, and there's no surgery here until Monday, we'll have to get her into Dewkesbury Hospital. I'll pop round and see Mr Clements, he runs the hospital car service. I won't be a minute. If he's at home he'll be only too happy to help."

"Let's hope he is then," said James as the good neighbour bustled across the square.

The ponies tried the stream water and made rude faces, then they began to snatch at roses and sunflowers.

"Oh, why can't she hurry up," complained Sarah. "I can't wait here all night. My mother'll be coming to fetch me for the Prince Philip practice."

"It might be an idea for you and Sarah and Lynne to go on and find where we're camping," Seb suggested to James. "Tina and I could cope with this end."

"Yes, we could try and find Mr Quale too," agreed James. "I suppose the school is through those gates."

"It looks very posh," said Lynne, gazing at the gates doubtfully. "Too posh for a school."

"Of course that's it," snapped Sarah, pushing past her and leading the way in.

"If you find him, don't forget to tell Mr Quale that the pony's still missing," Seb called after them.

The good neighbour, who turned out to be called Mrs Moon, reappeared in the passenger seat of Mr Clement's car, and Seb explained that the other trekkers should now be approaching the forest gate. Mr Clements, stoutly built and silver-haired, drove on ahead. Seb and Tina, suddenly aware that they and their ponies were tired, followed slowly. When they reached the cattle grid they found that the car had driven over and met the As a short way into the forest. Everyone gathered round as Amanda was helped off Saffron and assisted to the car.

Mrs Moon took a quick look at the wrist and agreed that it was broken. Seb told Amanda that the others had gone on to the school to find her father and tell him what had happened.

"You will tell him to try and find Robin?" pleaded Amanda in a shaky voice.

"Would you like us to ring the police or the people at your old house?" asked Alice.

"They won't keep you in, dear," said Mrs Moon, settling herself beside Amanda in the back. "You'll soon be home again with that wrist in plaster."

"It's Friday evening. We might have a longish wait," said Mr Clements, starting the car.

The trekkers waved as the car drove away.

"She's terribly worried about Robin," said Lizzie as they sorted out the ponies.

"Who wouldn't be?" asked Hanif.

"Her mother's dead," announced Tina. "The neighbour told us. She said it was quite recent."

"Dead?" Oliver sounded incredulous.

474

"Poor Amanda." Alice's mind was suddenly replaying the awful moment at school, the scene when her house mistress and the matron had broken the news of *her* parents' death. She could remember it vividly, the pain and the stunned feeling. She felt a sudden closeness to the white-faced girl.

"I hope her pony does turn up O.K.," she said. "I wish we had the telephone number of her old house."

James and Lynne had been very efficient. They had found the school caretaker, who was in charge, and he had shown them the two fields at the back of the headmaster's house. The Rookes' trailer was parked in the smaller one, which, once again, the tents were to share with the mares.

"It all looks very grand," said Tina in a hushed voice as Lynne helped her unsaddle Bowie.

"It's O.K., we don't have to be quiet. The headmaster doesn't come home until Sunday. There's hardly anyone here," Lynne told her cheerfully. "We're to use the loos and showers in the cricket pavilion," she giggled. "It's miles to walk and mostly for boys."

"Did you find Mr Quale?" Seb asked James.

"No, he was somewhere in the school building and the caretaker went to look for him. We told him to say that Amanda was on her way to Dewkesbury Hospital and that the pony was still missing."

"I wish we could do something about looking for Robin," said Alice, "but I suppose Mrs Moon was right. Amanda will soon be home from hospital and able to telephone all the horsey people who live near her old home."

"Twenty miles is a long way to go on his own *and* at night. I hope nothing awful happens to him," said Hanif gloomily.

CHAPTER FIVE

Day III: "She Wouldn't Listen."

It began to rain in the night and the fierce drumming on the tents wakened the campers from their deep, exhausted sleep. Tina was heard hoping that Bowie was all right, Oliver moaned that his socks were getting wet again, Rupert's sleepy voice advised putting them inside his sleeping bag, James murmured that he hoped it would stop by morning. Then they had fallen asleep again.

In the morning they were wakened by urgent neighs from the ponies. The campers peered out reluctantly. It was still raining, falling in a heavy, lifeless, unrelenting downpour. The ponies, soaking and shivering, were watching the tents and seeing someone stir, they burst into another chorus, demanding breakfast.

Groaning, the trekkers dragged themselves from their warm sleeping bags, bumping into each other as they searched for their macintoshes, pulled on their gumboots and crept out, bent shrouded figures, into the teeming rain. The ponies neighed again, trying to hurry them as they ladled feeds into buckets.

The mares' field had a shelter, which was quickly appropriated by Rupert and Lesley, but Stardust, spurning creature comforts, neighed endlessly for Sparkler who, wet, cold and miserable, was refusing to be caught. The other ponies were all tied up and attacking their feeds with the desperation of the starving, but Sparkler, nervous of having his wet ears touched, was trotting circles round an exasperated Sarah. The rest of the trekkers were trailing across the vast, green expanse to the cricket pavilion, except for Hanif. Having failed to light the wet cooking stoves he was moving them to the shelter, staggering backwards and forwards across the field with stoves and sodden cardboard boxes full of frying pans and food. He had coaxed the stoves into action by the time Alice and James reappeared with kettles and the plastic container, full of water from the cricket pavilion tap.

"Owing to exceptional weather conditions, breakfast will be late," announced Hanif to the shrouded, anonymous shapes which drifted hopefully into the shelter.

"We can put the bedding rolls in the trailer and the tack in the tents," suggested Seb. "Then when breakfast's over the tack can go in the shelter while we take down the tents."

"Great," said Alice, "but don't pack our clothes— remember that the cooks aren't dressed. I've found a tin of hot chocolate, Lynne," she went on. "Shall I make it with these cartons of longlife? I think they belong to your lot."

Eventually breakfast was ready and they ate it standing in the shelter, squashing Rosie and Stardust into a corner. Sarah said they should be tied up outside like the others, but Rupert pointed out that they acted as central heating, combining with the stoves to create a comforting fug.

"One thing is, there's no point in grooming," said Oliver, his mouth full of sausage and fried bread.

"Better pick out the hoofs and make sure they've still got shoes," Lizzie told him.

"The cooks had better pack and dress," said Hanif. "My stepfather will be here at any minute. Can we leave the rest of you to wash up?"

"I've got to catch that stupid pony," said Sarah, edging her way out.

"Help with the washing up," suggested Tina, "and then *we'll* help *you* catch Sparkler."

"You're always getting out of the boring work," grumbled Oliver. "If you ask me you're the laziest person in the Woodbury pony club."

"We don't ask you," snapped Sarah. "You're pathetic. You're a useless rider. And Janet Green says you'll never be any good for the Prince Philip because you're too conceited to learn,"she added as she stormed out into the rain.

"You asked for that," Rupert told Oliver.

"Yes, it's best to ignore her," added Lizzie.

"Your sister gets more and more poisonous," Seb told Lesley.

"What's the matter with her?"

"She's always like that."

"She's not usually *quite* as bad," argued Tina, "but I think Netti keeps her in order."

"I think she's worn out. It's daft doing the Prince Philip on top of a trek, too much for anyone," said Lynne.

"And she misses half the fun going away in the evening," added Oliver.

"Silly old Rooke, it's her fault," observed Rupert, taking a mop to the greasy plates. "Oh, sorry, Lesley, I forgot you were there."

"That's all right. I hate my mother," snapped Lesley.

Sarah was still trying to catch Sparkler when Mr Franklin arrived.

"Why doesn't someone help that kid with her pony?" he asked in a disapproving voice. "Surely one of you older ones could catch it for her?"

"At risk of being scratched and clawed, by Sarah," Rupert told him. "She's in a vile mood this morning."

"We did offer," added Lynne.

"One of the most important aspects of group activities is learning to get on with each other," Mr Franklin told them severely.

"Could you tell Sarah Rooke that?" asked Seb. "She's being really impossible."

"To an outsider, it looks as though you are all ganging up against one member of the party."

"But one shouldn't take things at face value, should one?" said Rupert.

"Have you seen Mrs Rooke? Did she tell you about Amanda Quale?" Alice asked hastily.

"And is there any news of the lost pony?" enquired Tina.

Mr Franklin shook his head. "I haven't heard from Mrs Rooke." He looked at his watch. "She's late. I hope she hasn't had car trouble. The rain's causing havoc on the roads; flood water in all the hollows and abandoned cars everywhere." He turned back to watch Sarah, trailing round the field, shaking a bucket of pony nuts at the disdainful Sparkler. "What are you going to do if you *can't* catch him?" he asked.

"No problem," answered Hanif briskly. "We take Stardust in. They're in love."

"Then why in heaven's name hasn't someone done it already?" demanded Mr Franklin.

The pony club members looked at each other and giggled.

"We don't like to interfere with the power structure of the Rookery. Well, only as a last resort," explained Rupert. "We're afraid of being pecked."

The rain was still teeming down and Mr Franklin retreated to his car while they tacked up. Alice and James went over to ask him for their envelopes and then retreated to the shelter to work out their routes.

"Want some help?" Rupert asked Sarah.

"I hate you all!" she screamed at him.

"Come on, Lesley, we want Stardust at the gate," Rupert called. "Can't waste any more time on this dotty pony."

Lesley, already mounted, dithered, unwilling to oblige, but Stardust, seeing the open gate, took charge. Neighing

479

an affectionate greeting, she cantered through. Sparkler rushed to meet her, as they whinnied, nose to nose, Lesley leaned forward and took his head collar. Sarah hurried over, clipped on the headcollar rope, and led him away without a word.

Everyone who could, crowded into the shelter while they waited for Sarah to tack up.

"We've got two map references again," Alice told the As. "The first one's on the White Horse. You know, the horse cut out of the turf, high on the Downs."

"High's right," said Hanif, who was looking at the map. "It's a mountain."

Mr Franklin came running through the rain. "If the weather doesn't pick up I think you'd better skip the second task," he told them. "I must go now, but Mrs Rooke's arrived. She's chatting to Sarah by the trailer. Take care, I hope it clears up for you."

"We've got the White Horse too, but second. Our first one's down by the canal," said James, as Mr Franklin ran back to his car.

"Let's see if Mrs Rooke has any news of the Quales," said Alice.

"No, I haven't seen them. I called in last night but they weren't back from the hospital," Mrs Rooke answered Alice, as Sarah mounted and the cold wet ponies, heads bowed, tails tucked in snapped at each other irritably.

"Do let's start," pleaded Oliver, shivering inside his enormous macintosh. "Tiger's back is all hunched up. He's going to explode soon."

"Keep his head up," instructed Lizzie.

"Ought we to thank someone?" worried James.

"You can do that for us, Mother, can't you?" said Sarah. "The ponies can't be kept hanging about any longer."

They set off up the school drive at a brisk trot and swept through the imposing gates into the square.

"We turn right here," said James.

"Yes, but the As want to call on Amanda first," answered Alice.

"Do they?" asked Lesley.

"Yes," said Lizzie firmly.

"So do the Js," added Seb and Tina.

"It won't take a minute," said Alice, dismounting. Seb followed her over the bridge and they huddled together in the porch until a tall, stooping, sad-looking man answered their knock.

"We came to ask how Amanda's doing," said Alice. Mr Quale spoke quietly and the waiting riders couldn't hear what he said.

Then an upstairs window opened and Amanda's face, pale with red-rimmed eyes, looked out. She held up an arm, in plaster to the elbow. "You were right," she said, "about it being a broken wrist. It's better now it's in plaster, though it still hurts a bit."

"Any news of Robin?" asked Tina.

"No," she shook her head. "He hasn't turned up in Crofton yet. The police haven't heard anything; he's completely vanished." They could tell from her voice that she was trying hard not to cry.

"We're going over the Downs to Bewley, so we'll watch out for him," said Lizzie.

"And we'll be going along by the canal first," added James.

"Thanks. Dad's going to drive me round the roads in a minute, and this afternoon he says he'll search the forest."

"We've got the telephone number," said Seb, taking Jigsaw. The rain was falling harder and the ponies milled round restlessly, trying to turn their tails to the rain and protect their heads.

Alice and Seb climbed hastily into their wet saddles. Then James led the way past the church and turned left at the school gates.

When they left the road it was to take the path by the river, a narrow track, between the river and the steep, hanging woods which offered some shelter. They rode for two or three miles before they came to the place where the groups had to part. The Js were to continue beside the river, the As to turn right, up a slippery chalk track which skirted the woods.

The steep, slithery climb was hard work for the ponies. The riders sat well forward and tried to guide them to where there were footholds, and all the time the rain lashed down.

"We turn into the woods here," said Alice, at last. "The path goes straight for a bit and then there's a hairpin bend and we start climbing."

"Anything to be out of that rain." Hanif patted Jupiter. "He hates it."

To Alice's relief the hairpin bend appeared where she expected it and they climbed on steadily. The second bend appeared; this was the leg of the path that should bring them out on top of the Downs, but after a few metres it ended abruptly at a wire fence. And, on the other side of the fence, stretching in all directions as far as the eye could see, was a new plantation: row upon orderly row of young trees.

Alice's heart sank. "I'm sorry," she said, "but this oughtn't to be here. It's not marked on the map."

Hanif shook the fence. "We're not going to break that down."

Lesley, peering through her misted glasses, asked, "Can anyone see a gate?"

"We must have taken a wrong turning somewhere," said Lizzie.

"No, I don't think so," said Alice, dismounting to check the map. "Look," she pointed with relief. "This path's supposed to go all the way to the top."

"She's right," Rupert looked over Alice's shoulder,

then he kicked the fence. "This has no business to be here."

"Maps can't be wrong," snapped Lesley.

"They go out of date," Hanif told her.

"You mean it's an old one?"

"No, I expect it's the latest, knowing my stepfather, but even the latest can go out of date."

"We'll have to go back," said Lizzie.

"Oh no," wailed Oliver. "It's not fair. Stupid, rotten map."

"Don't be like that, Ollie. You're beginning to sound as spoiled as Sarah." Lizzie's voice was disapproving.

"Why don't we try to get *round* the plantation," suggested Alice. "Otherwise it means going back to the path up the side of the wood and right round the outside."

"Miles," wailed Oliver.

"Yes, miles," agreed Hanif looking at the map. "Of course we may find another brand new wire fence joining this one, but *I'm* willing to risk it."

"Yes, it's a lot warmer in the wood," agreed Rupert, "we'll probably expire from hypothermia if we attempt the outside route."

"The worst of it is we were nearly there," said Alice.

They rode on in a depressed silence. There was no proper path, but, Hanif, who was in the lead, picked his way through the trees staying as close as he could to the fence. They couldn't see where they were going, but Alice, who was keeping an eye on the compass, said, "We should be O.K. as long as we don't start going downhill."

Hunched in their mackintoshes, feeling cold and miserable, the four following riders had lost faith in the leaders, but, having no alternative to offer they could only grit their teeth and suffer in silence. Alice and Hanif were equally wet and miserable, but noticed it less, because of their preoccupation with finding the way. The responsibility of leading lay heavily upon them both, now

483

that errors of route meant miles of misery for ponies and people.

"I can see light ahead," called Hanif. "I think we're arriving somewhere."

They had reached the corner of the plantation. As they turned it they joined a well-defined path.

"This looks hopeful," called Hanif, letting Jupiter trot on.

"Yes, and it's uphill," agreed Alice. "If only we can get out at the top."

Eventually, at the top of the hill, the path led them to a hunting gate, which opened on to the Downs, shadowy greyish humps glimpsed through a sheet of rain.

"Do we *have* to go out there?" asked Oliver.

"We do, if we're going to find the White Horse," answered Alice.

"What about eating a little lunch first," suggested Rupert. "Wasn't there a rumour that we've all got Mars bars? And the rain might slacken off a bit."

"Yes, we have, I looked," Oliver told him.

Alice turned to Hanif. "O.K., snack time?" she asked. "Saffy seems to have found some tasty brambles."

"Yes, but I don't think there's much hope of the weather changing. The sky's solid cloud, not the hint of a break anywhere. I think we're in for an English wet day."

Fortified, they rode out of the wood and found themselves at the mercy of the stinging rain. The ponies bowed their heads, the riders pulled up their collars and drew down the peaks of their caps.

"We need to go back a bit," shouted Alice, "to where the proper path should have come out, then we'll connect up with the path to the White Horse. This way."

"Are you sure?" asked Lizzie.

"Fairly sure, if we've come out where I think we have." Alice handed over the compass. "North is behind us, so if we turn right in a minute we'll be going due west."

"Oh, don't say we're lost again," wailed Oliver as Lizzie stared doubtfully at the compass.

"Oh come on, trust Alice, she hasn't done too badly so far," Rupert told them.

"It's no good asking me. I can't see a thing," said Lesley as they battled forward into the wind and rain.

They kept close to the wood, which provided some shelter, until they found the old path emerging from under a new barbed wire fence. Relieved, they turn westward and, forcing the reluctant ponies on, they trotted across the sodden Down.

"See that sundial thing?" Alice pointed excitedly. "According to the map there's one of those on top of White Horse Hill."

"It's a trig point," said Hanif.

"Where's this white horse then?" demanded Oliver truculently.

"It faces west, it's on the far side of the hill," Alice explained.

"You mean we've got to go down into that valley and then climb all the way up again?" Oliver exclaimed.

"Fraid so, but at least we'll be more sheltered when we're down there."

Out of the southwest wind, the valley was much warmer, and the rain lost its sting, while the shivering ponies were appeased by being allowed to canter up the two legs of the zig-zag path which climbed White Horse Hill. But, when the trekkers came over the crest they were higher and more exposed than ever; they found themselves torn by the wind, blinded by the horizontal rain.

"Do keep Tiger's head up," shouted Lizzie, noticing his mutinous eyes and hunched back.

"It doesn't look much like a white horse to me," answered Oliver in a disappointed voice. "Just a lot of bald chalk."

"It's meant to be seen from a distance. It's a landmark," shouted Hanif.

"I can't see a thing," complained Lesley.

"*We* can't see much," Rupert told her. "What were we supposed to identify, Alice?" he shouted, battling with Rosie who was refusing to face the rain.

"An appendage," yelled Alice, who had dismounted, and, turning her back on the wind, was trying to read the sleeved map. "The grid point is about halfway down the hill, not directly below the trig pillar, but to the left, from where you're standing."

"The horse's tail," shouted Rupert promptly.

"Of course, you're brilliant!" yelled Hanif as he tried to control the rain-maddened Jupiter. "Come on, let's go."

"The shortest way to our next place is along the top of the Downs," called Alice as she struggled to mount a prancing Saffron, who seemed to have grown by at least a hand, "but there's another way along the valley, it's quite a bit longer."

"Let's take it, we can't stay up here," shouted Hanif, as Jupiter cantered sideways across the hilltop.

"Yes, this is unbearable," yelled Rupert.

"You *must* keep Tiger's head up, Ollie," called Lizzie. "He's sure to try to buck going downhill."

Sheltered from the worst of the weather, the ponies became calmer.

"This valley's called Brett's Gap," said Alice as they rode down the zig-zag path. "Eventually it joins the track beside the wood, the one up from the river that we were on this morning, but much further along, and it goes all the way to Bewley."

"So if we decide to skip the second 'task' it'll be easy going," observed Hanif.

"Oh, *do* let's skip it," pleaded Oliver.

"We'd better wait and see what the weather does," suggested Lizzie. "It might clear up."

"I know one thing, I'm never going to volunteer for an expedition to the Antarctic," announced Rupert.

"*I'm* never going to volunteer for another *trek*," vowed Oliver.

"Oh cheer up, Ollie, it may be fine tomorrow," Lizzie told him consolingly.

"And yesterday was gorgeous," added Alice, trying to recall the warmth of sunshine, the blue sky and smells of summer.

"And you've only yourself to blame. You would come, though we all advised against it," accused Lesley.

Alice was thinking of Amanda. "I do hope Robin's reached his old home by now," she said aloud.

They emerged from the gap and took the well-trodden track coming up from the river.

There were trees, fences, ploughed fields and a barn.

"It's a different world, still wet, but otherwise civilized," Rupert was saying when a yellow, plastic sack blew suddenly across the track, scattering the ponies. Rosie and Jupiter swung round, cannoning into the ponies behind, and then fled up Brett's Gap; Rosie launching herself into a series of wild bucks. Tiger twisted and dropped his shoulder as he turned, depositing Oliver in a muddy puddle, before racing in pursuit. Stardust turned too, but swerved away to the left and, passing beneath a clump of trees, a low bough caught Lesley in the face and chest, sweeping her off backwards. Neighing loudly, Stardust seized her opportunity, and galloped down the track towards the river.

Saffron and Rajah had shied and scattered with the rest, but then, realizing that the windborne bag was harmless, they stopped and stood gazing after their fleeing friends with pricked ears and rather superior expressions.

Lizzie hurried to Oliver, so Alice went to Lesley's aid. "Are you all right?" she asked.

"No, I am *not*," snapped Lesley, who was groping

around on the ground. "A branch caught me right across the face and swept my glasses off; I can't see a thing."

Alice choked back an inclination to say, *not again*. "If you'll come and hold Saffy, I'll search for them," she offered.

"They're probably smashed." Lesley looked round short-sightedly, "Where's Stardust?"

"Gone to find Sparkler, I'm afraid. Full gallop down the track," answered Alice.

"Well, can't someone go after her?" demanded Lesley.

"In a sec. Ollie came off too and the boys are rounding up Tiger."

Alice was still searching for the spectacles, when Hanif and Rupert returned with Tiger. Lizzie had loaned Oliver her handkerchief and was directing the wiping off of mud from his face. Rupert knotted his broken reins.

"Stardust will be halfway back to the school by now," Lesley announced indignantly. "Isn't it time someone went after *her*?"

"Yes, O.K.," agreed Alice. "Will you come too, Hanif? And can someone else search for the specs?"

"Shall we go on slowly and let you catch us up?" asked Lizzie.

"Yes. We'll be as quick as we can. You go straight up this track."

The Js had found their first objective without difficulty. They'd ridden along the river path until the river met the canal in a series of weirs and locks. The grid reference pin-pointed a working water mill and their question asked "Whose name is on the building".

"Easy, F.J. Sprotley." James read the miller's name from a board above the door.

"Wouldn't this be a lovely place on a fine day," said Tina, shivering inside her macintosh.

"Great, I'd like to come without a pony and have a look at the locks," agreed Seb.

"It's such a shame it had to rain," moaned Lynne. "My hands are freezing."

"It'll be worse on the Downs," warned James. "We'd better eat our lunches before we get up there."

"In that wood, where we parted from the As," suggested Lynne. "It kept off quite a lot of the rain."

"If we can wait that long," said Seb as they trotted back along the path. "It's taken ages to get here."

Seb managed to wait and, when they reached the wood, they led the ponies in among the trees and dismounted where the tangle of leaves overhead seemed most rain-proof.

As they ate, Lynne tried to be nice to Sarah, who had been very silent all morning.

"How are Sparky's stings," she asked. "Have they all gone down?"

"I haven't looked," answered Sarah. "Stupid pony," she added, taking her new map and compass from her saddlebag.

"They've nearly gone," said Lynne, running her hand over the grey quarters. "How's the one on his chest?"

"Oh, do go away, you're making him fidget," snapped Sarah, "and I'm trying to look at my map."

Hurt, Lynne went back to the others and they all ignored Sarah until it was time to move off.

"O.K., Sarah?" James called, as they tightened girths, mounted and started slowly towards the river path.

"Why are you going *that* way?" demanded Sarah.

"Because that's the track that goes up to the Downs. The one the As went up this morning," James answered patiently.

"But we want to go up through the woods."

"Yes, I know, and a bit farther on there's a way into the woods and a path that goes all the way up to the Downs."

"Why can't we just go up there?" Sarah pointed. "There's no point in going out of the wood and then coming back in again."

"Because there's no path." Seb sounded impatient.

"Who needs a path? We can just ride up through the trees."

"No you can't. It's too steep and the soil's very slippery under the leaves. It's quicker, and easier for the ponies, to go up the track."

Sarah stood undecided.

"Let her try," suggested Seb. "She can go that way if she wants to."

"No, she can't. We have to stay together. And look what happened yesterday," answered James as he rode on and then turned up the steep chalk track between the wood and a ploughed field. Sarah followed slowly.

They had almost reached the turning into the wood, when they heard frantic neighs. Sparkler raised his head and neighed back, and then with a squelch of hoofs, a chestnut pony appeared, cantering towards them, saddle empty, reins and stirrups flying.

"It's Stardust," said James, as she pulled up with a long skid and hurried to Sparkler, whinnying with the joy of finding him.

"Oh hell. Now what's happened? Shall I go up and see?" asked Seb.

James looked worried. "We're not supposed to split up, and they may be miles away."

Tina had caught Stardust. "I hope Lesley's not hurt," she said as they continued up the track, hoping that some of the Js would appear.

"That's our path," said James, pointing. "But we'd better go up a bit further."

Sarah had stopped at the entrance to the wood. "Aren't you coming to look for Lesley?" asked Lynne.

"No, why should I. It's her own silly fault for falling off."

"But she may be hurt," objected Tina.

"Who cares," said Sarah.

490

"Come on, Sarah, you know we have to stick together," called James, looking back.

"Well, you can stick with me then," shouted Sarah.

"Don't be silly. We can't leave Stardust roaming around and, even if your sister isn't hurt, we can't leave her to walk miles," protested James.

"I can, do her good. *And* I've got my own map now, so I don't have to stay with you."

"Yes, you do. David will be furious if you go off on your own."

"Who cares."

"Go on, James, call her bluff," said Seb. "We have to find Lesley."

"Yes, I expect Sarah will follow if she sees we're really going," agreed Tina.

"I don't know what's got into her," said Lynne, as they trotted on up the track.

"She should be expelled from the pony club." Seb spoke severely.

Lynne giggled. "Not much hope of that, with Mrs Rooke secretary."

"We could have a new secretary."

"Not many people want to take it on," Lynne told him. "It's a lot of work. I know David had trouble finding someone when he became D.C. . . ."

"There they are," James's voice was full of relief as he caught sight of ponies coming down the track. "Only two of them. Looks like Alice and Harry," he added, staring through the rain.

Stardust was neighing for Sparkler. Sarah hadn't followed the other riders, but they'd forgotten her as they cantered on to meet the As.

"Is Lesley O.K.?" asked James when they were within shouting distance.

"Yes, fine, except for a bashed face and lost spectacles," answered Alice. "Thanks very much for

491

bringing Stardust back. We thought she'd gone to find Sparkler, but where is he?"

James looked back and groaned. "That means she's started up through the wood on her own."

"She's getting more ghastly minute by minute," complained Seb.

"Well, she'll get a shock in the wood," said Hanif and went on to explain about the plantation and how to make the detour round it.

"It's almost quicker for them to go up Brett's Gap, now they're here," suggested Alice, pointing up the valley. White Horse Hill is the one with the trig point pillar thing on top," she went on, "but you can't see it until you're almost there, because of the rain."

"We'll have to go back to the wood because of Sarah," James explained, "but thanks for the information about the path."

"Thanks for catching Stardust. See you," called Hanif as they parted.

"I hope they've found those wretched specs," said Alice, dragging the reluctant Stardust. "Could you go behind, Harry, and chivvy her along?"

When they came in sight of the barn and the trees, Alice's heart sank, for the scene was unchanged. Oliver and Lesley were still pony-holding, the older Wheelers still circling the grass, searching for spectacles.

"You haven't found them then," said Hanif.

"No, not a sign, they've vanished," answered Lizzie.

"Lesley won't let us give up and go on," complained Oliver indignantly. "I'm freezing and we haven't even had lunch."

"Well, they must be there somewhere," said Lesley, "but I suppose we'd better give up now. I'll have to manage somehow."

Rupert, making faces of exaggerated delight and wide smiles, hurried to take Rosie. Lizzie gave up the search reluctantly.

"Your pony, all in one piece," said Alice, handing Stardust over.

"Thank you. I wish we could say the same about my glasses," snapped Lesley.

Hanif, who was standing on the other side of the track, looking round vaguely, suddenly gave a shout. "I've found them! They're hanging from that bough." He rode over and reached up into the wet leaves.

"Be careful. Don't drop them," entreated Lesley.

"It's all right, here they are," Hanif rode back triumphant.

"And we wasted all that time," groaned Rupert, as Lesley glared round at them.

"Lunch," said Alice.

"I was wondering if we could shelter in that barn. It's fairly empty," suggested Lizzie, "and it would be better than standing in the rain."

"Why not," agreed Rupert, "I don't see any angry farmers around."

They went through the tubular metal gate and let the ponies drink at a water trough before leading them into the shelter of the barn. It wasn't a very comfortable picnic for the riders, standing in dripping clothes, but the ponies, eating the sandwich crusts and apple cores, quite enjoyed themselves. Then Stardust began to neigh, and, looking out into the rain, the As saw Sarah and Sparkler standing on the track, Sarah was looking at her map.

"What's up, Sarah?"

"Are you lost?" they called to her.

"No, of course not. What are you doing in there?"

"Eating our lunches. There's a water trough, if you want to give Sparkler a drink."

Alice gave her reins to Lizzie and went out to open the gate. "Didn't you meet the others?" she asked. "They expected to catch up with you in the wood."

"No, the stupid map is wrong. I had to come back."

"We were stuck at the plantation too, but we found the way round. We told your lot where to go. Now you're here you'd better go up Bretts Gap," she pointed.

Sparkler had seen the water trough and dragged Sarah over to it. Stardust rushed to nuzzle him, whinnying with love. Sarah spread her map and set her compass at the ballcock end of the trough.

"Oh, do take that stupid pony away," she snapped at her sister. "Can't you see that I'm trying to check my bearings."

"White Horse Hill is up there," Alice pointed again.

"How can it be, when north's over there," snapped Sarah, turning her map to agree with her compass as Alice mounted.

"North is over there, actually," said Hanif, pointing.

"And Bewley's straight up this track. That's where we're going," added Rupert.

"Thank you very much," said Sarah sarcastically. "I know you're trying to muddle me up, but I'm not that stupid."

"No, truly, Sarah," Lizzie looked at her anxiously. "The only way to find the Js now is to go up Brett's Gap, but it might be better to come on with us."

"No *thank you*," said Sarah, in a rude voice.

"You're wasting your breath," Lesley told Lizzie. "*She* won't listen or take advice."

"But we can't just leave her. David said we were to stick together," protested Lizzie.

"Who cares what *he* says?" asked Sarah, bundling her map into her saddlebag.

Lizzie looked shocked.

"We care," said Hanif.

"He's responsible for us," added Alice.

Sarah didn't bother to argue. She rode through the gate, leaving the As to shut it, and kicking Sparkler into a canter, set off up the track. But she didn't make for

494

Brett's Gap, she took a track on the left which ran along the top of the ploughed field.

"She's going in the *opposite* direction," observed Hanif.

"Do you think she's lost her reason?" Rupert assumed a grave voice.

"No, she's always like that," Lesley shouted to be heard above Stardust's lovelorn neighs.

"She's either dotty or Mrs Rooke's bought her a dud compass," said Alice, shutting the gate.

The As, revived by their lunch, cantered up the track towards Bewley. It was still raining, but not so hard, and when they reached the path which would lead them to their second grid reference, even Oliver agreed that they might as well make the detour and carry out the task. The new track headed south and was more or less parallel to the one Sarah had taken.

"It's a building," said Alice, "because the question is, 'Who lived in this building?' And it's at the top of this track. Then it seems quite easy to get to Stoke Farm."

"It had better be," said Oliver. "I'm freezing, starving and have two sore knees."

"I've been wet for so long I've forgotten what it's like to be dry," observed Rupert.

The building proved to be a small thatched cottage.

"What do we do? Walk in boldly and ask the owners' name?" asked Hanif.

"No, because it's *lived*," answered Alice.

"There's a notice." Lizzie pointed to a low wooden sign beside the gate.

"William Harcourt, poet of rural life 1839–1871", they read, "lived here. The cottage is open to the public on the first Saturday in the month 2–4pm." Lesley wrote down the whole inscription, while Alice and Hanif looked at the map.

"We're on the edge of the Downs, then," said Hanif.

"Yes, and near the horrible new motorway," agreed

495

Alice. "But look, if we go round behind the cottage the track goes on round the bottom of Bewley Down to the village. We go along the road a tiny way and then take the lane to Stoke Farm."

"Right, last lap, everyone," called Hanif, mounting.

They found Stoke Farm. The house, built of timber and brick, was old and beautiful. The square of farm buildings was in the process of being converted, into cottages and garages it seemed, though there were a couple of looseboxes.

"No animals," said Tina.

"And no machinery," added Lynne. "I think it's stopped being a farm and the land's been sold off."

Then, to their surprise, James's mother appeared from one of the looseboxes. Dark haired and pretty, she was wearing a bright yellow plastic macintosh with a hood.

"At *last*," she said. "Where have you been? Mrs Rooke said you would be here by four. I've been having kittens."

"Problems, problems," answered Hanif, dismounting stiffly.

"Adventures, people falling off, bridleways blocked," expanded Alice.

"Do you know where the ponies' fields are?" asked Rupert.

"And where the loo is," demanded Oliver.

"Yes, the loo is in the half-converted cottage," she pointed across the yard. "You can use the bathroom; it's not decorated yet, but they've switched on the immersion heater for you."

"Hot water!" exclaimed Lesley, as Oliver threw his reins at Lizzie and ran.

"As the weather's so awful, and I knew you'd all be soaking wet, I commandeered a loosebox and turned it into a kitchen," Mrs Morgan went on. "I managed to get the cooking stove working and the soup's hot when you're ready. I've brought dry clothes too; every Mum has sent a bag of them."

"What luxury! We didn't expect this," said Hanif.

"Especially *soup*," Rupert smacked his lips. "Come on Dozey Rosey, let's find your field and give you your tea."

"I don't suppose the Js will be long," said Alice, "but we're a bit worried about Sarah. When's Mrs Rooke coming?"

"She's not. The Prince Philip practice is cancelled because of the weather."

"You don't want to worry about my sister, Alice," snapped Lesley. "I don't."

They settled the ponies. The mares' field was small and square, the geldings' large and windswept. The tents were to share a plot of rough grass behind the stables with a row of uninhabited beehives.

The soup, served with chunks of new bread, tasted delicious, and the tired trekkers felt inclined to sit on bales of straw and discuss the day's adventures, but Mrs Morgan handed out plastic bags of dry clothes, neatly labelled, and insisted that they went into the next door loosebox, in relays, and changed.

"Put your wet clothes in the bags and I'll take them home for you," she said, and then looking out at the damp dusk falling over the Downs, added "I can't *think* what James and his lot are doing."

"They lost quite a lot of time bringing Stardust back when Lesley fell off," Hanif explained reassuringly.

When they had changed, the As began to erect the tents. They worked quickly, now that everyone knew what to do, and the rapid darkening of the early, drizzling dusk, spurred them on. Their own tents were up and they were starting on the Js, when Mrs Morgan came over.

"I *must* go now," she said in a worried voice. "My sister and her husband are coming to supper. Will you give the others their dry clothes?"

"Yes, of course, don't worry," Rupert told her in a soothing voice.

"The MacKenzies, the people who own this place, have gone to London for the evening," Mrs Morgan went on, still worried. "There's only a French au pair girl looking after the children, I don't think she'll be much use in an emergency, but David is coming over later. Anyway, if there *is* any trouble, remember that we're all at the other end of telephones, so don't hesitate to get in touch."

"We'll do that, and thank you for the lovely soup and dry clothes," said Alice.

"Yes, thanks very much."

"The soup was great."

"Terrific," they called, hammering in tent pegs and fixing guy ropes.

The tents up and furnished with bedding rolls, they hurried back to the loosebox and the luxury of electric light. Hanif and Oliver began to organize the supper, Rupert to write up the log, while Lesley went to sample the hot water in the almost converted cottage. Alice and Lizzie looked round the bare loosebox and decided on improvements: they fetched planks and empty oil drums from the building works and constructed seats round the walls and then, pushed three straw bales together for a table, with black plastic sacks as the table cloth. With both doors shut and the four cooking stoves in action, the loosebox was becoming quite cosy when the sound of hoofs in the yard sent the As rushing out to greet the Js.

"You're late."

"We've put the tents up."

"James, your mother was here. She's brought everyone dry clothes."

"The Js looked down at the welcoming group, their faces illuminated by light from the stable. "Sarah hasn't turned up then?"

"No, we met her, but she wouldn't believe us when we told her she was going in the wrong direction."

"We've been looking for her for hours," said James, dismounting. "Where's Mrs Rooke?"

"She hasn't come, the mounted games practice was cancelled," Alice told him. "Mrs Morgan came instead."

"Oh hell, this is serious. We really *have* lost Sarah." Seb sounded gloomy.

"It wasn't our fault," Lynne told Lesley, "but your mother and David will probably think it is."

"It was fatal, giving a poisonous little kid like that a map and compass of her own," added Seb.

"Where *exactly* did you see her?" asked James, moving into the light and holding out his map. The As crowded round to show him.

"You mean she went off up that track? Towards the motorway?" asked James in a worried and baffled voice.

"Yes, she insisted that she was heading north," explained Hanif, "I suppose she had her map upside down, but when we tried to sort her out, she wouldn't listen. She seemed to think we were deliberately confusing her."

"She never listens," said Lesley, "but you needn't fuss. She'll turn up, worse luck."

"I'm not so sure. It's getting late and dark," James's solemn face was very worried.

"You see, she could have got here quite easily, because her track crosses the one running from east to west, the one that brought us here from the poet's cottage." Alice pointed out to James and the other As.

"What are we going to do?" asked Seb. "Telephone Mrs Rooke?"

"No, David's coming over anyway."

"David, great," said Seb sarcastically. "He'll go raving mad."

"We're dry and our ponies have been fed and had a rest. We could go and look for her," said Alice.

"Yes, we could eat first and then, if she hasn't turned

up, we could ride down the track by the motorway," agreed Hanif.

"And along the track she took and back by the main track, which we *told* her to take," suggested Lizzie.

"The As to the rescue," Rupert's voice was mocking. "I'm willing."

"It looks a bit dark," said Oliver.

"We don't want Ollie, do we?" asked Lizzie. "He's got sore knees."

"We certainly don't want Tiger," Alice answered.

"I don't think Lesley should come. I'm sure she can't see in the dark, not efficiently," Rupert added.

"Yes, and if your specs are swept off by another branch in the dark we'll never find them," agreed Lizzie.

"Could you be in charge of the telephone, Lesley?" asked Alice. "Mrs Morgan said there was a French au pair looking after the children. The owners are out. Would it be an idea if someone went over now to ask if Sarah's telephoned?"

"And don't you think we ought to tell your mother?" Lizzie asked Lesley.

"No I don't. What's the point? Sarah will turn up eventually and we'd only be making trouble for ourselves."

"As long as nothing really awful has happened," murmured Tina.

CHAPTER SIX

Lost In The Night

The Js turned their ponies out, agreeing to postpone their feeds until the As were ready to tack up for the search, then James and Lesley went to the house to see if the au pair had any news of Sarah.

There was no news, and supper was rather a gloomy meal with everyone listening for the sound of hoofs and watching darkness fall with growing foreboding.

"Something *must* have happened to her," said Lynne through a mouthful of beefburger and mashed potato. "I mean she should have realised where she'd gone wrong and found her way here by now, surely?"

"I expect she's going round and round in circles," suggested Oliver gloomily.

"Poor Sparky," said Tina.

"The trouble is that the Downs were deserted. On a normal Saturday there would have been dog walkers and picnickers and other riders," Rupert pointed out.

"And once it's dark there won't be any visible landmarks to set the map *by*," added Hanif. "I don't suppose she knows about the stars, and she obviously can't read her compass."

"And she's not carrying her torch. We all packed them in our kit bags," observed Tina.

"We'd better check *our* torches," said Alice, starting on apple pie. "We need at least four good ones."

"What's yours like, Ollie? Mine's already a bit faint," admitted Lizzie.

"Ollie's is useless, it has intermittent bulb failure," answered Rupert. "He's always borrowing mine."

"I've got two, and there's my stepfather's big one," said Hanif. "I think I'll put that in my saddlebag."

The As ponies were surprised at being caught and tacked up again and, except for Jupiter, were reluctant to leave their fields and friends. Stardust neighed even more forlornly when she found that Rosie was also deserting her.

"Keep it up," Seb told her. "With luck Sparky'll hear you and bring that stupid girl home."

"Don't disappear for hours," James told the search party, "I mean, she may turn up or we may get news."

"No, we'll ride round the triangle of tracks we were talking about," agreed Hanif. "There's no point in wandering about the Downs."

"Unless we hear a cry for help, or Sparkler neighing," added Alice.

"I've got the first-aid kit," said Lizzie.

"It's surprising how quickly one's eyes become used to this murky light. I'm beginning to see quite well," observed Rupert, when they had left the comforting lights of the cottages scattered alongside the road and taken the dark, deserted track which led to the Downs.

"And the ponies are all used to sleeping out, so it can't worry them," said Lizzie trying to sound confident.

"And it's actually stopped raining at last," Alice pointed out.

"Yes, it looks as though the clouds are clearing," Hanif gazed round at the sky. "We might get a moon and some stars."

"And Sparkler is *grey*," added Alice in an optimistic voice.

"He'll glimmer through the gloom," agreed Rupert. "Do you think it's time I tried a shout?" Without waiting for an answer, he began roaring, "Sarah. Sarah, where are you?" at the top of his voice.

They all listened anxiously, straining their ears, willing

a reply, but only the squelch of hoofs, the wind sighing over the Downs and the repetitive bark of a bored dog in the village below, broke the silence of the empty air.

They called at regular intervals as they jogged along the track, and then, coming to the wooded area near the poet's cottage, they stopped to switch on torches, for the path running through the trees was suddenly pitch black.

"I don't think I'd want to be out in this alone and torchless," said Alice.

"Poor Sarah, I do hope she's not hurt," sighed Lizzie, switching off her borrowed torch, for the other three were powerful enough.

"Poor Sarah nothing," said Rupert contemptuously. "She brought it on herself."

"I know, but I can't help feeling we should have done more to stop her," explained Lizzie.

"But what? She wouldn't listen."

"Knocked her out and tied her up with headcollar ropes," suggested Rupert. "It would have saved us all this trouble now."

"Give another yell," said Alice.

Rupert yelled and the wood rang with the alarm calls of startled birds making for safer perches.

"Sorry," he shouted after them. "I didn't know you were there."

The poet's cottage was dark and deserted. They crossed the track they'd come up that afternoon and entered unknown territory, an even darker path, hedged in by scrub and roofed by low, dripping branches, lying in wait for incautious riders' heads.

Lizzie switched on her torch. "Two of us had better shine upwards and two downwards," she said.

When they emerged from the wood they found that the track now ran beside a post and rail fence, new and raw, which stretched away out of the torch beams' range. The riders, able to see their way in the softer darkness which shrouded the Downs, shone their torches over the fence into the natural ravine below.

"That must be where the motorway's going," said Hanif.

"What a shame, it'll ruin the Downs," sighed Lizzie.

"I wonder if there's a way through, or across," puzzled Alice, flashing her torch along the fence.

"Once they've built the road there are usually bridges or tunnels underneath for farmers and locals," said Hanif. "I don't know what they do while it's *being* built, though."

"We must be getting near the track Sarah took. Give another shout, Rupert," asked Lizzie.

"Right." Rupert dropped his reins, cupped his hands and gave a yodelling cry which wavered away down the valley. Then, above the suck and squelch of the ponies' hoofs, they thought they heard something.

"What was that?"

"It could have been an answer."

"It was quite a way ahead and down in the valley."

"Give another yell, Rupert."

"No, hang on until we're a bit nearer. If it's Sarah and she's hurt we don't want to wear her out with shouting."

Shining the torches through the fence they saw that they had reached the spearhead of the motorway works and a canyon had been cut through the Down, leaving deep scars, cliffsides of chalky soil where the green hill had been hacked away.

"She *can't* have got down there," said Hanif, leading the way at a steady trot.

"I'll try again," decided Rupert. "Can we stop, Harry? We'll hear better if we can keep the ponies still."

"Sarah, are you there?" he yodelled.

"Yes, down here," came the answer, faint but clear.

"How did she get there?" asked Hanif, trying to shake the wooden fence, but finding it strong and solid.

"Better go on, there must be a way down," said Alice.

"We haven't reached the track she took yet," Lizzie reminded them. "When we do we may be able to follow her hoofprints."

"She may have ridden full speed at the fence and poor old Sparkler, not realizing, jumped into space," suggested Rupert.

"Let's hope not," said Alice as they all rode on grim-faced and worried, imagining a crumpled pony and crushed rider lying in the canyon below.

They came to a north-south running track, which they knew must be the one they had seen Sarah take. It ended abruptly at the fence. But their track went on, only now it ran between two fences, and a huge stubble field stretched away into the dark on their left. Then, suddenly, a torch beam illuminated a broken section of fence, they all surged towards it. The top rail was broken, the lower rail still intact. They were on lower-lying land now, for they had come over the Down, and so the canyon was less precipitous, but the slope was still steep and slippery enough. "It looks as though children have been using it as a slide," thought Alice.

Hanif had got out the large torch and flashing the long beam into the canyon, he found Sarah and Sparkler.

"Are you hurt?" Rupert shouted.

"No."

"Why don't you come up again?"

"Because Sparkler fell over and his bridle's broken and he won't go up. I've been trying for hours and he won't. I'm stuck."

"Isn't there a way out if you go eastwards towards the river?" called Hanif.

"How do I know? It doesn't look like it, the fence goes on and on. I'm stuck and you'd better go and get help—you've been long enough coming!" shrieked Sarah in hysterical fury.

"If she's going to be like that she deserves to spend the

night there," said Hanif, his relief releasing a wave of anger.

"There's no point in taking another pony down," decided Alice, who'd been investigating the slope. "If someone will hold Saffy I'll go down on my feet and see if I can help her to get him out."

"O.K. We can send reinforcements down if needed," agreed Hanif.

"Be careful, it looks slippery and we don't want any sprained ankles," said Lizzie anxiously.

"Easier on two legs than four," shouted Alice, slipping and slithering her way down and landing in a heap at the bottom. She got up with a mud-soaked bottom, but still holding her torch, and waved to the anxious faces looking down. Sarah wasn't coming to meet her, so Alice sloshed through the chalky white mud which came over her ankles. She shone the torch on Sarah, who'd evidently been crying, and then on Sparkler, he looked tired, depressed and his stomach had run up, but otherwise he appeared undamaged.

"What's the good of *you* coming. You won't be able to do anything," sneered Sarah. "Have the others gone to fetch help?"

"Let's have a look at this bridle," said Alice, taking the tangle from Sarah, who was holding Sparkler by the reins round his neck, which were still attached to the running martingale.

"I've told you, it's broken." Sarah's voice was petulant, but Alice went ahead with her inspection. Both cheek pieces had snapped, but the head collar was intact. "How did it happen?" she asked as she began to unbuckle the reins.

"He fell over."

"He slipped down the slope and fell?" asked Alice, puzzled by the broken bridle.

"No, the stupid pony put his head too low or something,

the martingale rings went over the pelham rings and stuck. When he found he could get his head up he went mad, really mad, he reared right up and fell over backwards and everything broke!" Sarah's voice rose to a scream and then broke into hysterical sobs.

"Well, you're not hurt and he looks O.K.," said Alice briskly, as she knotted the martingale rings round the neckstrap. "Now can you shine the torch while I undo the stud billets on the bit? I'm planning to join the four reins on to the headcollar rope, and I think they'll be long enough to tow him up the slope."

"I've told you, it's no good. I've been trying for hours. He keeps pulling back and then you slide all the way down."

"How are you doing? Want any more help?" Rupert's voice boomed down to them.

"Hold on, nearly ready for action," Alice shouted back. "Can you put the remains of the bridle in your saddlebag?" she asked Sarah, and holding the torch between her knees she knotted one rein to the headcollar rope and buckled the second pair to the first. Then coiling up her long leading rein, she lead Sparkler across to the cliff.

"Will you see if you can climb up without Sparkler," she asked Sarah. "Then, when you're halfway up I'll throw the reins to you."

"What's the good of that?" Sarah interrupted. "He'll only pull me down again. I've told you—"

"Hold on," said Alice. "You're not trying to pull him. You're taking the reins to the people on the top and, if our collection isn't long enough, they can drop you down another headcollar rope. O.K.?"

"Yes, I suppose so, though I know it won't work," said Sarah, seizing her chance to escape and not caring if she left Sparkler behind.

As Sarah started her climb, Alice explained the plan to

the As waiting above. "I'll run with him as far as I can," she told them, "but I don't think it'll be far," she added, watching Sarah's slow progress, mostly on all fours.

"Let's show him the other ponies, that'll be an encouragement," suggested Rupert, persuading Rosie to lean over the fence. Hanif was trying to kick down the lower rail, but without much success.

Sarah had almost reached the top when the slack in the reins ran out, but Rupert, lying on his stomach, long arms extended, managed to join two more headcollar ropes to the reins with a reef knot.

"O.K. We're ready," called Rupert.

"Give me all the slack you can. He needs to take a run at it," Alice shouted back. She was talking encouragingly to Sparkler, giving him pony nuts from her pocket, trying to restore his courage.

"Coming," she shouted, running the few steps to the foot of the cliff and making clicking noises. They started up the slippery slope, Alice managed several yards before her feet slithered from under her and she had to let go. "Go on, boy," she shouted.

"Come on Sparky," they were calling from above.

Slithering down, Alice waved her arms ferociously and with a great heave of his quarters, Sparkler went on. His feet slipped and scrabbled for footholds, voices called him, Alice roared fiercely, he kept going, the As greeted him with a shout of triumph and pulled him over the low rail. The other ponies welcomed him with excited neighs.

Alice had gone back to collect Sarah's whip when she heard the other neigh. She shone her torch round and up at the opposite cliff. There was no pony to be seen, and yet she was sure she'd heard it, a weak, somehow appealing neigh, and it had come from close at hand.

"Come on Alice."

"What *are* you doing?" called puzzled voices from the

508

cliff top, as she hurried through the slimy mud, casting her torch beam in a wide arc.

"Oh, can't we just leave her? I want to go home," sobbed Sarah.

"That's a great idea, when she's rescued you," Hanif's voice was heavy with sarcasm.

"There, you've got reins," said Lizzie, giving Sparkler a pat. "I think I'd better lead you," she told Sarah, "because they're only attached to the headcollar; you haven't got a bit."

"I don't care what you do as long as we *go*," wailed Sarah.

"She's running round in circles," observed Rupert, watching Alice's light. "Do you think *she's* gone dotty?"

"No, not Alice," answered Hanif. "She seems to be looking for something, but what?"

"Shall I start home with Sarah?" suggested Lizzie.

"No, better stick together. Look, she's flashing her torch at us and shouting," said Hanif, straining his ears to hear.

Alice had sloshed round in a small circle and found nothing. She began to think she'd imagined the neigh, and yet she had been certain at the time. Just one more circle, she decided, towards the huge machines, earthmovers and bulldozers parked in a row, which she had glimpsed in the torchlight. She sloshed on. The mud was even deeper here, but the giant machines were standing on concrete, the foundations of the half-made road.

"Coop, coop, pony, are you there?" she called softly into the dark as her torch beam searched between the great yellow machines. She finished her circle and stood undecided. She knew that she ought to go back. Sarah was probably suffering from shock, Sparkler hadn't eaten since morning, David would be mad with worry. Then she heard a small scraping noise. A repetitive noise. There *was* something here. For the first time she felt afraid.

There was something close by her in the darkness and the mud. She felt like running. Running back to the others.

"We've found Sarah, that's all that matters," half her mind told her. "Don't take any risks, go back to camp." But the other half told her that she had to look, that she had to go over there by the far cliff and see what was hidden by the night.

She went slowly, hiding behind her torch beam, hoping that it would find some unfrightening object, but fearing what was about to be revealed.

Then, she saw the hoofs, the black tail, and ran forward. The pony was lying on its side, dark with sweat where he wasn't covered in mud. She shone the torch on him. He didn't seem able to get up, the ground around him was churned and scraped by his long and desperate struggles to rise. He could have colic, thought Alice, or a broken leg.

"Whoa pony," she said gently, and, kneeling beside him, she felt each foreleg in turn. They seemed perfectly all right. She moved over to check the hind ones and saw what had happened. There was a carpet of thick wire-mesh spread over the mud and one section had risen up and worked loose, somehow it had entangled itself round the pony's hoof and one mesh had jammed between his shoe and hoof.

"Lie still," said Alice, "and I'll set you free." But it wasn't as easy as she thought. She needed one hand to hold the hoof and one to pull the wire and then she couldn't hold the torch. She put it down and pulled with all her strength. The wire didn't move.

"Don't worry," Alice told the pony. "I'm going to fetch help, we'll soon have you free." Shouting and waving her torch she ran, splashing through the mud.

"A pony trapped—I need some help," she called. "Can you come. Bring the big torch."

When she was within conversation distance Lizzie said,

"Rupert and I are tying our ponies to the fence. Sarah's going to hold Saffy; we think Hanif ought to ride back to the farm and tell them what's happened."

"What *has* happened?" asked Hanif.

"There's a pony lying out there in the mud. He's trapped by some wire round his shoe." Alice made herself speak calmly. "I guess he's been there a long time, he looks exhausted. I think two or three of us may be able to free him, but we'll never get him up the cliff, they'll have to bring a trailer. The new road ends over there. Tell them to hurry, he looks very ill."

"A trailer and some wire cutters," said Hanif. "Anything else?"

"Whatever you revive ponies with, brandy or something," Alice shouted.

"I think it's Amanda Quale's pony. He's so covered in mud and sweat I can't be sure about his colour, but he could be roan, his tail's black and he's the right size."

"She told me that he had a white mark on his forehead, only it wasn't the usual star but a little crescent moon," shouted Hanif as he started campwards along the track.

Rupert and Lizzie slipped and slithered down, landing in the mud with aggrieved cries. Sarah was complaining from the cliff top, but they ignored her as they picked themselves up and hurried after Alice. Rupert switched on the powerful torch and it soon picked out the helpless figure of the trapped pony.

"Don't shine it in his eyes," objected Lizzie. Rupert switched to the diffused beam.

"Oh dear, he looks exhausted," Lizzie was shocked. "He must have been here for days."

"Twenty-four hours," said Alice who was inspecting his forehead. "It *is* Amanda's Robin."

"I don't think he'd have lasted much longer," Rupert was shocked too. "Look at his eye, it's sort of sunken and blank."

"Yes, he's given up," agreed Alice kneeling in the mud. "I hope he's not going to die." They gathered round the trapped hoof. Rupert shone the torch on it. Lizzie pulled at the wire.

"It should just come out," said Alice, "but the matting is pulling downwards all the time and as the pony's lying on the matting it's impossible to take the weight off."

Lizzie held the pony's leg and Rupert pulled at the wire, but the jammed strand didn't budge.

"I see what you mean," he told Alice, "and it's strong stuff."

"Supposing we all try to pull the matting up first?" suggested Lizzie.

"Or two of us lift Robin while one tries to loosen the mat, I don't think he'd mind," said Alice. "He's too tired."

"Yes, we only have to loosen it a little to take the downward pressure off," agreed Rupert. "If you two could raise his quarters about an inch, I might be able to pull up the matting just enough."

They tried. Robin did not object to the girls heaving at his quarters, but Rupert could make no impression on the wire matting.

"It's sunk deep in the mud. I suppose they've put it down to make a road for the trucks and lorries, otherwise they'd spend all their time having wheelspin in this sort of mud."

"What about trying to prise it up with that piece of wood?" asked Alice.

"O.K." Rupert handed the torch to Lizzie and began to dig with the piece of wood, attacking the matting where it had already come adrift. "At least I'll have a better handhold. There, now can you try lifting him again?"

The girls struggled to lift the pony's quarters.

"Great, it's moving," cried Rupert, tugging with all his strength.

"Can't hold him any longer," gasped Alice. "Sorry."

"I wasn't being much use, there's nothing to get hold of," said Lizzie. "I'm going to take that battered saddle off. We could slide the girth under his quarters and lift him that way."

There wasn't much left of the stirrup-less saddle, but the nylon girth was unharmed and, when they had passed it under the pony and through the slop of mud, they each took a buckled end and, pulling for all they were worth, managed to raise the pony's quarters a couple of inches.

"Quick, he's terribly heavy," Lizzie gritted her teeth and urged Rupert to greater effort.

"I'm pulling as hard as I can," he grunted as he jerked, tugged and heaved at the wire in turn. "It won't move. Sorry. It's come so far and now it won't budge another inch," he added breathlessly as the girls let Robin slip back into the mud.

"Do you think it's worth having another try?" Alice was asking, when the pony suddenly attempted to get up. He struggled to get his legs under him, and then, realizing that he was still trapped, seemed to panic and began to thrash and kick in a wild attempt to break free. The three flailing legs slashed mud through the air. Rupert grabbed the torch and retreated.

"Whoa, boy, whoa," called Alice, hurrying to the frantic pony's head. "It's all right, Robin, we'll get you free." She tried to calm him, but the frenzied, useless struggle went on, it was as though he was prepared to destroy himself rather than remain trapped. The pony club members watched, horrified and helpless, until at last the exhausted pony collapsed back into the slimy mud and lay, only his flank, heaving and shuddering with a frightening violence, showing that he was alive.

"He's going to have a heart attack in a minute," Lizzie's voice was shaking.

"Or break a leg. We'd better leave him until the wire

cutters come," said Rupert, shining the torch over the sweating, mud-soaked body. "I hope Harry's explained it's an emergency."

"It'll be another hour before they *can* get here," Lizzie sounded despondent. "They've got to find David or some other grown-up, hitch up the trailer, borrow some wire cutters. . . . And then there's Sarah," she added as a resentful cry shrilled from the cliff top. "She's had an awful day and we oughtn't to leave her on her own much longer."

"I'd forgotten all about her," said Alice, who was kneeling in the mud and massaging Robin's cold, clammy ears. "One of us had better take her to the farm or she'll go off on her own again and get lost."

"One person won't be enough. There are four ponies up there and Sarah's not in a fit state to lead one," Rupert pointed out. "And someone has to have a free hand for the torch."

"You two go then," Alice told the Wheelers. "Sarah can ride Saffy, he'll look after her and you'll be able to ride faster than if she's trying to control Sparkler in a headcollar. I don't mind staying if I can have the big torch."

"Are you sure?" Rupert swung the torch round, illuminating the waste of mud and the giant earthmovers. "It's a bit spooky with only mechanical monsters for company."

"I'll have Robin and someone has to stay."

Both Wheelers were worried. They didn't like leaving Alice on her own, but then a frantic wail from Sarah decided them.

"If you're *sure* you don't mind," said Lizzie, turning.

"I'll be fine," answered Alice, swopping torches with Rupert. "And, if Harry hasn't got a rescue party on its way, you'll be able to hurry things up. Tell them it's a matter of life and death."

"We will, don't worry." Rupert gave the limp figure of Robin a mournful glance and squelched after Lizzie.

While the others were sorting out the ponies on the cliff top the sound of voices and the flashing torchlights were company, but as they rode away, the voices and the lights faded and the darkness seemed very black to Alice. Lonely, she began to talk to Robin.

"I don't know if David can manage the trailer," she told him. "They may have to send for another grown-up. Of course James and Seb are there as well as Harry. They'll hitch it up for him and James is a practical sort of boy; it's a pity he's not old enough to drive. I'm going to learn the minute I'm old enough. Aunt Margaret simply hates having to drive me around, but there are years and years to wait. I've got to be patient. So have you, Robin. I promise that we'll get you free soon, you must just hang on a bit longer." Now that his flank had stopped heaving, the pony looked alarmingly lifeless. Gently, Alice eased his head out of the mud and, edging closer, rested it upon her lap. It lay, heavy and passive without even the flicker of the closed eye.

"Please hang on, Robin." Alice stroked the clammy cheek gently. She could hear nothing, but the wind sighing over the Downs, and see nothing but the wall of darkness round her pool of light, she began to will the rescuers to hurry, to drive faster, to reach her before the poor battered pony gave up and died.

At the camp, time was passing very slowly. The trekkers fed their ponies, washed up and unrolled all the sleeping bags. Then, for want of anything better to do, they decided to clean their tack.

Lesley, now as silent and anxious as everyone else, went across to the house again for news. On her return, she reported that the MacKenzies were still out, and not expected home until midnight. She'd telephoned the police, who said that no accident to a girl or a pony had been reported, and her mother, who was out, but she'd left a message with Julian.

"It's a good thing I wasn't in your group," she told James, "or I'd be the one to get the blame. As it is we'll all be in her bad books."

"But she can't really blame anyone but Sarah," protested James.

"She will, she'll twist it round somehow, because it's never Sarah's fault," Lesley answered.

"I'm going to stand up to your mother," announced Seb bravely, "and tell her just what a poisonous little creep Sarah is."

"You'll be wasting your breath. She won't listen. She's convinced Sarah's perfect, so anyone who criticizes her is jealous or spiteful; you can't win," said Lesley in a disillusioned voice.

They were halfway through the tack cleaning when they heard the sound of a car, and headlights beamed across the yard. Abandoning sponges, rags and dusters, the trekkers rushed out.

"It's a Land Rover."

"It's David." They clustered round the driver's door, all explaining at once.

"O.K., O.K. Hang on," David shouted them down. "I met Harry on the road and the latest news is that they've found Sarah and she's all right, but then Alice found a pony trapped on the new motorway. Apparently it's caught up in some wire and in pretty bad shape. They've asked for a trailer and wirecutters. So, if you'll hitch up the trailer I'll go and find out how we get on to this diabolical motorway from the police."

Lesley explained that she had already talked to the police about Sarah.

"Right, you come too," said David, as he backed the Land Rover up to the trailer, "and we'll give them an update."

While Seb and James hitched up, Lynne and Tina ran around collecting the main first-aid kit, a container of water, two buckets and a small feed. Only Oliver ran to welcome Hanif when he rode into the yard.

"How's this pony trapped, and do you really think it belongs to Amanda?" he asked.

"I don't know," Hanif dismounted wearily. "I didn't see him. Let's turn poor old Jupe out. He's had a long day."

With Jupiter in the field, grazing hungrily to make up for lost time, Hanif drank a mug of water and joined the other trekkers, who were waiting for David by the Land Rover.

"Do you know *how* this pony's trapped," James asked him at once. "Should we take spades and shovels?"

"Or send for the fire brigade?" suggested Seb.

"Alice said he was caught up in some wire and to bring wire cutters in case they couldn't free him, nothing about shovels."

When David reappeared, limping along at speed, they asked him about the wirecutters. "Yes, two pairs, large and small," he answered briskly. "Now, the police are going to meet me at the entrance to the motorway so I must get a move on. How many of you want to come?"

"All of us," answered Tina.

"Yes, we may be useful," agreed Seb.

"I told Marie-Therese I'd stay, in case there's a telephone call," Lesley told David.

"Oh good, you're doing a great job there. I had no idea you spoke French so well," said David gratefully. The other trekkers, piling into the Land Rover, didn't see Lesley blushing with pleasure.

James and Lynne were in the front, James with his map and torch at the ready.

"We have to cross the river," said David, settling himself at the special controls. "The nearest bridge is at Martlock, and I may need a bit of help with the way.

We're going to rendez-vous with a police car, and a vet," he added, as they turned into the road.

"Ponies!" shouted Lynne a moment later, as the headlights picked out Rajah's wise chestnut head. "It's them."

"Have they got Amanda's pony?" asked Oliver from the back.

"No, only four ponies and three riders," answered James as the Land Rover pulled up.

"Sarah's there, but not Alice," said Lynne in a disappointed voice.

"Take care," roared David as they flung themselves on to the road. "You're not on the Downs now."

While the pony club members questioned Rupert and Sarah, Lizzie rode round to David's window.

"We couldn't free him. We did our best, but it made him panic and start to fight again. You'll have to hurry, he's not going to survive much longer. It looks as though he's been struggling for hours and he's completely exhausted."

"And Alice has stayed on her own?" asked David.

"Yes, Sarah's a casualty too, she keeps crying. We *had* to bring her back, so Alice said she'd stay. Sparkler's bridle's wrecked, that's why Sarah's riding Saffy."

"But she's not hurt?" asked David.

"No, she says not. Sparkler's martingale rings went over his pelham rings and jammed. She says he went mad and then reared up and fell over backwards, but she was thrown clear."

"Well, Mrs Rooke's on her way, so she'll cope," said David. "I'll go on and see what we can do for this pony."

"Where's our trailer going," demanded Sarah tearfully as the Land Rover drove on. "*I* want it to take me home."

Alice had switched off the torch. She felt that she ought to conserve the battery for future developments and dramas.

For the moment all was quiet, Robin lying ominously still, his head heavy on her lap. The moon was up, her strange, silver light exposing the grotesque and shadowy forms of the earthmovers and bulldozers. They looked like huge beasts crouched, ready to spring, thought Alice, as the long, haunting cry of a hunting owl sent a sudden shiver down her spine.

It *is* spooky, she admitted to herself, and I'd probably be frightened if it wasn't for being so anxious about Robin; I'm too frightened that he's going to die before they get here with those cutters to care about spooky sights and sounds.

She looked at her watch. Thirty-five minutes had passed since the Wheelers had disappeared into the darkness, and almost an hour since Harry's departure.

"Not much longer," she said aloud, more for her own comfort than Robin's; he seemed to have abandoned hope, lost his will to survive. Alice shivered again, this time from cold. The damp of the slimy mud had seeped through her jodhpurs and her left foot was having an attack of pins and needles. She longed to move, to get up and stamp about, but if she disturbed Robin he might have another of his fits of frenzied struggling. She couldn't risk that, but she did wish that he would give some small sign of life. She began to massage his cold ears, willing him to live, to hang on until the rescuers came. She had found a handful of pony nuts in her anorak pocket and held them by his muzzle, hoping that their smell would rouse him, but there was no response.

At last she heard the sound of car engines and saw long, pencil beams of light probing their way up the unfinished motorway.

Several cars, thought Alice; it *must* be the Woodbury people, perhaps Mrs Rooke had come as well as David. There seemed to be three of them, they stopped and six headlamps illuminated the machines, taking away their moonlit mystery, exposing them as yellow mechanical giants. They also lit up a wooden building, labelled *Site Office*, stacks of huge drainpipes and other road-making materials. Then she saw why they had stopped. A tall, unscalable fence of link wire blocked their way.

Oh no, she couldn't bear it. After all that waiting to find that they couldn't get in; that poor Robin's ordeal still wasn't over. Perhaps they could throw the wire cutters over the fence, she might be able to free him on her own. She was gently easing Robin's head off her lap, when she heard familiar pony club voices. They didn't sound despondent. She switched on the torch.

"I'm over here," she called, and was answered by a babble of voices and she realized that it was all right, sections of the fence were gates and they were opening; the cars were being abandoned, the people were coming through on foot.

Hanif reached Alice first. "How is he?"

"Not too good. Have you brought the cutters?"

"Of course. David's bringing them."

"We've brought reinforcements: two policemen and a vet," added Rupert, as David limped over accompanied by a large macintoshed man who carried a case and a bag of tools. They looked down at the pony.

"Poor little devil."

"He's taken a pasting."

They bent to look at the shoe. Hanif took the torch from Alice and used it to spotlight the strand of wire.

"Be careful. He went berserk after we had tried to free him," Alice warned everyone, but Robin, half opening a dull and sunken eye, seemed past struggling.

"It looks cuttable," said the vet, taking the wire cutters from David, "which will be a lot less hassle than taking off the shoe. Will you steady the leg for me?" he asked James.

Tina, who was carrying a headcollar, squatted down

beside Alice. The vet cut the wire on either side of the shoe.

"You're free now," Alice whispered to Robin, but there was still no response.

The vet took a stethoscope from his case and, crouching in the mud, listened to Robin's heart, then he took a look at his eye.

"A combination of exhaustion and shock," he announced. "I'll give him a shot to stimulate him a bit and then we'll try to get him on his feet."

Hanif shone the torch for the vet as he prepared the injection. The two policemen had appeared and David was telling them Robin's story with occasional help from Seb and Lynne.

"He's not dead, is he?" asked Oliver, looking down at the motionless pony. "He doesn't seem to be breathing."

"No, he's not dead," said the vet, moving Oliver out of the way, "but he wouldn't have lasted much longer. It's a good thing your mates found him when they did. Now," he went on, the injection given, "we'll wait five minutes and then try to get him on his feet."

Alice was still rubbing Robin's cold ears. She told him again that he was free. David and one of the policemen had gone for the Land Rover and trailer, they were going to bring it to the edge of the concrete and the policeman had offered to do the reversing.

"Any sign of life," asked the vet, looking at his watch.

"He's twitched an ear," answered Alice. "Shall we try to put the headcollar on."

"Yes, come on, pony. Wakey, wakey," said the vet, shaking Robin's neck.

Alice and Tina slipped the headcollar on and then Tina propped up the pony's heavy head while Alice fastened the buckle.

"You lads go round the far side and get ready to give him a push," the vet told James and Seb. "We want him lying in the upright position. You pull his head to the left," he instructed Alice. "Not yet, wait until I've got his legs a bit closer to his body."

They pushed and pulled and suddenly Robin summoned up the courage to test his legs again and finding them free, tucked them under his body and with a great sucking noise, heaved his body out of the mud. "Let him lie like that," instructed the vet. "Let him rest for a couple of minutes."

Alice patted the pony and offered him a pony nut, but he didn't seem to want to eat.

"I'll get the water," offered Lynne. "We brought a bucket and one of the containers."

"Only a sip or two," said the vet. "We don't want him going down with a colic on top of everything else."

Robin didn't need much persuasion to get on his feet, but he climbed up very slowly and stiffly and then stood, his head hanging and obviously feeling very sorry for himself.

"He aches all over," said the vet. "Lead him on slowly."

Hanif shone the torch, illuminating the pony bit by bit. His near side was completely plastered with mud.

"Talk about revolting. I've never seen such a yukky pony in all my life," observed Oliver. "Am I glad it's not me who's got to groom him tomorrow."

Lizzie and Rupert welcomed the Land Rover party with a beautifully bedded-down loosebox and the news that the Quales would be over about nine next morning with a borrowed trailer.

"Amanda was asleep when we rang," Lizzie explained. "Her father said she'd been in a lot of pain and hardly slept at all last night, so the doctor had given her a sleeping pill. He's putting a notice that Robin's been found on her bed so that she'll know the minute she wakes up."

"He was very grateful when we said we'd look after

Robin for tonight, and that we'd already borrowed some straw and bedded a box down," Rupert went on." He was in rather a tiz about whether he ought to leave Amanda and come over here."

"How's Sarah?" asked David, when Alice had led Robin into his stable and was giving him another small drink.

"She's in there with her Ma," muttered Rupert, pointing to the kitchen loosebox. "There were some very loud caws at first but things have quietened down now."

"Sarah's insisting on going home," added Lizzie.

"Why on earth, is she feeling ill?" asked Tina.

"No, I think she's furious at having made a fool of herself. She tried to blame everything on her compass, but Rupert and I tried it and it's working perfectly. When we told her she flew into a terrible rage, threw it on the ground and stamped on it."

"What a waste," said Oliver. "She kept boasting about how much it cost. But I'm really glad that she's going home."

David was leaning over the loosebox door, watching Alice tempt Robin to eat.

"Well done, Alice," he said. "I reckon you saved his life."

With the excitement over, everyone began to realise how tired and thirsty he or she was and they persuaded Lesley to brave the kitchen.

"You're family, *we* can't go charging in there when they're talking," Seb told her.

"It was her own fault," said Lesley, emerging a few moments later. "She'd changed her bottom reins, she says the old ones were stiff, so she put on a different pair, but they had no martingale stops."

"Does that matter?" asked Tina.

"Yes, the rings can jam on the buckles or stud billets or even over the rings of the bit and when they do, the pony goes crazy. Sarah says Sparkler reared up and fell over backwards," explained Lesley.

"Yes, I was always warned not to ride without stops when Jupe had a running martingale," agreed Hanif.

"My mother's going to take Sarah home. She wants you boys to hitch up the trailer," added Lesley.

As soon as Mrs Rooke and Sarah had driven away, everyone gathered in the loosebox for tea. Lynne produced the last of her mother's cakes and Alice two packets of biscuits.

"I detect a feeling of relief," said David. "I hope you haven't been ganging up against Sarah."

"Absolutely not," answered Alice.

"I think we *should* have ganged up against her, on the very first day," argued Seb. "If we'd put her in her place then we wouldn't have had all this trouble."

"It wouldn't have done any good. You can't shame my sister," Lesley told him. "Nothing is ever her fault. Sparkler is being blamed for today's shambles. He's being sent back."

"Lucky Sparkler," observed Seb.

"But Sarah and her martingale stops were even better than Tristram's warble fly," Alice pointed out. "If she hadn't led us to the motorway, poor Robin would have lain there until the road-builders went to work on Monday. She really saved his life."

CHAPTER SEVEN

No Rosettes

Alice wakened early to glorious sunshine. The sky was blue and the whole world seemed to be steaming and sparkling under the sun, the stormy misery of the previous day forgotten.

Except for Jupiter, the ponies were lying down. He was standing on guard for both fields, thought Alice, as she pulled on her gumboots and anorak and crept to the stable yard. Robin was lying down too, flat on his side, and, suddenly fearful, Alice called to him. To her relief he raised his head and answered with a little whinny.

"I'll make you some breakfast," said Alice. She refilled his water bucket and helped herself to some more of Hanif's short feed; he was the only person with more than one feed left in his sack.

Robin had moved into the upright lying position and, with pricked ears and expectant eyes, looked like a convalescent eagerly awaiting a delicious breakfast in bed.

Alice offered him the water first, which he sipped delicately, and then put the feed in front of him. He lay, munching enthusiastically. "I think you're going to be all right," she told him.

Jupiter, hearing voices, woke the camp with a neigh, aimed at the boys' tent. It was a bossy neigh, demanding breakfast.

The trekkers emerged slowly with sleep-drugged eyes. They felt tired and flat after the night's excitement, and drifted slowly towards the bathroom or the loosebox kitchen, where the tack and feed sacks had been dumped in the absence of the Rooke trailer.

They had almost finished breakfast when the Quales arrived, complete with a borrowed trailer. Mr Quale looked even taller, thinner and sadder than before, but Amanda ran to the loosebox and cried tears of joy when reunited with Robin, who was on his feet and greeted her with a whinny.

"He's *caked* in mud, we ought to have groomed him," said Lizzie, buckling on his headcollar.

"The vet said he ought to be allowed to rest," Alice reminded her. They all looked at his swollen, shapeless, hindlegs with horror. "The vet couldn't find anything really wrong with them," Alice told Amanda. "He says they'll probably go down quicker if he's turned out and walking about, but not with other ponies who might chivvy him."

As they led Robin into the trailer, Mr Quale, who seemed rather vague about horsey matters, was consulting James.

"And you're quite certain that it was wasps which caused this extraordinary behaviour? He has never shown any tendency to indulge in bucking bronco acts before, but I don't want to risk another accident to Amanda, so if there's any likelihood of a repeat performance . . ."

"It was *definitely* wasps," James answered firmly. "Sarah's pony went crazy at exactly the same spot. Sarah thought he had been bitten by a snake, but, when I went to investigate, the wasps were pouring out of this hillock at the side of the path. I ran for it, but they got me a couple of times and Sparkler was covered in stings."

"Thank you, that's reassuring," said Mr Quale. "I'll get on to the foresters tomorrow and have the nest dealt with, before there's another accident. And you think the pony is on the mend?"

"Yes, he should be rideable by the time Amanda's wrist is O.K." said James, accepting his role as expert.

They heaved the ramp shut. Amanda was to travel in the car to avoid any danger of jolting her wrist.

"It's only a short way and Robin's used to trailers. I don't think he'll mind," she said.

"Well, I can only say how deeply grateful Amanda and I are to all of you." Mr Quale's sad gaze travelled from trekker to trekker. "First for helping her so effectively after the accident and then for finding and rescuing the pony. But for you he would still be lying on the motorway, a fact too horrible to contemplate."

"Yes, thank you a million times for saving Robin," said Amanda as she opened the car door. "I do wish I could belong to your pony club," she went on, winding down the window. "You seem to do such exciting things. The Northdown's rather boring."

"The Woodbury *used* to be the most boring pony club ever," Rupert told her.

"Yes, they do change," agreed Lizzie.

"It's the members who make them fun," said Alice.

"I think it's the officials who make the most difference," Oliver told Alice as they watched the Quales drive slowly away.

"The Woodbury changed when we got David. And think what a pony club run by Mrs Rooke and Janet Green would be like—dead boring."

"Shush, Mrs Rooke does a lot for us," Lizzie sounded shocked. "Look how good she's been moving all our stuff to the next camp every morning."

"But he's right," said Lesley. "My mother would be an awful D.C. and everything would be run to suit Sarah."

The trekkers felt very melancholy as they dismantled camp for the last time.

"I *am* looking forward to sleeping in a bed though," admitted James.

"And I won't miss cleaning those awful greasy frying pans one bit," said Tina, rolling up her bedding.

"It's washing in cold water that gets me down," observed Lesley.

"I hate all this putting up and taking down. Let's insist on caravans next year," suggested Seb, pulling up the last tent peg and letting his tent collapse in a heap.

"You haven't a hope if my stepfather's still involved," Hanif told him. "He *believes* in roughing it. Caravans don't develop the character like tents do."

"I wonder if the trek *has* had any effect on our characters?" mused Tina. "I think I do feel slightly different."

"I feel the same, only dirtier," decided Oliver.

"It hasn't gone on long enough to make permanent changes," said Rupert.

"I feel as though it had gone on for *ages*," objected Alice. "It seems weeks since we found the dog, and years since we were packing and trying to decide what food to bring."

Mr Roberts was their next visitor. He drove into the yard in David's cattle truck.

"Well, you had a rough time yesterday, but I hear you didn't do too badly," he said cheerfully as he climbed down.

"We survived," said Hanif, depositing another packed tent on the pile by the loosebox.

"In retrospect it's actually beginning to seem quite exciting," observed Rupert, "but at the time it was just problems, rain and mud."

"Hullo, Dad," Lynne came running. "What are *you* doing here? Where's Mrs Rooke?"

"Nursing young Sarah," Mr Roberts laughed sarcastically. "The rest of you look healthy enough." He glanced at the line of ponies tied along the fence. "They look fit too."

"Poor Sarah, but she did lead us to the trapped pony," Lynne told her father. "As Alice says, if she hadn't gone down to help Sarah she wouldn't have heard Robin neigh."

"That wasn't Sarah, that was fate," Seb objected. "I won't have a good word said for her. She's poisonous through and through."

"It's really my mother's fault," said Lesley. "She's always spoiled her."

When everything was loaded into the cattle truck, Robin's loosebox had been mucked out and Lesley had gone to the house to thank Marie-Therese and any MacKenzies she could find, Mr Roberts handed over the two sealed envelopes.

"One map reference and 'Lunch will be provided'" Alice read out in a puzzled voice.

"Both lots have got the same reference," announced Oliver, taking a look at the Js' instructions.

"I was wondering why you hadn't brought us any sandwiches, Dad," said Lynne.

"So was I," agreed Oliver. "Does that mean an extra good picnic? I'm a bit fed up with sandwiches and fry-ups."

"Could be," said Mr Roberts, climbing up into the cab. "See you later."

"We all go in one lot then?" asked James.

"Yes, it'll be rather fun."

"And with *two* leaders we might not get lost," said Oliver in a cheeky voice.

They pored over their maps.

"It's Hampton, our first stop," Alice told James. "But the other end of the village this time."

"We might call in and see our tombstone again," suggested Rupert, "just for old times' sake."

"Better get going," said James, folding the Js' map. "It's going to take a couple of hours."

It was a lovely ride. They took the track over the top of the Downs. The air was clear and they could see for miles. Larks were singing as they soared into the sky, and scattered over the Downs were walkers and riders.

529

Yesterday it was a different place, thought Alice, but she felt rather proud to have known it in its wilder mood.

The ponies, pleased to be part of a friendly herd and realising that they were heading for home, bounced along happily. The trekkers' minds had already gone ahead and were picking up the threads of everyday life. Alice was thinking of Shawbury and her return to boarding school. Seb and Tina were both busy with the problems of their new family and the prospect of a new house, while Lynne realised that she hadn't felt miserable about not being in the mounted games team for almost three days; it didn't seem so important now.

Hanif was wondering about his stepfather's view of the trek. He was going to grumble about the state of the cooking stoves, but they'd coped with the map reading and the tents, they'd survived the revolting weather and managed a few exciting adventures of their own.

"What did you think of all that map reference stuff?" he asked James.

"Great. It made the whole trek much more interesting," James answered enthusiastically.

"And it made me master the art of mapreading," added Rupert proudly. "Netti will no longer be able to boast that she's the only one of us who knows the way."

"I keep thinking places are north or south or east or west quite naturally now," observed Tina. "Before the trek I hardly knew that compasses existed."

"And I know that we're heading north now, because there are our shadows in front of us and it's getting on for one p.m.," announced Oliver proudly.

Soon they saw the square tower of Hampton Church, and the village spread along the stream, in the combe below them. It looked very familiar to the As, though this time they were approaching from the opposite direction.

"Look, that's your stepfather waving to us. Do you think he means us to go in there?" Lynne asked Hanif.

530

"Yes, but it's someone's house," he answered disapprovingly.

"Seb, in that field, there, by the stream," Tina pointed excitedly to a row of parked cars. "There's your father and my mum."

"My mum and dad are there too, and Paul," Lynne was waving.

"Netti's there and David and Julia, and I can see your mother, James," called Lizzie.

"Practically the whole pony club's there," said Oliver. "I hope they've brought plenty of food."

Mr Franklin welcomed them at the gate.

"The return of the travellers," he said. "Well done. Ten out of eleven staying the course isn't a bad score. You can water the ponies at the stream and I've tied some ropes between those four large trees; temporary horse lines, so you can tie the ponies up and enjoy your lunches. But I think David wants a word first."

Once through the gate, the trekkers scattered, trotting off to say hullo to their families.

Alice looked at Lesley. "Your mother and Sarah aren't here."

"No, but I don't mind. Do you mind that your uncle and aunt haven't come?"

"No, not really, they wouldn't fit in," said Alice. "But look, there are the lost dog's owners, Mr and Mrs Mottram, and they've got a little terrier on a lead—that must be Dirk." She rode towards them, Lesley followed and then they saw another familiar face. "Amanda," called Alice. "We didn't expect to see you."

The As soon gathered round Dirk, who bounced about cheekily on his short legs, while the Mottrams told how he had slept for a whole day after his experience, but was now completely himself.

The Js paid more attention to Amanda. They felt they had played some part in her rescue, while Dirk belonged to the As.

Then Mr Franklin came over to fetch them. "Can you gather round David? He's by the trestle table."

"If there *is* a competition, you As will have won," Seb told them as they strolled across the field. "You had a more productive trek than we did. All our dramas were connected with Sarah."

"We had Tiger and spectacle dramas," Lizzie reminded him. "It was just that our dramas led on to other things."

"It was chance, chance or luck," said Hanif. "I hope David's not going to go on about it."

"Welcome home, trekkers," began David. "You look very muddy and rather travel worn, but I hope you enjoyed your journey. We all think you did very well and I'd like to thank all the people who made the trek possible. Your three hosts, the pony club committee, especially Mr Franklin, Mrs Rooke, Mrs Roberts and Mrs Morgan and all the other long-suffering parents.

"Now, you'll remember that we did consider running an inter-group competition, but we soon realized that life was being exciting enough, and that you didn't need any artificial stimulus. We were particularly impressed by the way the two groups co-operated and helped each other in times of trouble. I think that sort of spirit augurs well for the future of the Woodbury.

"So we have no winners, but Mrs Mottram and Mr Franklin have generously provided useful momentoes of the trek for everyone who stayed the course. Now, if you'll come up to the table . . ."

"You go first, James, you're the eldest, then Lesley," said Lizzie, holding the eager Oliver back.

They trooped up to the table and Mrs Mottram handed out elegantly boxed compasses, with suitable remarks.

"They're better than the pony club ones. They've got built in magnifiers," exclaimed Seb, unpacking his.

"Terrific," agreed Rupert, looking pleased, "I'll never be lost again."

"If you remember to take it with you," snapped Lesley, zipping hers, unopened, into a pocket.

"We'll be able to get the hang of them now," Lynne whispered to Tina. "We never got much of a look in with James and Seb as leaders."

"They're good ones, better than Sarah's, but I wish there had been rosettes too," Oliver told Lynne.

"There is one thing puzzling me," James consulted Mr Franklin. "How did Sarah get a wrong reading on her compass? I mean she's not that stupid, and the compass was working perfectly when Lizzie and Rupert checked it, but there must have been something wrong if she went to the motorway instead of White Horse Hill."

"No doubt of that," agreed Mr Franklin. "Could it have been magnetic attraction? Was she near any metal when she took her bearing? The needle can be affected by anything metal: wire fences, pocket knives, car bonnets."

"I wasn't there," answered James. "Did you see any metal around, Lizzie?"

Lizzie thought back to the scene by the barn. Sarah was holding Sparkler, looking at her map. "There was a metal gate," she said uncertainly. "Oh yes, would a cattle trough matter? I remember now, she was using the lidded end as a table."

"You've solved the puzzle," said Mr Franklin.

"I shall take mine back to school," said Alice, examining her compass lovingly. "It'll remind me of the trek and all the Woodbury people. But it's sad for you, Harry, you've got two already."

"They really belong to my stepfather. This one is truly mine," Hanif sounded contented. "In a strange sort of way I feel that I've earned it."